Sleep Don't
Come Easy

Sleep Don't Come Easy

J.D. MASON
VICTOR McGLOTHIN

Dafina
BOOKS

KENSINGTON PUBLISHING CORP.
www.kensingtonbooks.com

DAFINA BOOKS are published by

Kensington Publishing Corp.
119 West 40th St.
New York, NY 10019

All Kensington Titles, Imprints and Distributed Lines are
available at special quantity discounts for bulk purchases
for sales promotions, premiums, fund-raising, and educa-
tional or institutional use. Special book excerpts or cus-
tomized printings can also be created to fit specific needs.
For details, write or phone the office of the Kensington
special sales manager: Kensington Publishing Corp., 119
West 40th Street, New York, NY 10018, attn: Special Sales
Department, Phone: 1-800-221-2647.

Dafina and the Dafina logo Reg. U.S. Pat. & TM Off.

ISBN-13: 978-0-7582-1380-8
ISBN-10: 0-7582-1380-8

First trade paperback printing: July 2008
First mass market printing: December 2009

10 9 8 7 6 5 4 3 2

Printed in the United States of America

Contents

The Lazarus Man

J.D. Mason

By the Light of the Moon

"**S**top and let me explain!" he said, gritting his teeth, struggling to keep her still. If she'd just stop fighting him he could think, and he could calm the fuck down and find some semblance of rationale in all this crazy bullshit.

He straddled her, pressing his weight down on her petite frame, but somehow, she found the strength to struggle, kicking him, clawing at the sleeves of his shirt, reaching up to claw at his face. She kneed him in the behind and she tried to scream. But he couldn't let her do that.

The thought never occurred to him that if he squeezed too hard, if he held his grip around her neck too long, that she might die. He hadn't thought that far ahead. It was all a matter of *now* and what was happening *now* and of what he needed to happen *now*. Words, images, revelations all flashed quickly in his mind, and he couldn't put together one cohesive train of thought or plan of action. Flesh melted in his hands. Bones and cartilage crushed in his palms, and the terror on her face was just one more image he couldn't see clearly enough.

He had never killed anyone. He'd done some terrible, dark things in his life, but he never believed he was the kind of man who could actually take someone's life. The look in her eyes begged him to stop, her mouth moved, breathless, pleading for him to let her go. She couldn't believe it was him. She never said it, but the stunned and horrific expression on her face shouted it loud and clear.

Snow fell quietly from the sky, dissolving in the heat of his breath. Illumination from the street lights in the distance cast a soft sheen across her, reflecting in her brown eyes the slow fading of life. She was a beautiful woman, quick to smile at a man, and say his name in that way that left him weak. She was the kind of woman a man loved at first sight. He had been one of those men.

It wasn't long before she stopped struggling, and with the final flutter of her lips, stopped begging for her life. It wasn't long before the life from inside her faded to nothingness, and all that was left was the hum from the outside world. Slowly, he released the grip he had on her neck, and crawled off her. High on adrenaline, he started to finally catch his breath, and let the cold night air cleanse him from the inside out. The surreal moment seemed frozen and him along with it, while traffic passed by over the bridge above them, and somewhere in the back of his mind, he realized that the rest of the world was still moving, still living, still on its way home.

He looked down at her, and then he raised his hands, and stared at these weapons of destruction he'd never even known were there. His memory drifted back to a conversation from earlier—moments before that changed the course of both their lives.

"Tell me it isn't what I think it is," her voice quivered, out of anger? Maybe shock? Disgust? "Tell me I'm wrong, and that this is all a terrible mistake! Please!"

She confronted him after everyone else had left. Why would she be so foolish? He wondered, shaking his head, and rubbing the weariness from his eyes. The weight of what he'd done started to bear down heavily on his body. He was tired all of a sudden, exhausted and empty.

"It's not how you think it is," he had tried convincing her. "I'm not a monster."

"You're fucking evil!" she screamed. "Worse than a monster, because you're real! Pretending to be someone else—I can't believe you would actually do something like this!" she sobbed, and then she turned abruptly to leave, and he knew. Oh, dear God! He knew she'd tell the world.

He grabbed at her, but missed. And for a moment, time held them both hostage, and their gazes locked onto each other's, and instinctively, they both understood what he had to do. Her eyes grew wide with fear, and his narrowed with determination. She ran for her life, and like any other frightened prey, she panicked, and ran away from safety instead of towards it. She ran down a path, into a part of the city abandoned this time of night. It was only a matter of time before he caught her.

He was surprised when he realized he was crying. Hot tears burned his face. Tears for her? For himself, perhaps? Tears for the depths of this mess he'd gotten himself into, for the corner he'd painted himself into, and for the loss of this beautiful woman?

Her body lay carelessly splayed on the dirty ground, and he gently took both arms and folded them across her midsection. He straightened each twisted leg, and pressed them close together, replacing the shoe that had come off in the struggle. He never meant to hurt her like this. It was an accident, but of course, no one would ever believe that. So he walked quietly away, destroyed and for the time being, relieved.

In the dark, they looked like lovers. *A whore and her trick—getting it on,* Lazarus thought, lying still like stone, and quiet as a mouse, watching the couple take care of business, struggling to recall what it was like to make love to a woman. He waited until the shadowed man crawled off her, caught his breath, and then left her lying there in the cold, night air, with the snow falling. She never moved. Lazarus watched her for what seemed like hours and she never moved.

Death wasn't a brand new song to him. Lazarus knew death, and he knew all the words to it, too. He'd seen it a million different ways, heard it in a thousand different sounds, and he'd smelled plenty of it. The shit stunk, like garbage, but on her it didn't. On her, it smelled damn good, good enough to eat and to drink and to sleep next to. She was one of them pretty women—picture pretty, like she shouldn't even be real. Soft pretty, like if you touched her, she'd disappear in a puff of smoke. She looked like someone had painted her, and the mothafucka had a hell of an imagination too. He chuckled, gazing down at her, gently touching the mass of tangled brown hair on her head. Lazarus leaned down close and inhaled. "Damn!" he said breathless. Truth be told, he was grateful for this moment. A woman like her wouldn't let him within two feet of her if she was alive. It took death to bring him this gift, and in a revelation, he smiled knowing that sometimes, even death had its moments.

He believed he'd seen her before, countless times or maybe only in dreams. He was blind to people most times because people were blind to him. He leaned down again and lowered his mouth to hers. The last time he'd kissed a woman—when was it? Back when he was a young man, and clean, and drove a fancy car. He'd fucked plenty, but he hadn't kissed many. Snow lighted on her face. He pressed his lips to hers and lingered there until he realized that she'd never be able to kiss him back. But then, what did he expect? A woman like her would cringe at him being this close, if she were alive. She didn't belong here with him, dirty, old, crazy Lazarus, kneeling over her, and wanting to kiss her one last time before they came and took her away. Angels. Or the police. Whoever got there first.

Ties That Bind

Fatema Morris had to pee. And then she had to throw up. She forced open her eyes, squinting and trying desperately to focus on the digital clock on the nightstand next to her bed. It was one-thirty in the afternoon. She groaned miserably, then slowly managed to sit up and swing her feet over the side of the bed. The jackhammer assaulting her head pounded so hard she fell back and covered her face with a pillow. A few minutes later, she still had to pee and the bed was spinning so fast, she really had to throw up. How the hell was she going to make it to the bathroom without releasing bodily fluids? The shrill sound of the phone ringing pierced her brain like an ice pick, damn near killing her.

"Hello," she answered, grunting irritably.

"Well, if it isn't Sleeping Beauty." She recognized his voice and immediately regretted answering that phone. "I was worried about you, sweetheart, and was wondering if you wanted me to send the coroner over to see if you were still breathing," he teased.

"I can't talk right now," she told him, as she hurried into the bathroom.

"You sound like shit," he felt the need to say.

Fatema didn't know which end to put into the toilet first, but ended up sitting down to relieve herself and started to hang up.

"I take it you don't remember last night?" he questioned, unaware of the peril she was in.

That question certainly got her attention, though. No, she didn't remember last night. She'd been drunk off her ass last night, so how was she supposed to remember anything about it?

She searched through the fog of her memories to try and piece together an evening in which she probably embarrassed the hell out of herself, and would undoubtedly end up lamenting. "Party," she mumbled. "The Christmas party at that little club in LoDo." Vague images flashed in her mind, but nothing cohesive. It suddenly dawned on her that he wouldn't be asking her about last night if he hadn't played some crucial role in it. "You were there?"

He chuckled, sarcastically. "Of course I was there, baby. You called me, and invited me to the party. Don't you remember?"

She hated when he did that condescending thing, knowing full well he knew the answer to the question before he'd even asked it.

"I did?" she asked, disgusted with herself. "Why would I do that? I thought you divorced me."

"As a matter of fact, I did," he gloated. "But that doesn't mean I don't still care. Besides, you were lonely, missed the hell out of me, apologized profusely for having been such a terrible and inconsiderate wife, and you were too drunk to drive and needed a ride home. So I accepted your apology and undying gratitude and love, and showed up like the knight in shining armor that I am."

Fatema slumped on the toilet, and shook her head. "You sure it was me who called?" she asked shamefully, hating herself more than she hated anyone, even him. "Why in the hell would I call you, Drew, of all people?"

"Now, now," he said, trying to console her. "What's a designated driver between divorced people?"

Her stomach made a gurgling sound, and the taste of last night's liquor rose like bile in her throat. Fatema reached up into the medicine cabinet and found the Pepto. She drank it straight with no chaser, right out of the bottle, and then wiped the pink mustache from her top lip with the back of her hand. One last question bubbled in her guts. "Did we fuck?" A dreadful feeling overwhelmed her, as she waited for him to answer.

"Like champions, baby," he said proudly.

Fatema nearly fell off the throne, but held on tight to the sink and caught herself.

"You rode with the best of them, cowgirl, slobbering all over yourself and me too, come to think of it. I swear, it was the stuff dreams are made of."

Fatema rolled her eyes and groaned.

"But don't worry," he assured her. "It's over, and regardless of what you might think, I knew I'd respect you in the morning. I'd like to think you feel the same way about me."

"I hate you, Drew," she muttered disgusted. "I hate you so much."

"Hate me!" he said aghast. "How can you? Last night you loved every inch of me, Fatema. You loved me from the top of my head to the soles of my feet and everywhere in between, girl—just like a porn star."

"Shut up!"

"You professed your love to me at least six times . . . no, more than that, but I lost count after like seven."

"Why'd you call me, Drew?" Fatema burped, threatening to vomit any second. "To gloat? To what? To make me feel like shit?"

"No." He sounded sincere. "To thank you, Fatema, that's all. I had a lovely evening and I wanted to let you know how much I appreciated it. And besides, I figured that as drunk as you were, you'd probably wake up feeling like shit whether I called or not."

She took another drink from the Pepto bottle. "I'm hanging up now, and if you ever call me again—"

"I thought you said you loved me?"

"I swear I'll wait outside your apartment and smash your girlfriend underneath the wheels of my Mini Cooper."

"Now that's just evil."

"You're evil! You're an evil, evil man, Andrew Vincent, and I never want to see you again!"

"Call me if you need anything," he blurted out quickly before she hung up on him.

By day, and when she was sober, she'd convinced herself that she was over her ex-husband, but sometimes at night or after she'd had one too many butter babies and tequila shots, she realized that deep down, she really wasn't, and something about alcohol and that eight pack of his resurrected ferocious memories and stirred her loins viciously enough to drop her to her knees. Like magic, his number rolled off her fingertips and into her cell phone and everything after that was a blur of resentment and regret.

They'd been divorced for less than a year, but she'd left him long before their marriage ended. She and Drew met when she hired him as her personal trainer, and he was a decent guy, good-looking, with dreams of a family, owning some real estate, and growing old together. Fatema dreamed of becoming the first black female correspondent on *60 Minutes*, hosting her own morning show in New York City, or being the next great White House correspondent and best friends with Michelle Obama. She put her career first, over their marriage, then had the nerve to get pissed off when she found out he was cheating on her with a tall willowy redhead from the gym.

Fatema sat at her kitchen table drinking her third cup of black coffee, still nursing her migraine and feeling plenty damned pissed at herself for the hangover, which could've been avoided, and for messing around with Drew's ass, which also could have been avoided had she been sober and in her right mind. She ran her hand through the tangled nest on her head and sighed. Her life had gone to hell, racing out of control at lightning speed, headed straight for a cliff, and she just stood there, watching the whole thing happen. Was it any wonder that she drank too much, or was still having an affair with her ex, who was damn near married to somebody else? Fatema had lost track of herself and her goals.

She was nine the first time she stood in front of her mirror talking into a hairbrush and pretending to be a reporter. Fatema had a goal back then, but she didn't have one anymore. She used to pour everything into her job, but one day she woke up and realized she had nothing to show for all her efforts except an ex-husband, a one-bedroom condo, and a Mini Cooper that she adored the same way other women adored children or animals. Fatema had emptied all of her passion into the stories she'd put entirely too much faith in, expecting to be rewarded for her daring insight and vision, only to have her passion doused the last time one of her stories was passed over for an award, and it dawned on her that it was the rewards that mattered to her more than the heart of a good story. Her motive for choosing this career had been skewed from the beginning and one day, she just accepted the fact that she'd become a reporter for all the wrong reasons.

She turned on the television to drown out the sound of her own nagging thoughts. Debra Byers was one of the premier anchors of Channel 4's evening news, and Fatema despised her. The woman looked like a rodent, sunburned, with a thin hapless look in her eyes. Deb was a robot with no drive or passion of her own, and yet, here she was, the news darling of Denver, Colorado, with her picture plastered on billboards and the sides of city buses. Success. How do you spell it? B-O-R-I-N-G.

"The body of a young woman was found early this morning by a driver crossing the Corona overpass, just off of Speer Boulevard, southwest of Downtown Denver. The woman has been identified as twenty-seven-year-old Toni Robbins, a city government employee who volunteered regularly at a local homeless shelter."

Fatema sat frozen with her mouth hanging open. She couldn't believe it. "No," she cried out, covering her mouth with her hands.

Toni's photograph flashed on the television. The young woman smiled, looking vibrant and promising. Fatema knew that picture well. She'd seen it many times on Toni's dresser years ago, when the two of them had shared a small apartment together in Denver's Capitol Hill neighborhood.

The lead detective, Bruce Baldwin, appeared on

screen. "The family of Miss Robbins was notified this morning," he explained stoically. "This case has our full attention, and we won't rest until the killer is behind bars."

"Toni was incredibly special," Nelson Monroe, Director of The Broadway Shelter of Denver, told reporters. Visibly shaken by her death, he worked overtime to maintain his composure. "She . . . uh," his voice cracked, "worked alongside me and my staff at the Shelter two, sometimes three days a week. Toni was a caring, generous person and something like this shouldn't happen to someone like her." He walked away, shaking his head. "It's a shame. It's terrible."

Deb Byers gravely finished up her report. "Police are investigating all leads in this case, and are asking anyone who might have seen or heard anything to call the number at the bottom of your screen immediately."

Fatema hadn't realized she was crying. Tears streamed down her face, and she struggled to catch her breath. Disbelief wrestled with the shock of seeing Toni's picture and hearing her name on the news in the same sentence with the word "killed." Who would do—why?

Her phone rang and she picked it up without thinking. "Hello?" she sobbed.

It was Drew. "Did you see the news?" he asked solemnly.

Fatema couldn't speak, but she didn't need to.

"Do I need to come over there?" he asked tenderly.

Fatema didn't answer, but she needed him, and he knew it.

"I'll be there in twenty minutes."

King of Kings

Never let them see you sweat.
Or mourn.

Or covet something you can no longer have.

Lucas Shaw sat in the study of his palatial Cherry Hills home, staring blankly at the fifty-two-inch plasma television mounted on the wall, watching the story unfold about the death of a young woman.

"Becoming Mayor is the first step, Lucas," his father-in-law told him a year ago after he'd won his campaign for the Mayor of Denver. "The senate is calling out to you, son, and I say you need to consider answering the call."

It was an idea he relished. One that was spoonfed to him by a man who only expected the best for his daughter because the best was what she was accustomed to. Senator Lucas Shaw was out there waiting for Mayor Shaw to catch up to him, and Lucas had been riding that locomotive to the ultimate prize for the last fifteen years of his career, allowing no one or anything to hinder his progress, until she came along.

His eyes glistened with tears as one news story melted into another, but all he could see was her face, smiling back at him. He heard her laughter in his ears, felt her touch on his skin, and tasted her in his mouth. Until she'd come along, Lucas had never known the truth of loving a woman, or being loved by one. He'd never yearned so deeply for anyone's company, or the sound of another person's voice. Toni had come into his life and threatened to derail him and everything he'd worked so hard to achieve, without even trying.

He closed his eyes and recalled the last time they were intimate. Lucas fought to reject this vision, but it wouldn't let him. She was such a beautiful woman; beautiful in a natural, quiet and delicate way.

He took a deep breath, and slowly released it.

"Nothing about us should work," she had said quietly, lying naked on top of him. He was inside her, rigid and long, wet with her juices. Making love to her was a thing to be savored and unrushed.

Her long, dark hair hung past her face and brushed lightly against his skin. Toni's caramel complexion glistened with perspiration, and her dark, wide eyes bore into his.

"Everything about us works," he assured her, gently rubbing his fingers along her spine, and down to the curve of her plump behind.

Toni arched her back then gazed back at him with a mischievous twinkle in her eyes.

"You're a married man, Mr. Mayor. And that doesn't work."

He pulled her to him, and filled her mouth with his tongue, then rolled her over, and braced himself over her. "I work hard for you," he insisted. "I will always work hard for you."

Lucas knelt between her thighs and took hold of her hips. He moved down and kissed the space between her breasts, then gobbled up one nipple, and then the other. Toni rolled her hips against him, and moaned her pleasure.

The best hotels.

The best restaurants.

The best . . . the best . . . the best.

She was his delicious secret.

She helped him to maintain sanity in an insane world.

She gave him peace, where there was none.

She loved him for who he wasn't, more than for who he was.

And then she dared to take it all away from him.

"I don't even know you anymore, Lucas. You're crazy, and I can't believe I ever fell for a man like you."

"What the hell is that supposed to mean? A man like me?"

"I've seen a side of you that—scares me, worries me—that doesn't make sense to me. You'll do anything to get what you want, and it doesn't matter who you hurt in the process. Does it?"

He had no answer to give, and she didn't wait around for one.

Lucas dried his eyes, and turned off the television. As if on cue, his wife knocked lightly on the door before opening it. "Don't forget we have to be at the Feldmans' at seven-thirty. It's six-thirty now, Lucas," she informed him, then left as abruptly as she'd come in.

He sighed, surprisingly relieved, yet brokenhearted.

The thought of living without her, knowing she was living in the same city, and working in the same building as he was, and knowing that he couldn't have her, had been incomprehensible. Lucas guessed the old adage really did hold some solace after all. He couldn't have her, and now, no one else could either. Unfortunately, he found comfort in that.

Invisible

T he cops reminded him of roaches, swarming around the place where they found that woman. Damn, he hated cops. But then, they didn't care much for him either, he thought, smirking. Lazarus watched from a distance, failing to blend in with the crowd, but managing to be a part of them anyway. That spot down there was his favorite place at night, next to the river because the sound of the water would lull him to sleep.

Lazarus killed a man and his little girl not far from here years ago when he was a young man. Back then, he drank too much when he drove, and smashed up his 1980 Thunderbird sedan and those people right along with it. He'd always thought it a shame that he managed to walk away. Spent plenty of time in prison, though, but he shouldn't have been the one to live.

He wondered sometimes if he had kids of his own. Lazarus couldn't remember children, at least none that looked like him anyway. His memory was sketchy at best, though, filled with blank and empty spots; he'd lost track of time, and eventually figured that time had probably lost track of him too, so him and time were even as far as he was concerned.

Eventually, the cold started getting to him and Lazarus knew he needed to walk before his joints grew stiff. Another reminder that he'd been living out here too long. Lazarus was fifty-nine or sixty. He wasn't sure which, but he knew he was one or the other. He was old enough in years, but his body felt like it was even older.

He enjoyed this time of year, though. Pretty Christmas lights hung overhead, folks stood in the streets singing for no other reason than the season, and bells rang from every goddamned where. Lazarus startled some people walking ahead of him when he let out a hearty laugh. They turned and looked at him, and he looked right back, and nodded his acknowledgment. Naturally, they hurried along to try and get away from him. Had his knees not hurt so bad, he'd have hurried right along after them just enough to scare the shit out of them.

As he scuffled heavy-footed along the 16th Street Mall, people instinctively made wide paths around him. Anybody else might've taken it personally, but Lazarus appreciated the extra room. "Got a lotta snow for this time of year!" he said much too loudly to no one in particular. Of course he didn't expect anyone to respond, but if someone had, he'd have ignored them. Lazarus never had been much of a conversationalist, and he didn't care too much for people. So most of his conversations were between Lazarus and himself, just in earshot of everybody else.

Everything he owned he carried in his backpack: some extra socks which didn't match, a thin, worn

coat that made a better pillow than something to keep
him warm, an empty pill bottle with his real name on
it. He ran out of pills a long time ago, but kept the
bottle to remind him of who he'd once been. And a
broken yellow crayon. He found it on the street once
and kept it because—hell—he liked yellow. And he
carried a key. For thirty years he'd been trying to remember what it went to. He held on to it, though,
just in case.

"Got snow I say," he muttered again. Cold seeped
in through the bottom of his boots. The soles had
worn thin and he needed to get another pair soon.
Sometimes they gave them away at The Broadway, or
he'd have to go digging around in the trash to find a
pair. People were wasteful, throwing away perfectly
good shit without even thinking about it, but it was
all good if it meant finding a decent pair of shoes.

He was tired as hell, walking from dawn to sunset,
stopping long enough to check for food where he
knew people sometimes tossed it. Stopping long
enough to stare at his reflection in the windows of
the buildings, wondering what he must've looked
like before he became the man he was now. Lazarus
stared at the ground as he walked. People dropped
things—change, something good to eat, and they
walked over that shit too, because they were too busy
to notice. He noticed, though. Lazarus noticed most
things, and by the end of the day, he had a nice
chunk of change jingling in his pocket. He stopped
in a coffee shop and ordered a cup of hot coffee and
a donut. Then Lazarus sat down on one of the
benches, and stared up at the Christmas lights above
his head.

He tried not to think about her. The police had
come and picked her up early, like he knew they

would. Lazarus had covered her up, nicely, though, with something to keep her warm. He'd been a hell of a man in his day, he thought proudly. Women like her practically threw themselves at him, because he was so good-looking. Too bad about what happened to her. Hell, he thought they were getting it on, which is why he let them be. If he'd known the moth-afucka was killing her, he'd have done something. His mind went blank as to what. He'd have done something. If the cops knew he'd been there, they'd probably think he did it. Which is why he wasn't try-ing to tell them a damn thing. They were always try-ing to throw his ass in jail for one reason or another. He wasn't about to make it easy for them.

"The police can't stand a mothafucka!" he spat, startling some woman walking past him.

The brotha cried when he walked away from her. Like his heart was broken and like he was sorry. Lazarus watched him leave, and turn one last time to look at her. He never saw Lazarus because it was so dark and Lazarus knew how to lie still so people would keep on walking and not bother him. Lazarus knew who he was though. His ass had been in the paper, and he'd seen him someplace else too, but damned if he could recall where. That woman looked familiar too. Only she looked even prettier when she wasn't dead.

Hidden Treasure

"My father is an important diplomat. I'm sure he has half the world out looking for me." Alina's Russian accent was almost too thick to understand, but Ivy listened intently, hoping that she was telling the truth. "I came here to attend American university—Brown," she continued talking in a low voice. "Have you heard of it?"

Alina was nineteen, two years older than Ivy, and she was beautiful, tall—at least five-ten, thin, with silky brown hair cut short, and crystal blue eyes. Ivy had lived in the basement of this old house for months, and she'd seen people from all over the world come and go. Most of them couldn't speak English and the few who did didn't say much because they were afraid and confused. Alina was different, though, and she spoke like royalty. "When my father finds out what's happened to me, he'll have their heads. All of them."

Across the room were two women and one man, sitting huddled together speaking in Chinese or some other Asian language. "They took my passport," Alina continued, hardly noticing that Ivy hadn't said a word. "There were four of us who came here to attend university, and they took all of our passports. When I protested, one of them hit me. Can you believe it? He hit me!" Her clear blue eyes clouded over and she pressed her hand against the side of her face. "I told him, my father is Ambassador Petrov, and if he finds out what you are doing to me—" Alina started to sob quietly. "What do you think they will do to us?" she finally asked Ivy.

"I don't know," Ivy shrugged. Alina had the benefit of being a diplomat's daughter, but Ivy was no one's daughter. She'd run away from home two years ago. Her mother had been a heroin addict and her father, whom she barely knew, had another family altogether and wanted nothing to do with her. Someone had offered her a ride once, and she made the mistake of taking it. She never knew their names, and the faces were always different. But Ivy was a commodity. She'd heard them call her that once, and she was a hot ticket on the Internet. They'd made her strip down to her bra and panties at the first place they stopped, made her swallow a handful of pills and took her picture. Not long after that, the men started coming and doing terrible things to her and there was nothing she could do to stop them. That's what they did to her. But she didn't tell Alina because her rich father might be able to save her and there was no sense worrying her needlessly.

Since Ivy had been in this place, though, she'd been pretty well taken care of. They'd starved her before, but here, she had plenty to eat, and the men hadn't come at all. But she wasn't allowed to leave. The people here were nicer than the rest, but it was still a prison and Ivy wanted her freedom more than anything.

"If she'd have gone for help, the police should've been here by now," Alina's voice quivered. "Don't you think? Maybe she's one of them. I think she might have been."

The night before, a pretty black woman had crept down the stairs and seen Ivy and Alina in the basement chained to the radiator by the ankles. She'd gasped at the sight of them, and started to speak, but the sound of voices came from somewhere in the house, and the woman ran away.

"I don't think she's one of them," Ivy whispered. "She didn't look like somebody who'd do this to us."

"She should have gone to the police, then. And she should have told them where we were and—"

Alina stopped speaking when she heard the door at the top of the stairs open. Heavy footsteps slowly descended down the stairs. Everyone in the room stared at the man as he approached Alina and Ivy and stood between them. He dropped a newspaper on the floor and without saying a word, left as abruptly as he came.

After he closed the door behind him, Ivy tentatively reached across the floor and picked up the paper. On the front page was a picture of the woman they'd seen the other night. She wouldn't be going to the police after all. Hope sank like a ship in Ivy's stomach, as she covered her mouth with her hand and stifled a cry.

Denver Woman Found Murdered

Ivy looked at Alina, who knew instinctively that no one would be coming to their rescue today.

The Gathering

After the funeral, family and friends gathered at the house where Toni grew up. Esther and Thomas Robbins were gracious people despite the tragic loss of their oldest daughter. Everyone ate and drank and reminisced about Toni, but Fatema didn't have much of an appetite. Since Fatema moved to Denver from Alexandria, Virginia to attend college, the Robbinses practically had become family, and Toni was as much her sister as her real sisters were back home. They'd grown apart these past few years for different reasons and in different directions.

Toni majored in sociology, but ended up working in the planning division for the city. She'd never gotten married or had children, but she was the one who loved the idea. Between the two of them, they both figured she'd be the first to settle down, but the task fell in Fatema's lap to everyone's surprise. They drifted apart after Fatema and Drew got married, but Toni had been her maid of honor, and she had been slated to be godmomma too, if Fatema had given into Drew's whim to start having babies right away.

The old Park Hill home, was still the most warm and inviting place she'd ever known. The Robbinses were stuck in an eighties time warp, with their decor. The pink and sea foam green striped wallpaper and that atrocious rose-colored carpet made her smile, recalling how wonderful it was that they'd left well enough alone. Fatema fought back tears the way she'd been doing all afternoon, when Tracy, Toni's younger sister, sat down beside her on the loveseat in the family room.

"It never ceases to amaze me how anybody could have an appetite after a funeral," she said, grabbing hold to Fatema's hand. "I don't think I'll ever eat again."

Tracy was five years younger than Fatema and Toni, and when she was a kid, Fatema couldn't stand her. Thank goodness they grew up. Tracy was a younger version of her sister, just more random. She wasn't as refined as Toni, choosing to wear sarongs, or tattered jeans, and pulling her natural hair back into a puff. She was as beautiful as her sister, though. Toni had been the shorter of the two, more petite, and Tracy was dangerously curvy. If she wasn't careful, she could easily cause a traffic accident.

"She called me about two months ago." Fatema swallowed hard. "Left me a message, and I never called her back. I kept meaning to, but—"

Tracy looked at her with tears in her eyes. "Shame on you."

Fatema squeezed her hand, and smiled weakly. "I know. I suck."

Tracy managed to laugh. "I always thought so."

This time, Fatema laughed. "You never did like me."

"You're like my sister, Fat Ema," she quipped. "And I didn't like her much either."

Fatema cringed when Tracy called her Fat Ema, but what could she do? They were both grieving the loss of the most important person between them, and it just felt wrong to protest.

"I miss the hell out of her."

"I'm lost without her," Tracy's eyes clouded over.

Fatema pulled the young woman to her and held her. "I know, honey. I know."

"She used to talk about you behind your back, you know," Tracy said, as she sat up and wiped away tears.

Fatema looked appalled. "She did? What did she say?"

"Said you were your own worst enemy and your biggest fan."

The two of them fell into each other laughing hysterically. People in the room looked at them like they were crazy.

"She was so right," Fatema nodded. "Looking at myself is like watching a train wreck. I don't want to look, but I can't help it."

"She loved the mess outta you, though." Tracy squeezed her hand. "And she knew you loved her too."

"How was she doing, Tracy?"

Tracy sighed. "Well, you know how she always hated drama?"

"Loathed it."

"She was drowning in it, Fatema." Fatema looked stunned. "She was a moody mess because of it too."

"Man problems?"

"Men problems," Tracy corrected her. "And work

problems. And I'm-not-happy-with-the-way-my-life-turned-out blues."

"She sounds like every other woman I know," Fatema said sarcastically.

"Speak for yourself," Tracy shot back. "Because I ain't tripping."

"Sorry. I forgot that you had your act together."

"Since birth."

"So who was she seeing? Anybody I might know?"

"Well, the brotha giving her the most grief is affectionately known as Mr. X because she wouldn't tell me his name."

"He was married?"

"Of course. He started tripping when she broke it off with him, though, blowing up her cell phone, blasting her with e-mails, even showing up at her job. But the other brotha had her thinking marriage and kids and the house in the suburbs. She was really feeling him. I think she loved him."

"What was his name?"

"Nelson. Cute too, girl!" Tracy exclaimed. "I met him once, and slobbered all over myself."

Fatema laughed, and the reporter in her stirred from her slumber, and that inquisitive thing she came by naturally made the hair on her arms stand up. "You think either of them might have some idea of why this happened?"

Tracy cut her off. "Girl, don't ask me. Toni was—I don't know. She'd been acting really strange lately. I don't even think Nelson knew where she was coming from half the time. We all met for drinks one night, laughing and having a good time, then all of a sudden, she gets real serious and brings up something she'd heard on the news about some missing Russian ambassador's daughter. And that led to conversations of other people's missing children and immigrants in this country and disadvantages and exploitation. I lost my buzz real quick. Nelson did too, from the look on his face, but since it was obvious the man had caught feelings over her, he entertained the conversation. I left. But, you know how she got sometimes," Tracy gave a sly grin. "Every once in awhile she got a wild hair up her behind to save the world and everybody in it and that sociology major came up like the resurrected dead or something."

"Yeah, I used to have to tell her to back off, because she used to try and drag me along."

"But she was all obsessed about this chick. I went by her place one day and she was on the Internet, reading all of these articles about her, Alina Petrov or whatever. She showed me some of the articles, and I asked her what was up, but she just said . . . she didn't know for sure."

Fatema drove home with the conversation she'd had with Tracy heavy on her mind. Toni had been dead for nearly a week, and the police still hadn't found the killer. Maybe she was just looking for a reason to butt in. Tracy hadn't told her anything all that extraordinary. Toni had a man she'd broken up with and who had her tripping. That was a broad term, "tripping," and it could've meant a lot of things. Jilted lover murders woman for wanting to leave him—seemed mighty clichéd for this day and age, but hey, it happened. And then there was the other thing making her "trip." That girl who'd gone missing about a month ago that Toni had become so enthralled with recently. How and why would something like that ever pop up on the radar of a city planner? Fatema wondered.

* * *

Tracy had been kind enough to give Fatema a key to her sister's condo. She needed to see it—to connect with her friend one last time. She stood outside the door with the key in her hand, daring herself to put it in the lock and open the door. Fatema didn't know how long she'd been standing there, but eventually she realized that today was not the day to go inside. She'd burst like a dam if she did, and there'd be no amount of objectivity in her.

"Tomorrow," she whispered to Toni's spirit. "I'll go inside tomorrow, T."

Nelson

There was a time in his career when Nelson Monroe waited hands and feet on the rich and famous. He was the very successful manager of a very successful five star hotel called The Menagerie in downtown Denver, and he was miserable. Ten years ago, he turned his life around and found his true calling. These days, he was a lot poorer, but his life had purpose now, and he loved what he did for a living.

Nelson could've written a book on his life. He'd literally come from nothing to become a successful young businessman, and the sky would have been literally the limit had he kept on that same path. But there was always something in him that would never fully let him enjoy his success. There was the sad part of him, lonely and afraid, that served a dual purpose. On the one hand, it drove him to work hard to finish school, get into college, and graduate at the top of his class, and find his own piece of the American dream. But on the other hand, it was the thorn in his side, the fly in his soup, that one thing that held a part of him at bay, standing on the outside of the window looking in.

His mother raised him and his brother. Nelson's father died when Nelson was young and he barely remembered the man. But he remembered being happy before his father passed away. He remembered feeling safe. His mother did the best she could, but it was never good enough. For years they lived on the streets, homeless, wandering, the boys were in and out of school. They slept in strange places and beds, and found food wherever they could. Those were his formative years, and they were as much a part of who he was as an arm or leg.

One Thanksgiving, for reasons he still didn't understand, Nelson volunteered at The Broadway to help serve food to the homeless, and he felt like a man reborn. A man with purpose. It was the happiest day in his life, and he said a quiet prayer that night, thanking God for his true calling finally finding him. He became a regular volunteer, helping out any way he could, from preparing and serving food, to purchasing supplies with his own money to help keep the shelter thriving. It was such a gradual and natural shift in his life, that he seemed to wake up one day and find that the hotel had become a distant memory, replaced by a run-down and tattered old church that had magically become his.

"Nelson, now, you need to get away from my stove 'fore you burn something up." Lois Anderson nudged him with her hip and took the spoon he was stirring in a pot from his hands.

"How many times do I have to tell you I know how to cook, woman?" he retorted playfully, relinquishing control to the older woman.

Lois immediately began to toss various seasonings into the simmering chili. "No. You know how to heat up, but you ain't no cook. That's my job."

"I'm just trying to help, Miss Lois." He softened his tone.

"Fine. You can help me by finishing up that budget you trying not to work on so I'll know what I got to work with the rest of the month. That's how you can help me."

Lois was like everyone's mother. A sweet, plump, feisty woman with a heart of gold and that tough kind of love that made you just want to do better. She'd been there longer than he had.

The kitchen was her domain, and off limits to everyone except—

A lump swelled in his throat just thinking about her. Lois was a valiant woman, but she'd been close to Toni, and even though she masked the sadness in her voice, there was no way she could hide it in her eyes.

"You miss her," he said, quietly. "Don't you?"

Lois continued seasoning and stirring, almost as if she hadn't heard him. "I do," she answered shortly.

A part of him expected Lois to turn to him, and fall crying into his arms, but then he remembered that Lois would do no such thing. She'd grieve, like all of them, in her own quiet way. Nelson left her to her duties, went back into his office and closed the door behind him.

He stared out of the window to the brick wall of the building next door, just across the alley. He'd given up his hope of ever actually having a "view" a long time ago. Through the years, Nelson had memorized every line, every brick of that building wall, and learned to meditate on it.

Toni had been so much like him. She lived and worked in a world that could never live up to her passion. And she'd been drawn to The Broadway because it filled the same void in her that it filled in him.

"The Broadway can break your heart," she told him late one night.

The two of them lay naked on the floor of her apartment. Nelson held her in his arms, and buried his nose in her hair.

"But I'm needed there," she continued quietly. "I'm doing something good there."

No one knew they were seeing each other. They were private people, and what mattered most to both of them were the people who came through The Broadway who needed their help.

"I love you," he confessed that night.

Toni stared back at him, and softly pressed her palm to his cheek. She smiled. "Good," was all she said.

Nelson blinked and a tear fell down his cheek. Life was a balance of the good and the bad. Angels were all around, but then, so were devils. The police had questioned him and his staff several times about the night she died.

Had she worked at the shelter that night?

Yes, but she left early.

Do you know where she went after she left the shelter?

Home. He assumed.

What time did you leave, Mr. Monroe?

His usual time around nine.

And where did you go after you left?

Stopped at the store for milk (he still had the receipt if they needed to see it) and then back to his apartment, where

he spoke briefly with a neighbor in the elevator on the way
up. And yes. He spent the rest of the evening at home alone.

Did she have any problems with anyone who
worked here or any of its residents?

No. Everyone loved Toni.

A knot tightened in his stomach.

Everyone loved her. He loved her more than he
ever thought possible.

In My Sister's House

Toni's parents couldn't bring themselves to pack up her apartment yet. Tracy left crying every time she tried. Fatema let herself inside, carrying boxes and packing tape. The Northeast Denver condo was impeccable, but Fatema wasn't surprised. Toni always had been a neat freak, bordering on Obsessive Compulsive Disorder, and Fatema had always been the opposite. Both of them used to drive the other crazy when they lived together, but somehow, they found a hallowed in-between space of acceptance that worked for them.

Toni had tastefully decorated in muted earth tones and textures; a sliver of her wild side came out in unexpected splashes of vibrant colors, fusing the peace of her abode, making everything look like it had fallen out of a magazine.

The police had been through her apartment with a fine tooth comb, and surprisingly enough, had been pretty respectful. Toni's laptop, which had been confiscated, sat on the coffee table. All of her personal files were stacked in a chair across from the sofa, instead of being placed back in the cabinet where they belonged.

Fatema turned on the CD player, knowing that she'd dig whatever song it played because Toni had great taste in music. Angie Stone serenaded her, as she slowly began packing, forcing herself not to get bogged down by sadness. She should've kept in touch. She should've called more. She should've returned Toni's calls. She should've kept better track of her friend.

While putting the file folders in boxes, Fatema accidentally dropped one, and all its contents spilled out onto the floor. Newspaper clippings going back several months of missing children littered the floor. She sat down on the floor and studied each of them before dropping them into the box next to her.

Fifteen-Year-Old Girl Missing
Eleven-Year-Old Girl Kidnapped
Sixteen-Year-Old Girl Found Dead After
Missing Three Years

Toni had been obsessed with this stuff. In some cases she'd even gone so far as to research some of these stories on the Internet, printing hundreds of pages of information and keeping detailed files on these girls. Gradually, Toni's research changed from stories of missing girls to the subject of human trafficking. Her files contained story after story of people from all over the world being coerced, tricked, or even abducted, and forced to work for next to nothing, enslaved and tortured, forced to live secretly under the most inhumane conditions.

In one of the files, she found the picture of the

Russian college girl who'd disappeared from an airport in New York City on her way to an Ivy League college. The woman's picture plastered the front page of the article. Her name was Alina Petrov, and she was nineteen years old. Her parents said in an interview that the last time they'd seen their daughter was when they said goodbye to her at the airport in London with several of her friends who had all been accepted at Brown. Upon further investigation, after their daughter was reported missing, Brown had no record of any of the students.

She knew the police had already gone through Toni's laptop, but Fatema turned it on anyway, hoping she could get a better idea of what Toni had been on to.

Of course it was password protected. And of course, Fatema knew what the password was. B-I-L-B-O. Toni had been a huge fan of J.R.R. Tolkien's book *The Hobbit* and named her first cat after the main character. Toni used that password for everything, even after that damn cat got run over by the garbage truck eight years ago.

She had no idea what she was looking for, but she started with Toni's e-mail account. She typed in BILBO again and instantly had access to Toni's inbox. There were hundreds of e-mails, mostly spam, a few invites, and notes from friends. And some very interesting strings from two men, Luke1963, and Mainman2. Reading through these e-mails was like reading the woman's diary.

Luke1963:
We need to talk. Please. Just talk to me. Meet me somewhere.
TBabe:

You're disgusting and you need help. I should've left a
long time ago. I can't believe I actually believed I loved
you.

Luke1963:

It's not what you think. You mean everything to me, and
without you, I'm afraid of what I'm capable of. Please
don't shut me out.

TBabe:

You're a greedy man, L. You want it all, no matter who
you hurt in the process, no matter what it takes to get it.
You are not my responsibility.

Luke1963:

You said you loved me. Love works through problems. It
doesn't run away from them.

TBabe:

Love doesn't do the shit you do. If you don't leave me
alone, I swear, I'll put it out there.

The string from Mainman2 weeks later, was vastly
different.

Mainman2:

Guess what's on my mind? Go ahead. I'll give you three
guesses.

TBabe:

Me.

Two more.

Me, me, and us.

Mainman2:

That's four things. But yeah. When can I see you again?

TBabe:

My place. Tonight. At 6.

Mainman2:

Do I need to bring anything?

TBabe:

Yes—your smile and that sexy way you talk to me that makes my toes curl.

Mainman2:

If I didn't know better, I'd think you were just using me for my body.

TBabe:

Got a problem with that?

Mainman2:

Do you love me?

TBabe:

More every day.

Mainman2:

No. No problem. But even if you didn't love me, I still wouldn't have a problem with it.

So who the hell were Luke1963 and Mainman2? Fatema checked Toni's contacts list, and found that Luke1963's profile was left blank, while Mainman2 had information filled in. She wrote down his name, Nelson Monroe, and his phone number.

Only You

More than a week had passed since Ivy saw the headlines of the woman who'd been murdered. The Asian people living with her in the basement had been taken away, but Alina was still there, and growing less talkative and more despondent by the day. The woman taking care of them never looked at them, and seldom said a word when she came down. Alina had stopped eating and this time the woman stared angrily at her when she saw the girl's food virtually untouched on her plate.

"I'm not going to keep bringing food down if you're not going to eat it," she said, gritting her teeth. Alina sat like a stone, as if the woman hadn't spoken to her at all. "Fine," the woman, turned to leave. "You can starve for all I care."

Dark circles had formed under Alina's eyes. She slowly raised them to Ivy. "The food is disgusting," she whispered.

"But it's food," Ivy said. "And she won't bring you any more."

"I'd rather die than stay here," she said defiantly. "Unlike you. You're like a pet, Ivy. You do what they tell you to, without protest or fight, and they keep you like a cat or a dog." Her venomous words hurt, and Ivy averted her gaze. "I'm no one's pet."

"They'll kill you if you misbehave, Alina," Ivy said quietly. "And besides, this place isn't so bad."

"We're living in a dungeon, held captive against our will. So what if they kill us? As long as we stay here, we are already dead." Alina turned her back to Ivy, and cried herself to sleep in her cot the way she did every night. Ivy stayed up until dawn, thinking about what Alina had said.

The next morning, the man bought down breakfast, but only for Ivy. Alina pretended to be asleep. He wasn't a mean man. He'd never raised his voice, or even touched Ivy the way other men had touched her. But Ivy wouldn't let her guard down too much. He'd killed that woman in the paper, even though he hadn't admitted it. And if he was capable of killing, then he was capable of anything. He glanced at Ivy when he set her plate down in front of her, and almost smiled. Ivy couldn't help herself and almost smiled back.

At first, she wasn't going to say anything, but what Alina had said the night before gnawed at her inside. Ivy wasn't a pet and she did know how to speak up when she had to. "You should let us go," she told him as he turned to leave. Alina slowly turned over, suddenly aroused from her deep sleep. "We haven't done anything wrong," she said quietly, "and Alina"—Ivy looked at her—"her family will be worried about her. If you let us go, I promise we won't tell."

"My father is a powerful man," Alina blurted out. "He can give you money, mister. Lots of money. Please. Please let us go."

The man took a deep breath and knelt down among them. "If I could," he spoke tenderly, "I would. But that's not in my power to do."

"We won't tell," Ivy's voice cracked. "You've been good to us. Hasn't he, Alina?"

Alina glared at her, then stared back warmly at him. "Yes. Of course you have."

The man traced invisible circles on the floor with his fingertip, entranced deep in thought. The girls looked back and forth at each other and then at him.

"I've made terrible mistakes," he said. "Too many of them that I wish I could take back and erase. I've done things I never dreamed I'd do and that I know I'll never forgive myself for."

"Mister, please!" Alina said desperately. "Please just let us go! Whatever you've done I'm sure can be forgiven if you help us. Please—this is monstrous! It's inhuman! And you're a beast if you keep us here!"

"Alina!" Ivy shouted.

Before either of them knew what happened, the man swung hard and hit Alina across the mouth.

He bolted to his feet, spun around and kicked an empty wooden chair across the room. Alina lay across the bed, wailing and writhing in pain and bleeding from her mouth.

Ivy sat frozen, holding her plastic spoon in her hand, unable to move. He turned back to her, and took her tray from her, then glared down at her. "You're alive because of me," he growled. "If you leave this place— they will tear you to shreds! Do you understand that? You think that I'm a monster? Yeah, well, the real monsters are out there."

"We're sorry," Ivy whispered, tears filling her eyes.

"I don't have to come here, Ivy! I've got plenty of people who can come down here and bring this shit to you," he said, indicating her meal. "I don't need to be here looking at you or the ice fucking princess over there! But I come so that I can see how you are for my own peace of mind. And when the day comes that I stop showing up here, that's the day you'll know that I don't give a damn anymore. On that day, you'll see what hell is really like."

Several minutes passed after he left that Alina finally stopped crying. Her lip was swollen and she had a deep cut on the inside. She refused to look at Ivy, and Ivy stopped asking her if she were all right.

Robocop

"Look, I'm not trying to be a nuisance, but it's been more than a week, Detective Baldwin," Fatema sat at his desk in the precinct, challenging him. She'd told him she was a reporter for the *Denver News*, and he had reluctantly agreed to talk to her. "Are there any leads?"

The man looked exhausted and overworked, and impatient. Baldwin was a tall, thick, solid man. He had dark circles underneath his dark eyes, and wore his hair cut close to take the emphasis off his receding hairline. He'd been the lead detective on some of the city's most prominent cases, and Fatema could tell, detective work was definitely taking its toll on the older man. "We have a few, Miss Morris. And I assure you, we're following up on each and every one." He forced a condescending smile.

She hated interviewing cops. They went out of their way to be vague and politically correct with their answers, talking circles around the facts. "I don't meant to insult you fine folks here at the station." Fatema pulled one of Toni's file folders from her messenger bag and laid it down on his desk in front of him. "I'm sure you've seen all of this before. Do you think it has any bearing on who could've done this?"

He searched through the files, then stared strangely at Fatema. "Where did you get these?"

"From Toni's apartment," she answered immediately.

He leaned back and studied her. "What were you doing in Miss Robbins's apartment, Miss Morris?"

Fatema shifted in her seat. "Her family asked me to go there, and to help pack up some of her things."

"I see. And why would they do that?"

She cleared her throat. "She was my best friend."

He closed the folder then handed it back to her. "This *interview* is over Miss Morris."

"Aw, c'mon, Baldwin," she almost whined, "just tell me if this stuff has anything to do with why Toni might've died. Was she on to something? Could it have been a lover? I know she was seeing someone. And who's this Nelson Monroe cat? Who's Luke1963? I know you know."

He sat quietly for a moment, then finally responded. "You came to me under the guise of a reporter, not a best friend," he said calmly. Too calmly. "I don't appreciate the deception, Miss Morris."

Fatema sat there while the man quietly admonished her.

"But I'll tell you what I have told the family. We are following all leads, including the ones we found among Miss Robbins's personal belongings. Solving Toni Robbins' murder is my number one priority and I assure you I won't rest until I've found her killer."

Fatema shrank a bit in her seat and rolled her eyes at the overly-rehearsed rhetoric rolling off his lips.

"Now, please take your papers and go. I have work to do."

Fatema's eyes teared up, and she felt like a child. All of her objectivity was gone. Toni wasn't a stranger, and that fact sorely affected her judgment and professionalism. If she'd been a stranger, Fatema would've dug in and taken the hard line with this man. She'd have challenged him, and put what he knew to the test. But Robocop here was all she and Toni's family had at the moment. And she felt weak and sorry for letting her friend down again.

"She was like my sister," she said quietly, wringing her hands together in her lap. "And I need to know what happened to her. I need to know who did this."

"Yes, ma'am. We all need to know."

"I read her e-mails." She sniffed and dried her face with the back of her hand. "She was seeing someone, and I think she'd broken up with someone else."

He leaned back confidently in his seat, as if he already knew this. "Do you know either of these men?"

She shook her head. "Toni and I hadn't spoken in months," she admitted shamefully. "Do you know them?"

His demeanor seemed to become less defensive, and he managed a real smile this time. "We know the man she was seeing, yes."

"What about the other one? The one she broke up with?" she asked too anxiously.

All expression washed from his face. "We're working on it."

He was lying. He knew who the man was, but for whatever reason, he didn't want her to know.

"So, what about all this human trafficking stuff? Modern day slavery?"

He nodded. "Alive and well, unfortunately."

"Even here in the United States? I always thought that was third world shit."

"The U.S. has a huge market for the business. But most people think like you. That it's happening somewhere else, and oh, it's a terrible thing for that poor ignorant country on the other side of the world. I suppose we choose to turn a blind eye to it because it's human nature at its worst. And that's awfully hard to look at."

"Toni was always down for a cause. Do you think she was actually on to something?" The reporter in her crept out just a bit.

"Maybe," was all he'd say.

"You won't tell me because I'm a reporter, huh?"

He leaned forward and stared sincerely into her eyes. "I won't tell you because you've just lost your best friend to a terrible crime, and if I can't tell you something concrete, something that can give you a small sense of peace and solace, then I'd rather wait until I know for sure that I can."

She sighed, then gathered her things to leave. "Thanks, Robocop. I'll let you get back to work."

Nice man. He was a fucking dick though when it came to answering questions, and she was no closer to any answers than she was when she first walked into that police station.

He watched her leave. Ten years and twenty pounds ago, he'd have definitely made a move on that one, but a woman like that was entirely too much woman for him these days. Baldwin had a swollen prostate, high blood pressure, and absolutely no fight left in him, and his idea of a good time was sitting at home

on a Friday night, watching old reruns of *Law &
Order*, eating cold pizza and drinking warm beer.
Baldwin admired Miss Morris's behind, and smiled
warmly as she left. She was a good-looking woman,
smart, and a damn reporter. He'd managed to hold
the best friend in her at bay, but something told him
that the reporter in her wouldn't rest until she managed to identify those puzzle pieces she carried with
her in that folder. Nelson Monroe would no doubt
end up getting a visit from Fatema Morris as soon as
she figured out who he was, which wouldn't be hard.
Mayor Shaw, on the other hand, would be harder to
identify. He and Miss Robbins had done a damn
good job of keeping his identity hidden, but thanks
to that creepy guy in IT, they found out about him almost immediately. He'd have done better to send
smoke signals if he wanted to keep this woman a secret.

Was there a connection between the human trafficking issue and this woman's death? It was possible,
but he knew, like every other police officer on the
force knew, that finding and proving that shit was
damn near impossible. The perpetrators weren't so
obvious as gang members, wearing something as apparent as colors to give themselves away. And the victims were often too broken and afraid to admit they
had been forced to do something against their will.
Hell, half the prostitutes they arrested were probably
victims, but they'd never admit it. It was a nasty business. One that left you feeling dirty just thinking
about it, and Toni Robbins had been so obsessed
with it, he wondered how she could've even slept at
night.

True Love

Lisa Shaw was a beautiful and elegant woman. Lucas struck gold when he met her. Lisa was a product of the black elite, coming from old money, and a genealogy filled with doctors, professors, a lawyer thrown in every now and then for good measure. They met at Howard University and developed a made-for-television love story that seemed too good to be true from the start. Lucas came from a working class family from Texas, who ultimately migrated to Denver. He'd worked hard to make something of himself, graduating at the top of his class, ending up at Howard majoring in law.

Tall, statuesque, with a honey-brown complexion, Lisa was his dream walking on long, lovely legs. She was refined, soft spoken, classy. He never understood what she saw in him. When she took him home to meet her family, it was obvious that they'd had higher expectations for their daughter. But she was in love, and he was a good man, and eventually, they stepped aside and made way for the inevitable nuptials.

Lucas had proven himself more than worthy to his

in-laws through the years, despite his insisting that he and Lisa move back to Denver. He'd passed the bar exam the very first time, become a junior partner at one of the city's top law firms a year out of law school, and gone on to start his own firm, which quickly became one of the elite firms in the country. When he ran for mayor last year, he won by a landslide over his opponents and the city embraced him like its long-lost native son. Lisa's family was even more proud of him than his own.

Dinner parties were her specialty. Lisa had been planning this Christmas party since the beginning of the year, and nothing was going to stop it from happening. She floated through the crowd wearing an emerald green velvet gown, looking like someone had written her in a novel. Diamonds sparkled on her earlobes and around her wrist and ring finger. Luscious lips parted and smiled, welcoming everyone into their home. Lucas could hardly keep his eyes off her.

Cherry Hills was Denver's priciest neighborhood, and she'd insisted on buying a house there from the moment she set foot in Colorado, nearly fifteen years ago. Lisa was used to the best, and he turned flips to make sure she never had to settle. An Italian Tuscan villa replica, a fifteen-thousand-square-foot home, with imported marble and African mahogany woodwork, a wine cellar and theater room, was all it took to put a smile on her face and keep it there. And a damn pool. A fucking swimming pool that no one ever used because what the hell was the point to having a pool in Denver, Colorado?

"The kids would love it," she'd exclaimed when she saw this place.

The kids used it a couple of times, but not nearly

enough to justify the expense of maintaining that sonofabitch.

"You have a beautiful home, Lucas," Don said coming over to him. The man was a martini shy of being drunk off his ass, and Lucas right along with him.

"Thanks, Don. I take it your lovely wife is enjoying herself?"

"One can only hope," he said, sarcastically. "Lisa is certainly the belle of the ball tonight."

"Yeah, well . . . it's what she does best."

The two men looked at each other, then raised their glasses to each other in a toast of unspoken solidarity.

She was the only woman he knew who could make love without messing up her hair. Lucas came, rolled off his wife, and sighed. Lisa played her role, crawled out of bed, took a long, hot shower, put on a fresh nightgown, and climbed back into bed next to him, grazing his cheek with a kiss, then turning over on her stomach to sleep. Moments later, Lisa's slow steady breathing let him know that she really had drifted off to sleep.

Lucas stared up at the ceiling. He felt restless inside, unsatisfied, bored. He had everything he'd ever dreamed of, and along with it, the realization that nothing was as he thought it would be. Every chess piece of his life was in place. His career, family, life— all strategically laid out, the perfect foundation to build his legacy on. Mayor Shaw. Senator Shaw. It was what he'd worked for his whole life. The son of a postal worker, and the next state senator. The only kink in this chain of events had been Toni Robbins.

Toni shined like a new penny to everyone she met, but Lucas knew another side of her. She'd threatened to make his life hell. Lucas swallowed hard. Relief that the drama with Toni was over was understandable, but relishing the fact that she was dead was despicable.

Lisa had had more than her share of champagne tonight, followed up with a couple of sleeping pills no doubt. Lucas eased out of bed, slipped on some jeans, a T-shirt, found his sneakers and quietly crept down the stairs. He'd purposefully left his car parked in front of the house to avoid having to open the garage. Lucas slowly turned onto the street, and breathed a much needed sigh of relief. Masturbating was more enthralling than fucking Lisa. Lucas needed something more. He squeezed his erection, and hurried across town for the kind of satisfaction his wife would never give him.

I Can See Clearly

"Spare some change?" Lazarus had a technique for this that worked with assholes like this mothafucka. He stopped in front of them, held out his hand, and looked them square in the eyes, daring them not to dig around in their pockets and give him what they had. He only approached the man because he went out of his way to look unapproachable, and brothas like him needed a reality check sometimes. *There's a thin line between me and you, man,* Lazarus thought as the man begrudgingly handed him a buck. *If you'd taken that wrong turn back in the day, instead of me, maybe I'd be wearing that expensive-ass suit handing you a lousy dollar.*

"'Preciate it," Lazarus muttered as he stepped aside and let the man pass. Familiar face. So familiar.

Mayor Shaw climbed into his silver Mercedes and sped away.

* * *

The police had left that yellow tape up around where they found that woman's body, but Lazarus decided to hell with the tape. He was sleeping in his spot tonight whether they liked it or not. He stretched out under the viaduct, smoking a cigarette and listening to the water trickling by from the river. It was cold out, but Lazarus was toasty warm, layered in extra coats and sweaters he'd found in some bags folks had left behind the Salvation Army store for donations.

All week long he'd seen that woman's face in the newspapers, and heard people talking about it as he passed them. He wished they'd shut up about all that. Hell, it was over and the man who did it wasn't the type to get caught. He'd walk around free as a bird for the rest of his life, maybe tormented inside about it, maybe not, but cops wouldn't touch a man like him. His type was too damn righteous.

Lazarus spotted a couple walking along the path near where he rested, talking in low voices, arms looped inside arms. Them fools were dumb asses walking down here at night. In the daytime, the path was filled with joggers, walkers, and people riding bikes. But at night, this wasn't a safe place to stroll. They looked like they were enjoying each other's company, though. The man looked like some makeshift knight in shining armor, and she looked like the fair maiden princess too in love to see straight.

Love was something he missed from time to time. He believed he'd had it at least once, maybe twice. The first time was a sistah with a short natural, big hips, small breasts, and slanted dark eyes that made her look like she was from some foreign place. Jolene was her name. Or was it Charlene? Maybe Maureen. Anyway, he loved her. Or she loved him. One of the two. But they were together back in the day. Lived together and everything, making love, and barbeque, and maybe even babies. There were too many blank spots in his memory where she was concerned, but the memories that remained were some damn good ones. She could cook her ass off and every Sunday was a feast with that woman—collard greens, home-made cornbread, none of that store-bought shit, smothered pork chops, homemade macaroni and cheese with the big chunks of cheese melted into it, and sweet, delicious banana pudding. Lazarus smacked his lips just thinking about it. He ate like a king back in those days, and fucked like one too. Jolene or Maureen was a loaded gun in bed. Dangerous! Fearless! And game for anything. He heard himself laugh. She would buck on top of him like a bronco. One time she bucked so hard they put a hole in the damn wall behind the headboard. Damn! He loved that woman.

His other love happened while he was in lock-up. Lazarus had put his name on one of those pen pal lists and all these women started writing to him. They fell in love too easily for his taste, but then when you're locked down for twenty-some odd years, the promise of love equates to the promise of pussy, so he let them all love him as much as they wanted. One woman though, sent him a beautiful picture of herself with her son sitting on her lap. She was a nice looking woman, on the heavy side, but not bad looking at all. The boy looked just like her, too. Handsome young man, with a bright smile and a fresh, greasy haircut his mother had gotten for him just to take the picture. Everything about that woman was sweet in her letters. She wrote him every week, six, seven-page letters about how her week had gone, and what she and her son were up to. Lazarus wrote back when he could. Back then, he signed his real name to his letters—Brian. And she surprised him and told him how much she'd always liked that name. Every now and then she even had the boy write. Lazarus would read his letters over and over until he could recite them word for word without even looking. The next day, of course, he'd forget them. That woman and that boy was the closest he could ever remember to having a family of his own. And he missed them.

Lazarus was a name he'd given himself. Somewhere in the Bible, Jesus came back and brought Lazarus back from the dead, and after that you never head anything else about the man. Lazarus spent a lot of time in prison wondering what could possibly have happened to a man who'd been dead for all that time, then been brought back to life. Ain't no way he could've been the same man he was before all that happened. And he just assumed that maybe, while the real Lazarus was walking around alive and breathing, maybe a part of him was still back in that tomb—dead as dead could be. That's how he saw himself. He was alive. And he wasn't. A part of him had died in that crash on top of this bridge years ago with that man and his little girl, which was why he was so drawn to this place. His soul lingered here. And that's why it felt like home.

Byline

"**M**orris!" Todd Bingham stood in the doorway of his office and called across the busy newsroom floor to Fatema.

Fatema stopped bickering at the sound of her name, but she didn't turn in his direction. "Shit," she muttered. Her colleague took her cue and slowly backed away.

"In my office," he demanded. "Now!"

She begrudgingly entered his office, and stood in the doorway.

"Close the door," he said sternly.

She did as she was told and sat down across from him.

"I thought you told me you were ready to come back to work." Todd leaned back in his chair, glaring at her.

"I am," she cleared her throat.

He looked like he didn't believe her. "Is that why you've been spitting venom at my staff all week?"

Fatema sighed in frustration. "I haven't been spitting venom, Todd."

"You're wearing your attitude on your sleeve." His cold steely blue eyes drilled holes in her. "Now, if you're not ready to come back here to work—then get your shit and go home."

She looked offended. "I told you—I am—"

"Then act like it, Fatema, and stop being a bug up everybody's ass."

She and Todd had had their share of knockdown drag outs, and Fatema gave as good as she got, but not this time. Before she realized what was happening, tears filled her eyes and the floodgates opened embarrassingly wide in this man's office. She had never cried on the job a day in her life! And she sure as hell had never given Todd the satisfaction of seeing her bawl, but here she was, grabbing a tissue off the box on his desk to wipe her nose.

"It's been two weeks and they haven't arrested any goddamned body." She blew. "How the hell could they go this long and not arrest anybody, Todd?" she stared pitifully at him.

He looked absolutely uncomfortable. "C'mon now, Morris," he tried consoling her. Todd shifted uneasily in his seat. "It's tough. I know. But you've got to give them time. They'll find the guy."

"She was one of my best friends."

"I know."

"Like my sister and I . . . we hadn't spoken in months, Todd. I was a horrible, horrible friend, because I should've . . . I should've . . ."

"Why don't you go home, Morris? Take a few more days off."

"I really need to work," she said, composing herself. "I need to stay busy."

He sighed. "Then stay busy, but stay off my staff's asses."

Fatema seemed to ignore him. "I have some leads I want to follow up on, if that's okay."

"What leads?"

"I don't know." As soon as she said it, she knew she'd lost him. "I went through some of Toni's things, and came across some interesting stuff."

"I don't do stuff, Morris," he said sarcastically. "And I don't want you working on your friend's story. Doesn't feel right, and I'm sure it's got to be unethical or something which could get me into trouble. Besides, I need you to finish that series on food poisoning in vegetarian restaurants I assigned to you two weeks ago."

She rolled her eyes. "I gave that story to the intern to write. Thanks for reminding me. I'll get on his ass."

"I didn't assign it to the intern," he said irritably.

"Toni was obsessed with that Russian college student who went missing a few months ago. Remember her? Toni had all sorts of clippings from newspapers and articles from the Internet in her personal files on the woman. What do you think that could mean?"

"Obviously it means you've disobeyed your boss and given my assignment to some idiot who doesn't know his ass from a hole in the ground, and I should fire you right here on the spot."

"She had tons of articles on people gone missing from all over the country, and this fixation with human trafficking. Didn't Abner write a story on that before he moved to Florida?"

"Let the police do their job. And you do yours, which means you will stay out of their way on this one, Morris, and let them solve your friend's murder. You are not the person for the job."

"Maybe it was the reason she was killed," she said despondently.

"Talk to the police, and tell them your suspicions, then."

"I did."

"And?"

"And they know what I know."

"I want you to go home, Fatema," he said with finality. She started to protest, but he put his hand up to stop her. "That's not a request. You're no good to me in your state of mind right now and I need reporters who can work on stories I assign to them."

"Todd?"

"Todd, my ass. You go home and finish grieving. Let the police do what they do best."

The way he looked at her told her more than she needed to know, and Fatema was wounded by his unspoken accusation.

"You don't trust me," she said, defeated. "I thought you said you let it go."

Todd sighed, put down his papers and leaned back in his chair. "Yeah, well, I thought I had, until now. You got desperate and crossed the line, Morris. Now you're desperate again. Do you blame me for being worried?"

"Yes," she said, hurriedly, "and no. I loved her, Todd. But I'm not desperate enough to make this up. Damn! Do you really believe—I have done some fucked up shit I'll admit, I'm pretty devastated over this, but Todd, I need to do this!"

One fake story and she was forever on the shit list. Integrity wasn't an option in this job, though. A reporter had to be trusted to report the facts objectively, concisely. People depended on them for the truth, and Fatema had blown her credibility sky high. He didn't trust her. As much as he tried to pretend everything was water under the bridge, Todd had lost respect for her, and it hurt.

"I think you may be looking for a story where there is none," he spoke quietly. "You miss your friend. You feel guilty about your relationship. I don't know, Fatema. I just don't think I can trust your judgment right now."

"Yeah," she muttered. "My judgment."

"If it were any other victim, if—" She looked at him, begging him to trust her. "But after what happened—"

"I said I was sorry, Todd." She sounded like a kid.

"That's not enough and you know it."

"I panicked."

"To say the least."

She shrugged. "But thank goodness you caught me. Otherwise, I'd have made a complete fool of myself."

"And me. And this paper. And I can't risk letting that happen."

Tears flooded her eyes. "Well, if you don't trust me, why don't you just fire me, then?" she said, more out of frustration than anything.

The twinkle in his eyes assured her that he wasn't ready to go that far. "What? And lose the best creative writer reporter I have?"

"Fuck you, Todd." She tried not to smile.

"Oh, don't I wish . . ." He grinned, and nodded reflectively. "Yeah."

"Don't make me file harassment charges," she quipped.

"A man can dream. Can't he?"

She laughed.

"You used to believe in me, Todd," she said softly. "I hate it that you don't anymore."

"So do I, Morris."

"Then let me work on this. I swear, when it's all said and done, I'll bring you something front page worthy."

"I'll see you in a week, Morris," he said with finality. "If you aren't willing to come back on my terms, then maybe you need to consider not coming back at all."

The City's Finest

Lucas's assistant escorted the burly detective into his office. Baldwin held out his hand to the mayor and introduced himself. "Pleasure, Mr. Mayor. Detective Bruce Baldwin. I'm honored to meet you sir, and thank you for your time."

Lucas motioned for the man to sit down. "Well, when you told me you were investigating Miss Robbins's homicide, Detective, I cleared my afternoon calendar to make time."

The mayor had a terrible habit of deciphering a man by his suit. Detective Baldwin's suit looked as if he'd slept in it, and he was definitely fast on the way to outgrowing it. Baldwin had an exemplary background with the Denver Police Department spanning thirty-five years, starting out as a traffic cop. He'd worked his way up through the ranks to detective, working in the narcotics unit, street gang task force, and finally landing in homicide, where he seemed to be planted until retirement. Early in his career, he'd been awarded numerous citations and awards, but in the last ten years, there was nothing.

"He's a good cop," Baldwin's captain told the mayor when he called to inquire about him. "Could've been a great cop, but he seems content with just being good."

Baldwin followed the rules. He never made waves, and kept to himself according to the captain. "Been married a couple of times, I think. Even has some kids, but he doesn't say much about any of that," he volunteered.

"What can I do for you, Detective?" Lucas purposefully tried to look intimidating as he sat behind his large desk. Right before his eyes, Baldwin shrank in comparison.

"Well, sir," said Baldwin, nervously clearing his throat, "I, uh . . . wanted to ask you a few questions regarding Miss Robbins. I came to the offices here a few weeks ago and questioned a few of her co-workers, but I didn't get the opportunity to speak to you."

Lucas nodded. "Unfortunately I've never had the pleasure of working directly with Miss Robbins," he said, smugly. "She worked in the Small Business Development Department, I believe, and suffice to say, we've lost a valued member of our team."

Baldwin adjusted his tie, and pulled out the note pad he carried inside the breast pocket of his coat. "Some of her co-workers said that she told them she was seeing someone." He waited for the mayor to react, but the man never did.

"I wouldn't know, sir."

Baldwin hated being here. The room was too big. Everything about this cat was too big, and it left Baldwin feeling unnaturally small. He never had liked politicians or lawyers or rich people. Lucas was all three and this pompous mothafucka was doing everything in his power to punk Baldwin in that unspoken way between men.

He was too damn cool. So to gain some ground, Baldwin decided it was time to unnerve this bitch. "Luke1963," he read from his notes, then looked at Shaw. To the naked eye, the man didn't flinch a muscle, but to Baldwin, the fool might as well have done a Tom Cruise from his chair to his desk.

"I beg your pardon?" Lucas asked.

Baldwin looked down at his notes again. "Luke1963. That's your e-mail address, isn't it, sir?"

Shaw stared unblinkingly at the detective. The man wouldn't be asking if he didn't already know the answer, and lying would only serve to make Lucas look like an idiot. Where'd he get it? That was the question Lucas Shaw knew the answer to without even asking.

"We found the e-mail address in Miss Robbins's laptop, Mr. Mayor, along with some rather incriminating e-mails between the two of you."

Baldwin waited for Shaw to react, but the man never did. He held on to every bit of his mayoral dignity the whole time. Only now, it was Baldwin's turn to sit up a little straighter.

"I guess you knew the victim a little more intimately than you originally recalled?"

Shaw didn't appreciate the sarcasm. He was still the mayor and this mothafucka was nothing more than a fuckin' cop. "If I did, that's none of your goddamned business, Detective."

"It is if it has anything to do with this case, Mr. Mayor," he responded coolly, meeting the mayor's gaze with his own. "From the string of e-mails, it looked to me like Toni Robbins ended the relationship and you weren't too happy with that. I'm sure you know, being one and all that, some lawyer could take that shit and run you into the ground with it."

"There was nothing to run into the ground." He was calm. "I had an affair, and it ended. It ended long before she was murdered."

"Some people might think it could be the reason she was murdered."

Lucas chuckled. "Please! You think I'd be so stupid as to kill-for pussy, Detective?"

Baldwin laughed. "Oh, no sir. But reading those e-mails, Mr. Mayor, it sounded like you were strung up by the balls for more than just pussy. A man doesn't beg and plead the way you did unless he's got some deep feelings, sir. But—that's just my opinion, of course."

"I cared for her, deeply. Maybe I did love her. But the bottom line is, there are plenty more where she came from—if I were looking."

"So, you're off the market, sir?" Baldwin smirked.

Lucas hesitated before answering, wondering if he should even bother to justify that snide-ass remark with a response. "I'm a married man, Baldwin. I made a mistake, and I've learned my lesson. My wife means the world to me."

Baldwin easily read between the lines. "Yes, sir. Repentance is the way to heaven." Baldwin stood up to leave without waiting to be asked. "Thank you again for your time, sir, and my best to your wife and family," he told the mayor before leaving.

"That's it, baby," Lucas whispered to the young woman working her own brand of magic in his lap with her mouth. "Take good care of it, sweetheart. I'll take good care of you."

She was a nameless prostitute who barely even spoke English. "Sucky? Twenty-dolla?" She didn't give a damn who he was and she was deliciously young. She could suck the hell out of a dick, though, and Lucas rested his head against the leather headrest of his car, savoring the sound of jazz filtering through the speakers, and the warmth of her sweet mouth.

The lure of young women was an addiction for him. Not young enough to be illegal, mind you, but young. Toni didn't understand. Love had nothing to do with it. His wife wouldn't understand. He didn't even understand. He would never touch a child, but he knew he'd come dangerously close, and it disturbed him more than he could admit to himself. He guessed this one to be eighteen maybe, give or take a year—or two. He firmly grabbed a handful of her silky, black hair, and groaned out loud when he came. She told him it would cost him twenty dollars. She'd done such a good job, he gave her a hundred.

Breaking News

"This just in," the polished CNN news anchor reported grimly. "Tragically, the body of a young woman was found today in an abandoned warehouse located in a city just north of Denver, Colorado. Police have confirmed it to be that of Alina Petrov, the Russian college student reported missing by her parents when she didn't show up for classes at Brown University. No official word yet on the cause of death, but police are calling this a homicide."

"I don't believe this is a coincidence, Drew." Fatema felt as if she'd been kicked in the stomach by a mule, hearing the news of the discovery of that woman's body. The story was on every channel, and finally she couldn't take it anymore, and Fatema turned off the television, pulled out a bottle of Merlot, and called her ex-husband—just to talk. Drew was fast becoming a crutch, and even though she could see it, and she knew it was a mistake, Fatema couldn't seem to bring herself to stop it from happening, before it even got started.

There was a time when he'd been her best friend, and she could talk to him about anything, and he *got* her. He really *got* her; even when everybody else around her thought she was a loon, Drew had a knack for knowing exactly what she meant, or what she was trying to say, or what she was going to say. Somewhere along the line, shit went awry between them, but in a crunch, he was still her friend, butter babies or no butter babies.

They sat next to each other on the sofa, shoulder to shoulder, sipping on wine, forgetting all about the fact that he was seeing another woman, and that she hated him for it. But she could never blame him for leaving her for someone else. She was just pissed that he couldn't have picked somebody less superficial than the red-head.

"Toni had pages of files on that Alina Petrov—search queries, pictures. And now both of them are dead all of a sudden? Does that sound right to you?"

He took a drink of wine, before responding. "Don't ask me to be the investigative reporter, Fatema. I'm just a jock, and for all I know, it could simply be coincidence. Didn't you say she had all kinds of articles and stories about missing people?"

"She did, but—I don't know. Something in my gut tells me that there's more of a connection here."

"Maybe there is, but for the life of me, I can't see what it could be."

She leaned forward and sighed deeply. "The cops still don't have any leads, at least none that they're willing to talk about."

He rubbed his hand across her back. "They're working on it. It's going to take time."

"You sound just like them." She finished the wine in her glass and filled it again. "I tracked down this guy I think she was seeing. Nelson Monroe. He works at the shelter where she volunteered."

"Thought you said she was seeing some cat named Luke?"

"She broke up with Luke, for Monroe, I think. Anyway, he's a do-gooder like Toni from what I hear. She was really feeling him, too."

"You talk to him?"

She shook her head. "Not yet. We're going to talk over coffee on Thursday. The police have really been grilling him, and for the most part, he's all talked out. I think they were getting pretty serious." All of a sudden, Fatema choked up. "It's so unfair, Drew—for one human being to think they have the right to take life away from another. Toni—that young woman—they both had their whole lives ahead of them, and—"

Drew pulled her close and held her in his arms. Fatema had him trained, or sprung or something, because all she ever had to do was call, and he came running. They'd been divorced for almost a year, and despite the façade of having moved on, he always kept one foot in Fatema's doorway, waiting for the opportunity to try one more time. Fatema might've been blind to it, but Aisha, the woman he had been seeing, wasn't. He never told Aisha that he still saw Fatema, but he never had to, and the thing is, he never denied it either.

Detective Bruce Baldwin didn't believe in coincidences either. Toni Robbins was on to something. He suspected she wasn't even really sure of what that something was, but she had pieces of a puzzle that she had no idea how to put together, or maybe she did, and maybe that's why she was murdered.

The press hadn't reported it yet, but the woman had been sexually abused and there was evidence of drugs in her system. Speculation among police was that Alina Petrov was too visible; her picture had been splashed across every newspaper and on every news channel across the country from the moment she'd been abducted. Someone didn't want to be found with Alina, and the only way to make sure that didn't happen had been to discard her.

He slowly flipped through copies of Toni's files, seeing face after face of abducted women and children. Locally, a prostitution ring operating under the guise of a massage parlor that had been closed down a few months back housed half a dozen illegal Korean immigrants, all female, forced to sleep on dirty floors, allowed to eat a can of soup a day, forced to have sex with patrons, and beaten or tortured if they refused. He remembered the case. The women were terrified victims who refused to talk, fearing they'd be deported or killed. He came across another article about a group of men from Mexico, forced to work eighteen-hour days in peach groves for pennies with hardly any food to eat, and no medical care for those who became ill.

If Miss Robbins was always down for the cause, as her sister had put it, then she picked one hell of a cause to be down for. One as ancient as time itself, and the pessimist in him settled into the fact that this modern day slavery would certainly outlast him.

New Friends

The television didn't do him justice. Nelson Monroe was incredible to look at, with a genuinely charming personality. His hazel eyes and strikingly white teeth were a dramatic contrast to his dark complexion, and shoulder-length locks added to the exotic appeal of the man. He reminded her of one of those men immortalized on the covers of romance novels.

"Sorry I'm late," he said as soon as he sat down. "Traffic."

The waitress appeared as if by magic. "Hi. What can I get you?"

"Just coffee," he said, taking off his coat.

"And are you still good?" she asked Fatema, without ever taking her eyes off Nelson.

"I'm fine. Thank you."

Fatema wondered if he truly knew how mesmerizing he was to women, but from the indifferent look on his face, she figured that was her answer. Involuntarily, a comparison between Drew and Nelson formed in her mind. OK, so it was lame of her to compare every man to her ex-husband, but until she got a new husband, Drew was all she had to work with in recent years. Drew was that pretty kind of handsome, chiseled, and defined. Nelson, he was grown-man handsome. Rugged? No. Just earthy. Almost as if you could smell a breeze coming from him. She made a conscious effort not to stare.

"I didn't see you at the funeral," she said during the conversation that came surprisingly easy to both of them.

"I was there," he said, quietly. "Saying goodbye was difficult."

"Yeah," Fatema said reflectively. "Still is."

"She used to talk about you all the time. Had some pretty interesting stories."

Fatema looked frightened. "What did she say?"

He laughed. "Don't worry. Nothing I could sell to the tabloids."

For some reason, she found very little comfort in that.

"How long were the two of you seeing each other? If you don't mind my asking."

"Not long enough," he said sadly. "She started volunteering at the shelter about six months ago, and I fell for her the first day I laid eyes on her." He smiled. "She wasn't feeling me like that, though."

Boy, please! She wanted to scream. If she knew Toni the way she thought she knew Toni, then she knew without a doubt that she was feeling him too.

"Did you ever meet her family?"

"I met her sister, Tracy. Spitting image of Toni."

"Yeah, well, don't let her hear you say that. She's got a major case of the don't-compare-me-to-my-big-sister syndrome."

"Yeah, but you could tell she was proud of her, though. Looked up to her like she was the big sister."

Fatema smiled. "This is true. I think we both did. I'm older than Toni by three months, but she was always the more responsible one, and most of the time, I tried to do whatever she told me because she was usually right."

"She usually was." He sounded melancholy.

"It was pretty serious between you two, though?" Fatema probed further.

He nodded. "It was on its way to becoming very serious. I'd never met anyone like her before. Toni and I were on the same page about a lot of things. I've been in plenty of relationships where women come into it believing they can handle my commitment to The Broadway, until they get a taste of what that really means."

"They couldn't handle it?"

"They could as long as it didn't interfere with the weekends, evenings, holidays." He laughed. "Those are the peak times at that place, and I have to be there. Toni understood that, and there were many times when I'd look up on Thanksgiving or Friday evenings, Sunday mornings, and see her coming through the door, ready to don an apron and get to work. It meant almost as much to her as it does to me. And she wasn't fronting. She genuinely cared."

Fatema broached the next question carefully. "Did she ever talk to you about a man she called Luke that she may have been seeing at one time?"

He hesitated before answering. "Yes. She told me about him."

"Did she stop seeing him because of you?"

"No." He shook his head. "He was married."

"And she came to her senses and cut him loose?"

"She cut him loose, and I'm sure his marriage had something to do with it, but there was more to it than that."

Fatema smiled. "She fell for you." She winked.

He smiled back. "Eventually."

"Good for her."

"Luke is the mayor, Fatema," he reluctantly admitted. "Lucas Shaw."

Fatema's chin dropped. "*The* mayor?"

"The one and only," he confirmed.

"She was screwing the mayor," she said making sure to keep her voice low. "And she dumped him because—why? Because he's the mayor *and* he's married?"

"She stopped seeing him because he's the mayor, and he's married, and he was cheating on her."

"Who?" she asked, confused.

"Toni."

Awe washed over her face. "Let me get this straight. He was cheating on his wife with Toni, and then he was cheating on Toni with somebody else?"

Nelson shrugged.

"I need something stronger than coffee," she exclaimed.

He laughed. "Yeah, me too."

All sorts of thoughts ran through her head, like what the hell was Toni doing sleeping with the married mayor in the first place?

"Did she ever tell you what she saw in him?" Nelson was the wrong person to be asking this question, but it just sort of fell out of her mouth before she could catch it.

"I think he just happened to come along at the right time in her life, to be honest. Toni was vulnerable and lonely, and he worked it."

"Toni was gorgeous, Nelson. How the hell would she ever have time to be lonely? Men fell at her feet."

"Not necessarily the right men, though."

Okay. She could see that. Toni always could get a man, but thinking back, some of them fools should've been neutered at birth to prevent reproduction. And she usually fell for them and she usually ended up regretting it.

"He's a successful man, rich, powerful, and she fell for him. And she hated the fact that she'd fallen for him. So, when she found out that he was sidestepping on her too, she called it quits, only he wasn't trying to hear it."

"He's got nerve!"

Nelson laughed. "He didn't want to let her go, and he let her know that all the damn time. I asked her if she wanted me to step in and run interference, but she was afraid of how it might affect the shelter as far as funding and grants go. I didn't think it would affect it one way or another, but it was her business and she asked me to stay out of it. What choice did I have?"

"For the life of me, Nelson, I can't believe she ever let herself get involved with someone like that. I mean, so, he's not a bad looking brotha, but he's married. She's always frowned upon any woman who would stoop to that level, and here she was doing the same thing she condemned other women for. All I can think is that he must have some serious game, or she must've been mighty desperate."

"Honestly," he sighed, "I think it was a bit of both, and I think that if she were here, she'd tell you the same thing."

"She was at the shelter the night she died. Were you there?"

"Yeah. And I feel like shit about it, too. She was getting ready to leave. It was about eight-thirty and I offered to walk her to her car, but she told me not to bother because it was in a lot a few blocks away. I told her to wait for me, and then one of the volunteers interrupted us and when I turned around, she'd left already."

Fatema shook her head. "Stubborn."

"Very," he agreed. "She said she was going home. I told her I'd call her later, but—"

"The police seem to think she was running away from someone, but I'm confused. Both her car and the shelter were in the opposite direction," she said, thinking out loud. "If she were headed for her car, then what would make her run in the opposite direction? And what would make her run past the shelter if she knew you were still there?"

"You got me," he said, frustrated. "The cops have been grilling me since it happened, and I don't know what to tell them, Fatema. Because I don't understand it either. I was there for at least another half hour, and then I went home."

"They say she was killed between eleven and three in the morning. It's like, she never left?"

"Maybe she stopped at one of the bars for a drink or met someone," he speculated. "I'm just guessing."

Fatema had speculations of her own. "I wonder where Shaw was that night?"

Nelson couldn't believe where she was going with this. "You don't think—I mean the man had it bad for her, Fatema, but I don't think he had it bad enough to—he's got too much to lose to do something crazy like that."

"He's got too much to lose to be cheating on his wife too, but that didn't seem to stop him. I'm not saying anything except that maybe he's the reason she didn't go straight home. I'm not saying he did this." But she was thinking that it was a possibility. Men killed women they loved all the time. It was that if-I-can't-have-you-no-one-can syndrome. It was a stretch, but Fatema was just considering it. That's all.

"Well, it's possible, I guess. She worked a few blocks from The Broadway too, so maybe she saw someone she knew and they stopped off for coffee or something."

"Maybe. I did a story a few years back for PBS called *Invisible People: The Plight of the Homeless in America*. Did you ever see it?" she asked, hopeful that someone saw the damn thing.

His eyes lit up. "That was you? I watched it a couple of times. Even taped it."

"Really?" she asked proudly. "Yeah, that was me. My hair's different now, and I've actually lost a few pounds."

"I thought you looked familiar. I kept wondering where I'd seen you before. It was a great piece, by the way. Very informative and real. You really touched on some issues most people don't want to acknowledge."

"Thanks. I really tried to—anyway, we filmed a few days with a man named Lazarus. Lazarus was absolutely fascinating.

"He'd spent twenty-three years in prison for a vehicular homicide that occurred when his car collided with another, killing a man and his six-year-old daughter. Lazarus suffered some pretty serious head injuries, but he survived and went to prison, and ended up living on the streets after he got out."

"I remember."

"Well, he actually used to live under that viaduct

where they found Toni's body. Years ago, it was where he used to sleep almost every night. Apparently, he had his accident not too far from there and there's this spiritual connection or something that draws him to that place."

"You think he could've been there that night?"

She sat back and folded her arms across her chest, and gloated. "If he's still alive, then I'd be willing to bet money on it. It's dark in some of the corners and nooks and crannies down there, Nelson. A person could hide there and not be seen."

"Well, if he was there, why do you think he wouldn't stop something like that from happening?"

"He's crazy."

Nelson looked at her like she was grasping for straws.

"I know it's a long shot, Nelson, but I think it could possibly be a lead of some kind. Lazarus is crazy, but he's a creature of habit too. He may have been there and he may have seen something. Even if he didn't actually witness the murder, maybe he saw someone chasing her, or maybe he saw someone leaving the scene."

"Do you think you can find him?"

"Like I said, he's a creature of habit, and I spent two days following the man around with a camera. I don't think he'll be hard to find."

"If he's still alive," Nelson reiterated.

"If he is. Yes."

Partners in Crime

Dan Goodwin was the closest thing to a friend that Baldwin had. They'd partnered together briefly on a couple of cases during their careers, and tolerated each other's company well enough to enjoy a beer together every now and then. Goodwin worked in vice, and every now and then, their paths crossed and they sometimes helped each other out.

"The world ain't big enough for coincidences," Goodwin said, gulping down his beer. "Your dead woman and my dead woman are connected some kind of way. We just need to figure out how. Found this on the Russian woman's wrist." He pulled a piece of paper from his inside coat pocket, unfolded it and spread it out on the table in front of Baldwin. It was a photocopy of the front page story from the newspaper edition with Toni's picture on the front. It looked as if the newspaper had been torn into thin, even strips, and then pieced back together to reform the picture.

Baldwin nearly spit out his beer when he saw it. It was damn near the whole front page article and photograph of Toni Robbins the day after her body had turned up. Baldwin stared stunned at Goodwin, who sat back smirking.

"Them patient motherfuckers in Forensics carefully removed it from my victim's wrist, then pieced this crap back together until they came up with this. Looked like a paper chain a kid would make or something."

Baldwin nodded. "Toni Robbins had an obsession with this Russian girl. Kept files on her, and newspaper clippings."

"If that Russian chick's daddy hadn't been some kind of big time ambassador, she wouldn't have had anything on her. Do you know how many Eastern European girls disappear every year that nobody knows about?"

"How many?"

"Too many. The man has clout, and so his daughter gets media attention. Some poor farmer's or factory worker's kid goes missing, and you never hear a thing."

"So why did this one land in your lap? Was she prostituted?"

"Or about to be. Her body was found in a massage parlor that had been busted before for prostitution. But according to the M.E., this girl was in overall too good a shape to have been hooking, and if she was, it hadn't been for very long."

"What killed her?"

"Somebody beat the crap out of her. She bled to death internally, after she was raped by half a dozen guys. We figured that whoever took her found out she was too hot a commodity to move, and rather than do the decent thing and let her go, they just disposed of her."

"What's your take on this human trafficking issue? I think my vic might've thought Petrov was kidnapped for something like that."

"Well, it's real, and it's real ugly. Big money, too. To think that in this day and age, shit like that is still going on blows me away, but—hey. I'm just a halfway decent guy who doesn't think selling human beings is the way to go, so—"

"How's the climate here for stuff like that?"

"Like it is in just about any other city. Alive and well. Some of the feds have their eyes on some places around here that they consider hubs. Major international airport, not too far from the southern and western borders, it's not a bad place to transport bodies in and out of. Some of the sickest shit in the world goes on in these circles, man. One task force in Wisconsin, of all fucking places, found evidence of kids being bought and sold over the Internet like people buy designer purses and computers off eBay. They move them around from city to city, selling and reselling them until they're all used up. Once that happens, they're sold overseas for cheap."

"All for prostitution and pedophiles?"

Goodwin shook his head. "Domestics, factory and farm workers, and yeah, prostitution and porn. I wouldn't be surprised if our Russian princess showed up in an erotic thriller on DVD or the Internet before too long."

"Maybe my vic was on to something after all, then. Somebody found out and shut her up."

"I wouldn't doubt it, my man. These people don't mess around, and if she did know, I wouldn't put it past them to kill her."

"You got a lead on somebody here in town?"

Dan Goodwin looked defeated. "It's like trying to

grab a handful of wind, Bruce. Just when we think we've got it nailed down, it blows up in our faces. But yeah. We think we might be narrowing in on a ring here in town. And who would suspect modern day slavers transporting merchandise through Denver 'Cornball' Colorado? But hell, we're talking a ten-billion-dollar-a-year industry, man. And we both know how well money can keep a secret."

Resurrection

"Larue! Miss Larue!" Lazarus laughed at the sight of her and held his arms open to welcome her embrace. She was a portly woman, and so short the top of her head pressed against his stomach. She was the color of mud, with a head full of short wiry, silver hair and she had never had teeth as far as he could remember. He didn't know too many people, but he knew Larue. She squeezed him tight and laughed, happy to see him too.

"Where you been, boy?" She slapped her hand against his chest. "I ain't seen you 'round in a long time. Almost had me thinking you was dead or in jail or something."

He was touched by her concern. "Aw, baby. Marry me," he teased.

"Fool! I'm already married!" she spat back.

"Well, then, where your man?"

Larue laughed. "Hell if I know!"

She was the one who told him to come here and

get him something to eat. "Always talking 'bout how hungry you is," she scolded him, the whole time they walked. "I keep telling you to come on over to The Broadway and get you a bite to eat. Always got a hot meal here. Always."

"You know my mind ain't what it should be," he reminded her. "You know how easily I forget sometimes."

"Act like you got some manners when you walk in this place, boy." She patted his arm while they stood in the long line. "These people got tables and napkins and shit. Like they a real restaurant. Even say grace sometimes to bless the food."

"I don't know no grace," he joked.

"Well, if you wanna eat, you gone know her tonight."

Lazarus and Larue didn't say another word to each other after they sat down to eat. Damn! This was good. Lazarus tried to take his time to savor this meal. Fried chicken, mashed potatoes and gravy, a biscuit, and a salad—which they could've kept and replaced with another piece of chicken or some more of them potatoes as far as he was concerned.

"You folks enjoying the meal tonight?"

Lazarus looked up and saw the brotha with the long hair.

"Yessuh, we shore are," Larue blurted out, licking her fingers, and swirling her tongue around the edge of her lips. "Ain't this some good food?" She nudged Lazarus in the arm.

The man smiled at Lazarus, but he didn't smile back.

"Fool," Larue whispered loud enough for Nelson to hear. "Say something. Tell him how good this is."

Lazarus continued eating, and Nelson knew when to leave well enough alone. "I can see you're both enjoying it. You folks have a nice evening."

When Nelson was out of earshot, Larue nudged Lazarus again. "What the hell is wrong with you, man? He the one feeding us."

Lazarus took one last bite then pushed his plate away. He never said a word to Larue, and suddenly got up and walked out.

His memory was sketchy but some things always managed to linger. He never liked that brotha. Lazarus had been to that place before, but damn if he could remember when. And he didn't really know for sure until he'd seen that spooky-eyed bastard come by the table. Lazarus knew his type. One of those do-good brothas who believed that if he saved the world, it would turn around and save his ass right back.

"Never happen," he muttered as he walked. "You black like me, man. Still."

He sucked on his teeth, then used the toothpick he'd picked up on his way out of that place. Where the hell did she come from? Lazarus' chin dropped at the vision coming towards him. Damn, she was fine. Smiling. Strutting. Shaking her hips. Her eyes locked on his, and as she passed, he smelled her perfume, and it dawned on him, that she was supposed to be dead. He turned around to go after her, but he stumbled and fell. When he looked up, she was gone.

"Did you hurt yourself?" he heard a child ask. Lazarus turned around and saw—

"What the hell?" he blurted out, then scrambled to get to his feet. Her father stood in the distance, calling out to the little girl, but Lazarus couldn't hear his voice. He saw the child run towards her father and jump into his arms. The man stared at Lazarus one last time, before turning away and disappearing into—the lights.

The driver in the car coming towards him, hit his brake, screeching the tires, and furiously honked his horn. "Are you crazy? Get the hell out of the street!"

In his confusion, Lazarus stumbled to the curb and for the next two days, he wouldn't even be able to remember his own name.

The Honorable

There was no denying Mayor Shaw's handsome appearance and charisma. Fatema had never interviewed him personally, but she'd attended enough press conferences featuring the city's dynamic mayor and his appeal and charm were intoxicating even in a crowded room. So, how come she didn't like him? Fatema had been turned off by the guy ever since she found out he was running for the position because he reminded her of a sheet of ice, too slick and too cold. His façade was transparent to her, but he was the darling of the state of Colorado, so he probably could've cared less about what she thought of him.

His stark, white shirt created a powerful contrast to the jet black suit he wore. The mayor wasn't wearing a tie, which was way too sexy a gesture on his part, as far as she was concerned. And yeah. She could see how Toni could've fallen for him, married or not. Toni had always been attracted to men in powerful positions. "Give me a man in a suit anyday," she'd once slurred over martinis.

"You can put a monkey in a suit," Fatema shot back. "That don't mean it ain't still a monkey."

Toni had frowned and stared, offended, back at Fatema, and then the two of them clinked glasses, and laughed hysterically.

True to form, the good mayor didn't know how to say no to an interview. She told his assistant half of the truth—that she wanted him to share his personal thoughts on the death of one of *his* people. The assistant worked her magic and freed up the mayor's calendar the very next day, and in the blink of an eye, Fatema found herself sitting across from his massive mahogany desk, quietly shocked and appalled at the way he overtly checked out her legs.

"This office is doing everything in its power to aid the police in their investigation of the tragic loss of Miss Robbins," he spoke slowly, perfectly pronouncing every syllable and vowel, sounding more like the President of the United States than the mayor of a city in the Midwest. She nodded politely, surmising that this cat's ego was so big he probably did have his eye on the White House. He'd taken it upon himself to lead this whole conversation from the moment she stepped through the door, reciting a speech he'd probably had written for him and practiced in front of his secretary. The more he spoke, the more angry and resentful she became, envisioning this bastard pumping poor Toni full of himself, then giving her the shake down after she told him to get lost. Now, she was *Miss Robbins*, a fine and upstanding city employee, whom he regretted never having had the opportunity to meet. *Bull!*

"You never met her?" she asked quietly, staring him squarely in the eyes.

He smiled smugly. "We may have spoken briefly in passing, but other than that—"

Lucas didn't like the way she asked the question. Or the way she glared at him when she did. He also couldn't stop his palms from sweating. Toni was never far from his thoughts. She was like that word or phrase on the tip of his tongue that drove him crazy because he couldn't shout it out when he needed to most. She left him for all the wrong reasons, and if she'd just been patient—if he'd been more discreet—or just a different type of man altogether, he knew he could've been the man she committed herself to. She was the one he wanted. Toni tormented him from the moment they met, a constant reminder of the one thing he couldn't have that he craved more than almost anything. He met her too late, during his campaign, when the wheels of motion had been set in place for his candidacy for mayor, on the road to his ultimate goal of becoming a senator someday. His life had become an open book and there was no way he could've re-written the chapters with her in them, and not risk losing everything he'd worked so hard for all his life. Given time, things between them could've been different. Somehow, some way, they could've made it work. His indiscretion got the best of him, though. Lucas had an appetite that never seemed to be satisfied. He slipped up once— only once with Toni, and she never forgave him for it.

Fatema Morris was taller than Toni. She was almost as tall as he was, and she was darker than he would've preferred, but despite his best efforts, he couldn't help himself. She was a good-looking woman, thick legs, narrow waist, long, black hair pulled away from her face. He found himself staring at her lips, full and moist, fighting back images of slipping his tongue between them, and then slipping his penis between them. He hated himself for being so weak.

"It will probably surprise you to know this, Mr. Mayor." She leaned forward slightly, and ran her hand over her bare leg. The thought crossed his mind that she did it on purpose. "But I knew Toni."

Lucas wasn't aware that all expression had faded from his face. "Is that so?"

Fatema nodded and smiled. "We went to college together, and she was my maid of honor at my wedding."

"Oh," was all he said. Lucas's heart pounded hard, but he refused to let loose his composure.

"I got the impression from her that the two of you did know each other," she said, cautiously. "But I don't know. Maybe I misunderstood her."

"I think I'd have remembered meeting as beautiful a woman as Miss Robbins. I meet so many people, though, that, we may have met and I just . . . don't remember."

Fatema grimaced and noticed that he did, too. To challenge him would be a waste of time. Denial was a river he'd rather drown in then finally admit the truth, and she had no doubt that Lucas played this game of "he said-she said" better than she ever could. His smug attitude made her skin crawl, though, and before she left his office, she wanted him to know that she knew he was lying.

"She told me not long ago that she'd been in love, but that he was married, and after a while, she felt it best to walk away." The light in his eyes faded, and she knew she'd touched a nerve.

"Sounds personal," he said quietly.

"Oh, it was. He'd done something to her that really

turned her against him. Something she couldn't stomach."

"I have another meeting to get to, Miss Morris," he said, bitterly.

"Of course." She smiled, and stood to leave. Lucas stood too, and Fatema pretended not to notice his erection. "Well, thank you so much for your time, Mr. Mayor." She reached out to shake his hand. "I'll see myself out."

Lying mothafucka! She thought gritting her teeth as she closed the door behind her. But what did she expect? The man was married. The man was mayor. And the man had been lovers with a woman who'd been murdered. Yep. He made a great politician.

My Kind of Girl

What was this, a fucking tag team? Baldwin had no sooner hung up from speaking to the sister, when the best friend makes a beeline straight for his desk. Fatema plopped a gigantic purse down on the corner of his desk, sat down, folded her arms, crossed her legs, and burned holes in him with those lovely brown eyes of hers.

"I take it you never received any of my messages," she challenged.

He was the police. Obviously she'd forgotten that small fact somewhere along the line, and felt obligated to speak to him like he was any fool off the street. He'd just had this conversation with Toni Robbins's sister, and he'd been cool and appeasing and apologetic and reassuring. He couldn't guarantee that same attitude would carry over in so short a period of time from the last one.

"It's been nearly a month, detective. Tell me you have a lead. Tell me you have a suspect, a theory, a consensus—something."

Baldwin cleared his throat, and worked a small, quiet miracle to maintain his composure. "I'll tell you the same thing I just told her sister, Miss Morris. We're working diligently on this case."

"So, what do you have?" she blurted out.

He stared at her.

Fatema shrugged. "Tell me what you've found out so far. Reassure me, Detective Baldwin, that you are working diligently on finding out who killed my friend, so that I can walk out of here knowing that justice will be served and soon."

Bruce Baldwin worked hard to come across as a much nicer man than he really was. Time in this job had taken its toll, and his patience had worn painfully thin through the years. He didn't like her tone or her attitude and he almost didn't give a damn that her best friend had been murdered. Almost. It was that "almost" that kept him from throwing her ass out of his precinct. He didn't like most people in general, and Miss Morris had moved up to the top of his list in a very short period of time.

"If I had anything concrete to tell you, I would. But at this point, to do so would jeopardize our investigation, and—"

"Well, let me tell you what I found out during my own investigation, Detective," she interrupted him. "Toni was having an affair with a city official. A high ranking city official who happens to believe his shit don't stink and he's slick enough to get away with fucking around on his wife. A city official whose entire career would go down the toilet if anybody found out, and whose lovely wife would probably financially rape him in the ass and take everything he owns if she ever knew. This same city official had a lot to lose should Toni come forward and reveal this little secret. And I'd bet money that he was probably dancing on tables when he realized that threat had been eliminated. I'm talking about our beloved mayor, detective," she said, smartly. "Or is the police department buried too far up his royal highness's ass to consider him a suspect?"

That was it. Baldwin bolted up from his chair, grabbed her purse, and took hold of Fatema's arm, then pulled her into an interrogation room, despite her loud protests. He slammed the door shut behind them, and threw her purse on the table.

"Sit your ass down!" he growled.

His voice echoed and bounced off the walls. Fatema reluctantly did as she was told.

"What the hell are you doing, fucking with my investigation?"

"I'm trying to find out who killed Toni!"

"No! I'm trying to find out who killed Toni!"

"But—"

"But—I want you to stay out of my way, Miss Morris!"

"I'm just trying to—"

"I don't give a damn what you call yourself trying to do! This is my fucking case, and nobody—I mean, no fucking body is going to interfere with my shit! Is that understood?"

Shit. Tears. Where the hell did she pull those from?

Baldwin had never been a match for tears, and he took a deep breath to compose himself. He pulled out the chair across from her and sat down.

"I don't want him to get away with this," she sobbed. "Toni deserved better."

"I understand your frustration, Fatema." It was the first time he'd called her by her first name. "Believe me. I'm frustrated too."

"She was having an affair with Lucas Shaw. I found out from—"

"I know," he spoke calmly. "Mayor Shaw has been thoroughly questioned."

She stared desperately at him, hoping for answers.

"All I can say is that he's not immune from this investigation. You've got to believe me on that. Hell," he said sort of smiling, "I didn't vote for his ass."

Fatema managed to smile back. "Me either."

"The deeper I dig into this matter, the more complicated it becomes," Baldwin explained. "I have reason to believe we're dealing with more than just a romantic tryst gone bad. I wish it were that simple. If it were, then this case would've been solved a long time ago. But I believe there's more to it than that."

"What makes you say that?"

"I'm not at liberty to say." Disappointment washed over her. "But solving this case is my top priority and I'm using all this department's resources to find out who did this. You have to help me by staying out of my way. I don't need a best friend or even a reporter putting this investigation at risk."

"Well, what do you expect me to do? I'm only doing what comes naturally. I'm an investigative reporter, and I snoop. I dig. I find out things."

"So do I, but you don't see me trying to write a newspaper article."

Okay, so he had a point. "Touché," she sniffed.

"When this case breaks," he reassured her, "—and it will, I'll stake my career on it—when it breaks, believe me, I won't leave you in the dark."

Fatema bit down on her bottom lip, and reached

across the table taking his hand in hers. "Thank you," she mouthed.

Her touch was like a bolt of electricity surging through him. Bruce had perfected the art of keeping the world at bay. Even when he fucked a woman, it was placid and uneventful. But Fatema's warm hand affected him, and it made him uncomfortable. He pulled away from her, but she didn't seem to notice.

"Oh," she sniffed again, and pulled a tissue from her purse. "There's a man named Lazarus. He's an old homeless guy . . . kinda crazy, but . . . nice man. I interviewed him a few years ago when I was working on a documentary for PBS about the plight of America's homeless. Did you see it?" she asked hopefully.

"Afraid not."

She shrugged, disappointedly. "Anyway, I spent two days with my cameraman and Lazarus underneath that viaduct. He lived there. Had lived there for years, and swore he'd never leave. Anyway, I don't know if Lazarus is alive or dead, but I'm willing to bet that if he is alive, he probably still lives underneath that bridge. I was thinking about looking for him, and that maybe—I don't know. Maybe he saw something. It's a long shot, I know." She answered the question before he even asked it. "But that place was his home, and he had me convinced that he would never leave."

She left with a much better mind-set than she had when she walked in. Baldwin watched her leave, and wished he could've been a different kind of man who could have gotten a woman like that. It was a short-lived fantasy that he noticed on the faces of half the men in the precinct who also watched her walk out.

Prayers Go Up

Lazarus needed new boots. Sometimes he would find them outside in the alleys and dumpsters. People threw away good boots all the time, wasting good shit because they could. He dug through one of the smaller trashcans and found a half-eaten sandwich, wrapped in tin foil. He smelled it, flipped up the bread on top and examined it closely, and then he covered it back up and slipped it into his pocket.

He kept digging through dirty papers and dumping garbage bags, until he found a nice sneaker. It was worn and dirty, but had a good sole on it. Nobody ever threw away just one shoe, and he searched long and hard for the other.

"She's been here too long. You've been allowed to keep her long enough. I've got a buyer." Ivy sat with her knees drawn to her chest, staring blankly down at her bare feet. She'd never seen this man before, but he talked about her like he knew who she was.

The other man paced back and forth, glancing in her direction. She didn't have to see him to know when he watched her. She'd been with him long enough to feel it. All the other girls who'd come through here never stayed long. It had been weeks since she'd last seen Alina, and every now and then Ivy let herself wonder if Alina was dead or alive. She'd rather believe that someone had found Alina and saved her, and taken her home to her family where she belonged. And maybe one day Alina would remember Ivy and tell someone where to find her and they'd come take her away, too. But those fantasies were fleeting and reserved for the darkest part of the night or for warding off nightmares.

"I've done everything you've asked," the desperate man argued. "He said she could stay . . . as long as I wanted . . . needed her to."

"Yeah, well, he's out of the picture, now, and you're dealing with me. She'll bring some good money, man. You've taken real good care of her."

"What happened to him?" They were so careful not to say names, or places, or dates, or times. They spoke in code that through the years, she'd learned to recognize. "Is he dead? Did he get arrested?"

"Not relevant. One week," the other man told him, starting back up the stairs. "I'll send someone to get her in a week."

Living in this cold, dank basement was hell, but it was her hell, and had become her home. She'd memorized every nook and cranny, every spider web and mouse. She'd counted the threads on the bedspread. And she knew him. If she had to be a prisoner, then she wanted to be a prisoner here, because here she still had hope that she'd find a way out one day. If they took her someplace else, chances are she'd never get away.

"After they use you up, and there's barely anything left," one girl who'd come through this place told her, "they sell what's left of you overseas. Nobody ever hears from you again. Nobody knows where you are, and you die there. That's what I've heard."

Hot tears filled her eyes. Ivy couldn't remember the last time she'd cried, but the thought of leaving here terrified her and threatened to steal away the last bit of hope she clung to. If she remembered how, she'd have prayed and begged God to save her. But God didn't come to basements and He certainly would never hear her small voice when everyone else was shouting to Him from the rooftops.

At first, she thought the noise outside the small window over her head was a rat or a cat or dog until he spoke.

"Good. Good. Where the other one? Don't nobody throw away one without the other."

No one ever came down that alley. Cars and the garbage truck drove through it long enough to empty that dumpster, but no one ever stopped by her window before.

"That's nice. I like that. I like that. I do—for real."

The light coming from the lamp near her bed wasn't very bright. She picked it up and held it up so that she could see better out of the window. He must have seen her too, because he stopped, stepped back and stared back at her, and for what seemed like an eternity, their gazes locked and each of them froze.

Lazarus couldn't tell if she was real or not. Light bounced off dull green eyes and translucent skin. Stringy brown hair framed her thin face, but she had the most beautiful lips he'd ever seen, full, pink—they

looked like pillows. White girl. White girl with big lips.
He smiled. "Ain't that some shit," he muttered. It was
the way she stared at him that sent a shiver through his
bones. Tears glistened in her eyes and filled them with
more sadness than he'd ever seen before. Lazarus
caught his breath, and he wanted so badly to turn away
but he couldn't.

"Ahhh!," he heard himself say. He clutched at his
coat, and pulled it tight around him.

His gaze fixed on her pretty mouth that was moving, but without sound. He studied her, absorbed
this image haunting him from that small window,
seeing her narrow fingers spread flat against that
dirty glass, and all of a sudden, he realized what she
was saying.

Help me. Please. Help me.

Man on Fire

Fatema had been called into her boss's office as soon as she'd walked in. She hadn't even put away her purse yet when he commanded her presence and demanded that she close the door behind her.

"So, imagine my chagrin when I get this call from the mayor's office"—he feigned a quick smile—"asking me when the mayor could expect to see his interview in the paper." Todd swiveled back and forth in his black, worn leather chair wearing sarcasm like a cheap, wrinkled shirt.

She was definitely in trouble and from the look on his face, for real this time. "Todd, I—"

He held up his hand to interrupt her. "Funny. I don't remember telling you to interview the mayor. As a matter of fact, the last story I think I assigned to you had to do with food poisoning at a vegetarian restaurant in Cherry Creek or something mundane like that, you know—to help you get back on track and all because I've been so concerned about your well-being."

"I needed to talk with him," she said desperately. "I have reason to believe that he and Toni—"

"Fatema, I really don't give a damn what you believe right now." Todd's face turned red.

"But—"

"You put my ass and reputation on the line! You put this paper's reputation on the line!"

"What? All I did was tell him I was a reporter! I never said that I was going to print anything!"

"The man is expecting an article about him! And he believes it's going to be published in my paper, Fatema! He's the fucking mayor for crying out loud, and you really put me out there this time."

"He's the Mayor of Denver, Colorado, Todd, not Jesus!"

"Do you want to keep your job?" he blurted out.

Fatema was taken aback. "What?"

"Because if you don't, I've got a dozen other reporters out there foaming at the mouth for your job!"

"You firing me?"

"You fucking act like you want to be fired!"

"I don't want to be fired! My best friend was murdered, Todd. I need to know what happened to her. All I'm doing is trying to put this thing together to find out who did this!"

"Yeah, well, last time I heard, the police department does that very thing. They're pretty good at it, too, from what I understand."

"He had an affair with Toni," she said, gravely. "Todd—if anybody benefited from her death, he certainly did."

"And you know this—how?"

"I read her e-mails."

"E-mails signed by Lucas Shaw, Mayor of Denver?"

"No! But it's him. Nelson told me—"

"Who the hell is Nelson?"

"The guy who runs the homeless shelter. He and Toni were seeing each other after she broke things off with Shaw, and Shaw was pissed."

Todd sat for a moment, taking it all in. "This isn't the *National Enquirer*, Morris."

"I know that. And I'm not trying to turn this into a Jerry Springer episode. But I needed to meet this guy and get a feel for him, and honestly, he's shady, Todd."

"Well . . . duh! He's a politician. Of course he's shady."

"But I mean when it comes to Toni."

"Did he tell you outright that he and your friend had an affair?"

"Of course not."

"Then you have nothing, Fatema."

"I have his e-mails. And the police questioned him too, and they wouldn't do that if they didn't feel he wasn't somehow involved in all this."

"I don't print speculation," he explained, sounding more serious than she'd ever heard him sound before. "Shaw is a pisshead, and I don't need flack from his office."

"I'm not afraid of him."

"This isn't about you, dammit!" He slammed his hand down on his desk. "This paper is my baby, Morris. And it's been in circulation a very long time, mainly because—my father and his father believed in the sanctity of alliances and goodwill and not making unnecessary waves in this city. The Lucas Shaws of the world will come and go, but my integrity, the integrity of this newspaper has to be solid or else you might as well wipe your ass with it."

"So we should kiss his ass?"

"No. But we shouldn't lie to get fake meetings with the man and then turn around and print shit we don't know is one thousand percent true or not."

"I know this is true. I know he had an affair with Toni while he's been married and that he's a snake who probably killed her and may just get away with it because everybody in this damn town is afraid of him!"

He stared at her before asking her again. "There was a time when I believed you were as passionate about this business as I am, Morris," he said solemnly. "You lived for the next great headline, got high on being the first to break that big story, but lately—"

"Lately, a lot's been happening in my personal life," she finished quietly. "My divorce, questioning the real reason I ever wanted to be a reporter in the first place, and now this."

"You've had a lot of distractions this past year."

"No, Todd. I think this past year I've had the misfortune of running into my life and actually having to face it once and for all, instead of ignoring it by pouring my heart and soul into this job."

"It didn't used to be just a job to you."

"You're right. But maybe that was the problem. I was so into my work that I let everything else slip away from me and reality is just starting to set in and it hurts."

He leaned back and tapped a pencil against the desk. "Then maybe you need to step back—walk away for awhile and figure out where it is you want to be."

She never bothered saying goodbye. It seemed a silly thing to say when she wasn't sure if she was really walking away for good or not. She mentally calcu-

lated how much money she had in her savings and
401K, wondering how much she had to live off if she
decided not to come back and go running off to find
herself once and for all. Fatema quietly gathered her
purse and coat and left without any idea as to what
she'd do next.

When They Come For You

That Lazarus character was right where she said he'd be, underneath that viaduct where Toni's body was found. Ever since Fatema Morris told Baldwin about him a few days ago, he'd been obsessed with finding the man. It was a lead. A slim one, but Baldwin had nothing else to go on and he was getting more and more desperate.

"We just want to ask you some questions, man." Baldwin and two other officers surrounded Lazarus wildly swinging a baseball bat he kept close by for safety. The uniformed officers prepared to remove their weapons, but Baldwin stopped them.

"Back up off me!" Lazarus shouted. "Back up!"

Baldwin motioned for the policemen to take a few steps back away from the old man.

Lazarus's appearance matched his name. He looked like something biblical with long hair matted and growing in thick clumps long past his shoulders. His dirty gray beard had grown long enough to touch his chest. He was a tall man, dressed in thick layers of clothing he'd probably found in the garbage. Back in his day, he was definitely a man to be reckoned with. But now, Lazarus was a frightened and disillusioned old man, and quite possibly, the missing link Baldwin needed to finally solve this case. If it were true, then the world was truly a fucked up place.

Fifteen minutes later, Baldwin realized that all the reasoning in the world wasn't going to resolve this situation. The three policemen strategically surrounded Lazarus, confusing him, and throwing him off balance, until one of them lunged at the old man and tackled him to the ground, giving Baldwin and the other cop a chance to subdue Lazarus and handcuff him. It took all three of them to practically drag him to the squad car and load him up in back.

At the station, Baldwin didn't dare remove the handcuffs from the old man. Lazarus sat on the floor in the interrogation room, staring ahead at nothing with a cold, dark, angry expression on his face. Baldwin counted his blessings that the man was too far gone to know his rights. The old man smelled like raw sewage, and Baldwin tried breathing through his mouth, until he realized that the foul scent tasted just as disgusting. He sucked down black coffee and broke the law and lit up a cigarette. Everyone standing on the other side of that two-way mirror would just have to cut him some slack, or come in here with him to endure this shit.

"You're not under arrest," Baldwin told him. "I just need to ask you a few questions, Lazarus, and I'll let you go."

Lazarus didn't respond.

"A woman's body was found near where you live a while back," he explained slowly, uncertain as to whether or not the man understood what he was

telling him. Looking at him, Baldwin felt himself slowly losing faith in what he'd hoped would be the big break he needed on this case. "Did you see her, Lazarus? Did you see the woman? Young. Pretty."

Lazarus didn't move or even blink. From where Baldwin was sitting, he wasn't even sure if the man was breathing.

"I really need your help on this, man. I need to find out who hurt her. I need to catch that person so that he can't hurt anybody else. If you saw any-thing—anything at all—"

Lazarus closed his eyes slowly, then turned his face towards the wall, and never said a word.

A psychologist came in to try and get him to talk, but Lazarus was silent.

"We can't hold him," Baldwin's captain told him. "He hasn't broken any laws."

"He's crazy," Baldwin interjected.

"We can't hold him for being crazy, Bruce. Maybe he isn't talking because he didn't see anything."

He hated making the call, especially after his "I know what I'm doing" speech and "You need to back off and let me do my job" tirade.

"It's me," he said over the phone. "I need you to come down to the station as soon as possible." He hung up before she had a chance to ask why.

Fatema hadn't seen Lazarus in over three years. "Emmy Man," her colleagues used to call him be-cause she'd been so hyped by the whole plight-of-the-homeless-in-America documentary she hosted and Lazarus in particular as her leading man, and no one could tell her she wasn't getting an Emmy for him. Well, she didn't get one, but that's not to say he wasn't

the most fascinating human being she'd ever met. The man was as flaky as a pastry, but damn if he didn't make for a good story.

She stood next to Detective Baldwin, staring at Lazarus from the other side of the two-way mirror. He looked so old. But his eyes were still young, hard, but young, almost as if that was the only part of him not allowed the privilege of aging.

"What makes you so sure he'll talk to me?" she asked Baldwin.

"Well, he sure as hell ain't talking to me. You're my last hope."

"Don't sound so pessimistic, Detective. The man sitting in that room is the closest human being I've ever seen to divine. He walked away from a burning vehicle with a bad bump on the head and lived to tell about it—what little of it he can remember, anyway. Between you and me, all of our hopes could very well rest in him."

Baldwin followed her into the room, and stood in the corner out of the way holding a small recorder. Fatema sat on the floor across from Lazarus, but not too close. She remembered that he didn't want anyone sitting too close to him, and with the way he smelled, that wasn't a problem. Several minutes passed without a word being spoken between them. She'd spent a week following this man around, watching him, learning him, and knowing how and when to best interact with him. Lazarus had been like a school project, and she'd been fascinated by him because he had the gift of taking Fatema out of her all-about-Fatema zone, and it had been one of the most liberating experiences of her life.

The first thing she needed to do was to let him

know she was there, and she knew from experience that she didn't have to say anything for that to happen. Lazarus's brain worked on its own schedule. His neurons fired at a different rate than everyone else's, and sometimes, it took a few minutes for them to catch up with the rest of him. Other times, they fired off too fast and left him standing still wondering what the hell happened.

He saw her. He stared at her. Fatema smiled. "Hey, Lazarus," she said quietly.

There was a hint of recognition on his face, but she knew that it could pass quickly and without warning.

"You back?" he asked simply.

She nodded. "Yeah. Came to see you."

Baldwin watched with fascination, this whole beauty and the beast thing unraveling right before his eyes.

"Why the hell did they bring me, here, Sweet Thang?"

Out of the corner of her eye, she saw Baldwin raise an eyebrow, but Fatema ignored him. He'd called her that from the moment she'd met him no matter how many times she'd told him her real name. "You look like a Sweet Thang to me," he'd explained, his eyes twinkling mischievously. So between them the name stuck, and honestly, she kind of liked it.

Fatema searched her soul for the right words to say. With Lazarus, saying the wrong thing could send him soaring off into the mental unknown, and she could lose him if she wasn't careful.

"How's the baby?" she asked. He'd told her bits and pieces about that little girl who'd died in the crash. Fatema was convinced it was guilt that drove him crazy more than that head injury he'd suffered. He held a special place in his guilty heart for that child, and sometimes, you'd think she was his daughter instead of someone else's.

"Still haunting my ass," he laughed bitterly. "And doing a damn good job at it too. Ain't she sweet?"

Fatema smiled. "I thought you promised me that you were going to let her go?"

"It ain't me who won't let go, Sweet Thang. It's her and I am a slave to her will. That's my penance."

Baldwin stared perplexed at the two of them, confused by the code in their conversation.

"Believe me," Lazarus continued, "it's the least I can do." He bowed his head graciously.

"The police need your help, Lazarus," Fatema mentioned casually.

"Fuck the police!" he responded angrily, cutting his eyes at Baldwin.

Fatema quickly revised her strategy. "I need your help."

He grinned. "Whatchu need from old Lazarus, Sweet Thang?"

"The woman who they found dead underneath the bridge where you sleep sometimes—she was my friend." She swallowed. "She was like my sister, Lazarus, and I need to know if you might've seen anything or anybody—I need to know what happened to her."

The blank expression on his face told her that he had no idea what she was talking about. Lazarus studied Sweet Thang's face intently, looking for clues as to what she was talking about. Funny how he could remember events that happened years ago, but couldn't seem to grasp memories as recent as yesterday sometimes.

"Somebody hurt your friend?" he asked, concerned.

"Damn, Sweet Thang. When that happen? What did they do?"

Fatema remained calm, controlling her breathing and holding her gaze steady with his. "Somebody killed her, Lazarus. Right there, not far from where you sleep at night. She was really pretty, Lazarus."

"Like you?"

Fatema smiled. "She was prettier than me."

He surprised her and laughed out loud. "Naw, now . . . not too many women prettier than you, sugah! I'm a old man, but I ain't blind. You fine as hell, girl!"

She glanced at Baldwin, standing smirking in the corner. He nodded his acknowledgment.

"I wish I knew who killed her. I wish I knew who hurt my friend."

Out of nowhere, Lazarus blurted out his response. "Mothafucka cried when he was through. Hell, I thought they was fuckin'."

Baldwin straightened up, and he was about to say something but Fatema stopped him with a slight wave of her hand.

"You did see something. Didn't you, Lazarus?"

Small beads of sweat began to form on his forehead, and Lazarus's frustration was starting to come through. "I'd have stopped him, but I thought they was—I'd a beat his ass down."

"Who, Lazarus? Who did you see?"

"He could've gave me a five!" he blurted out. "Rich ass—came up off a dollar like he was really doing something!" He stared into Fatema's eyes.

He squeezed his eyes shut and saw a hell of a lot of people; Larue's toothless grin, that little girl's daddy carrying her off, rich men in fancy suits, dollar bills, and pretty, pillowy pink lips—on a white girl.

"Damn, she had a pretty mouth," he said with tears forming in his eyes. "Pretty, pretty lips," he whispered, shaking his head. "I need to do something. I need to help her because . . . because . . ." He hadn't helped any of the others.

"Who? Lazarus? Who did you see?"

"I saw 'em all!" he shouted. "Every last one of them bitches!"

Baldwin started to worry that Lazarus was losing control and would hurt Fatema and started over to him. "Time's up, Fatema." He helped her to her feet.

"I saw all of 'em, Sweet Thang! He gave me a god-damned dollar like it shoulda meant something and that mothafucka cried like he gave a damn about what he did to that woman! He can't see in the dark, Sweet Thang!" Lazarus shouted after Fatema as Baldwin practically carried her out of the room. "But I can!"

The Masses

It never ceased to amaze him how many people came through The Broadway on a daily basis. Some came just to get a decent meal, others needed a place to sleep at night. The Broadway was a converted church sectioned off into large rooms with little privacy. Women and children were housed in one large, dorm-like room, men stayed in another. Unfortunately, he had no accommodations for families yet, but Nelson had just purchased half a city block of dilapidated row homes and was desperately seeking funding for renovations. Nelson depended primarily on state and federal financial assistance to keep the main shelter operating, he leveraged what he got from them against private investors for funds to put towards making the row homes livable. It was an uphill battle to say the least, but a necessary evil in this line of work.

There were days when he didn't want to get out of bed in the morning. His work was discouraging at best most of the time, but Nelson was like a cursed man, driven and passionate about this, the only task he'd ever had that truly fulfilled him, and that tortured him at the same time. Toni was a breath of fresh air, because she genuinely felt what he felt and she had a need to do more with her life than just to work a nine-to-five, pay some bills and get by. He never thought it possible before he met her, but soul mates existed, and he'd found his. It was only a matter of time before they joined forces in marriage. He knew it, and he suspected she did too. But it was never going to happen and knowing that emptied him of expectation he knew he'd never get back.

Finding Lazarus was starting to become an obsession with Nelson. Ever since Fatema told him about the man and that she suspected that he might've seen something the night Toni was killed, Nelson had been looking for him to come through the doors of The Broadway. He slowly strolled up and down the aisles between rows of tables while people ate. Lois and her staff of volunteers had outdone themselves again tonight, the way they did most nights when they could afford it. The woman had a way with stretching a dollar, that's for sure. Stretched it so thin sometimes he swore he could see through it. Baked ham, green beans, cornbread, and butter beans were on the menu tonight. And for dessert, a local bakery had donated fresh baked cookies.

"Hey," he heard a woman shout. Nelson turned around to see Miss Larue waving at him. Of course, he had to say hello. She was one of his regulars.

"How you doing, Miss Larue?" He smiled graciously.

"I'm doing good now that I got me some of this good food. You know, I used to cook like this a long time ago back when I had a family." She sprayed bits of food as she spoke, and Miss Larue never bothered to cover her mouth. Nelson stood back at a safe distance.

"I'll bet you were a hell of a cook."

She nodded enthusiastically. "I sho was. 'Specially on Sundays. My Sunday dinners was too much." She laughed out loud. "Folks couldn't eat fast enough. And they loved my red velvet cake. You ever had a red velvet?"

"I haven't had a good one in years, Miss Larue."

"Boy! Mine was so good it melted in your mouth. You didn't even have to chew it, just let it melt, then swallow it down!"

"Well, maybe you could be so kind as to give Miss Lois the recipe one of these days," he asked hopefully.

Miss Larue looked shocked. "Oh, no. No recipe," she said emphatically, then pointed to her head. "It's all up here in my head. And I can't tell nobody how to make it. I just have to make it myself. Maybe one of these days I can come in and bake it for everybody."

Nelson knew she'd never show up, so he nodded. "Of course. Just let us know what you need and we'll make sure you have all the ingredients."

Miss Larue took a big bite of ham and chewed like she had teeth.

"By the way, Miss Larue, where's your friend? The man you brought with you a few weeks back?"

She stared at him blankly for a moment, honestly not remembering who he could've been referring to.

"Tall fella. Long hair like mine."

Somebody turned on the light. "Oh! You mean Lazarus."

Nelson's heart dropped down into his stomach.

"That's his name?"

She chomped down on some cornbread. "He ain't here," she said with her mouth full. "I ain't seen him since that day when he acted a fool all up in here. Lazarus is crazy," she rambled on, volunteering more information than she needed to. "He all right sometimes, but he flip out on you in a minute, and when he do, he act like he don't even know who you are. Me and him was sitting and smoking one day, and . . ."

The sound of Larue's voice trailed off as Nelson pretended to listen, nodding appropriately. But his mind strayed away from the conversation as soon as she said the man's name. He had no idea of how long she'd been talking before he interrupted her.

"Do you know where I can find him?"

She stopped eating and cut her eyes at him. "Lazarus?"

"Yes, ma'am."

"Why you wanna find Lazarus?" All of a sudden, Miss Larue appeared suspicious of Nelson. He'd crossed an invisible line, and he knew it. The people he served were welcome in his world, but he wasn't necessarily welcome in theirs. They were paranoid like that, defensive and guarded of what little they possessed, even if it was junk or a warm, safe place to sleep at night.

"I just need to ask him some questions, that's all."

"Like the police?"

"The police?"

"They hauled him off and asked him questions already about that woman who got killed under that bridge. That cute one who used to work in here. Remember her?"

"Yes," he said patiently. "I want to know if he saw anything. She was a friend of mine."

"Oh, I know she was," the woman said flippantly. "I

saw y'all all the time making them lovey eyes at each other cross the room. I ain't no dummy."

"Then you understand why I need to find him. If he saw anything, Miss Larue . . ."

"Lazarus don't know nothing," she snapped.

"Well, I need to ask him myself. He might know something. He might have seen something that night."

"Even if he did, Lazarus's crazy ass probably don't even remember what he saw. His mind come and go. It's like turning on and off a light switch. One minute the light might be on, then somebody come along and flick the switch and it's off and pitch black in the room. That's how he is."

"If you could just tell me where to find him, Miss Larue," he insisted, "I'd like to see for myself if he remembers seeing anything."

Miss Larue never said another word after that. Nelson stood there trying to get her to tell him where Lazarus was, but she finished her meal, gathered her bags and her coat and left.

The guilt he felt over her death consumed him. She'd left the shelter that night at her usual time of eight-thirty.

"You go straight home now." He kissed the tip of her nose, and held her close in his arms.

"Promise to be at my place no later than nine, Nelson," Toni said, draping her arms over his shoulders. "Any later than that, and you're not getting in."

He chuckled. "You said that last time."

"But this time I mean it. Pinky promise." She held out her pinky to him.

"Baby, I'm a grown-ass man and we don't do pinky nothing."

She looked at him like he should know better, so he reluctantly wrapped his pinky around hers.

She smiled. "See you at nine." And then she kissed him, and left.

"Hey, boss," one of his volunteers had said, patting him on the back. "The kitchen's cleaned and we're out of here."

Good people, he thought fondly. "Get home safely," he said solemnly.

Toni should've gone home that night. She should've gone straight home and been safe.

Said the Spider

It was after two in the morning and Lucas noticed the light coming from underneath the door of the study. Lisa was sitting curled up on the cream suede chaise reading.

"Kind of late for you to still be awake, isn't it?" he asked, standing in the doorway.

She looked up from her book, looking fresh and beautiful as ever. "The same goes for you, husband of mine. Bet you thought I'd be comatose by now from one of those pesky little sleeping pills I take way too many of. Didn't you?"

"Your hands are trembling, baby. I think many experts would agree that cold turkey isn't the way to kick a bad habit, pesky or otherwise." His sarcasm came through loud and clear as intended.

Tit for Tat. She was good at this game. "Speaking of bad habits, how've you been since the untimely death of your little plaything?" All expression washed from his face as he stared stunned at her. Lisa smirked."Oh, do give me some credit, Lucas. I'm not just another pretty face, and I must say, you seem to have bounced back pretty damn well for a man who's just lost his lover. Not nearly as broken up as I thought you'd be, but then, that poker face of yours is flawless—except for now, that is. Careful, dear. I can see what you're holding."

"So you know." He quickly tried to compose himself. "What does that mean? You want to divorce me and take everything I own?"

She laughed. "Oh, for goodness sake, no! Besides, baby, what you own is spare change compared to what I came into this marriage with, so don't insult yourself. This relationship works for both of us, believe it or not. But I felt it was time for you to know that Momma's no fool, baby. And I know so much more about you than you know about yourself. Scary, isn't it?"

"You think you know me." He clenched his jaw without meaning to. "Be glad you don't."

"Or else what? I'll end up dead under a bridge too?" Lisa got up to leave. "Honestly, Lucas, I think it's the other way around. You think you know me, but you have no idea. Don't fuck with me." She brushed her shoulder against his passing by him. "And don't you dare embarrass me, Luke. You're getting careless with your little escapades with girls young enough to be your own daughters. You haven't crossed the line yet, but you're beginning to get mighty close to it, and I won't suffer the embarrassment of a scandal. Either nip that shit in the bud—soon—"

"Or else what?" He turned to watch her leave.

"Or else, I'll have to nip you. Somebody killed that woman, sweetheart. And I can't think of anyone with a better motive and more to lose than you, Mr. Mayor slash Senator slash President of the fucking United States of America. And what comes after that? Oh, yeah." She turned and smiled at him one last time before leaving. "God."

Lisa was a vision in her long ivory silk gown and robe flowing behind her as she left and disappeared into the darkness of the living room. The image was chilling and sent a shudder down his spine.

My First Love

Fatema couldn't fall back on being intoxicated this time to use as a reason to see her ex-husband. She was stone cold sober, and well, she missed him. Lately Drew had come through for her in a big way, reminding her of all those sentimental reasons she fell for him in the first place.

"Do you think you might be able to stop through for a bite to eat?" Drew was in his car, no doubt on his way home to his girlfriend, but Fatema didn't even bother to ask.

"You cooking?" He sounded shocked.

"I can," she said reluctantly.

"Chinese or Greek?" he asked.

She smiled. That man knew her all too well and it filled her with tons of warm fuzzies. "Chinese."

She felt awkward the moment he got there and Fatema suddenly wished she had a good buzz going. Inviting him here was crazy, but it was also a relief. A crazy relief—that was one hell of an oxymoron. They ate in silence for the most part, smiling politely at each other, then burying their faces in their plates to avoid conversation.

It was Drew who broke the silence first. "So, what? You want me to take you back or something?"

Leave it up to him to know exactly what to say. Relief quickly set in and Fatema felt like her old self again. "Hell, no! I just wanted some Chinese food and I knew I could sucker you into bringing me some."

Drew almost choked on his sesame beef, he laughed so hard. "Bullshit! You want me, woman. Admit it so that we can both move forward."

"Somebody in this room already has moved forward. How's whats-her-name anyway? Still anorexic?"

"She's fine, and bulimic—thank you very much. But at least she's in shape which is more than I can say for you, cutie. Getting a little wide in the hips there, aren't you?"

Fatema threw her napkin at him. "Fuck you, Drew."

He leaned forward and gazed longingly into her eyes. "Absolutely, baby. Any damn time you want."

She rolled her eyes. "You make me sick sometimes."

"But not this time. Right?" He looked too smug for his own good.

As hard as she wanted to be, Fatema couldn't help herself and something vulnerable rose up inside her. "No. Not this time."

He looked relieved all of a sudden. "How you been?"

She shrugged. "I kinda lost my job."

"You got fired?"

"Kinda. And I kinda quit too."

"Why the hell would you do something like that?"

"Well, Todd got mad at me, and—"

"Todd is always mad at you. He's never kinda fired you over any of the shit you've pulled. I thought you were his golden girl."

"I'm no golden girl, Drew." Melancholy set in. "I just—I don't know what I want anymore. And that's fucked up because my whole life I thought I had it all figured out, and my life's a mess."

"It's not a mess. A little chaotic, but—"

"But it's a mess. My career is stagnant. My best friend who I neglected for the last year has been killed. I lost my job, and a long time ago, I lost my husband and my other best friend."

"Strike that. You may have lost your husband, but you will never lose your other best friend." He reached across the table and laced his fingers between hers. "I'm a phone call away, Fatty. You know that."

"Stop calling me that. You know I hate that."

"What? It's a term of endearment."

"Coming from a personal trainer who lives in the gym, Drew, it's an insult."

"But you're not fat, Fatty. You're fine, Fatty. I wouldn't call you Fatty if you weren't fine—Fatty."

She couldn't help but laugh. She'd never thought she ever wanted to ask him this question out of fear for what his answer would be, but she decided that she needed to man up and just come out with it. "Do you love her? Do you love Bulimia Woman?"

"I care for her."

"But do you love her, Drew?"

"What difference does that make now, Fatema?"

"I just want to know."

"Because?"

"I just want to know."

"Because—why?" he asked, coaxing her to say what she didn't want to say. "Come on, baby. Say it." Drew smiled knowingly, as if he could read her mind. "We'll say it together. Because I," he spoke slowly, hoping she'd chime in. "Want—you—to—take—me—back—Drew—darling."

"Why's it have to be you taking me back? Why can't it be me taking you back?" she huffed.

"Because you're the one who told me to get out."

"After I found out you had a girlfriend!"

"Ah, but I didn't have a girlfriend."

"Liar!"

"She wasn't my girlfriend until after you threw me out, thinking she was my girlfriend," he explained.

"So you say. Why should I believe you, Drew? Why should I have believed you then?"

His expression turned serious. "Because I told you, Fatema. And it was the truth. And by virtue of me being your other best friend, you should've believed me."

The man was downright convincing and it panged her to think, that just maybe, he really had been telling the truth. "It was more convenient not to believe you," she responded quietly.

"Yeah." He looked hurt. "Nobody knew better than I did, how much of an inconvenience I could be to you sometimes."

"I was preoccupied—and obsessed with my career back then. I wasn't a good wife."

"Yeah, well, my ass was too damn needy—back then. And I just wanted you to want to spend time with me. Talk about an unreasonable demand."

"Not so unreasonable, Drew. And certainly not needy." She wiped tears from her eyes. "Besides, as hot as you are, I need my ass kicked for not spending more time with you and them pecs. My goodness!" She laughed.

He flexed his pecs right on cue. "Let's do it."

"No!"

"That's why you invited me over here, isn't it?"

"I'm not drunk this time, Drew. Go home to your woman, and thanks for the fried noodles."

"Aw, c'mon, Fatema," he begged. "Girl, I need you. I got blue balls just thinking about your ass. You know what happens when a man gets blue balls and don't get any."

Fatema grabbed his jacket, helped him up from his chair and escorted him to the door. "That blue balls shit hasn't worked on me since I was fifteen, Drew."

"You told me I was your first."

She smiled. "Night, Daddy-O." Fatema kissed him softly on the lips, and smiled up at him. "And yeah," she finally admitted, "I think I do want you to take me back." She closed the door, and felt good for the first time in a long time.

Jigsaw

"*I'd have stopped him, but I thought they was—I'd a beat his ass down.*"

"*Who, Lazarus? Who did you see?*"

"*He could've gave me a five. Rich ass—came up off a dollar like he was really doing something.*"

"*Who? Lazarus? Who did you see?*"

"*I saw 'em all! Every last one of them bitches!*"

"*Time's up, Fatema.*"

"*I saw all of 'em, Sweet Thang! He gave me a goddamned dollar like it shoulda meant something and that mothafucka cried like he gave a damn about what he did to that woman! He can't see in the dark, Sweet Thang! But I can!*"

Detective Baldwin played the recorded conversation between Fatema and Lazarus over and over again, looking for answers to a murder from the ramblings of a confused old man. He sat in the room with Fatema and Paul Woodstone, the department psychologist, hoping that among the three of them, they could find key information in something he said.

"In this conversation, Lazarus has no sense of time," the psychologist explained. "The past, present, future, all run concurrently to him, and his speech reflects that. He could be talking about something that happened now, or something that happened ten years ago, all at the same time, but to him, it's all here and now."

"Yeah, but there are times when he's coherent," Fatema interjected, "And I can sit and have a conversation with him like I'm having with you now."

"Well, we know that he saw something." Baldwin scratched his head. He played a segment of the tape again.

"*. . . that mothafucka cried like he gave a damn about what he did to that woman! He can't see in the dark, Sweet Thang! But I can!*"

"You think he's talking about the murder?" he asked, looking at Fatema.

"I want him to be talking about the murder, detective," she admitted. "But with Lazarus, it's hard to tell."

"*That one in the bottom, though. I think she need me bad.*"

"He kept saying that he thought they were lovers," Fatema interjected. "That one on the bottom . . . could've been Toni." She looked from Baldwin to the psychologist. "I'm just guessing."

"Lazarus more than likely did witness this murder," Paul said conclusively. "But honestly, whether or not you'll ever get anything conclusive enough to actually go on to help solve it is highly unlikely, Detective."

* * *

The psychologist left and Fatema and Baldwin took the conversation to the coffee shop around the corner.

"That fact that Lazarus has seen this man before is key, Bruce."

"Are you kidding me? It's a mess. It's like dangling a piece of meat in front of my face and never letting me take a bite."

"But you have to think, who does he see on a regular basis that he would recognize?"

"Fatema, the man is a panhandler downtown. That limits it to a couple of thousand. Lazarus has been seen everywhere, including the 16th Street Mall all the way over to the capitol and even the city and county building. We found him wandering the back alleys of Lincoln Avenue. He's like a fucking roach."

Without thinking, she slapped him across the face, then gasped, shocked by her own actions. "I'm sorry." Hell, she'd just assaulted a police officer.

Baldwin glared at her in disbelief.

"I'm so sorry, Bruce. I didn't mean to do that."

"I could lock you up."

"I know. I know and I'm sorry. It's just that, well, Lazarus isn't a roach to me. He's a sad man who is guilt ridden over killing a child. Don't ever call him a roach in front of me. Please?"

He composed himself, and then pointed at her. "Consider this a freebie."

"Yes, sir," she said amicably. "I just reacted. I'm sorry."

"You said that, already."

Uncomfortable silence loomed between them, until Baldwin finally said out loud what he'd been thinking ever since he laid eyes on Lazarus.

"What if he did it?"

"Who?"

"Your man, Mr. Ball of Confusion," he said, acutely.

Fatema started to laugh, like he'd told a joke, but the look on his face told her that he was dead serious. "You're kidding. Right?"

Baldwin shrugged. "No, I'm not."

"He's an old man, Bruce," she argued.

"A strong old man. Took three cops to get the cuffs on him."

"He wouldn't do this!"

"How do you know? You said yourself that he lives there. He's always there. And we're sitting around here questioning him on who he might have seen do this. Well, maybe the reason he can't tell us is because he's too out of it to tell us it was him."

"That's ridiculous," she snapped.

"Why? Why is it ridiculous? Because he's a nice old man who shared coffee and a fire with you one cold night years ago? I'm beginning to think I may have just let my number one suspect walk the hell out, Fatema!"

"Sounds to me like a desperate attempt to pin this murder on the person most likely to get your ass off the hook."

Baldwin was offended. "You haven't given me one good reason why I shouldn't arrest him for this."

Fatema picked up her purse to leave. "How about evidence? You don't have any more on him then you do on anybody else, Baldwin. And I swear, if you go after him, without a shred of evidence, I'll print some shit that'll ruin what's left of your career and make you look so shit faced, your own mother won't be able to tell which end is up."

* * *

Fatema drove home fuming and racking her brain about who in the world Lazarus had seen before who could've killed Toni.

Baldwin's statement haunted her. *Lazarus has been seen everywhere, including the 16th Street Mall all the way over to the capitol and even the city and county building.*

The city and county building. Mayor Shaw worked in that building. Wild ideas started to run through her head. They scared her.

"No way he could be that dumb," she muttered, referring to Lucas. Absolutely not and she felt like an idiot for even letting herself go there. Sure she didn't like the man. But to think he'd risk everything he had to cover up an affair by killing someone was just crazy. Not to mention, it was way too clichéd. Toni had broken it off with Shaw, though. Unless she was threatening to tell his wife about the two of them, there was no reason for him to kill her. Unless. "Unless he didn't want her to break it off," she muttered again. Shaw reminded Fatema of one of those men used to getting everything he wanted. He didn't seem like the kind of man who would take no for an answer either. What if the fool found out she was seeing someone else? Would he stoop so low as to kill her over it?

"Come on, Fatema," she said out loud. "That's so Lifetime movie-ish it's ridiculous." Or was it? Was it possible that he could've killed her over something else? "Unless she knew something about him . . ." For a man like Shaw, mistresses could come a dime a dozen. Toni's fixation with the kidnappings kept coming to mind, and Fatema was starting to wonder, if maybe, just maybe, Lucas Shaw might've somehow been involved.

There she was again, letting her imagination run wild. Fatema sighed deeply, then concluded that maybe Todd was right. Maybe she should write a book to release all this pent-up creative energy she had coarsing through her veins. Imagine, the Mayor of Denver, head of a human trafficking ring.

Fatema couldn't help herself and laughed out loud.

Demons

Lucas couldn't sleep. And after the incident with his wife, he felt it best to stay as close to home as possible—dutiful husband and father. He was a man obsessed by perfection and his whole life, everything about him from his thoughts to the way he spoke and dressed had all been carefully thought out and meticulously planned. He'd been a steady train on a straight and narrow track and there'd been few incidents in his life that had been unplanned.

Rigidity was second nature to Lucas, and until he met Toni Robbins, he'd been satisfied with that. She shook things up, though. She coaxed him off that track and showed him the excitement of spontaneity and taught him that rule breaking was not only intoxicating, but necessary.

He was drawn to her from the moment he saw her, but of course, she resisted because she knew his situation. To this day, Lucas had no idea what kind of spell she'd cast over him, but he was a man fixated and obsessed with getting to know this beautiful young woman, even if the affair had to be brief. In fact, he expected it to be. He counted on it. Lucas stepped up his game. He had to if he wanted to break through the barriers his marriage and position placed between them, and in time, his charm wore down her defenses and it all started with a kiss late one night in his office.

"Do you have any idea how long I've been wanting to do that?" he asked her.

"As long as I've wanted you to," she whispered. "But I can't do this, Lucas. I wouldn't want it done to me, and I won't do it to her."

He believed she meant it, and if he had one chance to make love to her, then he decided to make it happen right then and there. He lifted her up on his desk, kissed her drunk, and slid her panties down to her ankles. She freed him from his pants and guided him in between her soft folds and they made love slowly, thoroughly, as if they both knew this would be the one and only time.

But addictions are hard to break and once wasn't enough for either of them. It was the first time he'd ever cheated on Lisa, and it was like a drug, and he knew that he would never be the same man she married again. He took chances with Toni, sneaking out of the house late at night after his wife fell asleep, taking her on out of town conferences and speaking engagements. They'd even made love in his Mercedes, and in Lisa's. Toni would feel shame, but he felt exhilarated and rejuvenated like he was alive for the first time, ignoring every rule he'd ever lived by.

Toni bought him to life, and eventually unleashed a monster. He got to the point where he needed more than Toni. There were some things she wasn't willing to do. Some acts she refused to participate in, and he began to suspect her interest in him waning.

The first time he stepped outside of his relationship with Toni was at a speaking engagement at a law professionals' conference in Chicago. Lucas retired to his suite and he was restless. Toni had refused to come along on this trip. He felt anxious and overwhelmed by his desire. Lucas ached for a release, but not the tame kind. He didn't want to be considerate or charming. He didn't want to know the woman's name and pretend he cared. He wanted to get his nut, and he wanted it without the burden of caring one way or another how he got it.

He turned on his laptop and began surfing the Internet for porn sites. With each one, he became more aroused and more frustrated. He cursed the thought of jacking off, and his mouth watered for the touch and taste of a female. Somehow he landed on a compelling site that intrigued him. The website listed advertisements where a man could purchase what he needed. There were even pictures. He came across one in particular that caught his eye, of a young woman. Her age was advertised as eighteen. She was Hispanic, lean yet soft. She wore a pair of thin lace bikini panties, and a cutoff white tee-shirt that revealed the slight curve of her breasts.

"I'm waiting . . ."

Was all her ad said. And below was listed a code for him to click on. When he did, the response was almost instantaneous.

I want to meet you. How soon can we get together?

He pulsated and throbbed so hard, pain shot down his legs.

Tonight, he responded. *Now.*

In an instant, an address was sent to him.

Angela's picture didn't do her justice. She was petite, with doe eyes, satin black hair that hung down to her lower back, and she didn't speak a word of English. For three hundred dollars, she treated him like a god, and Lucas came back to his room just before dawn and slept better than he ever had.

His fetish followed him home, and he went out of his way to be careful. He wasn't about to lose his wife. He loved his mistress. But he craved something that neither one of them could give him.

When Toni discovered his secret, the look on her face crushed him. Her disapproval crushed him. Her rejection devastated him. But Lucas knew that as much as he couldn't stand the thought of losing her, he was too far gone to turn back and be anything but that thing he'd turned into.

"I don't know what this is," he said, desperate to get her to hear him. "I don't know how I let it go this far, baby."

"It's sick, Luke. It's disgusting!"

"I know it is, but it doesn't change how I feel about you."

She looked at him like he'd lost his mind. "So that's supposed to make it okay? I'm supposed to be cool because of how you feel about me? You pay for prostitutes and I'm supposed to act like it's just a bad habit?"

The only thing he remembered about the rest of that conversation was seeing her walk out the door screaming that she was through with him, and she should've stopped seeing him a long time ago. She cried when she said it and Lucas couldn't wait for her to disappear so that he could finally get to the Internet.

She needed time. He'd give her time. He needed counseling. He needed intervention. He needed to stop and take a long hard look at the destructive path his life was heading in. He needed some sex.

A feeling of dread filled his stomach. Lucas took a sip of bourbon, and relished the warmth of it going down. He felt like throwing up because deep down he knew that he was hanging on to everything he'd worked so hard for by the skin of his teeth, and he was one wrong move away from losing it all if he didn't get his fetishes under control. He chuckled bitterly, because Lucas had lost control a long time ago.

The Season

Lazarus knew enough to be respectful. Hell, this was the holiday season and the city was filled with holiday things: lights, bells, folks singing, and kids. This time of year, there seemed to be millions of them, in every size, shape, color, holding on tight to momma's and daddy's hands, and all of them laughing and looking happy and glad to be together. The shit was almost sacred, and Lazarus did whatever he could to disappear into the shadows and stay far removed from this picture postcard scene. A man like him didn't fit into all this, and he saw no reason to mess it up for everybody else. He watched, though, like he were watching a movie, and oddly enough, he enjoyed every minute of every scene unfolding in front of him.

He couldn't remember if he'd had any kids of his own or not. Lazarus couldn't fathom anybody running around calling "Daddy" after him. It didn't seem natural.

"Whe . . . where's my . . . where's my baby . . . where is . . ."

He shook loose the image of the man whose car he'd hit, lying bleeding on the ground, reaching out his arm for his daughter.

Lazarus saw her, though, her small head twisted towards Lazarus, staring wide eyed at him, like she really wasn't dead. And then he saw nothing. Just black and dark and memories of the yellow ribbon and pink barrettes in her hair. And nothing.

Tonight was a good night. Lazarus wouldn't let dark thoughts take away his good night. He closed his eyes, and squeezed everything negative as far away from him as he could. Lazarus had something to do. He had to have a clear head and steady thinking to take care of some business because he hadn't taken care of it before. And he owed her that. He owed all of them that.

That damn cop had pulled him in to jail and fuckin' fed him questions he was supposed to swallow and throw up answers to.

Did you see the dead woman? Did you see who killed the dead woman?

Lazarus blinked away the blurred memory starting to form in his head. Tonight wasn't the night for all that. Lately his thoughts were riddled with shit that didn't make sense. He thought about the dead woman too much. He'd seen her time and time again, but never the way he did that night, close. And he thought about the girl with the pretty lips, living underground out of the light and fresh air. She looked pale like a ghost, her eyes empty. He'd passed by that same alley where that building stood a couple of times today, and each time, he thought of going back to see if she was still there. But maybe she was just a bad dream like everything else.

He'd failed people. Lazarus had failed far too

many people in his life. He'd failed that woman who
ran where he slept and then died there. He even
failed that damn policeman that he hated, and Sweet
Thang who smiled so nice whenever she spoke to
him. He remembered her, but from where? God was
testing him. He tested Lazarus over and over waiting
for the moment he would pass. And suddenly it
dawned on him why he was left here in this place to
rot. It made sense. He couldn't believe he'd been
missing it all this time. He couldn't believe he'd been
so dumb and so blind. That ghost with the pretty lips
was another test. Oh, Lord! He'd almost missed it
again. It was another test to not fail. Maybe she was
real. Maybe she wasn't. But it was up to him to show
up for once in his life and see what it was like, not to
fail.

He stood up, stomped the feelings back into his
legs, and walked back to the last place he'd seen that
ghost—with the pretty lips.

Among Friends

"Dinner was great, Fatema," Nelson took a seat in the chair across from her in the living room. "You're a great cook."

"Actually Banquet is a great cook," she quipped. "I'm just good at following directions, then putting everything in some nice cooking dishes and making it look like I made it. The truth be known, Nelson, I'm more of a heat and serve kind of girl."

He laughed. "Well, you work a mean microwave, then."

"How you getting along?" she asked him, unable to look past the sadness still lingering in his eyes.

Nelson shrugged. "Oh, you know. Time heals all wounds. And I'm just biding my time. You?"

"Some days are better than others. For me, the frustration comes in not knowing who did this to her and why. I can't believe it was just random."

"But maybe it is," he said reluctantly. "Maybe Toni just happened to be at the wrong place at the wrong time and somebody took advantage of that. She could've just been convenient."

"You really believe that?"

"I don't know what to believe." He sighed deeply. "I miss her. I want her here with me, and knowing that's never going to happen again, well . . . like I said, I'm waiting on time to come in and save the day."

The two of them sipped quietly on wine as they reflected on Toni in their own ways. "Between the two of us, everybody used to believe I was the mischievous one." She smiled.

"You weren't?" he teased.

She rolled her eyes. "Toni was good at looking like Miss Goody Two Shoes on the surface, but that girl had a wild streak in her that rivaled mine any day. She just had a better handle on hers than I did. Did she ever tell you about the time that we streaked across the DU Campus one night after a lecture and mini-concert by Quincy Jones?"

He looked stunned. "Never mentioned it."

"Well, we did, in front of at least a thousand people, wearing Hello Kitty masks and white sneakers," Fatema laughed at the memory. "Toni was the brilliant one, but she was mean too. We ran across the lawn and then disappeared around the back of the Fine Arts building, where Miss Brainiac had the foresight to hide some sweat pants and a T-shirt."

"For the two of you?"

She scowled at him. "No! And then she left me shivering behind the bushes, dodging security for two hours while she took her time going back to our apartment to get me some clothes."

Nelson laughed hysterically.

"I told her, 'Why don't you just bring the car around so I can jump in? Don't worry about the clothes.' And she came back with some lame excuse about not wanting security to take down her license plate number and use it to track her down."

"Oh, she got you good."

"By the time she came back, I was covered in goose bumps and bug bites, and I didn't speak to her for a month after that."

"You think she did it on purpose?"

"I know she did. She was pissed because Troy Johnson asked me out, and she had it bad for the brotha. It was revenge. Pure and simple. That woman had an evil streak in her."

"So do you know if the police are making any progress yet?"

Fatema rolled her eyes. "Baldwin's ass moves as slow as molasses in the winter if you ask me. Most of the time, I have to wonder if he even gives a damn."

"I'm sure he's doing the best he can, Fatema. He didn't have much to go on."

"Well, he did manage to find Lazarus. You remember I told you about him? The cat who lives under the bridge where they found Toni?"

"Yeah. Yeah, I remember."

"He dragged poor Lazarus down to the precinct in handcuffs, then questioned him about whether or not he saw anything."

"They get anything out of him?"

Fatema smiled and winked at Nelson. "Not until they called in the cavalry."

"The cavalry?"

"Yes. The cavalry. Moi!"

"Oh, really?"

"Lazarus and I go way back. I told you about the documentary I did with him in it? Well, I spent a good couple of days following that man around and studying him like a book. There's a way to talk to him and there's a way to listen to him, and if you don't know how to do either, then you can't communicate with Lazarus. He's like a jigsaw puzzle with pieces scattered all over the floor. All the pieces are there. They're just not put together."

"Well, what did he say? Did he see who killed Toni?" he asked anxiously.

She hesitated before answering. "He did. I think."

"You think? What does that mean?"

"He saw something. I think he saw her running and someone chasing after her."

"But did he say who?"

"Sort of."

Nelson's frustration was starting to show. "Fatema."

"He led Baldwin and me to believe that he'd seen the man the night Toni was killed, and that he'd seen him before that."

His expression turned to stone. "Does Baldwin have a description?"

She shook her head. "No. Lazarus never described him, and eventually, Baldwin had no choice but to let him go."

Nelson took the long way home, thinking long and hard about Lazarus and who or what he might've seen. That old man was the key to solving Toni's murder. He had all the answers, but the problem was, no one knew how to get to them. If he'd been there, though, why hadn't he helped her? Why hadn't he tried to stop it from happening? Was he so far gone that he could just sit there and watch a man take a woman's life, and not think anything of it?

Lazarus would come back to the shelter eventually. Instinctively, Nelson knew he would. People like him were habitual and when he got hungry enough, he'd be compelled to visit again.

Ivy

The sound of voices woke her up. The light from the street lamp in the alley filtered into the basement, as she strained to hear what was being said.

". . . sample the wares . . . quality merchandise . . . don't make this difficult . . . more than generous . . ."

Moments later she heard the door at the top of the stairs open. Ivy's heart beat hard and fast, but she closed her eyes, steadied her breathing and pretended to be asleep. The next thing she knew, she was being pulled up by her wrists and dragged across the room to the bed behind the curtain.

Rape wasn't rape if you didn't make a big deal about it. Ivy had learned long ago, not to make a big deal about it. Some men didn't like that. This one was one of those men. He worked on her until he got a reaction—tears that she couldn't stop even if she wanted to. Thankfully he was the only one this time. The other man stood in the corner of the room and watched. When she looked back to him, though, he turned away.

"You keep this up, and she won't be so quality,

man," he told the man raping her. "I'll be upstairs when you get done," he said before leaving.

They were taking her away from this place. Ivy sat in the corner of the room on the floor after it was over and willed herself to stop crying. It hadn't been so bad here. Ivy knew that there were worse places than this for girls like her and she dreaded even thinking about it.

A shadow crossed the small window and caught her attention. At first she was scared, but then she saw it again. She stood and slowly approached the window. That crazy old bum she'd seen the other day stood across the alley and stared back at her. Tears burned her eyes again as she pressed her hands flat against the glass, hoping he wasn't as crazy as he looked, and that he knew she was in trouble and needed his help.

He stood like a statue, watching her watch him.

Go get help, she wanted to scream. Get somebody! Get the police!

Snow fell lightly to the ground around him and on his eyebrows and beard, making him look like a poor excuse for Santa Claus. Then suddenly, he surprised her and walked towards the window. The old bum dropped down to his knees and peered at her, then squinted trying to see into the room behind her. He looked even more ancient up close, except for his eyes. His eyes were clear, and young, and inquisitive.

He jerked and looked down the alley like someone was coming, and the old man quickly rose to his feet, and disappeared. No! Don't go! Ivy nearly choked on those words, as she watched him leave. Ivy had been really brave for a long time. But she didn't feel so brave now, and she crawled into bed, buried her face in the dingy pillow and cried herself to sleep.

Fall from Grace

The television was on, but while Bruce stared at it, he had no idea what was on it. He was losing it. That heightened sense of situations and people that led him to solve the kinds of cases that left other detectives shaking their heads. Ten years ago, he was a bloodhound. Bruce found evidence where it looked like none existed. He pieced together the puzzles of events and lives and circumstances of crime scenes, studying them from the perspective of a man with a gift that could only come from God.

He'd solved cases more difficult than this. And it pissed him off because on the surface there was absolutely nothing extraordinary about the murder of Toni Robbins, and solving it should've been a piece of cake. Everybody was starting to look at him sideways. His captain, colleagues, and the media were taking advantage of the fact that time had stopped being on his side.

What's taking so long to solve this case, Detective?

Do you have any leads on who might've killed this woman?

The public wants answers, Detective Baldwin. What do you have to say?

He said nothing, because he knew nothing. Anybody remotely suspected had an alibi, and he was beginning to think that maybe her death was random after all. As he'd done so many times before, Baldwin closed his eyes and mentally retraced Toni's last night alive.

She'd gotten off work at five, walked six blocks to The Broadway Shelter, played kissy face with her man, chatted it up with some other volunteers, and said hello to some folks waiting in line to eat. At six, she helped to serve the evening meal. Seven-thirty, she read stories to some kids, reassured some woman who, along with her four kids, had been evicted from her one-bedroom apartment, that everything would be all right, said good night to the staff and boyfriend, and finally walked out of the door, headed back to her car parked in a lot halfway between her job and the shelter. She was found early the next morning underneath the Corona and Speer overpass.

Denver's honorable mayor was attending a fundraiser the night she was killed, as attested to by three hundred of his fondest admirers and lovely wife. Nelson Monroe left the shelter around nine–thirty. He gave one of his volunteers a ride home, stopped at the ATM on his way home, and held a brief conversation with a neighbor on the elevator who lived next door to him.

No evidence had been found near the crime scene. Not a damn thing. There had been shoe prints in the snow, but by the time the cops showed up, snow had covered them and the city's finest had trampled over any potential evidence buried underneath it. Whoever killed her wore gloves. He didn't rape her, or hit her, or abuse her, other than to choke the life out of her. It was almost as if he were careful. Baldwin opened his eyes. It was almost as if he cared. Before he had a chance to decipher this revelation, his phone rang.

"Yeah," he said gruffly.

It was his friend from vice, Dan Goodwin. "Tell me you can be up and out the door in thirty seconds or less."

"Why? What's up?"

"Man! You are not going to believe who we got in handcuffs for soliciting sex from an underage girl he found over the Internet."

Baldwin bolted up from the sofa. "Where?"

He was out the door and in his car speeding across town with the light flashing in the window. Baldwin headed west towards Lakewood, to a seedy motel on West Sixth Avenue. All he had to do was follow the parade of lights illuminating the scene like it was a holiday party. News cameras were out in full force, and in the back seat of one of the squad cars he passed, Baldwin caught a glimpse of a man he thought looked like Mayor Shaw. He stopped, leaned down and peered at the man to be sure. Shaw glanced at him, then turned his head away.

Goodwin spotted Bruce. "Baldwin!" He waved him over. A female officer was escorting a frightened Hispanic teenage girl to another squad car. The girl was trembling despite the blanket she'd been wrapped in.

"You have got to be kidding me," Baldwin said dismayed.

Goodwin shook his head. "I wish I was, man. This is some shit for sure."

"How old is that kid?"

"Fifteen. Doesn't speak English either. Her mother sent her here to live with relatives, only the girl never made it to any relatives."

"How the hell did he find her?"

Goodwin looked shocked that Baldwin would be so naïve. "I told you, man. The World Wide Web—www.younghotchick.com. It's all the rage among pedophiles. Or hadn't you heard?"

Bruce scratched his head. "Sounds like some fucked up eBay shit if you ask me."

"Not quite, but . . . our mayor here has been busy. Careful, but not careful enough. He's a pompous sonofabitch, though, thought he was too slick to get caught."

"How long have you been on to him?"

Dan chuckled. "Hell, we were never on to him. We just got lucky as hell. Went fishing for a good-sized trout and came out with a fucking shark."

"Who called the piranha?" Baldwin asked, referring to the media.

Goodwin gave him a sly look. "He pissed me off."

Baldwin stared at him in disbelief. "Remind me never to get on your bad side, man."

Lucas was numb. The whole scene unraveled around him like a movie he was watching on late night television. News cameras surrounded him, flashing lights in his face, pointing fingers, shaking their heads, talking so fast, their tongues couldn't keep up. He hadn't known that girl was so young, but he knew she was young enough. He'd told himself that if she looked too young, he'd walk away, but deep down, he knew it was a lie. His wife had taken one of her sleeping pills so she'd get the news first thing in the morning like everyone else in the city. Lisa hated drama. She hated when things weren't perfect and to be embarrassed in any way. He watched them put that child in the back of that patrol car and breathed a sigh of relief. If he had touched her, he would've never been able to forgive himself.

Lucas had always dreamed big. He'd dreamed of becoming a national hero, a figurehead, respected, admired, loved by everyone who'd ever shaken his hand. The reality of what he'd become was a hell of a lot more frightening.

Daily Bread

Todd had left her a message on her cell phone at four in the morning:

"Where the hell are you? One of the biggest scandals in the history of Denver just came to light and you're no where to be found. When you finally peel your ass out from between those sheets, turn on the television to any damn channel you please. The story's gonna be on every last one of them."

She sat in front of the television for hours, flipping channels, watching report after report, commentary after commentary on the incriminating acts of the city's mayor. He'd fallen like a star from heaven, and still managed to look like a rock star, even in his mug shot. The man's smug expression dug deep down into the core of Fatema, and she cringed just thinking about the fact that she'd spent any time alone with him at all, and that Toni had actually been intimate with the creep.

One woman outside the precinct where he'd been taken reported:

"Inside sources say that the mayor has admitted to soliciting what he thought was an adult woman, and that he had no idea the girl was underage and being held against her will."

Of course, every so-called expert who'd ever taken a high school psychology class had to chime in with their opinions:

"It's highly unlikely that he didn't know. Pedophiles are predators. They hunt for their prey and they know where to find it. I doubt his claim that this was his first encounter with a child."

"It's a disease. And men like Lucas Shaw hide behind the order in their lives, and their success, covering up the truth of who they are and choosing to turn away from their transgressions rather than to face them head-on and take action to correct the behavior."

Toni knew. Somehow, she'd found out and that was the reason she'd left him. Fatema shuddered and tears unexpectedly stung her eyes.

"Oh, dear God," she gasped.

In the e-mails she'd saved on her computer, Toni had called him disgusting and told him that he needed help. If a man like Lucas Shaw had felt threatened that his secret would get out, how far would he go to stop it?

They flashed his photograph and images of him being escorted into the precinct in handcuffs. Fatema fixed on his face, particularly his eyes—cobalt, hard, and even after everything that had unfolded on national television, she saw in his eyes a man who was convinced that he was still untouchable.

* * *

That afternoon, she hurried over to The Broadway knowing that Nelson would be there. It was relatively quiet at the shelter, except for the sound of pots and pans clanging in the kitchen.

A few of the volunteers were busy preparing dinner when she walked in. "Hello." Fatema smiled. They looked as stunned as she felt. "Is Nelson here?"

"He's in his office," one of them responded quietly.

Nelson's door was open. The man was like a stone, sitting with his back to her, staring out of the window at a brick wall on the building next door.

"You heard?" she asked, trying not to startle him.

He didn't turn around.

"We own that building," he said, solemnly. "The plan is to make it livable to give people a place to stay until they can get back on their feet." Nelson sounded so defeated.

"I really believe Shaw killed her, Nelson." Fatema walked up behind him and pressed her hands on his shoulders. Nelson reached up and touched one of them.

"That's some pretty messed up shit." His voice cracked.

Fatema sat down in the chair across from his desk. Neither one of them knew what to say exactly and so they sat reflectively not saying anything for some time.

"I think Toni knew about him," she said quietly. "I think she found out what he was doing."

"Maybe she did," he said simply.

"And," she continued hesitantly, "I think he killed her because of it."

Nelson stared at her. "You think he's a child molester and a murderer."

She shrugged. "Don't you?" She waited for an answer, but Nelson's answer came in the form of an averted gaze. "It's the only thing that makes sense, Nelson. She didn't stop seeing him because he was married. She stopped seeing him because he's, for lack of a better term, perverted. The man solicits children on the Net. He's mayor of a big city. His career is planned out all the way up to the Senate level. Not to mention the wife and kids. Who else would have a better reason for killing her?"

"They say that kid was a sex slave, bought and paid for a hundred times by men like him. Do you think he knew?"

"I don't know. But Toni must have suspected something because she was obsessed with human trafficking. Maybe that's why."

"Do you think the police suspect him?"

"If they don't, by the time I'm finished talking to them, they will."

"They need to solve her murder, Fatema." Nelson looked like a man weighted down and tired. "I feel like someone's left the door open on my life, and until it's closed, I can't move forward."

Fatema walked over to him, and held him. "I know, Nelson. I feel the same way."

"She was the one. Know what I'm saying?"

"Yeah. I do."

Fatema eventually left on a mission to see Bruce Baldwin. If he had any kind of common sense whatsoever, he'd have figured this out by now, and she'd be wasting a trip. Heading west on 14th Avenue, Fatema spotted Lazarus crossing in front of her half a block ahead on Delaware Street. Without even thinking, she turned abruptly onto Delaware and quickly pulled into an illegal parking spot on a side street a few blocks behind him. Fatema jumped out of the car and hurried to catch up with him. For an old man, Lazarus moved fast, and for every two of her steps, he took one. She called after him, but he didn't stop. The thought that Baldwin had suspected Lazarus for murdering Toni had been absurd, and she couldn't wait to look him in the eyes and make sure he knew how out of line he'd been.

"Lazarus!" she called again. The old man seemed to pick up the pace, until Fatema was practically running. He turned right onto Washington, and right again. By the time she caught up with him, Fatema was out of breath.

"Hey, Lazarus," she said, still struggling to keep up with him. "Where you going?"

He ignored her and never said a word. There was something determined about him. She knew he'd heard her by the way he glanced at her out of the corner of his eye, but he seemed to be a man on a mission, and he didn't deter her from coming along. Fatema followed without saying another word. He led her back to West 14th and they walked for another four blocks into an alleyway between Lincoln and Sherman. Fatema recognized the back of one building as being The Broadway Shelter. Suddenly, Lazarus stopped and stared down at a small window of the basement of an old brick townhouse. She realized she was standing right below Nelson's office.

Lazarus stared fixated on a small, dark window near the dumpster and he waited. Moments later, a ghost appeared. Red rimmed eyes, oily brown hair, a narrow face with sallow skin stared back at first him, and then Fatema. Tears streamed down her face as she mouthed slowly, *Help me.*

"Is she real, Sweet Thang?" Lazarus asked, staring at the girl. "Or is this old man just seeing things?"

"She's real, Lazarus."

"She got some pretty lips," Lazarus said.

"Yes," Fatema responded, stunned. "She certainly does." She looked up and saw Nelson's office.

Redeeming Me

"Is she ready to transport?" The little man couldn't have been any taller than five-three. Nelson towered over him by almost a foot, and yet, he shrank into a shadow of a man as soon as the little man came into the room. Behind him stood another man, larger, who never said a word.

Nelson sat hunched over one of the tables in the empty dining hall, with his hands in front of him. He was exhausted, mentally and physically drained. "What happened to the other girl?" he asked with his head lowered, talking into his chest.

"What?" the man asked irritably.

Nelson slowly raised his head. "The Russian girl? You didn't have to kill her, man."

The little man looked annoyed, and the bigger man glared at Nelson. "You give me what I came here for. Nothing else is any of your business."

He'd been obedient, dependable, reliable in the past. He'd done everything he'd been told to do because that's what they paid him for. Nelson fell into a trap of his own passion a year ago, believing he was helping people who couldn't help themselves. Yes, they were illegals, but yes, they also deserved a chance at a better life and if that better life waited for them in America, then why shouldn't he help them? In the beginning, it seemed to be the perfect arrangement. Nelson got paid good money to further his good cause that allowed him to do good things for good people down on their luck. The Broadway had been a labor of love, and it had nearly taken everything from him to keep it up and running. State and Federal aid helped, private donations came in when they came in, and they helped, but Nelson had bigger dreams for The Broadway than just a place for people to eat and spend the night. The Broadway was supposed to change lives, to provide a safe place for people to start over from scratch, and give them the resources to begin again. The money these people paid him helped him to accomplish so much. It wasn't until a young girl was gang raped in the basement of one of his row homes that he realized what was truly going on, and by then, it was too late, and Nelson's good intentions, naiveté, and self-absorbed ambition blinded him to the truth and made way for these people to be delivered straight into hell.

"You stalling, Monroe?" the little man asked, sarcastically. "I'm taking my product with me, tonight. You can either take me to her, or we can use your head to bash in the door. How do you want to play it?"

"She's just a kid, man," Monroe protested. "Look, I've done my part, and all I'm asking is just let me have this favor. Ivy doesn't deserve this. None of them do. But can't you just let her stay here a while longer? I swear, she'll be here when you come back for her, if that's what you decide to do."

The big man stepped towards Nelson, and he knew what his ultimatum was.

He'd been working up the courage to save Ivy. Nelson should've just let her go, but he knew that if he did, when they came back for her, and if she was gone, they'd kill him. It was his ass he cared more about than hers, and at that moment, Nelson realized that he was a bigger hypocrite than anyone he'd ever known.

He stood slowly. "I'll get her," he said quietly.

Nelson left through the kitchen and through the back door of The Broadway that led into the alley. He didn't have to turn around to know that the two men weren't far behind.

He was fumbling with the keys in his pocket, when he looked over at the small window and noticed it had been broken.

"Hey!" the big man shouted.

Nelson looked down the alley and recognized three people running away; Fatema, Ivy, and Lazarus. Tears filled his eyes, and he shouted out to them. "Run!"

A shot was fired. Lazarus fell to the ground.

Nelson turned to the two men behind him, and before he could say another word, the large man hit him in the face with a black, gloved hand, and Nelson crumpled to his knees.

In an instant, both ends of the alley were blocked by police cars, and the two men tried to get inside the back door of The Broadway that locked automatically. Nelson still held the keys in his hand.

"You all right?" Baldwin asked, rushing over to Fatema.

She nodded. "Yes," she said, out of breath, and that's when she noticed Lazarus, lying face up on the ground.

She started to hurry over to him, but Baldwin held

her. "Let me go!" she screamed, struggling to get free. "Please!"

Ivy stood shivering in the cold in her bare feet. One of the officers wrapped a blanket around her and put her in the back of a squad car.

"Lazarus!" Fatema fell to her knees next to Lazarus. "Oh, God! Oh, dear God!"

Blood seeped out from underneath where he lay. Lazarus stared up at the sky with a strange smile on his face, and then he looked at Fatema, and held up his hand to her. "Sweet Thang," he said, and laughed out loud, then coughed uncontrollably.

"Shhhhh," she cried, squeezing her hand in his. "It's going to be all right."

Baldwin radioed for an ambulance from behind her.

"I know it is, girl." Tears slid down the sides of his face, but he wasn't crying. "It's better already."

"We're going to get you to a hospital," she told him. "And you're going to be fine."

Lazarus swallowed. "No, Sweet Thang." He stared up at the sky again. The snow had just started to fall, and Lazarus breathed a deep sigh of relief. "I did the right thing," he told her. "This time—I get to go to heaven, too," Lazarus chuckled, and then he stopped.

The police questioned Ivy for what seemed like hours, and then finally took her to the hospital for overnight observation.

Fatema made sure to say goodbye to her before they took her away, though.

"You're safe now, Ivy." She hugged her. "Nobody's going to hurt you like that again."

"He kept coming back," Ivy cried into Fatema's shoulder. "I didn't think he'd come back because I thought he might just be another crazy old bum, but he came back."

Fatema smiled. "He was a crazy old bum."

"I think the bastard called himself taking care of her," Baldwin told Fatema, before he went in to the interrogation room to question Nelson.

She watched from the other side of the two-way mirror, still in shock that he would have anything to do with something like this. Nelson told Baldwin everything about how he got involved in the human trafficking ring. Money made him do it. That was a lame-ass excuse, she thought, listening to him try and justify this craziness. And he gave names, numbers, e-mail addresses. Nelson broke down the whole operation as it related to his part in it, and hearing it made Fatema's skin crawl.

"The Russian girl stayed for a few weeks before they took her away. They filmed her before they did."

"Filmed her?"

"They—some men came into the basement, and they—they filmed what they did."

"Who killed Toni, Nelson?" Baldwin finally asked.

Nelson's handsome features melted into a pathetic lump of flesh in that room. And he sobbed like a baby. "It was an accident."

Fatema bit her bottom lip, and let the tears flow freely for her friend's memory.

"Tell me what happened," Baldwin probed.

Nelson tried to compose himself enough to explain the events of that night. "She left at her normal time. We were supposed to meet up later at her place, after I left."

"But what happened?"

He shrugged. "She came back. I had gone to check on—them before I left. I went back to my office and she—she came back."

"She confronted you?"

Nelson nodded. "I tried to talk to her, and get her to just listen. She wouldn't listen to me, man, she just—"

"She ran?"

"We argued, and yeah. She ran. I just wanted her to calm down—to be still so that I could talk to her. To explain."

"Are you saying that you killed her, Nelson? Is that what you're telling me?"

Nelson broke down crying. "I loved her. And yeah, man," he broke down and sobbed. "I did it. I killed her."

Fatema took a deep breath and held it and then left the precinct without saying a word to anybody.

I Will Love You Anyway

The coffee tasted unusually good this morning. Fatema stood on the balcony of her apartment looking out in to the city, thankful that for the first time in a long time, she could look ahead of her instead of at the past.

Drew came up behind her, wrapped his arms around her waist and nuzzled the side of her neck. "How's the coffee?" he asked, knowing the answer already.

She rolled her eyes. "You know it's good." Fatema took another sip.

The night Nelson was arrested was the night she called him to come over. That had been a week ago, and this time, he'd never left.

"Some things are just right," he told her that next day. "You and me, Fatty, we're right, and no matter how hard you fight it, there's nothing you can do to change it."

"Oh, yeah," she retorted. "And what about what's-her-name?"

"Who?"

She hit him on the arm. "Your girl, Drew. The woman you live with?"

Drew laughed out loud, then winked. "I ain't lived with that woman in three months, Fatema."

"Quit lying!"

"I'm serious," he said, sincerely. "Do you honestly think I could live with a woman and be on call for you every hour of the day the way I am?"

"I don't call you like that, Drew."

"Think about it, baby. In the middle of the night, 'Drew,' " he mocked her voice. " 'Can you come over?' Early in the morning, afternoon, Saturdays, Sundays, holidays."

"That's so not true!"

"Oh, it's true, girl. And like a magnet to metal, my dick drags me over here whether I want to come or not, and ain't shit I can do about it. If I was still living with whats-her-name, don't you think she'd have cut my ass by now?"

Fatema couldn't help but laugh. "I would've."

"Damn right you would've, and so would any woman."

"Well, why didn't you tell me?"

"What? And let you know I was available? I liked having you think I was with somebody. You look cute jealous."

"I have never been jealous."

"Quit playing, Fatema. We're talking serious here, and keeping it real."

"I'm being real, Drew. I have never been jealous of that woman."

"Yes, you have."

"Have not."

"Have too."

"Have not."

The argument went on like that for several minutes before Drew shut her up with a kiss.

He felt good being here, and he was right, though she'd go to her grave first before she'd ever admit it. But the two of them belonged together.

Toni's death was a wake up call. Fatema had spent too much time letting other things get in the way of what was really important in life. Maybe if she'd been a better friend, she could've seen the trouble Toni was headed in and could've stopped it from happening. The two of them had always been able to talk about anything, and Fatema would always feel a sadness in her heart for not being there for her friend when she needed her most. But from Toni and Lazarus, and even Ivy, Fatema learned not to take one second of life for granted. And to pay attention to that small voice inside telling her that Drew was the best thing ever to happen to her.

"I got the laptop all powered up for you, girl," he said softly in her ear.

Fatema laughed. "You really think I should do it?"

"I do. And from what you said about Todd, I'm sure he'd agree."

"Todd's just hating because he's not as good at creative writing as I am."

"Well, the sooner you get started on writing this novel, the sooner you can show him just how good you really are. Got a title yet?"

She hesitated in answering, quietly reflecting on the title of her first book. "Yeah. *Lazarus Rising.*"

Tomorrow's Edge

Victor McGlothin

One

The night before lightning struck, Vera Miles witnessed one thing she never thought possible. When she came up empty after trailing a client's husband over a week, it appeared out of nowhere like a flash. It had to be the first time in history a black woman became fighting mad because her man was *not* sneaking around. Most of them, still in the market for a good man, would never have considered the thought of dismissing a good man, so Vera knew right off that something about Sylvia Everhart didn't fit. The hired snoop stood in her client's plush office, which was excessively decorated with fine furniture and extravagant original artwork, wondering why the woman glared at her with clenched teeth after hearing that her husband Devin had not cheated nor displayed any evidence to suggest he was the philandering type. Even after Devin Everhart babysat a few drinks at an upscale, happy hour mix-and-mingle joint, he kept to himself, despite several women offering a menu of after-hours innuendo they assumed he was there to get.

For seven days, Vera followed Devin from his office building to a residential hotel a few blocks away, where he rented a room on the first floor. During that week, he ordered fast food and stepped out for quick bites, then returned to his single room with double beds, but always alone. Having been a private investigator for more than three years, Vera found it easy to make rational assumptions when shadowing a person for any length of time. She rarely had to guess whether there was a weakness for gambling, a predilection for sexual deviance or struggles with the bottle, because habits, especially bad ones, always had a way of showing themselves, like a stubborn pimple dabbled over with several layers of makeup. Before too long, it was bound to rear its ugly head.

During the previous week, Vera grew to appreciate the kind of man Mrs. Everhart's husband was, probably more than she'd care to admit. Not only was he nice to look at, he had proven to be a conscientious worker who believed in being on time for the nine-to-five grind and back on the clock after lunch at exactly an hour on the dot, with no deviations. Most women would have been smart enough to admire his dependable and responsible work ethic. While contemplating the drastic measures other women would have gone through to snag a quality mate like Devin, Vera found herself staring at a family of college degrees on her client's wall. Coincidentally, she tried to figure out how a woman with so much book sense suffered miserably when it came down to the good old fashion common sense necessary to cherish a fine man like hers.

Maybe Vera had tipped her hand by allowing myriad unprofessional thoughts to slow dance around that notion in her head too long. Perhaps Mrs. Everhart read those thoughts clearly enough to recognize Vera's lustful deliberations with her husband in mind. Whichever the case, Mrs. Everhart was mad as hell and didn't have any qualms about letting Vera know it when she finally switched her gaze from the client's accomplishments to the client's strained expression. That was the first time the private eye noticed how the woman's head seemed too big for her frail body. It had a lot to do with her outdated Mary-Tyler-Moore-flipped-up hairdo nesting above her shoulders and the fact that Sylvia Everhart was swelling with a rising tide of contempt. Seeing as how being hit with contemptible behavior from clients typically came with the territory, Vera shrugged off Mrs. Everhart's evil eye like water down a duck's back. After all, her client wasn't necessarily a bad person despite her soured disposition. Actually, under other circumstances, she might have even been tolerable. The woman's complexion was a shade lighter than Vera's, more of a toffee-brown hue. However, her spindly legs and slight build packaged into a perfect size four was enough to make Vera dislike her from the beginning. In fact, Vera considered all skinny women to be evil until proven otherwise. So far, not a single one of them had been given the benefit of the doubt. Not one.

After another long bout of silence, which was attached to that lingering glare Mrs. Everhart had propped up with a healthy dose of attitude, she decided to work her strategy from another angle. "I see," she said, looking Vera over as if she wasn't close to being satisfied with her abilities as a PI and just as displeased with the snug fit of the navy colored corduroy slacks hugging her curvy hips. Vera, whose figure floated between sizes ten and twelve depending on the cut, was partly to blame. At the time, she was an everyday twelve, hoping to get by with half a wardrobe that should have been given up, let out or traded in. And Vera should have given it a great deal more thought before leaving the house with that particular pair of dress slacks wrangled over all her womanly goodness. True, it was an error in judgment to think that no one would have noticed, but that was beside the point. Mrs. Everhart's disapproving sneer overshadowed Vera's first mistake of the day. She'd graded Vera with her narrowed, condescending eyes, which pushed Vera farther away from observing professional courtesy and much closer to opening her mouth with something she had been dying to say.

"Perhaps," Mrs. Everhart continued, after a pinch of silence skirted by, "perhaps you didn't adequately apply yourself on my behalf, Ms. Miles."

"Vera," the PI whispered uncomfortably, after having been chastised.

"Excuse me?"

"I said Vera. Call me Vera."

"Like I was saying, *Ms. Miles*, I've paid you good money and I expect good results." That inflated head of hers begun to bobble slightly from side to side as she pressed hard with an ink pen against her checkbook. "Why don't I sweeten the pot? Some people need more inspiration than others to try harder." Mrs. Sylvia Everhart reached out her hand, accessorized with a host of diamond trinkets. "Here is a check for two thousand dollars. Perhaps doubling your weekly fee will entice you to get out there and bring me something I can use," she spat irritably.

A prideful disposition kept Vera from taking the

check which dangled from the tips of the rich woman's skinny fingers like a doggie treat offered from a doting master. The only thing missing was the customary pat on the head that generally followed such a gift. Pride that Vera's grandparents instilled during her upbringing wouldn't allow her to bow and shuffle. It made her feel like a pooch presented with scraps from the eccentric woman's table, one with far more money than couth. That's when Vera sized her up for another reason. She figured Sylvia to be about five-five, a few inches shorter than herself, and guessed that she was at least thirty pounds lighter. Before Vera realized it, she'd imagined how silly Mrs. Everhart would look face down on the mean streets of Dallas after tossing insults then immediately being introduced to the concrete on the heels of it. But, they weren't on the mean streets and there was no real reason for Vera to get all worked up behind some stuck-up rich chick, black woman or not. Besides, no one would have known about the stack of situational ethics Vera kept tucked deep down in the bottom corner of her purse had she taken the money, added two-thousand digits to her bank register and then sat at home on her butt watching Tru TV for a week. There were a number of ways to get even with the stick figure of a woman whom she couldn't stand but violence was the first one that came to mind. No one would have been the wiser, except Vera and that stubborn pride of hers. The same pride that made her strong some times played her like a fool. This was one of those foolish times.

"On second thought, Mrs. Everhart," Vera said, declining the money, "why don't you keep that money to buy yourself a clue? And if you happened to smarten up, you'd use it on a gang of marriage counselors to help you keep that good man of yours. I've had the pleasure of watching him for a solid week and he was a model husband, even when presented with some pretty nice can't-miss opportunities, if you know what I mean. Now here's something else you probably didn't know. Most men are generally as honest as their options but not Devin—he appeared to be a man who was missing his wife and wishing he was home." Sylvia put Vera in the mind of a toy poodle when she marched her child-like frame toward her in an angered rant.

"That shows just how little you do know, Ms. Miles. *Mr. Everhart* left home on his own accord, so I know he's out there running behind some tramp willing to degrade herself by doing the things men fascinate themselves with. I'm not into greasing his ego or anything else for that matter. I don't have to and I won't."

Vera couldn't believe her ears or her reaction. "Well, maybe you should have. Then your man might've stayed home." Those eleven little dirty words just slipped right out of her mouth before she could tell them to go sit down and mind their own business.

"How dare you!" Mrs. Everhart yelled, from somewhere above the top of her lungs. "Get out!"

Vera swore that all three of the wall mirrors in that office were going to shatter against the woman's loud screeching pitch. Laughing in her client's face behind a teenaged-style tantrum was Vera's next thought commingled with one that served the situation a tad bit better, so she went with the latter. "Okay, I'll leave, but not before I tell you what I think the problem with you really is. Uh-huh, it seems to me that you were hoping your breakup was brought on by what some other woman was doing, but then you looked at me like I had on two different colored shoes when I showed up and informed you that Devin had not taken up with anyone else. That's disturbing, because it forces you to look at yourself and open to other folks' questions as to why your man ran off. I might be wrong but I doubt it. The way I see it, *Sylvia*, this is a big mess you've gotten yourself into and there isn't anyone else around to blame it on."

Suddenly, Mrs. Everhart's top lip began to quiver. She was so mad that Vera nearly giggled at the mere thought of that swollen head of Sylvia's popping off at the neck.

"Are . . . you . . . finished now or should I call the police to have you removed from my building?" Sylvia threatened.

"Yeah, I'm through but don't think about stopping payment on the check for the work I've already put in, or I'll be back and not as pleasant as I've been today."

Vera was well aware that people didn't like paying for bad news, unless it was wrapped around some want ads and grocery store coupons, so she raced to the nearest Wells Fargo branch to tender the check that was burning a hole in her pocket. She might have played a fool for the occasion, but she'd never once been mistaken for stupid.

It was just Vera's luck that the windows at the in-store branch were closed, so she cussed the bank's employees under her breath for closing down on time as she headed up the aisles to shop for a few female necessities. Getting over her last client's upsetting idea of what a marriage was supposed to be still troubled Vera, so she cussed Sylvia Everhart's silly ideologies altogether. Several shoppers threw strange glances her way and each of them was extremely close to getting cussed out too. That's what usually happened when CRUMBS (Clients, Reasonably Upset and Meaning to Bust Somebody) didn't get what they wanted via Vera's investigation services. They'd smart off to her face and she'd cuss them out later, behind their backs.

That night, Vera applied all five of her bedtime beauty secrets then slid beneath the covers to rest her troubled mind. She closed her eyes, repeating her personal PI Anthem while trying to feel good about the money she had made, until the sandman climbed into bed right along with her. *Once the case is closed and the money is made, don't matter win or lose. Some bills have been paid.*

Two

Tuesday morning found Vera hiding beneath the covers and dreading the cool air hawking from the other side of her handmade quilt. Whispers of fall had just rolled in and cast their mesmerizing spell over the city after another long blistering hot Texas summer. That crisp morning air reminded Vera of the first time she nestled herself in 450-count linens, on sale from Neiman's, when 270-count standard hotel type sheets had been good enough before then. She had grown accustomed to the way quality bedding made her feel pleasantly pampered, so she wasn't ready to give up her hiding place just yet. Instead, she lay there with the covers pulled up to her neck, while frowning back at the slender rays of sun peeking through the slits of the Venetian blinds. They didn't mean any harm and generally didn't cause any, so Vera said her hellos to the early coolness of the day and the sunshine's grandeur. Then, she smiled and gave thanks to the Almighty for providing her an avenue to keep the lights on the little extras of life, like 450-count linen sheets.

Vera made some money doing what she loved, some money, although it wasn't enough to multiply on its own. She spent most of her time figuring out ways to catch up on overdue notices while trying to keep her small investigation company afloat. Other than uncovering other people's dirty deeds, Vera came across an occasional insurance fraud case to make the ends meet. Before she hung her own shingle, it was a ten-year hitch as a parole officer for the state. It was safe, too safe. What she truly missed was a job she'd signed on to do with a crew of bounty hunters. Albeit a very brief stint tracking dangerous bail jumpers, it almost got her killed, more than once.

With a few regrets and a lot of bad boys to fret, Vera decided to try her luck at becoming a first rate snoop. Being a private eye put food on the table and presented her with a slice of life that most folks could have only imagined. Because danger and uncertainty often traveled the same paths she walked along, Vera trained herself to be Everywoman in order to survive. She'd learned to play the cold-fish and the queen-bitch, wearing attitude on her sleeve like it was part of a uniform. Mastering her piercing stare coupled with a certain amount of gruffness in her voice, Vera managed to maneuver her way into some very important back rooms, when batting her big brown eyes didn't get her past the front door.

While working cases for former CRUMBS, Vera learned a lot about people and their various bad habits; some of them made television crime shows play out like *Mother Goose* tales. Catching miscreants doing God knows what was always toughest when

Vera had to settle in and videotape their indiscretions. She'd filmed men with men, women with women, men with children and too many deviants with animals to remember. Sickness had taken on a whole new meaning since Vera started working for herself at Miles Above Investigations. The hardest part was doing the job without becoming the job. Unfortunately, the thin line narrowed each time she had to hold the camera steady in order to film an entire reprehensible act in wide focus while collecting the evidence. Having to play it back later, to be dissected on a conference room big screen monitor in a room filled with clients and high-priced lawyers, disturbed Vera down to her core. Private investigating was a dirty line of work to get caught in, one that rarely allowed her to walk away unsullied.

It was 8:30 that morning when Vera snatched her hair back in a ponytail just before leaving her comfortable three-bedroom home to meet the day. It was a red-brick fixer-upper, a money pit that she felt the need to rescue, like taking in a stray dog then later discovering it needed shots and a battery of other expensive veterinary treatments. The house at 9904 Newhaven belonged to Vera and it was well worth the ten grand of remodeling she had poured into it. After springing for a new roof and replacing the light fixtures in every room, Vera had something to be proud of. More than that, it was the first real thing she ever owned. At first sight, she knew that it was something that needed saving and she needed something to save. That's what the Realtor called a match made in real estate heaven.

The Silver Streak, Vera's metallic-colored '97 Ford Explorer, was another story altogether. Her grandfather always said, "Buy American and keep our jobs at home." So, Vera purchased an American automobile and learned something right away. Her grandfather's advice about waiting around until a good man found her wasn't the only thing he was wrong about. It seemed that Vera should have kept her pocketbook at home instead. It was a fact that The Streak got her from point A to B, but then so did walking.

Vera came by her SUV one Saturday afternoon after answering an advertisement for a traveling automobile auction which took place on the other side of town. The man who ran the event sold out of his entire inventory of thirteen vehicles by slashing prices. Twelve of the vehicles he unloaded were stolen property. The only one that hadn't been boosted had been pulled out of a flash flood in Houston. Based on the hill of maintenance bills Vera had accumulated over the past two years, she guessed that The Streak couldn't swim. The thought of passing it on to another chump crossed her mind all the time, but she figured on keeping it around as an, albeit costly, constant reminder that anyone could be a sucker if the odds were right.

Almost laughing at herself, Vera wondered when someone else would try and sucker her as she sneered at the cashier standing on the other side of the teller window. Seven-hundred dollars minus the five-buck non-account holder fee tacked on for cashing Mrs. Everhart's check suggested the bank was first in line. At least she saw that one coming. Vera climbed back into her vehicle wearing a crooked grin. She felt good about having a few extra dollars in her pocket, just a few. She knew all too well that a little money was a whole lot better than none.

Driving up to the oatmeal-hued brick covering the small building Vera leased on lower Greenville Avenue reminded her that she hadn't eaten breakfast. Since there weren't any potential clients on the schedule, or money coming in, she let the sinking feeling pass right on by when pulling into her personal parking space on the tiny back lot. Vera frequently parked behind the building, making it easier to duck out on bill collectors or unhappy persistent clients. Parking on the street out front was another option when her financial situation improved. Had she accepted that additional check from silly Sylvia Everhart, The Streak would have been lounging curbside for at least a week.

At the back door, sounds of Ms. Minneola Roosevelt's transistor radio tickled Vera's ears. At seventy-two, the receptionist motored along rather well for a woman with her mileage. Outliving three husbands was proof that she more than adequately handled her own back in the day and more than likely still could.

"Ms. Vera, that you?" was her first salutation of the day. "Good mornin'. I thought I heard you coming in through the back." Although it was uncomfortable having a senior citizen addressing her with immense respect, Vera understood her assistant was reared in another time where the boss was treated with a manner of reverence despite the age difference.

The older woman closed the door just after stepping inside Vera's small office that was separated from the rest of the building by a thin layer of sheetrock. The doorknob brushed across Ms. Minnie's wide behind. Vera pretended not to notice when the woman lunged forward because of it. "There's one of them CRUMBS of yours out there in the waitin' area," she announced sharply. Her top lip turned up as if she'd smelled something rank. "But I can't find him on the calendar nowhere." The receptionist parked her thick fist on her broad hips awaiting directions on how she should proceed.

Vera smiled, greeting one of her favorite people. "Good morning, Ms. Minnie," she offered, studying the woman's soft round face and dark brown worried eyes. "Is everything fine out there?" Vera placed her purse on the floor near her feet where it would be concealed by the office desk. When Ms. Minnie didn't utter a single sound, Vera questioned with her eyes what was bothering her receptionist.

"Ms. Vera, this man's been here since I opened up this mornin'," Ms. Minnie answered, with an uneasy glance behind her.

"Yes, and?"

She swallowed hard before continuing. "And, he's white." It was then Vera considered the sort of tragedies that warned Ms. Minnie to be cautious of strange white people, especially white men. A change of the millennium had nothing to do with her changing her mind about that. "Ma daddy always told me that a white man showin' up unannounced can't do you nothin' but harm, even if he was to be sellin' somethin'," the elderly woman added for Vera's sake.

"Yes, ma'am, I understand," Vera responded, keeping in mind what Ms. Minnie had likely witnessed at the hands of white racists. "Please send him back and I'll deal with him."

Slowly rocking her sturdy frame on the soles of her black orthopedic shoes, Ms. Minnie stalled. She contemplated sharing numerous apprehensions, in hauntingly grave detail, but Vera stopped her short of a lengthy history lesson.

"Go on now, Ms. Minnie," Vera hastened. Then, she glanced down at the top drawer, which cradled

Vera's chrome-plated .38-caliber pistol. "Go on now," she insisted.

Ms. Minnie's past had called out to her, beckoning her to heed the cautions. The old woman listened.

Vera should have, too.

No

Nor sir on blue jeans either piped Cleo on her
house.

Ma. Mamie standing stand out of the backroom.
Have it your way sass... She old woman stared
out pondering... ...

Three

When Vera's visitor wandered into her office, he wasn't at all what Vera expected. There were no manicured nails, no expensive timepiece, no exquisitely tailored Italian suit to marvel at and no seventy-dollar salon-styled hair job to impress her. At nine-fifteen in the morning, the visitor's five o'clock shadow wore him like a two-day hangover refusing to let go. A slight grin almost came over Vera when she envisioned Ms. Minnie tucking tail and running from what she used to call "common folk" before the crafty PI remembered the last time she underestimated a stranger's strength and guile. It was a slight miscalculation in judgment that landed Vera flat on her back with a pint-sized bail-jumper leaving tracks on her chest after knocking a door off the hinges to make his getaway. With no intentions of being the same fool twice, she saddled this stranger with a long once-over from head to bootheel. Other than the barely noticeable scar that lay along the ridge of his right eyebrow, the man's face was as handsome as it was perfectly symmetrical. Had it not been for his long, thick blond mane in desperate need of immediate attention, he could have easily passed for a male fashion model, only without the fashion. Movie stars would have stood in line for a chiseled jaw line like his or paid through the nose for a surgically enhanced reasonable facsimile.

His faded Wrangler jeans were authentic, the first pair of those Vera had seen since leaving her hometown of Waskom, Texas, a speck on the map near the Louisiana border. Every so often, she'd run across some store-bought tourist who paid too much to look the part. This drifter's twice-broke cowboy boots were the genuine articles. Hand sewn and full grain leather throughout. His weathered Stetson hat and the reddish tint in his tight skin were both bona fide. Vera could tell that he'd acquired the leathery complexion from long days under a sweltering sun, not hours in a tan-in-the-can ultraviolet chamber. Growing up country in a small farming town, Vera could still differentiate between fake ranch hands and fake tans from a mile off. Her visitor was the real deal.

An initial assessment double-crossed Vera. Everything about this man screamed second-hand, loud and clear. From his well-worn denim jacket, with faulty insulated lining, and plaid cotton shirt, she guessed that each stitch of his clothing had previously belonged to someone else before he'd shoved a fist full of wrinkled dollars across a thrift store counter to claim them for his own.

Although never having been physically drawn to white men herself, Vera had to blink twice when he asked if it was all right for him to sit down. Motioning with her hand, Vera conveyed to him that it would be fine with her for the time being. He nodded a thank-you and then took a seat across from her desk.

"So, tell me, Mister . . . what can I do for you?" Vera asked, before their names had been exchanged. Procedurally, Ms. Minnie would have photocopied the potential client's ID before passing it on to Vera. It was a security measure to verify she was meeting with the person he or she claimed to be. However, there was no recognition of protocol this time around, because Vera's trusty receptionist wouldn't have anything to do with this client including a suitable introduction.

"Rags, ma'am. I've never been a Mister anything," the cowboy answered eventually, while adjusting his posture as if Vera was a new schoolteacher mispronouncing his name. "Everybody calls me Rags." His twang sounded airbrushed or watered down, less Texan than Vera expected. She picked up hints of a formal education and polished diction trapped beneath a farm boy veneer. The dry coarseness surrounding his voice threw her for a loop. If she hadn't been looking at him when he spoke, she would have been willing to bet her life that those words came from someone else, someone much older and less appealing.

"Look, it would help if you told me your real name," Vera advised him. "I like to know who I'm dealing with."

"Unfortunately, Ms. Miles, I don't have the answer to that." He leaned forward with a hopeful expression, tucked behind a mask of uncertainty. "You see, I can't seem to remember anything past two years ago when . . ." he said, before his words trailed off. Moments later, he made up his mind to continue with his jagged explanation. "I'm afraid I might have killed someone but I can't recall much about it."

I'm afraid and *I might have* sounded even more like the products of a formal education to Vera, but she had run across slews of scholarly criminals before, so she took a moment to reconsider that notion as well. Suddenly, she wished she had listened to Ms. Minnie's ancestors, when they whispered to her earlier. A strange white man had all but admitted to killing someone and there Vera was trying to figure out what to do next. Having been caught off guard, she lowered her right hand from its resting place on the desk. As soon as she began to ease the drawer open, Rags's eyes melted into pleading green pools of sadness.

"Please, Ms. Miles, don't. That won't be necessary. I didn't come all this way to hurt nobody." The cowboy easily sniffed out Vera's move before she had the chance to pull it off. Because his words appeared as authentic as his boots, she decided to return her hand to the place where she'd moved it from. "I just need to catch up to some answers and I believe you're the one who can lead me to 'em."

"Me, why me?" she asked utterly confused.

Rags shrugged his square shoulders. "I can't rightly say. I just know that I hit town, walked around for a few days and ended up here."

Vera sat motionless, thinking she must have been crazy to let the thought of getting involved in this case run around loose in her head. Since putting on a game face was as natural to her as putting on a coat of lipstick, she was smooth and effortless. "Look, Mr. Rags, or whatever your name is, I would like to help you out, but I'm a businesswoman. Charity doesn't pay the rent, which means you'll have to find another agency with a pro bono program to climb into that bed you've made. I don't have time to hear any more of what's troubling you."

"Troubling me?" he repeated, with a whiff of disbelief. "Ma'am, I can deal with trouble but this is something bad. I can't hardly get no sleep and it won't let my soul rest at all."

Vera was intrigued but not enough to go out on a limb that didn't appear to have a bag of money dangling from it. "I am very sorry for you, sir, but I—"

"I have money," Rags offered abruptly.

Vera's eyebrows arched dramatically. "How much money?" she asked, in a direct manner that didn't allow room for being lied to.

"Will two thousand be enough for you to hear me out?"

"I'm listening," her shaky voice replied. Vera wanted to get to the bottom of Rags's claims and his pockets before he had the chance to wave that two grand in front of another somebody, who wouldn't be sharing it with her. All she could see were dollar signs, the ones that she'd recently allowed to slip through her fingers after succumbing to a moral dilemma and a temporary overwhelming case of scruples. Rags had her full attention, full and undivided.

Vera watched him cautiously, this man who wrestled the greenest ripest Granny Smith apple she had ever seen out of his raggedy pocket. When he blushed like a child who'd just won a first place blue ribbon, Vera endured a massive letdown. She'd been on the edge of her seat, silently hoping to get a good look at something green and something to deposit. After noting her immediate and apparent disappointment, Rags quickly set the apple on the corner of the desktop nearest to him before pawing through his pockets again. The second expedition proved more fruitful as the cowboy snatched his hand out to make an impressive showing.

Vera's mouth popped open when he displayed a swollen knot of crisply rolled bills, big-faced bills. Even though he counted out twenty Ben Franklins, which moved her like a strong West Indian breeze, she couldn't stop thinking how large his hands were. They were oddly big and thick for a man with such a wiry build. Suddenly, Vera was moved by something else, an irritation that she couldn't explain. She loitered between two unsettling states of mind. If those were the hands of a killer, why was he so willing to part with such a large amount of folding money when it appeared that he couldn't afford a decent haircut? That's when Vera determined that she'd better watch her step more vigilantly. Treating all men as guilty until proven innocent had worked for her up until then and it was a step in the right direction. Whether Rags was the murderer he believed himself to be or not, a rush to judgment suited her just fine. Experience had taught her that every man was guilty of something.

Before Vera knew it, she had gone and popped her game face back on and it was staring Rags up and down again, this time for a different reason. Vera's intuition had her sizing him up. Rags was almost six feet in height, two inches taller than her. A speedy notion came on like the flu. If bad came to worse she might have to plant her size ten in a place that guaranteed a level playing field. She recognized a certain anatomical truth—the one thing that makes a man could also break a man, if her aim was right. The immediate concern was a stack of bills sitting atop the desk longer than Vera was comfortable with.

The man calling himself Rags had picked up on that too. "If you're worried about where this money came from, don't be," he insisted thoughtfully. "Nobody's gonna come looking for it." In as much as five minutes, he'd read Vera's mind accurately. The time had come for her to return the favor. The wandering stranger didn't flinch when he saw it coming.

Vera's eyes begun to burn after two minutes of matching Rags's sullen gaze in an intense competition of unyielding stares. She had reason to be scared, but Rags needed to see if she could hold her own when it came down to getting what he was after. It appeared that time stood still. Neither of them had planned on looking away as the standoff in Vera's office became unbearable. Rags noticed how her left eye began to twitch in the same instant that she counted beads of sweat mounting on his forehead. It was a game of nerves, a thrilling game, which Vera championed while standing against hundreds of hardened criminals fresh on parole. She didn't fold in the midst of their plans to rattle her with their jailhouse bravado either. A long hard gaze was commonly utilized on the inside as a dire form of intimidation. Some of Vera's parolees brought that thuggish manner of diminishing their adversaries with them after stepping outside the prison gates. During ten years of matching her street survival skills against murderers, molesters and malcontents, Vera had never lost a single game of nerves. Not one.

She collected the money when Rags blinked first.

Vera could not have predicted what had begun as a study in white, would have somehow culminated in her professional defining moment. Rags had stumbled into her life like a slow ride. Not the kind that ends when a woman climbs down off the man she loves but one just as rewarding, the kind that ushers in self-reflection and internal growth toward a clearer point of view with a keener eye. Rags represented something Vera had longed for since receiving her PI license. His peril offered the opportunity she'd been waiting on, a chance to discover what she was made of. Rags was the slow ride Vera needed.

four

"It's always the same," Rags mumbled softly, his head bowed. "Every time I close my eyes for too long, I see it happening but can't do anything to stop it. The scene never changes. The rain is falling. It's cold and damp. My chest hurts, full of guilt, I imagine. The man I see is older than me and heavier. He looks tired, tired of life, tired of living. He's been running. His face is sweaty and flushed. Guessing from his terrified expression, he's very surprised to see me. Maybe he surprised me too. I don't know. But I shut my eyes because of the rain, I think. My eyes flutter open then I shoot twice. The man says something to me, sounds like 'Why?' " Rags glanced up at Vera as if to say he was sorry before his eyes returned to their hiding place. "I wish I could tell him why, Ms. Miles. I wish I knew why. I really wish I knew."

After hearing Rags's story for the third straight time in an hour, Vera determined that he had been truthful with her. She couldn't be sure of more than that but she was certain of his honesty. That much she did know. Rags didn't deviate from the sequence of events in any of the episodes he recounted as best he could, from the depths of his horrible dreams.

Vera fought off her own uneasiness each time the man cringed at the same place in the story he told. It was difficult to determine which parts to jot down and which to commit to memory, because in all probability, a man's death was involved and that meant the same for her client or at least his freedom.

Confronting death was often the cost of doing business in Vera's line of work. Dead men didn't bother her. There wasn't anything to fear from a man whose blood had run cold. Vera had seen a number of dead men with their dim-lit eyes frozen wide-open, their pursed lips punctuating silence and their bloated bellies rotting with their last supper but none was as ghastly as her first.

When Vera was a small child, her father caught a slug in the back of his head. The bullet came from his own gun. He'd found his way home one night, stumbling drunk and wearing the smell of another woman's loving commingled with her cheap perfume and hard liquor. Vera's mother was barely twenty-one. She'd vowed that her love for him was stronger than life itself. After losing his job at the oil refinery, it didn't take long before he'd lost his way. Spending the twilight hours on the Louisiana side of the Texas border caused his death. A heartbroken woman who couldn't swim through her tears was the effect. The day following the murder, they found Vera's grief-stricken mother swaying in a jail cell with a bed sheet securely fastened around her neck. It was proof that she truly believed in her vow. The sheriff's deputy wiped away a stream of tears, when explaining regrettably to Vera's grandparents that their only daughter was gone. Vera couldn't say she remembered either of her parents. That white man blubbering on her grandpa's front porch she remembered in the worst way. It was the first time she'd seen a grown man cry and the only time it moved her in a debilitating manner, until peering across her desk at Rags choking back his salty sentiment. Wedged in an awkward position, Vera realized it was her turn to look away.

Before Rags left the office he'd worked hard at remembering as far back as he could, but the details were so sketchy that Vera almost dismissed the chain of events entirely. Fortunately she didn't dismiss a single thing her client told her. Besides, a PI could never anticipate when or where pertinent clues would fall from the sky. With any luck, it wouldn't be long before it started to rain them down on Vera.

As Rags told it, his story sounded like a mystery straight out of a true crime book. Over two years had passed since his life, as he knew it, had begun. On a windy February morning, in a small central Texas town, Vera's client was found, discovered in an abandoned hunting cabin by one of the local farmers. Dehydrated, malnourished and left for dead, Rags's head had been thoroughly wrapped in hospital bandages, filthy and in such desperate need of changing that they appeared to be tattered strips of cloth. After the farmer rescued him and collected what appeared to be his meager belongings, the name Rags was given to him by this simple-hearted farmer who saved his life. The name stuck, even after Rags had survived his fate in the wilderness and was nursed back to health. Twenty-six months of good country living, hard work and bad dreams held him in check, until he woke up one morning with an itch needing to be scratched. He struck out on his own after losing an internal battle with his conscience.

Vera empathized. When her bills weren't paid on time, she could hardly sleep a wink either. Now that she had some folding money in her purse and a head-start on handling the next month's financial obligations, Vera had plans to catch up on the sleep she'd missed over the previous week. She couldn't have been more wrong if she tried. Vera was on a collision course with the realization that sleep didn't come easy when it became slick around the edges of life. With no leads, nowhere to begin and a possible death sentence hanging over her newest client, Vera soon began feeling like a bad joke told in reverse, the tail chasing the dog.

Impatient thumps on the front door forced Vera to investigate why her receptionist hadn't attended to them. As Vera hustled past her desk, she glared at two very tiny, delicately crafted, origami-styled paper dragons sitting on the corner of it. Rags had skillfully folded a couple of one-hundred dollar bills, while knitting together holes in his tattered memory, be-fore Vera convinced him to rent a room nearby and cool his heels, while she did her best to figure out just how she was going to prove herself worthy of the money he'd let her hold and how to go about getting her hands wrapped around more of it.

Glow Raines was skulking on the other side of the self-locking glass office door wearing snuggly fitting slacks and riding boots with a tight knit sweater be-neath a brown three-quarter-length jacket. Vera ap-preciated her friend's taste in clothing, but the way Glow appeared with the greatest of ease gave her the willies, just showing up out of the blue the way she did. Glow wasn't the kind of woman to stand around waiting on a formal invitation to mix in. Every time it came down to making things happen, she was always right there on the spot. Even though Glow was quick with a knife and worse with a harsh word, she had to be one of the most interesting creatures God ever allowed to walk His earth.

Although Vera didn't spend too much time with other people's faces up in hers, unless it was necessary, Glow's lifestyle intrigued her to the point of envy. She worked more scams, hustles, and con games than anyone Vera had assisted with their parole. So, she had to decide up front whether she would let Glow's pick pocketing, card-sharking, slick maneuvers, attractive features, flawless reddish-brown toned skin or small waistline anchored by a perfectly sculpted behind get in the way of them getting along. It was a tough predicament to say the least, but common sense won out over petty jealously. Besides, Vera recognized how much better it was to befriend Glow than to secretly despise her from afar. They were both better off once she did.

"So what did you do to Ms. Minnie?" Glow asked Vera, while she casually unfolded a miniature cash dragon.

"Never mind that, Glow," Vera scoffed. "I'm going to step out on a limb and guess that you met my new client on your way in?"

"I might have bumped into him, once or twice," was her lascivious reply. Glow's sly expression accompanying the second dragon she'd lifted from Rags caused Vera to double back inside her office and purse the paper beasts that belonged to her. She didn't mind her friend fleecing her clients as long as it didn't keep any money from landing in her pocket.

The satisfied grin on Glow's face revealed that she

was either up to something or she'd just pulled it off with little to no difficulty. It reminded Vera of the first time she laid eyes on the inexplicable Glow Raines, who was working one of her angles. She was outfitted as an old homeless woman, draped in full costume with a pregnancy-inspired empathy suit beneath a weathered trench coat. Even more impressive, Glow was done up in theatrical makeup and a black stocking cap pulled down over an old fashioned going-to-church-style wig. The miniature shopping cart Glow used as a prop was filled with aluminum cans. That overstuffed fanny of hers was two throw pillows.

Vera had watched the woman through the window before and was willing to bet that she panhandled three to four hundred dollars a day. That's when Vera discovered how hordes of businessmen in a hurry found it in their hearts to pitch in a few bills each to help a supposed senior citizen down on her luck. Up and down the sidewalk Glow trod and waggled, back and forth and back again. Watching her from the window, Vera took notice when it appeared that the homeless woman's steps quickened as the day wore on, instead of dragging to a slow crawl. With nothing better to do, Vera shadowed her on foot, casual-like, for six blocks. She laughed out loud when Glow stepped into an alleyway, ditched the collection of aluminum cans and swaggered up to a self-parking lot. Vera was still laughing when Glow sped past her in a new BMW hosting the same satisfied smile she had come to know so well. After what she'd witnessed, Vera couldn't wait to see her again, knowing right off that Glow had a certain degree of competence that came in handy in a pinch and the gall to use it if necessary. The following week, Vera shadowed Glow to the same destination, struck up a conversation, applauded Glow's craftiness, and then shared a hearty laugh. After a sixty-dollar retainer, as a show of good faith, Glow agreed to pitch in on cases every now and then. More than two years had passed since they'd thrown in together, formed a part-time business association and become the best of friends.

Since bumping into Rags, Glow had introduced herself indirectly and became somewhat fascinated that a stumble bum like him had enough loot to play with some of it. "Why'd you let that man scare off Ms. Minnie, Vera?" Glow asked. Her question was anchored to a soft frown.

"I didn't let him do nothing," Vera answered, her eyes staring past Glow's face. "She's got some hangups, from her childhood I'd bet. You know times were different then. Ms. Minnie never did learn to trust white people, even though things have changed."

Glow eyed the cuticles on her right hand then sighed behind the weight of an ensuing thought. "Well, maybe because Ms. Minnie hasn't seen enough real change to change her mind about things. I mean, the past ain't so easy to forget. Uh-uh," Glow contended seriously, with a stiff head nod. "Not for any of us."

"Glow, please. Girl, you're making my head hurt. Before I knew what hit me, this strange white man shows up at my doorstep, then you come in with some of his money in your pocket and now you're trying to hand me baggage that ain't none of mine."

After Glow stood up and rubbed the rise of her slacks with an opened palm, she eased her behind down on the corner of Vera's desk like an alley cat. "Vera, I don't like mincing words any more than you do, but we've got to talk about what brought that cowboy here and what baggage he's carrying."

Vera ran down the story Rags had told her. Glow

listened attentively. She almost flinched when Vera spit the word murder out like a poisonous pill. "Yeah, Glow," she reiterated. "The man just walked right in and said he might've killed somebody maybe a couple of years ago but he can't be sure. Ain't no statute of limitations on murder and I don't have a single clue why he ended up at my front door now." Vera witnessed Glow's hazel eyes narrow with suspicion. "What is it, Glow?"

"Something is wrong about this whole scene. What if he's fixing to burn somebody down and plans to leave the ashes at your feet? Just think about it. You don't know him from Adam. He could be planning to do his dirt and leaving you to clean it up."

Vera considered what her friend said then she tried to shake it off. "I don't know. I've got a bad feeling about the case but it's got hooks in me already. You're right about one thing for sure. Something is very wrong about this whole scene, very wrong."

Five

Vera agreed that the case was shaky at best before saying her goodbyes to Glow, then locking up her office for the day. With money in her clutches and nowhere to begin, Vera hopped in the SUV. She cruised around town for over an hour. Mindless driving calmed her nerves. Eventually she found herself parked outside of a place that made her feel almost as safe as the gun she carried for the same effect. The 3rd Round Bar and Grill was a decent eatery with thirty tables and a dozen televisions. The sports bar specialized in everything fried and all the discussion about boxing that an enthusiast could hope for. Bertram "Bullet" Manning, former light heavyweight champion, owned the place. He would have still been in the ring if his last opponent's lucky punch hadn't detached the retina in his left eye. Bullet's near-perfect physique, chocolate-smooth skin and teeth that sparkled like diamonds in a coal mine made it easy for Vera to love him; telling him that she did was the hard part.

"What you know good, Bullet?" Vera said, as she approached the bar area.

"Hey, Champ," he replied, behind a warm smile. "Here you go. Just the way you like it," he added after pouring a tall glass of cranberry juice over ice.

Vera wanted to hop across the bar, tear that tight black T-shirt from his muscular chest then wrap her thighs around his waist. Wrestling his pants down to his ankles occurred to her too, but she chuckled at her midday fantasy instead and let it pass. "Oomph, just the way I like it, tall and dark," Vera replied scandalously, while leering at him the way he liked.

"Oh, Vera," the waitress hissed nastily, as if it pained her to speak. Vendetta Lewis was an ex-stripper who had it bad for Bullet and she hated Vera. There was no use in pretending that Vera gave a damn about her either.

"Vendetta," Vera replied sharply.

"I didn't know you'd come in," the younger woman lied right off the bat, having seen Vera enter the building. She had also watched bitterly as Bullet flirted, all the while wishing it were her at the opposite end of his sensual gaze. Spending days on end with the famous boxer she admired presented several challenges for Vendetta. Watching him fall all over himself for a frumpy lady PI had her spitting mad. She'd hoped Bullet would have shared the softer side, and whispers with her that he reserved for Vera. That was merely one of the reasons she couldn't stand Vera. The other went a lot deeper than extreme envy. Vendetta was determined to despise Vera for saving her from a prison term by persuading the lead detective that Vendetta killed the night club owner, who also happened to be her baby's father, because his continual battering had taken its toll. Vera knew what it was like to shoulder a man's brutality, that's why she helped the waitress rearrange the crime scene before the police arrived. Although the homicide was ruled self-defense and the case dismissed, Vendetta was up to her neck in misplaced hostility every time Vera walked through the restaurant doors.

" 'Detta, why don't you cover the bar for a minute?" Bullet suggested, as a way to separate the women and engineer some private time. "Vera's got something on her mind that needs some massaging."

The woman sneered at Vera begrudgingly. "I don't see why—" she started to say before getting cut off at the pass.

"I said, Vera needs my help," Bullet replied firmly, although smiling in the wake of her blatant insubordination. "There's no need in arguing about it."

"Yeah, I need Bullet for a minute, *'Detta*," Vera added, to rub salt in the wound. "I could always use some massaging."

The women exchanged strained glances but Vera was giggling on the inside. Bullet wasn't wrapped around her finger like Vendetta assumed, but it made Vera bubble over having her think he was. As they headed toward the manager's office, Vera couldn't help herself. She lagged behind just long enough to get in one last dig. "Don't worry," she said, feigning genuine concern for the waitress's well-being. "I'll let him out once I'm done with him."

"Cow," Vendetta spat under her breath.

"Skank," Vera replied, loud enough to be heard clearly.

"Why do you do that every time you set foot in the 3rd Round?" Bullet asked, as she walked through the door.

"Do what?" Vera asked in a ridiculously coy tone that made Bullet laugh.

"Don't try that with me because you ain't that slick. You antagonize that girl, then bounce. I'm the one who has to spend the better part of her shift calming her down afterwards. She's still got some self-esteem issues."

"What about me?" Vera whined seductively. "Who's gonna calm me down?" She closed the door behind her and turned the lock. "How long do I get you to work on my esteem?" Vera placed her arms around his neck, wishing they were her ankles instead. "If I pout like 'Detta does, would you spend the rest of the shift stroking my ego? That is the only thing you're stroking of hers?" When Bullet took too long to answer, Vera bit down on his bottom lip.

"Ouch, woman!" he yelled. "You bit me."

"Uh-huh, and that ain't the half of what I'll do if I learn you've been massaging anything else on that tramp out there."

"Ooh, I see what's going down." Bullet sucked on his bruise then laughed. "That green eyed monster's got a hold on you. Vera Miles is jealous."

"Vendetta ain't hardly anything to get jealous about. Pole-climbing shake-dancers are a dime a dozen. I just needed to remind you that love hurts sometimes."

"You saying you love me?" he asked, wearing a come hither grin.

"You're the one who said it, doctor, but I do agree with your diagnosis."

Bullet backed away when he felt his jeans stretching out at the zipper. "Whoa, that's as close as you've ever come. You must really be in trouble."

"Not in as much trouble as I'd put you in, if there was a deadbolt lock on that door," she teased. "Besides, you get me to acting a fool when you pull that thing out. You'd have to shut this whole place down and send your little girlfriend home with a bad case of get-the-hell-on."

Bullet chuckled as he ran his hand over his bald head, all the while looking Vera over curiously. "I could tell something was weighing on you the moment you pulled in. Now you're trying to steam up my office. What's got you all riled up?"

Bullet knew Vera better than she thought and she liked that. If there was any doubt, the gleam in her almond-shaped eyes confirmed it. "Well, since you're paying such close attention I guess it won't hurt to let you tag along this one time." Vera's smile grew when Bullet took a seat and folded his brawny arms.

"You're stalling. This must be about a man," he said knowingly. Vera's smile evaporated in the blink of an eye. Bullet sighed as if he had grown bored with being right. "Humph, thought so."

"Don't do this, Bullet," she objected. "Don't come down on me when you haven't even heard why I'm so pressed. It's not like I have some he-hoochie hanging on my every word like old 'Detta out there with her ear mashed against the door." Vera picked up a stapler off the desk and hurled it against the office door.

"Ouch!" screamed Vendetta from the other side.

"That's what yo' ass get!" snapped Vera in that direction.

"You put a dent in my door, Vera," Bullet shouted.

"Sorry."

"That's a damned expensive door, Vera."

She threw her hands up in an ultra-aggravated manner. "Calm down, daddy, I'll pay for it."

"Oh, you'll pay for it?" Bullet questioned. "Since when do you have the money to pay for anything?" As he awaited a response that neither of them wanted spoken into existence, Vera cowered behind two tiny words.

"That man." Never before have breathless whispers come charging out like a lion's roar. "My new client put a few dollars in my pocket to find the person he killed and that's what's got me bent."

Bullet was outdone then. "You know this guy? Y'all got history or something?"

"No," she hated to admit, fearing the next logical line of questioning. Her eyes darted away from his judgmental stare. "He just showed up out of the blue." Having gone out of her way for a woman in trouble like Vendetta was one thing, but for some man she didn't know made Bullet's jaw tighten.

"What? You let some man get you in deep with a homicide?" His head was smoking now. "Hell, it could be worse. It could be a white boy mixed up in this." Once again, Vera's gaze floated toward the floor. "Dayyyum, you've got to be kidding me."

"Bullet, let me tell you how it went," Vera said before he blew a gasket. "It's complicated but this is how it kicked off." She explained in detail what Rags shared, for the second time that day and it showed on her face. Bullet watched vigilantly as he listened to every syllable. By the time she'd finished, he fully understood why she agreed to take the case.

Bullet circled his desk in the cramped room. He pulled Vera close to him and held her tightly against his thick chest. "I know exactly what it's like to need you, Vera. While I'm not sure why this dude can't get the kind of help he needs from anyone else, he came to the right place when looking you up."

"Ooh, that's the man I can't do without," Vera cooed, her face nestled in his arms. "I knew you'd understand."

"Just promise me you'll be careful enough not to get yourself killed over skeletons in this man's past."

"Careful can get you killed in this business," she replied. "I will watch my step though. I can promise you that." Vera pulled away from Bullet's embrace. "Thank you so much. I really needed that."

"So, how do you plan to go about helping this Rags? I mean, where do you begin?"

Vera chewed on her bottom lip, like she always did when something had her in a tailspin. "I'm used to looking into the *who* to find the *what*. This time, ain't nothing I can do but look into what happened and work backwards for the who. If there was a victim, I need to find out as much as I can about how things stretched out." She looked up at Bullet, who was smiling now. "What?" she asked, longingly.

"That's why you're the perfect woman for the job," he answered quietly. "Always was."

Vera caught Bullet's double meaning and held it close to her heart. Blushing like a love sick teenager, she exited the office with Bullet close on her heels. It didn't even bother her that Vendetta glared despicably as she exited the restaurant. Even though there wasn't a name for what Vera and Bullet shared between them, that didn't mean she wanted the trifling waitress to have any of it for herself.

Six

Vera knew that uncovering anything about what Rags thought he'd done was a long shot at best, but she was paid to try. On the east side of downtown, she parked her vehicle on the corner of a quiet residential street where two-story wood-framed houses lined both sides of the road. She pulled out her gun and checked the bullet clip. She thought it funny how three pounds of chrome and steel made the difference in one person leaving the scene in a bundle of rattled nerves and the other in a body bag. Her clip held six rounds of fire. Vera hoped that Lucius Carnes wouldn't try something cute and force her to pump some of that fire in his behind.

The house Lucius hid out in belonged to his mother. Despite being one of the craftiest criminals Vera had ever run across, Lucius was the biggest momma's boy. Although there weren't any outstanding warrants chasing him at the time, he spent more than twenty hours a day inside that house. Vera approached it quietly, looking out for anything that seemed out of place. The square white house could have used a fresh coat of paint but then so could just about every house on the street.

Vera stepped to the side of the kitchen window. She leaned against the wood siding to hear what was going on inside. There wasn't a single sound, so she brushed a layer of dust off the plastic bubble-faced cover to examine the electric meter. The small wheels were spinning out of control as if every socket in house was in use. "Yeah, Lucius, you're in there all right," she heard herself say, before banging on the front screen door. "Luuucius," she sang, "it's your old friend Vera Miles. Get your ass down here!" She continued pounding with the heel of her hand. "I ain't going nowhere and neither are you, so open up," she hollered. "Come on Lucius, this is getting old and I'm getting fed up." After another few minutes of ratty-tat-tats sounding off, there was a trail of footsteps heading down the stairs. Vera chuckled. "I hear you in there. Open up so we can get down to business."

"Ain't nobody here, go away," a soft voice murmured from the other side of the locked door. "My momma say I can't have no company."

"Lucius!" barked Vera. "What's your momma gonna say when I drag your scrawny ass downtown and make you do the time still on your books at the county?" She listened to the silence that had him in a strangle hold. Within seconds, several locks began popping in a rapid manner. "Uh-huh, that's what I thought." Annoyed to no end, Lucius jutted his peanut shaped head out from behind the door. Vera grinned at the small man with a squirrelly build like she was glad to see him. "Now that wasn't so hard, was it? Good afternoon, Lucius."

"What's so good about it?" he asked, with his thick dry lips pursed and puckered.

"Come on now, step aside and let me in," Vera ordered, when he continued to stall. She nodded agreeably after he did as commanded, although with a great deal of reluctance. Lucius had the body of a young boy and an odd stagnant beige complexion which looked as if it never saw the light of day. Vera nearly laughed at his ostentatious outfit but she knew better. He'd have flown off the handle and clammed up if she poked fun at his pink taffeta ball gown and sash so she reserved her comments.

Lucius stood next to an exquisite Victorian styled sofa covered in navy velvet. He sneered at Vera with both hands propped on his hips. "I know what you're thinking," he hissed finally. "But it takes a real man to put on pink." Lucius was thirty-five years old but you couldn't tell it by looking at him, even if he happened to be dressed in men's clothing. He was a convicted white collar crook with a number of quirks. Vera knew that Lucius was ashamed of his cross-dressing fetish and that was the card she played when necessary. Also, the little man was terrified of serving out his jail sentence. Vera made it possible to get his previous conviction kicked down to probation after convincing the judge that Lucius wouldn't last a single day in general population with actual grown men. Besides, Vera's ace in the hole was the secret she held over that particular judge's head. As it turned out, she caught him on tape during her first divorce case. He and Lucius were two of a kind, down to their sequined thong underwear.

Several months had passed since Vera felt the need to call upon one of the foremost Internet pirates in the state. There was definitely a need for Lucius's specialized services whether he was interested in helping her or not. She peered up at the steep staircase leading to the attic and his domicile. "Well, let's get to it," Vera asserted, with a raised brow.

"Ooh-ooh, I hate you," Lucius huffed as he stomped past her in black patent leather Susie-Q shoes. "Come on up so you can hurry back down and leave."

Vera followed the peculiar little man up the stairs. She counted over ten photos of him as a child, dressed in intricate costumes ranging from superheroes to the Village People. Vera realized then that his mother was partially responsible for his condition. By the looks of it, she must have wanted a girl. Let Lucius tell it, his mother got her wish.

"Don't touch anything," he spat loudly as Vera grunted past the top stair. Once her head cleared enough for her eyes to focus, she understood why he was so particular about his belongings. There were rows of porcelain dolls along the back wall, all dressed in fabulous regalia. Boxes of swanky negligees had been pushed toward the far end of the completely refinished attic. The floors were covered with thick plush carpet. Three computer monitors rested atop a broad mahogany desk. Nearby a signed photograph of Marilyn Monroe caught her eye.

"Damn, Lucius," Vera marveled. "Look at all this stuff. You and Marilyn are living ghetto fabuloso up in here."

"That's why I said not to touch anything," he smarted, with an air of arrogance. "However, if you behave yourself, I'll let you fish around in my boxes of designer delicates."

Vera's eyes widened with anticipation when he

reeled off designer labels to choose from. "You can't have anything in my size?"

"Sure do, I have lots of voluptuous friends," he informed her.

"Oh, yeah, I'll be good," she giggled. "Don't worry, I ain't misbehavin'."

Lucius blushed brightly then waved his hand for Vera to take the seat next to his padded throne. "Now then, whose mainframe do you want me to crack? I know you're here to use me up and toss me aside."

"Don't be so dramatic," Vera argued. "It's not that serious. Look, I want to run a scenario by you and we'll see what pops."

Lucius licked his lips then smacked them approvingly. "Sookee-sookee, I like the sound of that. Well, go on ahead and speak on it."

Yet again, Vera was trying to avoid retelling Rags's story so she hit Lucius with an abridged version. "This client of mine is interested in a murder, an old one. It might have occurred in Dallas, maybe two years ago. The victim, fatally wounded, was likely a fat white guy." She shrugged her shoulders when Lucius exhaled through his frustration. "What is it, Lucius?"

"I don't know why I'm surprised. Might haves, maybes and likely? It would be easier to find out who really killed Kennedy."

"JFK? You could do that?"

"Before you get your panties in a bunch, let's see what we can dig up on your likely dead, fat, white guy." Lucius tapped into the Dallas Police Department computer system without much difficulty. He ran a search with the limited information Vera provided. "Imagine that, here I am looking for a man on the Internet again," Lucius mumbled while waiting. "Okay, adult white male. Who are you and why do I care since you are obviously off the market? Oh, yeah, that's right, Vera showed up, trying to knock a hole in my door."

The computer bleeped then flashed several pages with numerous rows of names on a flat blue screen. Vera shook her head. "I can't investigate that many cases."

"And the police can't do a damned thing right," added Lucius. "Look, homicides aren't tracked by race. Your client could be interested in any one of these poor men."

"Dammit, you're right," Vera agreed. "I have a hunch that the one I'm dogging isn't solved. See if any of them are still open." She watched the monitor as it reconfigured Lucius's search. This time, eleven names scrolled down the page. "Can you print that for me, Lucius?"

"As long as you don't get none of this mess on me," he answered, with a slight head tilt for effect. "If you've forgotten, I'm not even supposed to own a computer, much less hack into the police mainframe."

Vera accepted the list of names and a troubled man's concerns with them. "You have my word. I won't let it come back on you, Lucius." She fished through his box of ritzy negligees before making her way down the tower of stairs to her car. Since Vera couldn't decide on a black number with straps and strings and a teal-colored sheer ensemble, Lucius suggested she take both of them and do her best to loosen up. A lot.

Seven

On the following morning, Vera headed toward downtown. She called the office to check in with her receptionist but the phone rolled over to voicemail. "Ms. Minnie, this is Vera. It's after nine. Hopefully you're just running late. Look, I'm going to stop by police headquarters and I might not be in until late. Please advise callers that I won't be taking any new clients for a while. I'm just scratching at the surface and this case is more than likely a deep pit. Hey, call me when you make it in. Bye." By the time Vera closed her portable flip phone, she'd concluded that her trusty office manager was not in any hurry to assist with Rags's dilemma. She'd made her position on that loud and clear by disappearing the day before. Vera didn't like it but she tried to understand nonetheless. Sometimes it paid to be afraid.

At police headquarters, Vera waved hello to a number of officers she'd done business with in the past. Salutations with veteran members in law enforcement typically came in the way of warm smiles and cordial winks. Vera's smile grew noticeably wider when her eyes found Homicide Detective Donald Beasley stuffing his face with a heaping dose of crème-filled delight. Detective Beasley loved donuts and had been dieting unsuccessfully for as long as Vera had known him.

"Ahhh, now that's just sad," she teased, while approaching his cluttered desk. The large man raised his head slowly like a child getting caught with a hand in the cookie jar.

The dark-skinned cop with a receding hairline hesitated then bit down into a chocolate covered éclair. "I thought I heard the diet police marching in. It's Vera Miles as I live and breathe." He wiped his hands with a paper napkin then he pressed flesh with his visitor. "Sit down and take a load off." The detective shoved another piece of dough in his mouth and shuffled some papers on his desk. "Mm-mm, you look great, Vera. I suck at diets. What else is new?"

"Well, I went to sleep with you on my mind last night," she answered jokingly. "Guess what, you hadn't moved one inch when I climbed out of bed this morning."

Beasley laughed. "I'm flattered. Was it good for you?" he flirted playfully. "Don't tell the wife. She thinks I spent the night with her."

"You know what I mean, Donald. I caught a strange one this time and I could use your help. A man stumbled into my place and paid two grand just to hold my attention. It could be nothing but I'd bet it's a live one." The cop leaned his thick frame closer to hers with exaggerated interest.

"Humph, I'm all ears." Since Vera was one of the smartest private investigators he knew, there was reason to take note and listen to what she had to say.

"Here is a list of homicides." She handed over the copy she'd gotten from Lucius. Beasley took one look at the pages then folded them over.

"Where'd you get these, Vera?" he whispered gruffly. "This is privileged departmental information. Hell, it's even printed with departmental subheads." He exhaled then surveyed the immediate area. "You could get into a lot of trouble with these and I could catch a lot of grief."

"I know, Donald, and I'm sorry for putting you at risk but all I need is to be pointed in the right direction. Then, I'm out of your hair."

Detective Beasley grimaced. "I must be out of my mind. A beautiful woman struts into my office and pulls a list of fatal shootings out of her behind, then here I go." He glanced at Vera, who had her fingers pressed over her heart.

"Donald, you said I'm beautiful. Does that mean you'll look into it?"

"Keeping two women satisfied is harder than I thought. I always imagined that stepping out on my wife would be a whole bunch more fun that this."

"Don't short yourself. That was very good for me," Vera whispered softly, with her hand over his. "Thanks so much, Donald."

"You might want to hold your applause until the show is over. I don't even know what you hope to gain from this." He laid his outstretched hand down on top of the list. "What does this client of yours want to know, exactly?"

"Okay, here's where it gets kinda tricky. I need a needle in a haystack, a gunshot victim, white male, forty plus. My client thinks he has information on one of these murders," she said, as not to give away Rags's position.

"Good, bring your guy in and I'll interview him personally."

"No, I don't think he'll go for that. Besides, he may be mistaken altogether. I'd hate to get him involved unless it's absolutely necessary."

Beasley grunted his displeasure. "Oh, but it's quite all right to involve the hell out of me?"

Vera batted her eyes at him. "You're built for this, Donald, he isn't. Don't go breaking my heart. All I need to know is which of those homicides on that list are white male victims and are still unsolved."

"And that's it?" he said, finding it hard to believe her. "I won't be asked to divulge any forensic evidence or nothing like that?" He smirked at Vera when she shook her head to affirm his question. "Just so you understand I'm not paddling up the creek alone if this goes south. Okay, let's get wet." Detective Beasley ran the same type of search that Lucius had but he tweaked the information to shake out non-males. He watched Vera gnaw on her bottom lip. "You're going to tear a chunk out of it if you're not too careful." She stopped after realizing he was talking to her. "Where'd you say you got this list?" he asked again. "Never mind, I don't want to know."

Beasley circled three of the names on the paper Vera strolled in with. Afterwards, his countenance changed dramatically. One of the names he ruled out immediately because the victim was a biracial male. Another victim happened to be a white female who'd undergone a gender reassignment surgery. Beasley was sure of it because he caught the case himself after the body was discovered. The remaining name didn't ring a bell whatsoever but that wasn't unusual since there were holes in the police department's bookkeeping system. The officer informed Vera of that so she wouldn't get her hopes up.

After a round of pleasant goodbyes, Vera folded both pages into her purse and strolled toward the exit. Narcotics Detective Frank Draper casually passed her to get a closer look. He'd been checking out their interaction the whole time. "Beasley, you old dog," Draper jested. "First, you overdo it with the donuts and now this. What's the wife and five little Beasleys going to say about your juicy piece of action on the side?"

"Not that it's any of your business but Vera's an old friend, a PI looking into something for a client. I used to toss her a bone every now and again. This time she's just asking about unsolved homicide cases, gunshot victims and such."

"Maybe I can toss the lady PI a bone on occasion too," the white cop replied. "Any case in particular? I'm down with dark meat."

"Sorry, Draper, not that kind of bone. One thing I never liked about narcs, they all think everyone is out to score."

While Detective Beasley was protecting Vera's honor, she was stretching her legs. She walked directly over to the County Sheriff's Office on the next block. She experienced an eerie feeling that someone was following her, although there wasn't anyone suspicious lurking around as far as she could tell. The sheriff's office kept most undesirables away on general principle. Vera knew that criminals with a lick of sense steered clear of that area whenever possible, so she pushed past the glass doors and entered the building with the thought of being followed diminished.

After she cleared the metal detectors and received

her plastic visitor's badge, Vera stepped off the elevator on the forth floor. Cecelia Montez, a clerk with twenty years on the city's dime peered over a cubicle wall on cue, as if she'd been waiting for Vera's arrival. "Hey, Cecelia," Vera sang. "You've got to be up to something, looking that good in the middle of the week." The Spanish woman wore a pair of slacks tighter than anything Vera dared crawl into. Green polyester was stretching every which way but that didn't stop the spirited Latina from pulling a pirouette to show off her voluptuous figure.

"Holà, chica, I have an early lunch date," Cecelia told her. "My new man is young and greedy so I got to keep it hot and ready."

Vera patted her on the shoulder approvingly. "Ooh, I know that's right. You've got to keep the young ones on a short leash."

"Tell me about it. I moved him into my place last month so he wouldn't wander off. If he strays on me, his insurance better be paid up, because you know I don't play." Cecelia's bark was bigger than her bite; knowing that made Vera laugh even louder.

"Cecelia, you ain't gonna ever change."

"If it ain't broke, don't fix it," she replied, with a welcoming gesture for Vera to enter her cubicle. "Who's running from you now, chica?"

"Cecelia, I just signed on to help this guy find somebody, but he's not sure if his head's on straight."

The clerk frowned, nodding toward the sheet of paper Vera had taken from her purse. "What's that got to do with it?"

Vera explained as much of the case as she was comfortable with. Although she and Cecelia went back at least nine years, she'd grown way past tired of random digging and hoping to hit pay dirt. If this search failed to pan out, Vera was determined to hand her shovel over to Rags and send him on his way. After Cecelia punched in the name on the page, she hummed a soft Spanish tune mixed in with English-sounding words to amuse herself. Before long Vera was bobbing her head and humming along.

"Oh, here it is. Harold Newel, died over two years ago," said Cecelia, as she read notes off the monitor. "This man was into some real rude stuff. He had a lot of priors for drug possession but got it kicked each time. Either he had one hell of a lawyer or somebody was looking out for him on the inside. His luck was running good, for a while. Nine pops and no convictions; maybe he was on a cop's payroll."

"I thought paid informants got protection as part of the standard health plan," Vera said, jokingly.

"I don't know. Too bad poor Harold's friends couldn't pull him out of this one. He was found dead in a motel bathroom. Somebody wanted him gone for real. Four shots, two in the face, one in the heart and the other aimed a lot lower." Cecelia looked at Vera, hoping she hadn't gotten herself tied up with the people who ended poor Harold.

Vera winced when a morbid thought kicked her in the head. "I know I'm going to regret asking this, but do you have any crime scene photos?"

"I'll show you but I haven't eaten yet, so get what you need while I'm powdering up in the women's room." The senior clerk got up from her desk then excused herself without apprehension. She'd run background checks for Vera over the years so leaving her alone and unattended wasn't out of line. Cecelia's office worked with private eyes routinely, because they were known to get into places cops couldn't without a warrant.

While the clerk was away, Vera read the crime scene report. Harold Newel, age forty-five, dead. There were two paragraphs discussing articles of clothing and drug paraphernalia found in the motel room. After Vera scrolled down to view the crime scene photos, she gathered why Cecelia would rather not carry that vision with her throughout the day. A graphic tribute to blood and guts spanned across the screen. From the description Rags had provided, this stiff wasn't the one she was after. Harold Newel was short, thin and nearly bald. By the looks of the disfigured corpse, Cecelia was correct in that someone did want him gone for real. She figured it was the work of a deranged killer or a scorned lover with an axe to grind. Either way, Vera felt relieved that Rags wasn't the responsible party, very relieved.

Eight

Despite having studied the disgusting murder scene photos, Vera hopped in her vehicle with food heavy on her mind. When she wheeled onto Commerce from Record Street, the apparent dead end shadowing her investigation had to take an immediate back seat to the glaring feeling that something was terribly wrong. Vera wasn't incredibly happy with the sometimes undependable Silver Streak but she knew it was riding heavy, about one hundred and eighty pounds too heavy.

Vera pulled into a full parking lot, then slammed on the brakes. She waved off the lot attendant who'd scurried from his tiny booth, flailing his hand and shouting angrily that there were not any available parking slots. Vera's stern scowl didn't seem to stifle the man's aggressive approach or his animated gestures accompanied by a verbal assault in his native tongue, so she reached inside her purse. When she raised her handgun, the stubby man staggered back with both hands hoisted and his foul mouth shut.

"Get back before you get hurt," Vera advised him, through clenched teeth as she exited the truck. She pointed her gun barrel at the back driver's side window with her shooting hand, then flung the door open with her left. "You've got three seconds to get the hell out of my truck before I start blasting!" Vera didn't have to bother with the obligatory nonsense of counting. The man hiding in her back compartment raised his hands just as the lot attendant had moments before.

"Don't shoot!" he begged, climbing over the rear bench seat. "Don't shoot. It's me, Rags." He jutted his head upward slowly, exhibiting a horde of trepidation and a head full of blond hair. Vera recognized him, sighed deeply then lowered her weapon. A crowd had gathered on the sidewalk near the parking lot entrance. She holstered her firearm, snatched a handful of denim from Rags's jacket then yanked him out onto the cold cement. Rags grimaced as he cowered back against her SUV.

Shaking her head in disbelief, Vera was mad enough to scream. "You must be trying to die today!" she shouted at him. "I don't know what to do, shoot you or run you over?"

"Shoot him!" a young black man hollered from the host of onlookers. "He probably got it coming."

Vera considered it then she almost laughed. "Yeah, you probably got it coming, too," she answered flippantly at the stranger, before ordering Rags to get back into the vehicle through the front passenger door.

The same fellow who wanted to see some real action frowned when Rags hurriedly complied as he was ordered. "Ahh, man, I'd have capped that white boy."

"You wouldn't have done nothing," Vera replied

harshly. "Now get out of my way before I'm forced to handle up on you next." Without hesitation, everyone in the audience hustled away as she jumped in and threw the gear and her attitude into reverse. Vera made tracks toward the Interstate, weaving in and out of cars traveling much too slowly for her taste.

"And you," she huffed in her passenger's direction, "I could have killed you, fool. What were you thinking, stowing away in my ride?" Before Rags mounted an answer, Vera huffed again, warning him to shut up. "On second thought, don't say a damned word. You just sit there and be still until I get you out of here. If someone reported what went on back there, I might have some explaining to do with the police. I'd have to tell them what I'm doing with you in the first place. Hell, that don't sound like such a bad idea right now." She glared at Rags then slapped at the steering wheel with the heel of her palm. "Shoot, you got me mad enough to cuss. You're gonna pay for that."

Vera continued seething during the four-mile jaunt on the downtown turnpike. She stared at him intermittently along the way, doing the best she could to refrain from a battering of gutter-style tirades pushing to get out. Vera wanted to question him while issuing ruthless reprimands simultaneously but the venom in her mouth was too thick to dispense. "Ooh, I'm so unhappy with you right now," she hissed instead. "Have you eaten?" Rags shook his bowed head from side to side. "I figured as much. Don't let a lack of food make you stupid. Killing you would have been a shame, a damned shame."

Vera could tell her client was sorry for his transgression but that was beside the point. She tried to keep that in mind while idling along the street in front of Leftovers, the diner catty-cornered from her office building. "Let's get something straight, Rags," she said, in a noticeably softer tone than before. "I know it must be hard dealing with everything that's been pulling on you, but understand this, you just can't show up out of the blue like an old boyfriend who messed up a good thing and not expect to get your feelings hurt."

"You're right," he said finally. "I didn't want to get in the way, so I thought hanging around was the next best thing." He raised his head and looked into her eyes for the first time since she'd pulled a gun on him. "I don't expect you to understand. I can't say that I would neither. It's just that I feel you getting close to something. I don't know, an answer maybe."

After Vera discussed what his life expectancy would have been if he pulled another stunt like the last one, she informed Rags that she had been steady on the case with what little he'd given her to go on. With a tone of gladness in her voice, Vera shared that neither the city police nor the sheriff's department had any knowledge of a homicide victim fitting his description having been murdered in the time frame he was concerned about. Then, in an effort to make things right between them, Vera offered to return half of Rags's retainer. He refused it immediately.

"Ms. Miles, that money won't mean a thing to me if I can't get any closure on this."

Closure? Vera thought to herself. *There goes another peek at the flipside of the same coin.* She'd seen black men and women change directions like the wind when placed in an environment that offered a favorable outcome for doing so, but never once witnessed it from the opposite side of the fence. There was something different about Rags, something she couldn't put her finger on. He'd been beat down by the dreams that haunted him. Maybe that's what made him so humble. She couldn't know for sure but liked it nonetheless.

"Rags, if there is anything you left out or something you haven't told me, now is the time, because I'm flat out of places to look for a murder that no one seems to think happened except you. I say count your blessings and let it go." Rags pulled and tugged at corners of the piece of paper Vera had gotten from Lucius, the one with three names circled. She watched his fingers bend and fold the page with meticulous precision like he'd done it a million times. It was nothing short of amazing, to see his eyes dart back and forth two steps ahead of his hands. When his hands stopped moving, an expertly crafted paper alligator rested in them. "Uhm, Rags," Vera whispered, not sure exactly what to say. He remained silent a while then realized that he'd checked out mentally.

"Who's Harold Newel?" he asked quietly, staring at the letters encircled along the ridge of the alligator's back. Vera was speechless. Rags had rolled the dead man's name off his lips quick and easy, like he'd manipulated that ordinary sheet of paper. "I know this name," he said, his eyes locked on Vera's. "Why do I know his name?"

When she left Cecilia's desk, she was certain that her client was off the hook. Now she was backpedaling fast. "Did you kill him, Rags?" she questioned cautiously. It felt like waiting on the other shoe to fall, waiting to hear his answer, and praying that she didn't detect a lie when he did. "Did . . . you . . . kill . . . Harold Newel?"

"No, I didn't," he replied honestly. "But I'm sure I knew him."

Vera's head sank in her hands. "I don't believe this. Okay, take my cell phone number because I won't be in the office that much." She took a business card from her purse then wrote on the back. "Call me if you get froggy again. As for now, get something to eat and stay off the streets."

"Whuut?" asked Rags, with a lump in his throat. "Why?"

"For the same reason Newel's name jumped off that gator's back, reached up and slapped you. Sometimes you don't know how or why but you do know." Truth be told, Vera wasn't sure what she knew, but it was clear that Rags had been a party to deeds best done in the dark. If there was useful information about Rags's old buddy Harold Newel, that didn't make his criminal jacket, Vera had to find it.

After shooing her only client out of her truck, Vera called Glow during the short ride to her next destination. She tried to put into words how Rags's paper gator pushed her in a direction she didn't like traveling, toward the world of drug users and those who would do anything to keep illegal money flowing in. With mental notes swirling in her head, Vera found herself banging at a familiar door again. What she needed was a little more quality time, with Lucius.

While standing on the front porch and waiting for an answer at the door, Vera gently fingered the origami alligator. It didn't make sense to think that a man who'd create such delicate artwork could pump four holes in someone then leave them to bleed out in a cheap motel bathtub. But then again, there were still too many holes in a case that didn't make any sense at all. By the time Vera heard footsteps from the other side of the door, she had decided it was worth digging to China if that meant freeing Rags from his nightmares and what she'd determined was a tortured soul.

"So, you gonna open up, Lucius, or just stand there looking through the peephole at me?" she asked, with too much on her mind to be wasting time.

"What do you want now, Vera?" he answered, through the door. His tone was filled with a bitter measure of annoyance.

"I'm sorry to bother you again but I really need you, Lucius. Please open up so we can talk about it."

Lucius's eyes widened with surprise. He flicked the locks then whipped the door open in a flash. He was even more flabbergasted at Vera's demeanor. She wore a faint smile. She actually smiled at whatever that was in the palms of her hands. A vulnerability Lucius didn't know she possessed caused him to groan pitifully for her. "Ahh, are you okay?"

Vera nodded her head, but not too convincingly. "Hey, Lucius," was her stoic response. "Can't you tell? I'm just peachy."

"Well, seeing as how you've never been this calm before, I'd have to disagree with you. Come on in and tell Lu-Lu all about it."

"Lu-Lu?" mouthed Vera, as a crease appeared in the middle of her brow. She'd snapped out of her daze to find Lucius adorned in an Indian squaw costume equipped with knee-high buckskin boots. The tight suede dress was too ridiculous for words although she did manage to compliment his Navaho headband with the decorative feather glued on the side of it. "The feather is a nice touch, Lucius. It really makes the outfit pop."

He blushed accordingly then stepped aside for Vera to enter. "You don't think I overdid it? You know I do have the tendency to go overboard at times."

"Oh, no, you nailed this one." Vera chuckled. "Believe me. I'm impressed."

"Thank you, do come in and sit a while. I was just about to dine." Lucius served brunch, a gourmet-styled chicken and Belgian waffle dish with julienne potatoes on the side and mimosas to sip. He enjoyed Vera's company, the news she shared about Harold Newel, the Lazy 8 Motel, and Rags claiming he remembered knowing the victim. Lucius listened attentively to every detail. Before Vera offered to clear the table of flatware, he'd grown very interested in how this episode in her life was panning out. Only it wasn't merely a melodrama with bits and pieces of a make-believe puzzle to solve. A man's life had been taken; if Rags was culpable in any way, Vera needed to know it. For Lucius, it was simply too juicy to watch from the sidelines. He wanted in.

Over coffee, Lucius admitted to hearing about the Lazy 8 and what kinds of transactions went on there. Although he never would have ventured close to a place like that, he made two remarks that got Vera to thinking. "All kinds of things go on over there, you know. Rough trade and hard heads always did make for a horrible morning after. Everybody's got to make a living, but I wouldn't think of choosing one that might get you killed. From what I hear, you'd be lucky to leave that motel alive. I hope your client didn't remember the dead guy from a party they had at that place?"

Vera leaned back in her chair at the breakfast nook. "Lucius, you are a genius."

"I know that, but what'd I say to let you in on it?" he quipped.

"You reminded me that my client remembered something. He remembered knowing the dead guy."

"Yeah, so?"

"That means his memory is coming back. I'd bet that's why he knew to come to Dallas of all places."

"Why did he look you up as soon as he did?" Lucius gasped dramatically, his hand placed over his heart.

"He didn't. Rags said he was in town a few days then ended up at my door. Maybe he remembered something about me, too. Lucius, you ever heard of retrograde amnesia?"

Lucius smirked at Vera's question then answered truthfully. "Heck, no. Don't get me to lying. The human mind has always been one big riddle to me, girl. What makes retrograde any different from regular amnesia?"

"His memory is subject to come back a little at a time or all at once with a sudden jolt or a shocking experience," Vera told him. Her big riddle was working on her overtime now. "You also said a person would be lucky to make it out of that motel alive. Maybe Rags was just that lucky."

At Vera's behest, Lucius searched newspaper archives on the Internet. Side by side, they scanned over newspaper articles, looking for shootings that happened up to sixty days before Rags was found in that central Texas hunting cabin. Several stories had been written about the infamous motel, the goings-on there and Newel's death. However, they couldn't find one shred of evidence to implicate Vera's client in it. Once again it appeared Rags was innocent of murder.

Then Lucius ran across a front page headline about a dirty narcotics officer, shot down in the street two days after the other murder. Vera thought it peculiar that the article was sketchy at best. An exhaustive search did not produce any additional stories concerning Officer Warren Sikes's demise or impending investigations. If Newel and the slain cop were up to something that got them executed, it likely didn't have anything to do with Rags. However, if his dreams were tied to either crime, Vera was duty-bound to turn him in. There were no two ways about it.

After searching the police department's database, she climbed into her second-hand Explorer with the article and an outdated photocopy of Warren Sikes in his first year as a patrolman. He had the world in front of him. He was young, thin, and alive.

Nine

After brunch with Lucius, Vera was so off balance it felt like she'd misplaced her purse. Ms. Minnie hadn't called her cell phone and possibly did not intend to ever again. As she spent time thinking about the older woman's premonition, Vera's mind began to swirl. It all seemed so silly before, to go getting worked up over a white man who hadn't come through one of the normal referral channels. Typically, former clients who walked away from Vera's office with exactly what they paid for sent others her way. In the three years she'd been in business for herself, Rags was her first white unicorn; a white man throwing money at her instead of employing more reputable firms where he'd feel more comfortable. That was just another in the train of lingering questions still eluding Vera. She couldn't find one reason why Rags was drawn to her, not one.

Vera spent several hours, running personal errands, before heading back to the office. She parked along the street in front of her building. Her pockets were full but her head was ringing. A strange chill crept up her back as she turned off the engine. Once more, she experienced an unnerving feeling that someone had her under their surveillance. Vera quickly checked her rearview and side mirrors. No nondescript panel vans idled next to the curb as far as she could see. There wasn't one single unmarked police car on the avenue. Just before dismissing the thought altogether, Vera turned toward the opposite side of the street. Her tired brown eyes met with a pair of green ones staring back, from inside the small diner.

From the moment Vera dropped him off, Rags had been gazing out of the large window waiting for something to happen, anything that could have possibly helped him. Becoming increasingly consumed with despair and guilt, he had been renting the booth, biding his time and hoping that Vera returned with some news. Whether the news was good or bad didn't matter. Rags had grown darn tired of wondering what amends he'd have to make for sins of his past. Watching Vera stare at him as if he was a stray dog she didn't fully trust, Rags put ego and humility aside for the sake of truth. Just when it appeared Vera had decided to turn away from him, the beleaguered cowboy stood from the booth calmly as a plea for her company and an up-to-date report on her progress.

"Hell," Vera mouthed, as she marched across the street. "I must be crazy." She offered a faint smile to Rags through the window after stepping onto the sidewalk. After he felt sure she would join him, Rags returned to his seat at the booth. "Hell," she cussed again, while trying to guess how much more breathing she'd be allowed to do before someone was nailing shut her coffin.

"Thanks for coming over, Vera," Rags whispered, low and slow like a stubborn apology. "I thought for sure you'd see me, then turn tail and scoot in the other direction." When Vera didn't bother to sit or respond, he began to fiddle with a stale cup of coffee on the table. "Truth be told, I wouldn't blame you if you had."

Vera's hard expression softened after she took a seat. She signaled for the waitress to slide by with two fresh cups of java. Vera hadn't ever eaten at the greasy spoon because it didn't look all that clean from her office. Now that she was inside, the small restaurant didn't appear to be half bad. Each of the ten tables had been wiped down from previous customers and the floor was fairly spotless. "I wouldn't tell me that again if I were you. It's hard enough turning over rocks in someone else's backyard anyhow."

"I can't say that I understand," he muttered, uncomfortably.

"Meaning, the only rock worth a damn had a dead male prostitute under it." Vera neglected to share what she'd learned about the slain officer. If Rags had something to do with it, she didn't want to tip him off that she suspected it. "Look Rags, I'm working hard on your case. That hasn't changed. While there might not be anything to find, I'm going to keep looking anyway. But I need to know a thing or two from you."

"Like what?" he asked anxiously.

Vera thanked the waitress then sprinkled a pink packet of sweetener into the piping hot coffee. "Well, it would pay to know exactly how far you're willing to go with this?" She could tell by the way his eyelids shuddered that he didn't fully comprehend that question either. "What if I come across some very damning evidence that could send you to prison or worse?" Suddenly his eyelids closed like he was mulling over her answer. When his head fell forward, Vera leaned in to get a closer look at him. "Rags, you all right? Rags?" she said, pulling at his wrist lying on the table.

"Yeah, yeah," he whispered quietly. "I'm up. I'm up."

With both her eyes trained on his, Vera realized that he'd simply fallen asleep. Regardless of what she may have found underneath other unturned rocks, Rags was suffering from sleep deprivation. There was no telling how many days he'd been awake or what little rest he did get since arriving back in Dallas.

"What?" Rags grunted, with an oversized yawn. "Did I miss something?"

"By the looks of it, too little shuteye to go on this way," she told him. "I've seen what a lack of decent sleep can do to a person's mind. Believe me, the paranoia ain't pretty and that's just the beginning."

"I could pal around with you some. You know, help you while seeing how my money is being spent."

"No way in hell that happens," she objected. "I'm too busy to babysit you. That's not in my job description. I'd like to clear you or give you enough rope to hang yourself, if you want, but I have too many corners to turn to have you falling asleep every five minutes and slowing me down." Vera took two meager sips from her cup. "Rags, is there any chance you'd been involved with the police department as an informant, like that Newell guy?"

"Sorry, but I can't recollect what I was," he replied honestly.

"Yeah, you're right," said Vera, "you can't *recollect*. I'll tell you what you can and will do though, get back to wherever you're staying, lie down and close your eyes for as long as possible. You need it and I'll work better without having to check in on you."

"Just don't stop digging," he pleaded. "However it turns out. I need the dreams to stop. I need to know about me."

Vera stared across the table at Rags, his narrowed bloodshot eyes. He was very close to falling asleep again. "Uh-huh, you and me both," she heard herself admit aloud before leaving him with his head slumped on the table. Vera wanted to wake him but realized immediately that every bit of rest he managed to get was long overdue. The waitress informed her that Rags had been napping off and on. None of the customers seemed to mind and since he'd given the waitress a fifty-dollar tip on a six-dollar bill, she didn't mind either.

It had begun to sink in just how desperate Rags's situation had become. The way he'd internalized it couldn't have been healthy, Vera thought as she hustled back to her office. "I need to talk to you about one of the names on that list," Vera said into her telephone. "Harold Newel was clipped at the Lazy 8, that rundown gay motel off Loop 12."

"I know the place. Can't help but to," Detective Beasley said. "Lots of bad things go on down there." He wanted to say "I knew it," but didn't. He figured that Vera had her teeth deep in something and wasn't ready to let go. He'd been there before, foolishly following leads that seemed to go no place in particular although his gut kept telling him to push ahead. "Okay, I know how this works, Vera. You tell me something, hoping I'm interested enough to return the favor. Well, you're out of luck. That's not one of my cases and it's unsolved for a reason. There were no suspects and no reason to think the attack was anything but a jilted lover getting even. Gay druggies and murder aren't the combo you want to stand too close to, trust me. Homo-cides can get very nasty," he jested.

"Yeah, but," she started to say before Beasley cut her off playfully.

"Hey, I'm too old for wild goose chases. Didn't we already go down this road before?"

"There's more to it now," Vera answered, in a manner that forced the detective to put down his jellyroll. "My client knew that guy who got done in. I showed him the list of names and he recognized Newel's but didn't know for sure from where."

Beasley picked up the second half of his pastry then decided what Vera dangled wasn't enough to stop him from eating. "Maybe your guy was soliciting this Newel. Maybe they partied together back in the day. Who knows and who cares? I know I don't."

"Would you care if I told you that Newel had nine narcotics arrests, zero convictions?"

"You're saying he was protected, a snitch?" Beasley asked, while nibbling from the pastry. "And?"

"And two nights after someone clapped him, a narcotics detective was killed. His death was all over the papers, then dropped from the front page like it never happened. You probably knew him, a thirteen-year vet named Warren Sikes. From where I stand, it seems like a janky coincidence. Someone clips the snitch, then . . ." she added, to stir the pot.

"Okay, now you've stepped over the line, Vera.

This is not a conversation I want to have and I'm not having it over this phone. I'm about to leave my desk. Don't go too far."

Donald Beasley called Vera from his cell phone in the back of the police dressing room. He searched among three rows of locker to make sure he was alone before explaining how Internal Affairs had the Sikes shooting under wraps from day one and added that the slain detective must have been dirty, because the departmental brass prohibited any of his friends from working the investigation. The entire case was sewn up tight and put away quietly. "Someone high up was looking down on that shooting and pulling all of the strings," he said, as an afterthought. "I'm surprised you don't remember it, Vera. Sikes was shot near your office. If my memory serves me, the botched robbery that got him killed went down at that diner. What's it called? The name is something kinda catchy, Midnight Snack or, oh, yeah, Leftovers."

Goosebumps ran up Vera's arms when Beasley informed her where the crime had taken place. The exact location wasn't mentioned in the articles she read. To think that Rags was probably still in the restaurant asleep made her cringe. The first thought that came to her was criminals returning to the scene of the crime. Now, there was a pressing desire to learn everything she could about the particulars of the case, including why Detective Sikes was shot and why the police department threw up the blue wall of resistance to keep a lid on the investigation.

With her heart rate climbing, Vera raced to her office window. She couldn't conclude if Rags was still renting a booth with outlandish tips, but she had a major concern, getting some answers without him doing something stupid like stowing away in her vehicle again, or worse. Vera thanked Detective Beasley for the information then thought long and hard what to do next. Beasley folded his flip phone closed and did the same. As soon as he exited the locker room, someone flushed the toilet a few feet away from where he'd discussed the "don't ask" police homicide that he shouldn't have, especially with the wrong somebody listening in.

Ten

Vera paced back and forth in her office, waiting on a phone call to set off her next move. She'd reached out to Glow with a voice message telling her that it was urgent she get back as soon as possible. Vera wouldn't go into detail because Glow would weigh her options if she had too much information. Vera didn't want to be put on hold while her girlfriend debated which was more pressing, picking up extra work on the side or hatching her own money-making scheme. When Glow came strutting, knocking at the door, in a black sweatsuit and running shoes, Vera had her answer.

"You got my message," Vera said, with a smirk. Her words came out more in the manner of a statement than a question.

"I'm here, ain't I?" Glow answered flippantly. She huffed then folded her arms. "Why didn't you leave word and tell me what you wanted? You know how I hate that."

"Hate what, Glow, me trying to put some money in

your pockets?" Vera spat, in a noticeably edgy tone. "Well, I hate it when I do leave you a message and then don't hear back from you for two or three days."

Glow's frown faded into a perfect smile. "I was just finished with my kickboxing workout and was about to set up this old guy at the Beverly Hotel, which would have taken about . . . two or three days." She snickered when Vera nodded her head knowingly. "Okay, so you figured me out. I'm here, what do you want me to do?"

Vera leaned back in her chair and interlocked her fingers beneath her chin. "I want you to sit on somebody for me. It shouldn't take but a day or two and I need a second set of eyes on him to make sure he doesn't cause any trouble."

"Who you want me to sit on?" Glow said, with a naughty leer. "Is he cute?"

"You've met him," Vera informed her. "Rags, the client you bumped into the other day."

"That fine cowboy?" Glow asked excitedly, as she took a seat across from Vera. "He's rough around the edges. It might be interesting at that."

"Not so fast, girl, hold your horses. There's something I need to spell out. I've been doing some digging and skeleton bones are starting to turn up. I told you about Rags's dreams. Well they might be the kind that came true. I can't prove it, but he's likely knotted in an unsolved murdered informant case and a slain cop who supposedly showed up at a botched robbery." Glow listened to everything Vera had gleaned from Lucius, Cecilia Montez and Detective Donald Beasley. While all the dots seemed to be on the same page, there was no clear connection as far as she could see.

At the end of Vera's pitch, Glow contemplated what risks were involved and then she had only one question. "How much you interested in paying me to sit on this guy?"

"Two hundred a day," Vera replied evenly, "if you're up for it."

"I'm up for it at two-hundred plus expenses." Although her slight negotiating maneuver didn't sound like much, it was a bone of contention. Glow once turned in an expense report for three grand, when she followed a kleptomaniac for Vera. Glow said she had to buy something to keep from looking suspicious in the mall herself. The tennis bracelet was returned immediately, along with the padded expense account.

"Let's make it three hundred then, and no funny business this time," Vera bartered. "Good, Rags is over at that diner. He's been dozing off for the past hour or so but there's no way he's staying put all evening. I tried to talk him into finding a place to lay his head but he didn't bite."

"Maybe you were saying all the wrong things," Glow smarted in a peculiar way that Vera didn't approve of.

Pointing her finger, Vera reminded her part-time associate to keep her guard up. "Glow, don't go getting in way over your head. We don't really know this man. I'd hate to discover he's a bad one and have you standing too close to do anything about it if I needed to."

Glow got up from her chair and noted the time on her sports watch. "It's four-thirty-two. My time starts now. I'll call you if he keels over or anything. Otherwise, go on and do your thing."

"Just one problem with that. Rags is squatting right where I need to be, in that curbside restaurant."

The feisty hustler winked at Vera and grinned. "Why didn't you just say so?" She turned around and strutted out of the door, a twinkle in her eyes. Vera watched as Glow entered the diner and cozied up to Rags. She waggled her finger an inch from his nose. He shook his head, with an objection in mind, but Glow persisted. Vera didn't have the slightest idea what she could have been saying to him, but thirty seconds of it got him to pull up stakes from that booth and out of her hair. Rags, still exhausted and short on sleep, stumbled from the seat he'd been perched on all day and followed behind Glow. After what Vera witnessed, she was no longer concerned about Glow being too close to Rags. Her charm would have rectified a bad situation if the knife she carried couldn't, if he turned out to be dangerous after all. Vera was certain of that. Once Glow had effectively removed her biggest obstacle, Vera was chomping at the bit to stay busy doing what she did best, scratching away at a headache one layer at a time.

After Vera watched her client and good friend drive away in Glow's sporty BMW, she marched across the street. It was four-thirty-five and the diner was nearly empty because the dinner crowd hadn't started to come in yet. Vera took the same booth where Rags had spent the better part of his day.

"What can I get you, sweetie?" grunted the weathered waitress. She had a full head of gray hair, appeared to be in her late sixties and too heavy to have any affinity for standing on her feet all day. Vera fiddled with the menu while selecting her words carefully.

"How ya doing?" she offered pleasantly. "I'd like a cup of coffee, no cream please. Oh, and by the way, how long have you worked here? I heard that a police officer was killed down the block a few years back."

The older woman placed her balled fist on her thick hip and laid her head back. "I've been working the day shift here a little more than two years but I seem to recall somebody saying something about that one morning. You'd want to speak with the assistant manager to be sure."

"Yeah, it was in all the papers," Vera added to make her interest sound strictly legitimate, as far as nosy customers went. "Is the assistant manager in today?"

"Uh-huh. I'll see if she can spare a minute whilst I get you going." The waitress waddled off like her shoes weighed ten pounds each.

Vera stared at the sign above her office, *Miles Above Investigators*. She chuckled when it didn't impress her anymore than the diner had in all the times she'd turned her nose up at it. What you see in life all depends on where you sit, she reasoned as a middle-aged white woman wearing dark polyester slacks and a tan blouse approached her table.

"Hey, I'm Linda," the lady hailed, looking Vera over suspiciously.

"Glad to meetcha, Linda. I'm Vera."

"Frances told me you were asking about the shooting that happened a bit ago. What can I do you for?" Vera knew that meant, "What's it to you?"

"I'm a private detective, that's my place across the

way," she answered, with an air of respectability. When Linda sneered at it, Vera quickly returned to earth. "Anyway, I was handling a case for a real estate company back then, looking to broker a lot of property on this block, then the deal fell apart because of what the buyer called a sensitive dilemma," she lied, to avoid suspicion.

"I see what you mean, a police officer getting himself shot up dead in the street, that's sensitive all right," the assistant manager contended. "It was a darn shame, too. I remember it like it happened yesterday." Linda's eyes grew dim like she was trying to recall what occurred during the incident. "Poor man lying in the street like a dog, just didn't seem right."

Realizing that the woman must have been on the scene, Vera tried to ease the question out as not to alarm her. "You were here, the night it happened?"

"Sure was, I was working the floor back then and I was the one who made the 911 after that colored fellow stuck up the place. I'll never forget it."

Vera was about to burst on the inside now that the former waitress was running off at the mouth. "Forget what, Linda?" she asked, using the witness's name to foster the rapport needed to get a scoop on everything the employee had.

"Well," said Linda, as the hefty waitress returned with Vera's coffee.

"Frances, you mind making that to go with a slice of blueberry pie?" Vera asked with the utmost sincerity. Vera handed her a twenty-dollar bill then insisted she keep the fourteen-dollar tip. She'd have emptied her entire purse in order to keep the waitress away from the table and Linda's recounting of the story.

"That's a good idea," Linda said, grinning from

ear to ear. "Honey, I dig your style. Let's talk about it in my office, nice and private like." Vera dug her style as well. She nodded mostly while Linda retold the incident that ended with a shooting and a slew of puzzling questions. "No, I won't forget it," Linda said, repeating herself. "As I said, a black fella come in out of the rain at around eleven o'clock and shoves this gun in the cashier's face. Of course she empties the register, per company policy. He snatches the bag and tears out of here. I'm a bundle of nerves while talking to the police operator. I'll give them some credit though, they got somebody down here quicker'n spit. Two police detectives come flying up in a four-door sedan with the lights glaring. It was hard to see what happened then because of the steam on the windows."

"The what?" Vera asked, although she didn't mean to interrupt.

"You know how it fogs up the windows when it's cold outside and raining, with the heat on inside?"

"Oh, yeah, condensation?"

"Whatever you call it, it was all over the windows, so we couldn't see a thing going on outside of those blue lights flickering." A sudden sadness washed over Linda's face before she continued. "Oomph, next thing you know, we hear what sounds like firecrackers popping off outside. Hell, I get down with the quickness, and crawl all the way to the front door. I know I shouldn't but I can't help myself. That's when I see him, the dead officer stretched out in the road, with his partner bent over him and crying like a baby. It was just plain awful."

"Yeah, I can imagine," Vera said, thinking of Rags's potential part in the murder. "Hey, Linda, that robber, the black guy, they ever find him?" Vera reasoned that Rags must have been in on the robbery as a lookout or a getaway wheelman.

"Nope, they didn't," Linda answered regrettably. "Detective Warren Sikes, that's the cop who died, his wife came by here seeing if we knew anything the police wasn't telling her. I never understood why they'd keep anything from her. Now those federal fellows, I wouldn't put anything past them."

"The FBI, they came around too?"

"Uh-huh, the day after the robbery," she replied, as if it was customary for them to poke their noses in a holdup. "It was all kinds of folks in for a while then I guess it was old news fast enough 'cause they all skedaddled after a few days." Since the police department had the investigation on ice, Vera needed another road to travel along.

"Linda, did the coroner's office send a hearse for Sikes's body?"

"No, I believe an ambulance zoomed in and carted him off. Why?"

"It's just a thought," Vera whispered quietly.

Linda assumed that Vera had been heartbroken by the story she shared. "I told you it was awful. I wasn't supposed to keep this past twelve months but I can't force myself to throw it out." Linda stood up and pulled a stack of pink copies from a black three ring binder. She flipped through the pages until she found what she was looking for. Unbeknownst to her, it was exactly what Vera wanted too. "Incident reports are to be trashed, per policy, but this one is hard to let go."

"You mind if I see that?" Vera asked, hoping the manager didn't.

"Hell, girl, take it," Linda offered. "If you don't, I may never have the nerve."

Vera read over it carefully. Linda did an outstanding job with the details. Everything she said was there on the carbon copy report, including the name of the emergency medical technician who arrived on the scene.

Linda felt relieved after talking about that terrible night, but there was something else she wanted to say before Vera left her office. "Hey, Vera, are you the kinda private eye that tails cheating hubbies?"

"If you know he's cheating, Linda, why would you need him tailed?"

"Shoot, honey, proof for when I haul his no-good butt down to divorce court."

Vera chuckled out aloud. "I'd be happy to get you all the proof you need. How about something in an eight-by-ten glossy?"

"I knew I liked your style, Vera," Linda howled, with her head thrown back. "I could tell right off you's a real peach."

Eleven

Before Vera exited the Leftovers diner with the incident report, she thanked Linda Klaus, promised to bust her philanderer of a husband then celebrate once they'd tarred and feathered his bony behind like Linda always wanted. They decided it was Vera's job to bring the feathers. It didn't matter how much Vera's business threatened to grow, she would always make time for cheating husbands. She was still laughing about the restaurant manager's penchant for getting even when she hopped into the Silver Streak with that golden nugget of information in her pocket, but she didn't expect to find any laughter on her next stop.

The clock read five-fifteen when Vera pulled into the parking lot behind Fire House No. 26. The name of the EMT on the two-year-old report read Susie Chow. Vera knew it was correct, because Linda proved to be quite the stickler for doing things by the book. The two-story building didn't seem any larger than most of the older homes in the area, a historical district north of downtown. The light-brown-colored fire station boasted neatly painted darker brown trim and a sizable lawn. A two-ladder fire engine had been backed into a slot on the side of the station. The image of lusty, muscle-bound firemen washing that fire truck, bare-chested and brawny, swept over Vera as she glided past it. What she meant as a private thought came out much louder. "Ooh, it's so long," she said to herself jokingly before strapping on her game face. "Uh-huh, yes it is."

"Yes, what is?" someone asked from the other side of a big screen TV in the downstairs common area. Vera stopped in her tracks when the man's voice came out of nowhere. The tanned, dishwater-blond-haired lieutenant raised his head eventually but Vera didn't mind the view from where she stood. His navy slacks gripped at his backside like a glove as he bent over sorting out wires. For a man of at least fifty, he was just as fit as someone half his age.

"Oh, nothing," Vera sang. "You weren't even supposed to hear that."

"Hear what?" another man replied, as he stepped out of the oversized kitchen. His broad shoulders and black mustache were solid accessories for his ebony-hued skin. Vera smiled uncomfortably at his developed chest beneath a tight blue pullover.

"Oh, y'all just coming out of every nook and cranny on a sistah," she teased.

"Can I help you with something, ma'am?" he questioned, when she didn't appear to be offering a reason for what could have easily been misconstrued as loitering.

"I'm Vera Miles, an investigator," she grunted, clearing her throat. Vera flashed her credentials then an awkward glance at the tall, dark and handsome newcomer. "I'm here to investigate a murder, a two-year-old cold case." That got the lieutenant's attention. He stepped in front of the grand entertainment center wearing a concerned expression.

"I'll take care of this, Rawls," he said, subtly ordering the younger black man to make himself scarce. "Ms. Miles, I'm Stewart Wilhort, the lieutenant here. Does this involve any of my men?"

"I certainly hope not. I'm looking for Susie Chow, an ambulance tech, or at least she was when the shooting in question took place." Vera stood a little taller when she felt the white man's eyes tracing her for all of the wrong reasons. She'd seen them before, curious leers leaning on the side of suspicion. "Well, is she still on staff here or do I need to make a call to locate her latest assignment?" Vera was bluffing. She hadn't planned on calling anyone that she didn't have to, nor was she in the mood to become a casualty in the war on sexism.

"Susie's still on board here," he informed here. "She should be pulling in soon. Her shift was over fifteen minutes ago. You can have a seat and wait around if you like."

I know I can, she wanted to say but didn't. "Thanks, lieutenant, I'll do that," she offered in the most professional manner possible, considering how he'd glared at her uneasily.

Nearly an hour had passed when the ambulance tech Vera had been waiting on finally arrived. Antsy and growing hungrier by the minute, she decided to facilitate what she called a rolling interview, where she persisted in getting the answers before witnesses had time to cook up new lies to hide old truths. Vera stood directly outside the driver's side door after the ambulance stopped. "Susie Chow," she huffed with a stiff jaw line to catch the attractive Amerasian woman with a short boyish hair style off guard.

The petite mobile medical unit driver hesitated when she saw Vera's size and serious stance. "What have I screwed up now?" she whined, while stepping down off the running board of her unit.

"I'm an investigator, Vera Miles, and hopefully nothing, unless you try to lie to me," she assured her plainly. "Lieutenant Wilhort said I'd find you out here."

"I'm surprised he knows I even exist, unless my dusting isn't to his liking," said Susie, as she unloaded rolled bandages and other supplies from the storage compartment inside the rear of the truck.

"Yeah, I know what you mean. I just met him myself," Vera said to get the ball rolling. "Men either look over me or look me over a little too closely."

"Yeah, you do know what I mean." Susie stuffed dirty gurney pads in a laundry bag then took a seat on the tailgate. "Since you're not here to rag on me, who's in for it?"

"Just tell me what you remember about a Dead on Arrival pickup you made a couple of years ago and I'll be out of your hair in no time."

"You kidding? Two years? That a lot of DOAs to sift through," Susie huffed.

"There was a shooting near the Leftovers diner on Mockingbird Road. A cop was shot in a robbery." The paramedic froze. Vera watched her eyes widen then grow dim as she traveled back in time just that fast, so she didn't ease up. "Tell me everything you remember about that pickup, everything."

"Funny, I've spent just about every second between now and then trying to forget it. I wasn't on the job a week when I got the call, shots fired and a man down. I was supposed to be with another tech but I bitched about getting my feet wet as quickly as possible. My partner sprained his foot the day before and there was my chance. Lieutenant put me with an old fart who didn't like driving. Said he'd sit on his duff to make the rent but never behind a wheel. I ratted on him and in return, I got stuck with a trainee. That guy, who died, he was a cop. And believe you me, that didn't help my situation. Gosh, there was so much blood," she recalled. "I didn't know a man's body could hold so much blood."

"Tell me exactly what you did when you initially arrived?" Vera asked, to keep her story moving.

"It was raining like crazy. Visibility was damn near zero and there I was weaving in and out of traffic to get there. Police cars were all over the place. They waved me through. I climbed out of the truck, sprinted out to him and tried to resuscitate. There was so much blood, so much," she mumbled, still in disbelief.

Vera nodded her head empathetically. "Okay, I'm with you so far. Keep going. Did he say anything while you were working on him?"

"What? That guy didn't have any vitals. He wasn't up to saying anything. Between the cops shouting at me, heavy rain falling and all that blood, there wasn't any way he had a chance in hell of making it. So, me and this trainee who washed out shortly after that, we roped him up and hauled ass back to the county barn." Susie noticed how Vera's face held a question when it shouldn't have. "I see the way you're looking at me. No, ma'am, he didn't make it. I wasn't sure of too much that night except one thing, that Warren Sikes was dead, deader than most if you ask me. His skin was white and ice cold. The FBI agents saw him when they trapped me at the medical examiner's office. They signed the forms and transferred his body to the morgue and everything. Don't believe me, go and ask them." Much like Linda, Susie was at a loss as to why the feds wanted information and access to the man's corpse, although she wasn't interested in causing trouble for anyone if she could help it, namely herself. Vera knew how life worked, and how there was always more than enough trouble to go around whether you stirred the pot or not.

With federal agents showing up after a policeman's shooting, a potentially guilty man running towards a death sentence and a desperate need for the right man's touch, Vera made two phone calls. The first one went to Ms. Mineola Roosevelt, her estranged receptionist.

"Hello, Ms. Minnie," she said calmly, when someone answered from the old woman's end. "This is Vera."

"That's just who my caller ID said you was," Minnie sniped.

"I can see you're still mad, but please come in tomorrow so I can attack this case head-on without wondering if I'm missing out on important calls."

"Ain't nothing to be mad about," the woman responded matter-of-factly. "Getting attacked from behind is what concerns me."

Vera almost smiled but she had something else fighting it off. "Don't be like that. I've been running circles around town and I'm still a ways away from knowing what I need to."

"Oomph, I knew exactly what I needed to do the moment that white man wondered in with cow puck on his boots and death in his eyes. I needed to find some other place to be."

"After all we've been through, I can't count on you being there for me? Ms. Minnie, we're a team. I need you."

"Vera, you know I love you like my own, but I ain't willing to get killed for nobody. I'd be glad to come back after you done dropped that devil as your client."

Vera sighed into the telephone, with a hint of apprehension in her voice. "I'm sure we can work out something tomorrow morning. Tell you what, I'll get you some new tires and help get your alternator fixed when this is all over. I have a hunch and should probably go to see the medical examiner this evening, but I'm behind on a lot of personal stuff that's got to be tended to today. Is there something we can do about this? You don't have to worry about . . ." Vera suddenly realized the she'd been the only one carrying the conversation. "Ms. Minnie? Ms. Minnie?"

"You still gonna do business with that white man?" Minnie asked quietly.

"Yes, ma'am."

Click.

"Hello? Ms. Minnie? Damn!" Vera cussed when she realized her savvy receptionist hung up the phone on her. "Fine with me," she fussed to herself. "I'll work it out anyway . . . with a plate of Chinese food and a little chocolate-chocolate cake on the side."

Bubbles floated in a tub of hot water in Vera's master bathroom. She didn't want to climb in alone but the message she left for Bullet at the sports bar hadn't been returned. She couldn't be certain he'd even received it, not with Vendetta on the clock and on his heels. Vera couldn't see how Bullet kept that woman out of his pants. She was shapely and attractive after all, in a strip-club-skanky sort of way that some men liked, although the thought of catching the heebie-jeebies should have made her considerably less appealing. Whichever the reason Bullet kept her in her place, Vera was grateful. She'd have been even more grateful had he returned her call then made his way over to her side of town.

Vera was neck deep in satiny foam when the telephone rang. She reached over the side of her bathtub to answer it. "Hmm, hello," she said, in a tired and subdued tone.

"I got your message," Bullet said, with a pregnant pause attached. "And I was wondering if you wouldn't mind some company."

"Yeah, that'd be all right with me," Vera cooed sensually. "I could use some attention, use something else too, and then you could kiss me all over."

Bullet chuckled while considering that entire scenario. "Sounds kinda nice, but what do I get for my troubles?"

"To see it happen," she answered, in a breathy whisper.

"I do like to leave the lights on and watch. Can I use my key? Good. I'll be right there."

Just as Vera closed her eyes, she heard footsteps coming her way. There wasn't any time to reach the gun in her purse or the one she kept in the lettuce crisper of her refrigerator. Her heart raced as she picked up the phone to call Bullet. "Pick up, please pick up," she panted. "Bullet! Bullet!"

"I'm putting some wine on ice," he hollered from her bedroom.

Now more aggravated than afraid, Vera shouted his name at the top of her lungs. "Buuuullet!"

He stuck his head into the bathroom, as if he hadn't just scared the living daylight out of her. "Baby, what's wrong?" After noticing that she was breathing fire, he realized an explanation was in order. "I was talking to you from the driveway the whole time. I thought it'd be kinda funny to surprise you."

"Well, it wasn't. You scared me. I didn't know who was all up and through my house. I could have shot you, Negro!"

"It ain't too late," he joked. "You want to shoot me in the bathtub or on the bed?"

"You just wait, I'm a get you," she grunted furiously.

"That's why I'm here, baby. I'm a get you too," he replied, oblivious to the drama he'd just caused her. She was into Rags's case much deeper than she wanted to be. Dead cops, black stick-up men, FBI, puddles of blood and God knows what else convinced Vera that she had better get to the bottom of it but quick. However, there wasn't anyone to interview tonight so she eased back down under the bubbles and smiled. There was six feet, two-hundred-thirty pounds of grown man putting wine on ice in her bedroom. Tomorrow would take care of itself she reasoned. She'd managed to get the night to working on her behalf.

Bullet lit two candles on Vera's wash basin then killed the lights. She watched with bated breath as he stripped down to nothing and then climbed into the bathtub behind her. "Ooh, hold on," she moaned. "Let me drain a little water and make it hotter for you."

"Uh-uh, ain't no need for that," Bullet growled in her ear. "It's plenty hot for me as it is."

She cut her eyes at him over her shoulder. "We got all night, unless you've got some other place to be?" Even if he did have other plans after she was finished with him, he'd better not acknowledge it.

"No, it don't get no better than right here." His answer came in a quick and easy manner that sounded so nice it had to be the truth. "I have been wondering when you'd get around to telling me what's causing that hitch in your voice."

"You think you know me?"

"Well?" Bullet said, as he sucked on the back of her neck.

"Quit that now." She squirmed. "Keep on and I won't be able to speak at all."

"Okay, two minutes, then I'm on to why I came."

Vera leaned back against Bullet's chest, her favorite place on the planet, and nestled her head against his neck. "You ever think about doing something that could get you killed?"

"Huh, you forget I made a living with my fists. I risked my life every time I climbed into the ring."

"Yeah, but you loved doing it. Maybe I'm just constipated."

"Right now?" Bullet asked, not sure what, if anything, to do about it. "I guess I could run down to the drugstore for you."

Vera laughed at him. "Not like that, silly. I mean in a rut sort of way. My business, I like it, but the hustle of making the ends meet makes me think sometimes."

Bullet stroked Vera's shoulder with his big hands in a compassionate manner that made her want to stay in that position forever. "What would you rather be doing?"

"Pretty much the same thing I'm doing now, only for more money," she told him honestly.

"Yep, I always said there wasn't any point in having your cake if you can't eat it too." Bullet went back to running his tongue up and down Vera's neck. "Your two minutes is up and I want some cake."

She squirmed again like before, moaning at the thought of it. "You . . . are . . . so . . . nasty."

"Just the way you like it."

"Uhhh-huh."

Twelve

The morning after Vera showed her man just how nasty she liked it, the sun shone through the blinds in her bedroom. An empty Chardonnay bottle on her nightstand and a head full of outstretched hair were the telltale signs that she got exactly what she needed—smooth wine and strong loving. She rolled out of bed, glowing with visions of what had transpired during the night swimming around in her mind. A hint of a grin played at the corner of her lips when Bullet pleaded for her to come back for another round.

"Uh-uh, I've got to get going this morning," she protested half-heartedly. "Besides you put enough work in for two nights."

"You know I love cake," Bullet said, licking his lips.

"So nasty," she whispered, while sliding beneath the sheets with him. "Okay, five minutes, but afterwards I've got to go."

Forty-five minutes later, Vera was making a second attempt at meeting the day, although her determination was quite a bit weaker than before. She stumbled to the bathroom and turned on the shower. "I like that man," she heard herself say, as streams of water cascaded down her breasts. "Y'all like him too, huh, girls? Yeah, he's my kinda freak." She couldn't help but envision a lifetime of late morning showers and good morning sex. Bullet liked her, that much was plain. How much she actually meant to him wasn't. Until it had the chance to show itself, what he had been willing to give her was exceedingly appreciated.

Vera left a note on the pillow next to Bullet as he slept, telling him that she enjoyed his company and his overwhelming fondness for cake. She wanted to close the note with an "I Love You" but thought better of it. Admitting those words might have set something into play she wasn't ready to deal with head-on, so she sidestepped it by writing "Love, Vera" at the end. After planting a gentle kiss on the crown of his bald head and feeling his warmth radiate throughout her soul, she tip-toed out the door and into the world that didn't bother with such pleasantries. Out there, she felt alone.

Elmer Williams, the Dallas County medical examiner, was singing a Billie Holiday tune, "Don't Explain," when Vera appeared in the basement of Parkland Hospital. He was in his late sixties and just as spry as ever. The graying goatee he wore was a nice accent to his soft brown skin. "Ahh, there she is," he sang with a smile bigger than Texas. "Come over here and trip the light fantastic with me." Vera giggled at him, then turned up her nose. She eyed his medical scrubs and latex gloved hands.

"No way I'm letting you touch me with those on. Ain't no telling where they've been this morning."

"See, now there you go. I haven't opened this one up yet," he informed her, regarding his next patient. A whale of a black man, seemingly in his late thirties, was lying flat on the metal slab with a white sheet draped over his waist. "You know I can't help getting my tour around the floor when you show up. Other women come to see me, too, but none of them have what you got, a perfect step. On top of that, you let me lead." Wearing the same non-committal frown, Vera pointed at his gloves. "Oh, all right," Elmer fussed. "Put your dancing shoes on." He snapped the latex from his mitts, then tossed them on his desk in the corner of the vast room.

Vera grinned at the older distinguished man and assumed a ballroom dancer's position with her arms held out mannequin-style. "Watch your hands, Elmer," she spat. "The last time I left here wearing your fingerprints on my tail."

"Sorry fo' that, must've slipped," he explained, and not too convincingly.

They danced around the room among stiffs stretched out beneath full drapes. The bodies didn't upset Vera, all of the bad deeds they were ever going to do had already been done. She was there to get closer to Rags's past and his potential fate. There was a good chance the medical examiner could help her with that, but first she had to pay the piper. Elmer was a pretty fine dancer, she thought. That's when she noticed he was humming another bluesy hit and guiding her around the cement floor with his hand on her behind. She stopped abruptly when it came to her that he'd become more excited than she could bear dealing with. "You said you'd watch your hands, Elmer," Vera hissed, as she backed away.

"Must've slipped," was his nervous response.

Vera pointed her finger at the bulge in his cotton scrubs. "And what about that?"

"Wait a minute now, I didn't have no control over that," he argued. "I'm sorry but what can I say? Had a hot date last night and the Viagra hasn't worn off yet."

"Elmer, you could have told me you were pill popping again. I'd have known better."

"I should have known better too, Vera," he apologized. "I don't want to let this little mishap to come between us." When she smirked at his choice of words, Elmer realized how it sounded. "Well, you know what I meant. Friends?"

"I guess," she pouted playfully. "Now put that thing away so I can ask about a case you might have worked a few years back."

Elmer shrugged on a long white lab coat then crossed his arms. "Is this good enough?"

"It'll have to do, won't it? Maybe you ought to button up so *it* doesn't get loose," she added to let him know that she didn't hold what happened against him. "Now, then, this may take some time to look up but I believe it was around December, twenty-four to twenty-six months ago. A white cop was killed, shot down while chasing the robbers of a roadside diner near my office. The paramedic that swooped him up from the crime scene says she brought him here. I need to know how many gunshot wounds he rolled in with?"

Elmer leaned his head back and stroked his goatee. When something came to mind, he nodded that he'd recalled it perfectly. "It was a cold and rainy night as I remember. I can't tell you any specifics about the autopsy though."

"Why not? The body was delivered here, right?"

"Yes, they brought him in and he stayed out in the hall due to the high overflow that night. Every time it pours cats and dogs like that, our guest room gets flooded from automobile accidents alone. There must have been twenty bodies to pass through here by sun-up."

Vera stood back on her heels. She didn't know whether to be disappointed or shocked beyond belief. "You telling me that y'all misplaced a dead cop?"

"Call it what you want, but forensic medicine is not an exact science and neither is cataloging corpses. He didn't up and walk off. I'd say somebody took him. And, by the looks of the blood-soaked sheets that EMT brought him in with, he would have been a mess to clean up."

"That's crazy, Elmer. I've got a client who thinks he killed somebody, maybe this cop and now there's no autopsy report to go on. I'd rather set his mind at ease and send him home with a clear conscience. Was there any remote chance the cop pulled through?"

"Sorry, Vera, not likely. If the wounds didn't kill him, he sure as hell bled out on the way over."

Vera thought she had come up with evidence either to clear Rags or sink him altogether. Now she felt like a woman who caught a close-out deal on shoes two sizes too small. The price was right but the pain was unbearable. "Okay, okay. Tell me about the federal agents that came snooping around after the body disappeared."

"What agents?" the examiner asked. "The policeman's wife, she showed up and pitched a holy fit about him being gone, then I didn't hear from her again. Actually, I expected to have my head handed to me on a platter by the police commissioner, too. I never heard a peep out of him either. It was the longest week of my life after I'd learned the dearly departed and misplaced was a city employee."

"This is too weird, Elmer."

"I always thought it was," he agreed.

"I've interviewed the waitress at the diner who called in the shooting and the EMT driver first on the scene; both of them claimed the FBI was all over it. It didn't figure that they'd pull a no-show at the morgue, where the medical examiner's notes could make their case for the murderer. I don't get it," she huffed finally. "I could have stayed in the bed for this."

"Sorry I couldn't be more helpful."

"Elmer, it's nothing against you. Thanks for the fox trot."

The medical examiner watched Vera's backside sway until she caught the elevator going up. "You're welcome."

The noonday sun shone brightly over the city area as Vera motored toward downtown. Still behind on her first meal of the day, she called Donald Beasley to arrange an impromptu lunch date. Before he answered the phone, Vera kept trying to make sense out of nonsense. There was a dead cop, whose body had been misplaced, ghost FBI agents and a gunman that no one pursued as far as she knew. Calling Rags with a stern suggestion to get out of town on the next thing smoking did occur to her, but that would merely ease her mind, not his. That's why Vera stayed on the job. Rags came to her in desperate need of help. She hadn't quit on a client yet, and he needed her more than any of the others had. As her grandfather used to say, Vera was determined to ride this bull until it bucked her.

"Hey, Donald, this is Vera. I'm rolling through your neck of the woods. You got time for a bite?"

"I wish I did," he said, as if in the middle of something important. "I'll take a rain check, but listen, since I can't do a damned thing about Detective Sikes's investigation, I want you to have what I've come up with. There's a man you'll want to locate. Sinton Johnson was one of Sikes and Draper's street informants."

"Sin Johnson's is a name I know. Draper, where have I heard that before?"

"Remember the guy you ran into when you came to see me? Yeah, that was Frank Draper, Sikes's partner. Vera, hear me now. People have been asking around about your involvement into Sikes's shooting, so watch your back."

"You saying somebody inside the blue wall has got something to hide?"

"Sweetheart don't kid yourself, we all got something to hide," he asserted jokingly. "It's just that some of us have a lot more than others."

Vera examined what her friend said and what it meant to her investigation. Unless she wanted to become a target for dirty cops, things had better get wrapped up soon. "Thanks, Donald. Sinton Johnson used to be a big shot until he got too deep into his own junk."

"And that's how Draper flipped him. Sinton's out there. Maybe he can shed some light on how things used to be, when Sikes was still breathing."

Vera parked next to a taco vendor on Commerce Street, across from the records building. "Got any idea where can I find him?"

"Nope, but I do know somebody who would. Draper's in the station house today. He could get you farther on down the road. He did take his partner's shooting pretty hard."

"You probably don't want to hear this, but Draper could be the reason his partner got blown away. If not, I can't let him know that I have a client who may have been in on it." Vera thanked Detective Beasley, then ordered two burritos to go.

Sinton Johnson was a player Vera knew from a time when drugs swam through the black neighborhood unopposed by the law. Crack cocaine hit Dallas without notice or regard to the lives it ruined. It caught the police department off guard and unprepared to keep the drug trade in check. Dealers lived like government project aristocrats, admired like top-billed movie stars. Sin Johnson epitomized men who came into immense wealth overnight. He spent money as if he had a license to print it. Vera wondered how he was getting along nowadays with a crack problem of his own. Going to Frank Draper concerning Sinton's whereabouts wasn't an option until Vera knew the whole story.

While dashboard dining wasn't her typical idea of grabbing lunch, Vera nibbled on bean and beef burritos, and used the time to think. She had gone out of her way to learn what happened after Warren Sikes was killed. Detective Beasley was on to something. Maybe it was high time to start looking into what went down before he died.

Vera contacted Cecelia Montez and asked how her boyfriend was working out, then laughed when she explained how he'd been evicted at the end of her .45 caliber revolver. He came home with another woman's panties stuffed in his back pocket. That wasn't enough to infuriate Cecilia, but learning that he was cheating with a size-six eighteen-year-old was a deal breaker. Vera had to catch her breath when her friend's tongue started spewing Spanish and broken English at the same time.

"Okay, chica, I get it," Vera chuckled. "He ain't coming back. Sorry I asked."

"Whatever, his cousin Ramón is way finer anyway. And from what I hear, he's packing, too," Cecilia snickered. "We're going out tonight after work."

Vera had a distinct feeling Cecilia already knew about Ramón's endowment first hand although she wasn't interested in calling her on it. "Go on then, keep it in the family."

"If you ever get tired of that big chocolate Bullet of yours, Ramón's got lots of brothers. I could hook you up, too."

"Nah, that's not possible. What I do need is a hookup on a last known address for Sinton Johnson."

There was a grunt on the other end. "Oomph, Sin Johnson? That's a name I haven't heard in a long while. Is he back on the streets?"

After Vera explained that's why she was calling, Cecilia pulled him up on the computer. She missed on the address but she did have information on usual hangouts and known affiliations. Vera nearly hollered when Cecilia mentioned Vendetta Lewis's name among Sin's old friends. "Vendetta Lewis?"

"Yeah, she used to be a mule when she was shaking her ta-tas at the nudie bar," said Cecelia. "I could see if she's in the system."

"No, that won't be necessary, chica, I know where to find that tramp. She works at the bar with Bullet now."

"Uh-oh, sounds like someone's been tramping around someone else's chocolate. Call me if you need backup."

"Good luck with Ramón tonight and try to keep your panties on, at least through dinner."

Cecelia giggled with her hand placed over the phone to muffle her outburst. "I thought you knew. I don't even wear panties."

"Uh-uh, that's too much information," Vera howled. "I'll get with you later. Bye, girl."

With two burritos sitting on her stomach like boulders, Vera figured to get some relief by cashing in that good deed she performed for the former stripper and get Vendetta to lighten up while giving up the goods on Sinton. "She'd better give up that chump," Vera grunted, on the way over to the 3rd Round. Unfortunately, some things were easier said than done.

Thirteen

The parking lot in front of Bullet's place was so packed that Vera spent several minutes waiting on a parking space. When she stepped inside, the wait for a table was just as long. The chattering crowd, saturated with fitness nuts, fell head over heels in love with Turkey Burger Thursdays. Although it was Vera's idea to add healthy alternatives on the menu, she'd planned on staying away on the days they were offered. Bullet stood behind the bar, mixing virgin frozen drinks and fruity cocktails by the dozens. He tossed a puzzled expression at Vera when she camped by the door with the other customers, then he waved her up to the bar area.

"I was going to wait my turn on a table," she said, eagerly approaching him. "I've been waiting on everything else. Why do workout weirdos act like there's only one restaurant in town with turkey burgers? I've had 'em, they taste like chicken."

Bullet filled three ten-ounce glasses with ice. He whipped up three Shirley Temples in a jiff and then grinned at Vera. "Hey, baby, and how is your day going?" he asked sarcastically. "I've got no complaints, because as you know I started it off with a bang. And, as you can see, my woman's idea was a hit, my customer base is about to pop and I even heard that people are outside fighting over parking spaces."

"Tell me about it, I was one of them not five minutes ago. Sorry to come in on a bad note." Vera thanked Bullet for the cranberry juice on the rocks he poured her while she looked around the restaurant for the Sinton Johnson associate she came to shake down. "Hey, where's Vendetta?"

"Uh-uh, don't start that today," he protested, fearing she was up to picking a fight. "We're too busy to fool with any unnecessary trouble."

Vera hopped off the barstool when she spotted Vendetta heading to the kitchen. "You don't feel me, Bullet, this is very necessary."

"Hold on, Vera!" he shouted, while trying to control his voice. "Damn, that woman's gonna get somebody hurt." He wanted to chase the bull traipsing through his china shop, but the drink orders continually rang in.

The waitress whizzed through the double swinging doors at the kitchen's entrance. She was in Vera's sights. Cooks and waiters took notice when Vera followed her prey into the frosty walk-in refrigerator. It was no secret that the two women couldn't care less for one another. Vera heard someone utter, "My money is on Vendetta. She's mean as hell," as the door closed behind them.

Vendetta spun on her heels. "What are you doing back here? Just because you sleep with the owner don't mean you get to harass the workers."

"Just like it's not any of my business who you

open your legs for, don't get to thinking who gets between mine is any of yours," Vera sniped in return. "I don't have time to play, li'l girl. I just want an answer to where I can get with Sin Johnson and I'm gone."

The waitress swung her hip to the side with one hand resting on it and a quart of salad dressing in the other. "Why should I help you do a damned thing when all you do is look down on me?"

"You can't think that. I put my ass on the line for you," Vera huffed, to remind the once wayward woman why she was not doing a major bid in prison. "I'm not asking for you to repay me, Vendetta. I'm simply asking for a li'l common courtesy."

"Good, because I don't owe you a damn thing," she smarted back. "Now you can do me the common courtesy of backing up out of my goddamned way."

Vera crowded her pathway even more then, daring her to make a move she'd regret. "Ohhh, by the way those veins are popping out of your neck you think you can take me? I ain't no pushover."

"And I ain't no punk," the waitress barked.

"Jump up and get beat down then," Vera threatened. She'd wanted to pop Vendetta in the mouth for a long time and this was her chance, especially since she wouldn't spill the beans of Sin's whereabouts. Vera drew back her right hand. Bullet ripped open the cooler door and caught her by the arm.

"Let it go Vera, Vendetta," he snarled. "I don't even want to know what's up, who started it or why. I just don't need it going down here. Vera, get on back out there." Bullet stiff-armed her when she prepared another plan of attack. "Vera, I done told you once. You shouldn't be back here in the first place."

Vera was shocked. She stared at Bullet peculiarly.

"You're a trip, taking her side." The cold glare in Bullet's eyes froze Vera on the spot. "Okay, okay. I'm leaving."

"You'd better run," Vendetta teased. "Next time your boyfriend ain't gonna be around to save you."

Bullet hustled Vera into his office and slammed the door. "What's gotten into you, Vera? You come up in here, my place of business, acting like it's a schoolyard?"

Seething, Vera cast her eyes toward the ground like a bad girl. "If you hadn't stopped me, I'd have mopped her ass up too. She should have told me what I needed to know and—"

"And nothing, Vera," Bullet protested. "Don't forget I own this place and I plan on keeping it that way. If you hurt that girl, it'll belong to her and her lawyers. Is hating her that important to you? You know better than anybody Vendetta's on probation. If she gets fired, there's no telling where she'll end up. Vera, I swear." He was outdone that she'd acted so selfishly.

"Not that it's an excuse, but I may have taken a case from a stone-cold cop killer. I think Vendetta used to run with the man who can tell me something about him. And when she tried to hold out on me after the chance I took for her, I wanted to slap some respect upside that cheap weave of hers. I'm sorry."

Pulling Vera close to him was as natural to Bullet as breathing, so he reached out his strong arms and drew her in. "Come here, baby. Why don't I talk to Vendetta for you?"

"Hellll, no!" Vera objected heatedly. "That'd be right up her alley, then you would be owing her. Hellll, no!"

"You've got a good point, Vera. However, I don't

want you to stay on this case if it's getting you
jammed up or second-guessing your first mind. You
can't think that about your client or you'd have
dumped him as soon as you suspected it. Can the
man, whose name you were about to beat out of
Vendetta, help you break it down?"

"I've got other ways of finding Vendetta's old
buddy. Shouldn't have to though," she said, pouting
for effect. "You've got a packed house out there. I'll
get out of your way and Vendetta's."

"That's my girl. Thank you for being the better
woman," Bullet cooed with a kiss.

"That's because I am the better woman," Vera asserted with utmost sincerity.

"Vendetta said that wasn't no weave," Bullet added,
while leaving the office. "Said something about being
part Indian."

"She was about to become an honorary Jackaho
until you stepped in. Okay, I'm going."

Vera left the restaurant as promised. The only
thing worse than a missed opportunity to beat down
her trifling rival was vacating the premises empty
handed. The list of hangouts she'd gotten from Cecelia didn't pan out either. After Vera called on several backroom dice parlors and local marijuana
dens, she found herself in the same predicament,
with no handle on what Warren Sikes was involved in
before his unfortunate demise.

Because Vera couldn't talk herself out of it, she
found herself pulling up to the home of Sharon
Sikes, where she expected to find the slain cop's grieving widow. The house was a step up as far as policemen's homes went, a two-story buff-colored brick
set-up with red shutters and trim. A sporty red Chrysler
coupe blocked a late model Mercedes Benz in the

driveway. At first glance it appeared that The Missus had moved on to a two-car family as well, until Vera read the name on a wooden placard nailed to the front panel of the house. *Sikes. The Missus hadn't remarried,* she reasoned. *Doesn't look like she's going it alone though.*

Vera knocked on the door for a few minutes then she beat on it louder when The Missus took her time answering. Suddenly and to Vera's surprise, a thin, fair-skinned black woman snatched the door open. She jeered at Vera before realizing that her visitor didn't scare easily or appear to be fazed by her attempt at warding off strangers. "Could you please not beat on my door? I do not except solicitations." She tried to cover her night gown with a housecoat but Vera had already seen it and made some definite observations. Sharon Sikes was a drunk and had probably been one for longer than she cared to remember. Bloodshot eyes centered in dark circles made that clear. This woman was a functioning alcoholic, who should have gargled with mouthwash before coming to the door.

"Good, because I have nothing to sell," Vera said eventually, while watching the woman's skinny hands tremble. She wasn't frightened, just behind on her liquor. "I'm Vera Miles, a private investigator. If you're not too busy, I'd like to ask you a few questions about your husband Warren."

"You could have called first," she grunted, before glancing into the house over her shoulder.

Vera didn't respond, blink or move an inch. She stared at the widow, with an intense gaze in her eyes. The thought of calling Mrs. Sikes for an interview didn't sit right with her. Vera discovered years ago how prior warning provided people the time to get

their lies straight. She was after pure and unadulter-
ated truth, the kind forced by showing up unannounced.

"I guess you're here now," Mrs. Sikes sighed, her
fingertips dangling nervously. "You may as well come
on in." It was painfully obvious that she experienced
a decent amount of agitation from being disturbed.
Vera picked up on another, more subtle, nuance
when the woman invited her inside. Sharon Sikes
hadn't gotten over her husband's sudden departure.
There was no other reason to explain her willingness
to discuss him while another man kept out of sight in
her home. Vera was certain of it once Mrs. Sikes returned from her bedroom with a pack of cigarettes
and a stiffer resolve. "So, what do you want to know
about Warren and who sent you?"

"Who employs me is highly confidential but I can
tell you that my next stop is the Federal Building.
There's a special agent on my investigation list," Vera
answered assuredly, in a tone so serious she actually
believed it herself.

"FBI?" she squealed, while flicking ashes into a ce-
ramic vase on the coffee table. "You think the feds
care that Warren's dead? He ain't any use to them
now."

"So he had decided to offer testimony?" Vera said,
as if she'd known it all along. "That explains why they
interrogated witnesses at the scene of his death."

Mrs. Sikes was deliberating now, whether to disre-
gard the marching orders from her bedroom associate and go after the answers to the questions she
hadn't asked for years. She sucked profusely on her
cigarette, then cocked her lips at the corner of her
mouth to exhale the smoke in the opposite direction
of her guest. "I went there, you know, to the scene," she

said eventually, with her eyes downcast and blank. "The next day, I went to the morgue first, but he wasn't there. How a place like that loses a body is beyond me. I couldn't have a decent burial for my own husband. The police department had this memorial service, you know. It wasn't nearly the same."

At a time perfectly scripted for waterworks, Vera didn't see a single tear fall from Sharon Sikes's eyes. "That's one of the questions I've been dying to ask you, and please don't take offense. You haven't changed your name, which wouldn't prohibit you from receiving Mr. Sikes's pension if you did. That leads me to believe you still love him."

The woman nodded slowly, then caught herself when reminded of a third party listening in. "None of that matters anymore, Ms. Miles," she answered sadly. "I was his wife, but gone is gone."

Vera had successfully lulled Mrs. Sikes into a false sense of security by exploiting a nostalgic love gone by. Her next question was pointed even closer to the heart. "Mrs. Sikes, it couldn't have been easy wondering if Warren's shooting happened like everyone, including the newspapers, reported it. I mean, that is why you showed up at the diner crying on your sleeve?"

The Widow Sikes clenched her teeth, once again torn over where to place her loyalties. "I'd been a cop's wife for ten years when the call came that I'd lost my husband. No woman wants to believe it'll be her phone ringing in the middle of the night." She lit up a second cigarette and inhaled deeply before pushing anxiety and smoke out of her body. "You can't imagine what I felt when no one had any real answers. Not the coroner's office and sure as hell not Warren's superiors. The blue wall went up and that was that."

Since the woman was on a runaway train with her

mouth wide open, Vera threw out a line of questions that begged to be asked. "Every cop's wife knows when he's in trouble on the job. I'm sure you knew about him agreeing to turn state's evidence. It must have been difficult being put aside when you needed answers the most?"

"You don't know the half of it. Warren was mad as a bandit one day, then the perfect mate the next. Yeah, I knew something was going on, I just never learned what exactly. Cops get real secretive like that at times. The police department brass didn't have two words to say when I told them his murder didn't look right to me."

"That's been bothering me, Mrs. Sikes. From what I hear you were playing the grieving widow but haven't sued the city, the cops or the county for misplacing your husband's body. If it had been me, I'd still be showing my ass."

The expression on Sharon Sikes's face could have melted ice. "How dare you question my love for Warren? He wasn't perfect but he was a good man and a good cop. I'd hate to mar his name or lose my benefits by causing trouble at police headquarters. Now, if you'd please leave, I'm done answering questions." Mrs. Sikes leaped up from her seat. She didn't look at Vera directly. Her shame wouldn't allow it.

"I understand how a woman's security plays a big part in what she's willing to put up with," Vera offered, while tossing a quick glance toward the closed bedroom door. "Believe me, I'm not one to judge." Vera left the moderately decorated home without asking a single question about Sikes's partner. She was interested to see how long the widow could avoid bringing him up as well. Considering how oftentimes partners shared secrets they didn't tell the wives,

Frank Draper's name should have come up at least once. When the slain cop's widow omitted bringing up the partner at all, Vera suspected there was more Mrs. Sikes chose to keep quiet about and that shame wouldn't let her reveal.

Fourteen

Vera stopped by the dry cleaners to pick up clothing after her chat with Sharon Sikes. It was two o'clock that afternoon when she arrived at her office building for the first time that day. Vera had just decided on taking a more aggressive approach and there were two ways to go about it—show up at Frank Draper's home and ruin his day like she did to Mrs. Sikes—or lean on Vendetta again to get Sin Johnson's whereabouts, despite Bullet's objections. She almost laughed when Frank Draper pulled his department-issued Crown Victoria behind her SUV.

The red-headed detective smiled as he stepped onto the sidewalk to greet Vera, who had two hands full of dry cleaning covered in plastic. "Vera Miles, we haven't actually met but I feel that we should have by now," he said, gesturing to carry her dry cleaning. "I'm Frank Draper, a narcotics detective with the city police, although I'm sure you knew that the minute I showed up."

"Yeah, I knew all right," Vera answered, trying to

determine how she would play the man who was undoubtedly trying to play her. She stood there, in a
non-committal stance, all the while watching his
every move. He grinned more than he should have,
as far as Vera was concerned. She never did trust a
man who shoved his big teeth in her face when he
should have come right out with what he had to say.
Draper was up to something and it didn't take long
before it revealed itself.

"Like I was saying, I feel kinda like we've already
met. With me spending seven years as Warren Sikes's
partner and you stomping around asking people all
sorts of questions about him, it would have been a
bunch easier if you'd have simply come and asked
me." There he went smiling again, that awkward fidgety smile that wouldn't have fooled anyone. It was
faker than a three-dollar bill.

Since the egg had been cracked, Vera had a split
second to settle on how to cook it. Seeing as how her
brains felt scrambled, she elected to keep it moving
with the white detective. "That's one way I could have
gone," Vera replied, while motioning toward her office door. "If I didn't want the truth, you'd have been
the likely candidate. Now, don't get bent out of
shape. I only meant that a cop's partner is always the
most likely candidate to lie on his behalf. Narcotics is
a tough job, Detective Draper. I wouldn't blame you
for covering Warren Sikes's behind, even after death.
When it's all said and done, a cop's reputation is all
he's got, isn't that the creed y'all live . . . and die by?"
She smiled to herself when his cheesy grin hit the
concrete.

"You seem to understand a great deal about loyalty
on the job for someone who's never been on the
force. I applaud that. I even respect it. Just tell me

why you're nosing around about my partner and whose dime you're on?" Vera ignored the question then slid her key in the lock. Draper crowded her in the door frame. He inched into her personal space and grinned again. "You need to watch your step when you're tracing someone else's."

"I'll keep that in mind," Vera groaned, while forcing the door open. "That's funny. It never stuck like that before." She studied the lock for a brief moment then went to put her cleaning down. Detective Draper was looking on when she discovered her office area was a wreck. Her file cabinet was overturned, documents were strewn about on the floor and every drawer was open. Someone had thoroughly ransacked the place. The way she looked at Draper indicated who she thought was behind it. "Oomph, I guess the cleaning lady has the day off." She chuckled.

"That's too bad, Vera," said the detective, with all of his teeth exposed. "There's never a cop around when you need one."

"Yeah, be sure to say hi to Mrs. Sikes next time you go jumping behind closed doors," Vera heckled, while staring him down until he backed out of the doorway with his hands raised in a faux defensive position. He'd gone out of his way to get under her skin and maybe uncover who she was working for. Either way, it worked. Vera was rattled. She locked the deadbolt and picked up the telephone receiver. Suddenly she slammed it down, fearing that the line had been bugged. Instead she pulled a small cell phone out of her handbag and pressed the number two on her speed dial. She was burning mad, feeling violated and pretty much pissed off. If Draper thought that trashing her office was enough to deter her, he had another think coming. When Glow picked up on the other end, Vera folded her arms defiantly. "Hey, this is Vera. Where are you?"

"I'm at home. Why, what happened?" Glow asked pensively.

"Nothing I can't handle. I thought you were supposed to be looking after Rags." Vera listened to a long bout of silence on Glow's end. "Glow, you there?"

"Yeah, I'm here. Sorry about that. I had to check on something," she uttered in a strained voice.

Vera, still trying to process the fact that someone trashed her place, was running short on good nerves. "Glow, this is the wrong time to trip, so don't play with me. Where in the hell is Rags?"

"Oh, he got tired of being led around by the nose so I put him up in a hotel not far from me. You know, the one on the tollway by that Cajun restaurant you like so much."

"Yep, I know that place. What name is he checked in under?"

"Mine. He don't have a last name or any real ID," Glow smarted back after being called out for sloughing off on her duties. "Don't worry about him, Vera. Rags has been sleeping like a baby. I got him a bottle of Hennessey and put his butt to bed. You won't have any trouble out of him."

"For the sake of us all, I hope you're right." Vera told Glow to get dressed and be ready to roll out in twenty minutes. She left the office like she'd found it, thinking of Ms. Minnie's words and the warnings of her ancestors. For the first time in four days she was glad her receptionist exhibited better judgment than she had and stayed away. Vera hopped in her vehicle, heading for Rags's hotel with her grandfather's voice in her head. "Baby girl, common sense ain't ever been all that common." The older she got, that tidbit of advice seemed to stand up that much taller. However that didn't make her feel any better about someone breaking and entering to prove it.

Vera did stop by the hotel to see about Rags and encourage him to hold on until she found Sin Johnson to satisfy her curiosity once and for all, but he wasn't anywhere to be found. His bed had been made, although the maid service hadn't gone over his room. Rags had gotten restless, fixed the bed as if he were at home, and then taken off. If he was in on the murder, Sin would have known about it. She was bent on finding him and closing this chapter in her life, hopefully without it being her last. Vera wouldn't stand for being pushed away from the truth any longer. It was time to find out one way or another. Learning whether or not Rags had anything to do with the tornado that blew through her office was sure to take a while longer to ascertain.

Glow was pacing the sidewalk in front of her apartment building when Vera wheeled around the turn. "Hey, Vera," she hailed from the cold cement. "They say it's gonna rain."

"Get in," was Vera's hurried response. "I don't give a damn about any rain, Glow. You told me you'd sit on Rags. Now, I don't know if he tore up my office looking for evidence or if Warren Sikes's partner had someone to do it."

"Sikes, that's the detective who got snuffed?" Glow asked anxiously, like his name finally meant something to her.

"Yep, he's the one Rags might've killed. And don't change the subject. I'm out here busting my tail and thanks to you we don't know what he's been up to."

Glow sat quietly, while taking her ribbing in stride.

She knew where Rags was the entire time and didn't feel like explaining anything to Vera. "I told you there were no worries about Rags," Glow asserted eventually. "Anyway, you didn't tell me somebody broke in your shop." She watched as Vera studied the road in front of her and the rearview mirror. "Who are you looking for now?"

"I don't know—nobody and anybody. I'm down to my last good nerve, though, that much I do know. Hell, Glow, I can't remember a case that I've worked for four days and still didn't know who the enemy was. I got a bad feeling about this one."

"What does that mean, a bad feeling?" Glow asked, hoping she wasn't suggesting anything negative about Rags.

"Meaning I'm a have to shoot somebody before it's done."

Glow leaned back against the vinyl seat, relieved. "Oh, then I'm good with that. You gonna shoot Vendetta? Because I ain't ever been able to stand her ghetto ass!"

"Uh-uh, can't pop her," Vera explained. "We need her for something big. Vendetta's got a line on Sin Johnson and won't give it up. Vendetta tried to front when I jacked her up in the cooler. This time, I'll run interference with Bullet while you stomp a mud hole in her behind."

Kicking back with an expression of satisfaction anchored on her face, Glow began to hum a carefree tune. "Backstabbers, hmmm, backstabbers." That was the one common thread Glow had against the woman she barely knew. Vera didn't trust Vendetta as far as she could throw her and disliked her even more. Therefore, Glow felt the same. That's what friends were for. Having a girlfriend who despised her nemesis on general principle came in handy during times like that.

When the ladies fell into The 3rd Round Bar and Grill, Bullet circled around the bar area, disapproving of Glow's presence in his place of business, as he put it. "No, no, no, not today," he fussed, waving his hand at Glow as if she was a mad cow not welcomed in the barn. "Vera, I know she's your girl, but we talked about this before." Bullet marched toward Glow until Vera grabbed him by the hand and led him toward his office.

"Baby, she ain't trying to cause no stuff up in here," Vera said, with her hands placed on Bullet's back. Once she had him to herself, behind closed doors, Vera put both hands down his pants. "Ooh, there's not a lot of room in there. Move that thing over so I can get my hands out."

"I know what you're trying to do, Vera," he complained. "And, it won't . . . whooo—work. Hmm, she's trouble, Vera. Glow is trouble, baby."

"Give me a minute and then you can tell me what you think about it." Vera unzipped his pants then pushed him down on the corner of his desk. "You think that door is locked?"

Bullet's eyes rolled back in his head. "Lawd, I sure hope so."

While Vera took care of Bullet, Glow made the best of an opportunity to do a number on Ven-detta. Inside the storeroom, things were getting heated.

"What, you think you're gonna do something to me in here?" Vendetta scoffed. "Your girl tried the same thing earlier and you can't find a scratch on my face."

Glow began to loosen her neck and shoulders like a boxer stepping into the ring. "Shut the hell up all that yapping and tell me where Sin Johnson is."

"Like I said," was all Vendetta managed to get out before she had been slapped twice and thrown on top of the potato sacks. Glow had a knot of the waitress's weave clutched in her fist and an ice pick at Vendetta's throat.

"Vera's a very busy woman with enough on her mind. She does not have the time it takes to fool with you. So, with that in mind, the words you say next just might be your last. Where is Sin Johnson?"

Vendetta deliberated over the severity of Glow's menacing intimidation. She closed her eyes then dropped the tough home-girl act when she realized it could have been the death of her. "Okay, I'll come out with it, just don't stick me with that pick. Sin is down there hiding from something in an old apartment complex in South Oak Cliff, on Overton Road. I can't say what the number is because he uses a few places at a time, but I can tell you how to go about looking him up."

"Why's a big-time dealer like Sin hiding? Who's he hiding from?"

"I don't know," Vendetta growled. "Everything I guess. Things done changed. He ain't a big shot no more."

"Okay then, that's good enough for now. Don't you feel better?" Glow asked, raising the heel of her palm from Vendetta's chest. "I know I do." There were two drinks sitting on the bar when Vera returned from her rendezvous in Bullet's office. Glow was calmly sipping from her favorite, a Long Island Iced Tea and urging Vendetta to hurry up with her friend's cranberry on the rocks. "I thought I made myself clear back there in the store room," she huffed. "Don't make me tell you twice."

Glow winked at Bullet once he'd gotten himself together and joined them. "Later, Bullet. I like your place. And Vendetta makes one hell of a LI iced tea." She and Vera sauntered out the front door like they owned the joint. Vera listened as Glow informed her where to look for the former prime-time dealer and how he had a predilection for Fat Man's Pizza, a large pineapple and chicken with pan crust.

Before parting ways at the curb near Glow's home, Vera thanked her. She insisted that Rags be found and followed again as quickly as possible. His chaperone agreed as she climbed down and shut the car door. "Don't mention it and don't waste any time on that. I know just where to locate Rags," Glow told her. "Go on and settle this so I'll know what I'm dealing with." Vera was at a loss as to what Glow had intimated but she sounded absolutely convinced that she had everything on lock. There was no arguing with her. Vera was just as thick-headed herself, so it was fairly easy to see where she was coming from.

Fifteen

Residential traffic began to thicken as Vera exited the freeway at Ledbetter Road on the south side. She took a left and headed east, traveling deeper into a vastly minority populated area which forty years earlier was relegated to "Whites Only." Rows of small wood-framed homes littered the landscape as far as the eye could see, with a few old and bewildered apartment complexes dotting the busy thoroughfare every other mile or so. Vera tried to imagine a time when Blacks and Hispanics were beating at the gates with aspirations of moving into the community but couldn't. The same neighborhood, now infested with prostitution, teen-aged pregnancies and rampant drug abuse featured scores of their offspring clawing for the chance to get out.

Sinton Johnson was partly responsible for the colossal decline of the once inspired community. For a time, he managed a notorious band of drug dealers, pushing crack to working class parents and school children alike. Oddly enough, Sinton was revered by those whose lives he ruined and dreams he stole. When Vera considered that, she thought long and hard about what she'd do if she found him. Men like him were brazen wolves who deserved to be hunted down and disposed of. How Sinton Johnson escaped that fate was beyond her. Lord knows he deserved it.

Per Vendetta's directions, Vera located the Fat Man's Pizzeria where Sinton supposedly ordered the same unusual pizza pie combination at least twice a week. It would take some posturing to get what she needed from the manager and Vera was prepared to shake it out of him if push came to shove. "Hey, tell the manager someone wants to see him," she requested boldly, in her best sister-from-downtown business voice. A young man standing behind the register finally acknowledged her.

"Yes, ma'am," the teenager answered quickly, with a resounding amount of respect in his voice.

Vera surveyed the restaurant's dining room, salad bar and an employee dealing dime bags of marijuana near the restrooms. She smirked when the young man saw her. He alerted his customer to move along when she continued to stare him down. Vera didn't usually give a flip about small time pushers, but there she was, getting angrier by the second over a gateway pot transaction. It was as if nobody cared for the great promise which was lost and the repercussions that reverberated throughout because of it. From that moment on, Vera was determined to find Sinton.

"Yes, I'm the manager here—Lester Parish," said the squat-built black man, with a receding hair line and dread locks dangling from the back of his head like stringy doll hair. He studied Vera while trying to bluff his way out of whatever stress she was bringing to his door. Vera remained quiet as she faced him, his arms folded, his demeanor surly and hesitant.

"And I'm Vera Miles," she offered eventually. "I received a tip that some of your employees are using this restaurant to push narcotics."

His eyes narrowed because of the way she phrased her words. "You're not a cop," the man said, uncertain of his statement.

"I'm investigating something bigger than you got going on here. If I get what I need from you, I'm a memory," Vera answered without addressing his question. The power of suggestion worked from time to time. Her bluff was stronger than his.

"I could deny any wrong goes on with my knowledge. Besides, it's just weed, you know."

"You sound like a man who should be read his rights. How much time do you think you'll get when these young punks roll on you? After they've been in the hole for one night without video games and cell phones, they'll be fighting each other over who'll give you up first."

It didn't take the manager a split second to decide which route to take. "Come into my office," he offered immediately. Vera followed the round-headed man down the corridor to a small alcove barely big enough to fit a desk and chair inside. He motioned for her to enter behind him. "Shut the door," he told her evenly.

"You're smarter than you look, Lester," Vera scoffed. She didn't have anything against him particularly, other than his use of underaged employees as drug distributors. "Do yourself a favor and keep up the act. Tell me where you deliver pizzas to Sinton Johnson."

"Sin . . . Johnson," Lester muttered solemnly, like

it was the name of a beloved warrior killed in battle. "Sistah, you must be doing dope yourself. Ain't nobody around here been near Sin. He's in too deep with the law and that makes him invisible. I don't have time for games. Now if you're here to shake me down, just say so. I ain't with the runaround." The manager had grown more mad than scared. Vera knew then he was telling the truth.

"Let me see your order receipts for the last two weeks," she said, going on Vendetta's tip. When the manager paused to figure out where she was headed with his receipts, Vera pulled her jacket back to reveal her .38. "Go on now, pull 'em down off that shelf." He nodded apprehensively then grabbed a black plastic three-ring binder.

"What kind of cop are you anyway?"

"The best kind, one that was never here if I find what I'm looking for," was her response. It must've sounded good to Lester, because he took a seat then shrugged his shoulders, waiting on instructions.

"All right, tell me what to do."

Vera separated two bundles of pink-colored delivery tickets. "Check those and I'll rummage through this set. You've been making chicken and pineapple pizzas for a man who lives in the area. Unless you have more than one customer who orders it at least twice a week, they've all been called in by none other than," she started to say before being cut off.

"Sin Johnson, I'll be damned," he said awkwardly. "Wow, lady, I can't believe it. I'd have remembered that name."

"Just check your stack. If anything else jumps out at you, tell me. I'll be out of your hair as quick as I can." Vera watched the stumpy man thumb through the thin sheets of paper like a bank teller counting money. Obviously he'd sorted through them often and kept the delivery copies on hand to discourage thefts by his drivers, explaining how they'd been jacked after selling the pies wholesale to their friends and family.

"Miss, ain't no Sin Johnson here at all," Lester informed her. "I took out the orders for chicken and pineapple, all phoned in by the same customer. Hmmm," he grunted. "This fella's got three different addresses, though. Says the name is Warren Sikes."

Vera dropped her bundle on the desk when she heard the name of the slain police officer. She almost smiled when it occurred to her that Sinton still had his legendary sense of humor, using the name of the man whose death he'd caused. No one would ever think to go traipsing in a black ghetto for a white man who'd been dead for two years. Vendetta said Sinton was hiding, that explained why he jumped apartments periodically. Now she had three places to search, three good places. She thanked the manager for his assistance and assured him that if he did get busted, the call wouldn't come from her. With a heavy dose of gratitude, Lester sent her off holding a special pizza pie with his compliments.

The sun was setting as Vera parked by the curb near a run-down building on the main drag. Since no one had answered when she knocked at one of the other two addresses on her list, Vera had a fifty-fifty chance to fall in on Sinton without someone tipping him off. The problem was both of the remaining apartments faced one another across a narrow courtyard and he could have looked out of the window to see her if she made the wrong selection. She caught a break when a woman scantily clad in a short sweater dress two sizes two small and over the knee boots exited the staircase near the end of the hall. "You on the stroll?" Vera asked, to be certain she was approaching a prostitute and not just some resident with bad fashion sense.

"That depends on who's asking?" the dark-skinned lady asked, with a curious expression.

"I'm asking," Vera replied, while holding the pizza box as if it were a tray of gourmet delights. "Are you working or not? I ain't got all day."

The woman sucked her gold teeth then adjusted the dress riding up her full thighs. "I ain't either. Time is money after all." That was her way of admitting to the oldest profession known to man. "What you got in mind? I can get with some girl-on-girl action."

"Well, I can't, so you need to back that up. How about you tell me something I don't know and I pay you for your time nonetheless? What do you charge for a date?"

The woman scratched at her red wig then gave Vera another once-over. "Sure you don't want to talk things over up at my place?"

"Hell, yeah, I'm sure. It's nothing personal but I'm running late as it is." Vera smiled cordially as not to offend the hooker. The lengths to which she had to go to get an answer for Rags had come to this, flirting with a streetwalker.

"I usually get thirty bucks to lockup with females. Paid in advance," she added, with her hand out. Begrudgingly, Vera slapped forty in her palm. "Cool, what you want to know?"

"Which of those apartments is Sinton Johnson staying in? And don't lie because don't nothing go down in the hood without working girls knowing about it."

"You're right, we keeps the four-one-one on things. He's been staying in that one over yonder," she answered politely. "How about you drop that box off and come see me about your change from this forty?"

Vera waved her off and pulled her gun. "Uh-uh, you should get gone. This might get ugly." Before Vera crossed the dirt courtyard, the prostitute was in the wind. Poised with a pizza box in her left hand and a pistol in the right one, she tapped the barrel of the gun lightly against the door with 2G stenciled on it. Vera held the box in front of the window when someone peeped out of the crease in some of the filthiest drapes she'd ever seen.

"What you want?" someone asked, while purposely staying out of sight.

"Got a pizza, man," she barked rudely, "Say here it's for Warren Sikes."

There was a string of silence on the other side of that door before the knob turned to open it. "I don't 'member calling for no pizza," came the answer from what appeared to be a disease riddled old man on his last leg. "It's right on time though. I didn't want to get out in the cold tonight."

Vera stared at him, a shell of a man too sickly to be a detriment to anyone but himself. She nearly apologized for barging in on the wrong apartment until something in the frail man's eyes spoke to her. "Sinton Johnson?" she called out, in a sorrowfully subdued tone. "Sinton Johnson, that is you." She couldn't believe her eyes. His once smooth skin was dry and ashy; all of his appeal had faded away. The ostentatious drug dealer who often boasted of having been in more women than a retired gynecologist had diminished into a diseased cripple. Vera hadn't seen a great deal of AIDS victims although the toll it had taken on Sinton seemed uncharacteristically devastating. Her heart sank into her stomach. All of the vile insults she wanted to level him with vanished into thin air. The flamboyant, good-looking ladies man she despised had become a humbled weak skeleton afraid of his own shadow. His dark sunken eyes dimmed even more when it finally occurred to him that Vera wasn't the pizza delivery lady.

Sinton took a deep breath then gazed at Vera's hand holding the gun. "You come here to kill me? Go on ahead and get it done." After Vera holstered her weapon, he lowered his head and shuffled back inside the poorly furnished hovel he camped in for the time being. Vera stood at the open door uncertain which way to proceed. "If you ain't gonna shoot me, bring that pizza in here. I'm hungrier than a hostage." Vera entered the small one-bedroom rental, holding her breath as much as she could. The stench of urine was overwhelming. "Put that box on the coffee table and tell me why you came after me. I hurt lots of people. You one of 'em?" He puttered around in the kitchen area, in a pair of brown run-over house slippers for a moment before returning with paper plates. Vera passed on dinner, respectfully.

"Sinton, I didn't know about the . . ." she uttered compassionately, feeling that his nickname seemed cruel at this point in his life.

"The bug," he said for her. "Yeah, I got it bad. I probably passed on worse than I got. Most of my old friends is gone." He slowly reached in the box for a slice. His eyes brightened when discovering it was his favorite combination. "How'd you know what I liked?"

"Sinton, look, I'm sorry to impose. I'm a PI and I

looked you up because of the brick wall I'm against concerning a shooting from a couple of years back." Vera still couldn't believe how low on the ghetto totem pole he'd fallen. Mixed emotions circled in her head about going forward with her questioning. However, she had jumped through hoops getting to this point. "Sinton, you were an informant for Frank Draper and Warren Sikes, the man whose name you're using."

He steadied his paper plate on his knees and wiped at his mouth with a dirty napkin. "Yep, I snitched for 'em. Sikes is dead though."

"Did you kill him, Sinton?" Vera queried, softly. He took his eyes from hers, shook his head then nibbled at the corner of the slice like a baby bird. "You know who did, though?"

"Wish I could help, but no," he whispered, like a repentant soul. "I was the one set him up for the fall." Sinton went on to explain how he, Sikes and Draper were all on the Guzman drug cartel payroll. He remembered how sweet life was with police protection and more money than he could spend. Eventually, he informed Vera that things got gritty when Frank Draper got too greedy. That's when all hell broke loose. Warren Sikes caught wind that Draper wanted to cut him out of the association and bring in another cop with a smaller share of the profits. Sikes had been seen having meetings with an attractive black woman, who turned out to be an FBI special agent. "After he started getting cozy with that agent, Yogi Easterland, we agreed he had to go," Sinton said. "Holding up that diner wasn't my bag at all but it did the trick."

Vera hadn't ever been closer to learning what actually happened and who pulled the trigger. All of her snooping culminated in the very next question. "Who put in the work?"

"All's I was supposed to do was run up on that cracker jack diner and stick a gat in the lady's face, so Sikes 'n' 'em would be the first police to show up. I wasn't in for killing no cop until Draper said he would handle the tough stuff."

"And did he?" she pried.

"I made it around the corner and was on my way when I heard two shots. Something told me to just keep right on moving but I had to see it for myself. Quick as I could, I poked my head out and saw it. Draper was leaning over him in the street. Even though the rain was coming down pretty good, I could tell that Draper had his hands over his partner's mouth. When that waitress chick started screaming, I booked out of there. I didn't find out for a month that Guzman put out a half-million-dollar hit on Sikes. I think the onliest reason Draper didn't take me out was because I never asked for my cut and let him keep it all to hisself."

"Is there any chance a third person was in it with y'all?" Vera asked on Rags's behalf.

"No way, couldn't have been nobody else. In the road, under the street lamp was Frank Draper shoving that smoking gun into his coat pocket. Wasn't nobody else could have done it." Sinton told the truth, as he knew it, although he didn't actually see the shooting. There was a slight chance that Rags could have been a party to it without Sinton having known. Either way, he was all talked out and wanted to be alone with his dinner. Vera left him with his favorite pizza and run over house shoes. She said so long to the contempt she'd felt for him after deciding it wasn't worth the effort and Sinton couldn't have cared less either way. He had enough troubles living with his declining health and personal pitfalls.

Sixteen

As Vera pulled away from the curb near Sinton's apartment, she held a clenched fist up to her mouth. She wouldn't have had the words to describe what she'd witnessed if her life depended on it. Not only did she leave with an indelible picture of a dilapidated man tattooed on her brain, Vera also left with two major holes in her case. Every time she grew closer to locking the case airtight, another gap turned up like a bad penny. There wasn't one eyewitness to the police officer's shooting and no death certificate existed to authenticate Detective Sikes's murder. If only his body had stayed put long enough for the medical examiner to pronounce him dead on arrival at the hospital, but no such luck. Someone had to go and snatch it; or was it something else instead? With a sick feeling in her stomach, Vera remembered what Sinton said about Sikes's turning state's evidence and working with the FBI. The next and only logical place to go for further information concerning the missing body was the agency that had nothing to do with the crime but couldn't seem to stay away from it.

Vera slammed on the brakes then hit a U-turn several blocks from downtown. Rush hour traffic poured out into the streets as nine-to-fivers made beelines toward the freeways while she sailed past them in the opposite direction. "Yogi Easterland," she said into her cell phone when someone answered on the other end. "My name is Vera Miles. Please tell her it's important." The operator asked Vera to hold after explaining it was after hours. Vera turned her lip upward smirking at the idea of federal agents punching a time clock.

"Special Agent Easterland speaking," hailed someone who sounded professional and tired.

"Oh, hello," Vera said, when the woman took her call sooner than expected. "You don't know me but I think we really need to talk. I'm a private investigator with one question no one has been able to answer."

"May I ask why you think I'm the one who can?" asked the agent, again professionally standoffish.

"Because I just left a funky ass apartment rented by Sinton Johnson where he told me you were chummy with a narcotics officer named Warren Sikes who got himself clipped before you could pimp him to roll on his partner and the Mexican drug lord Bolda Guzman," Vera rattled off quickly, leaving no doubt how serious and tired she was. Her chest heaved out while waiting on the agent's response.

"If your objective was getting my undivided attention, you succeeded. Surely you know where to find me, Ms. Miles. How quickly can you get here?"

Vera killed the motor in the parking lot across from 1 Justice Way and stared at the FBI regional headquarters building in front of her. "I'm already here. Meet me in the lobby."

"Will do," agent Easterland replied sharply, "One thing. Unauthorized firearms are not permitted. I'll have to ask you to leave yours behind."

Smiling wearily, Vera sighed, "Will do."

A heftily built security guard greeted Vera at the door, waved her through a metal detector then signed her in at the reception desk. She collected her purse, after he'd rifled through it. It was a mere precaution, she assumed, so she didn't argue. When Vera snapped her bag shut, she heard someone call out her name. Expecting an FBI agent with a line-backer's frame, she turned toward the elevators. Vera found it difficult to hide her surprise. The woman with an outstretched hand was gorgeous. Her sleekly fitted navy slacks were tailored, Vera guessed, and her button-down blouse had to have been plucked from a designer store rack. At nearly Vera's height and two sizes smaller, Yogi Easterland looked like a fish out of water. Her cinnamon-hued skin was flaw-less and full-bodied shoulder length hair put Vera in mind of a fashion model playing a role. Although she would have been considered more cute than pretty, the agent gave her visitor an inferiority complex. "Yogi Easterland," she said, after a thorough once-over.

"Yeah, come on up, Vera," the attractive woman replied, with a firm handshake. On the elevator ride to the sixth floor, Vera chuckled to herself or so she thought. "Something funny?" Easterland asked, her hands situated on her narrow hips like they were nailed there.

"No, it's just that you weren't what I expected. Uh-

uh, not by a long shot." Easterland's hands fell to her sides as her defensive smirk faded likewise. "Sorry, but I bet you get that all the time."

"You don't know the half of it," she confirmed lightly. "This is our stop." The elevator doors opened to a command center. Computers and cubicles lined the floors throughout. Several agents, all of whom resembled well-dressed insurance salesmen, fiddled with telephones and paperwork. Each one was oblivious to Vera's presence.

"Wow, this is it, huh?" she marveled. Vera knew that anything she wanted to know about anybody could have been accessed via any one of those computers. "Nice." She followed the agent into a glassed-in office then took a chair opposite her at a desk cluttered with files. Moments after they were both seated, Easterland shrugged silently.

"Like I said on the phone, you got my attention, now what?"

Vera wrestled to get comfortable in her chair. She frowned, leaned forward then slumped back in her seat. "Agent Easterland, can I call you Yogi?" The agent nodded that it was okay. "See, Yogi, I'm working for a man who thinks he's killed someone. He has these terrible dreams replaying it in his head. Only thing is, I've busted my rump trying to find a gunshot victim fitting the bill." Vera explained what Rags told her about the overweight white man he believed himself to have shot and that Sikes was the closest to a possible match.

"So," Yogi said, shrugging again. "What does that have to do with you ending up in Sinton Johnson's rat's nest and how does that factor into my business with Warren Sikes, Frank Draper and Bolda Guzman?"

"That's what I came here to ask you," Vera told her, with a befuddled expression. "I've exhausted every possible lead, one right behind the other, and your outfit keeps coming up on the tail end. I know you visited the diner involved with Detective Sikes's murder. I know you interrogated the EMT who pulled him off the streets that night and later hustled to the morgue searching for the body." Vera was bluffing on the last tidbit of information but it made sense that the FBI wouldn't take anyone's word that Sikes, their prospective witness, was dead. They were more thorough than that.

"You almost had me, Vera," Yogi said, chuckling under her breath, "then it occurred to me. If you knew for a fact we were at the morgue the night Warren Sikes got dropped, you wouldn't be sitting here now or have subjected yourself to, as you put it, Sinton's funky ass apartment, now, would you?" She let out a deep sigh, staring out over the illuminated Dallas skyline. "Before I tell you what you really want to know, it needs to be crystal clear that what I divulge is strictly off the record. You were never here."

Vera was sitting then, alert and salivating for what had eluded her the entire time she'd been working on Rags's behalf. "Understood," she said, agreeing fully.

Agent Easterland clasped her thin fingers together, settling them on her desk. "First of all, none of this is any longer privileged information because the case involving Sikes, his partner Frank Draper and Bolda Guzman was dropped when the old man fell on a knife, seventeen times. Guzman's younger brother got tired of sitting on the sidelines watching Bolda have all the fun. I guess you could say he took over the family business." It was Vera's turn to shrug, when she failed to grasp what Yogi's story had to do with her case.

"And that affects my client how?"

"I'll lay it out, then you can draw your own conclusions. True enough, we were dogging Sikes's steps. He was on our witness list and about to leave his cheating wife to flip on that dirty partner of his when he was wounded." The crafty agent let the last comment float in the air trusting that Vera had the wherewithal to take it and run. She grinned when Vera did exactly that.

"Wounded?" Vera queried, with her brow furrowed. "You said wounded, not killed." That was the first time she'd heard anyone say without one-hundred-percent certainty that Sikes was dead, real dead.

"Yes, I did," Yogi acknowledged. "We tried to stay close to Sikes, knowing there was a leak in our department. Guzman had deep pockets, deep enough to get at one of our own. There was a hit out on Sikes, a big one. We were set to grab him ourselves and stash him in a safe house until the trial, then he went down." Vera's mind was working overtime. She closed her eyes to get a clearer picture.

"Are you saying that Sikes didn't die and that you still have him? With Bolda Guzman off the chopping block, he's not worth much anymore. Hmmm, at least that gets my client off the hook."

"Well, it's a bit more complicated than that," Agent Eastland said matter-of-factly. "This is where things get tricky." Yogi fixed her eyes onto Vera's like a snake charmer, with a straightforward and compelling gaze. "Not long after Sikes's body was taken to the hospital, we located him, mainly to check his clothing for vital information, mind you, then I saw his eyelids flutter faintly. There were so many automobile accident victims needing attention that no one noticed me and my partner wheeling him to the back freight elevator. I made a call, had Sikes transported to another hospital and operated on as a John Doe."

"So that nobody would know if he survived?" Vera concluded correctly.

"Now you're catching on. Miraculously, Warren Sikes pulled through by the skin of his teeth. Because we didn't know who to trust, after the life-saving surgery, I had him transported to a hideaway in the country for safekeeping. There're a lot of people capable of murder when the price is high. We even went to great lengths to conceal his identity. It was my idea to requisition plastic surgery on Sikes's face. He wasn't a bad looking guy but we couldn't take any chances."

"So what did you do with Sikes once Guzman got clipped?" Vera asked, following the story as best she could.

"Someone must have discovered where he was. We had two agents babysitting him when they were lured back to the city with manufactured orders. They left him in the safe house alone for five hours before learning they were duped. When they returned, Sikes was a ghost. No one's seen him since."

The smile on Vera's face ached it was so big. "Thanks, Yogi. Now there are two people I know who're going to sleep a lot easier tonight. I owe you even though I was never here."

"I'll remember that," Yogi replied softly. "It's funny how the police never caught on to our little ruse with Warren Sikes. You must be one heck of a P.I. to get this far."

"I try," answered Vera. "Lawd knows I do try."

"It's a shame about Warren Sikes though. He was very good with his hands," the agent added, as she thought back on a time past. When she caught Vera looking at her sideways, she backpedaled quickly. "Oh, not like that, Vera. While his face and wounds were healing, he made these intricate origami animals out of one-dollar bills, even with his entire face bandaged. It was the most peculiar thing."

Vera thanked her newest associate, then caught the elevator going down alone. She grinned again thinking how Yogi would have been thoroughly impressed with what Sikes could do with one-hundred-dollar bills. Telling Rags that he hadn't killed anyone didn't come close to the kick she planned on getting when sharing what she didn't go to FBI headquarters for and didn't hear first hand from Yogi Easterland. It was almost laughable the way Vera had been chasing her tail when the answers to Rags's nightmares had always been right in front of him. The laughing stopped immediately once Vera had settled into her car, shoved her gun back in her purse, and put on the turn signal to exit the deserted downtown parking lot.

The thunderous sound of glass shattering from her front passenger window nearly caused her heart to seize. Instinctively, she threw her arm up as tiny fragments of glass flew her way. Vera grunted with her other hand clutching the steering wheel. "Ehhhh, get out! Ggget Ouuut!" she screamed, clawing at Frank Draper's arm.

He tossed Vera's purse on the floor board then shoved his pistol against her temple. "Shut up and drive, bitch!" he growled. "All of your goddamned snooping around ends tonight. I'd just as soon put a bullet in your head right here but you're gonna take me to the man who hired you."

With her gun inside the bag on the floor beneath Draper's legs and his revolver pointed at her, Vera had to think fast. She couldn't lead him to Rags even if she wanted to because she had no idea where he was. If there was going to be any bullets flying, Vera wanted a shot at leveling the odds. She clenched her teeth and pretended to do as instructed. "Okay, just keep that cannon out of my face. I'll take you where I'm supposed to meet with him. It's a little ways but he'll be there, at a bar called The 3rd Round."

Seventeen

On the way to Bullet's restaurant, Vera pondered several ideas to get Draper out of her vehicle and warn Rags about him. Since none of them included getting shot while trying to escape, she held her mind in check and a watchful eye on a loose cannon. The parking lot was stacked with patrons there to watch the college football special pitting two highly ranked teams. Somehow a busy collection of strangers made Vera feel safer. Perhaps they could have caught a bullet or two meant for her. At least Draper wasn't as likely to pull the kind of stunt that resulted in getting his own partner gunned down in the streets. Vera was counting on that when the dirty cop escorted her through the front door, with his gun hidden under his jacket.

"Get cute and get dead," he barked venomously.

"I'm not stupid and neither are you," was her answer to his callous threat. Draper was filled with desperation and Vera prayed it hadn't poisoned his brain. Going off half-cocked with beer-guzzling bystanders looking on was almost inconceivable, almost.

Vera took the last available seat at the crowded bar area among scores of football fans adorned in Texas Longhorn burnt orange paraphernalia, locked onto the big screen televisions and cheered an early touchdown against the rival team. The detective stood behind her, on the lookout for anyone who appeared out of place.

"Where is he?" Draper whispered in Vera's ear, just as Bullet returned from the storeroom with a stack of beer mugs. He paused. Seeing his woman all cozied up in his bar with a strange white man practically body-checking her was anything short of believable.

"Hey, Vera," he said cautiously, after setting the extra mugs aside.

"Bertram," she answered sharply. No "Bullet" or "baby," but Bertram. The restaurant owner and former boxing champion was thrown for another loop. The only time Vera had called him by his given name happened when she thought they were going to be parents. Come to think of it, Bullet surmised, she was scared then, too. He tossed a quick glance at Draper and considered beating him to a bloody pulp on the spot. Vera saw the rage of emotion building inside of Bullet.

"Hey, Bertram, it's kinda tight in here tonight. Can you get me my usual, two fingers of Jack Black with a coke back." Now Bullet was extremely concerned. Vera's usual was cranberry juice on ice or a glass of wine if she really wanted to let her hair down. Hard liquor had ruined too many lives too close to her. She'd never go for it. Not in a million years. If Vera was making sure he got the message she was in trouble, message received.

"Yeah, I got that," Bullet said with a hitch in his voice. "You want me to break out the old stuff. I know you like a stiff drink with some age on it."

"No, thanks," Vera replied, calmly chewing on her bottom lip. She'd read his every thought and warned against his reaching across the bar to break Draper's neck. "That'll be good enough for me. Want to see what my friend is having?"

Bullet stared at Vera's menacing white shadow then forced a smile. "And what can I get for you, sir?"

"I'll have what the lady's having," Draper ordered. "Double down on the Jack Daniels, neat."

Noise in the bar ebbed and flowed with the activity on the tube. Each time the customers roared with exhilaration or groaned disappointedly, Draper's anxiety rose. "I thought you said he would be here. If this is your idea of a joke, I'm not the humorous type."

"You don't see me laughing either. He'll show. Look, I need to use the restroom," Vera informed him just as their drinks hit the bar. She reached for her purse while stepping off the bar stool. Draper opposed her leaving his sight. He rested one hand on her bag then grabbed her by the arm. Vera snatched her arm from his grasp. "I wasn't asking your permission. I said I've got to use it."

"Go on then, but hurry back. I'll stay here and watch your purse."

"That won't be necessary."

"Oh, I insist," he snarled politely.

No one but Bullet seemed to notice what could have been an everyday lover's spat. He was fuming. "Is there a problem?" he shouted pointedly, above the noise. Vera slid something from the leather bag into her pocket when Bullet added the diversion she needed.

"No," Draper replied, realizing his tiff with Vera was causing a scene. "Just a misunderstanding is all." He forced a smile then motioned for her to go ahead. Vera cast a scowl in Draper's direction as if he'd outsmarted her. He settled down on the stool she vacated and raised his glass. "I'll be waiting right here."

"I'm sure you will," Vera hissed before winking at Bullet to put him at ease. She headed down the stairs then disappeared in the hallway toward the restrooms. When Vendetta passed her, with tray in hand, she stopped to give Vera a piece of her mind. Before she had the chance, Vera had sprinted off toward the exit.

Draper sipped on his drink for a few minutes longer than he should have. When it occurred to him that Vera had been gone a while, be became fidgety. After looking over his shoulder then at his watch repeatedly, he leapt off the barstool then headed in the same direction Vera did several minutes before. He stuck his head into the ladies room but a frightened woman screamed at him to leave. Draper saw Vendetta on her way into the kitchen. "Hey, do me a favor. I came in with a lady but she hasn't come out of the restroom. Can you check for me?"

"Unh-unh, I've got tables and people waiting on me," she refused. "Maybe your date wants some private time."

Draper pulled a twenty-dollar bill from his pocket. "Here, take this. I just want to make sure she's still in there. She's a tall black lady named Vera."

Vendetta tucked the money into her apron before handing out the bad news. "Sorry, mister, but Vera ain't in there. She hustled her fat butt out the back door about two minutes ago. She's in the wind by now."

The detective's mouth was wide open when he returned from the alley empty. Draper bolted back to the bar area to find Vera's purse gone. He ranted loudly while racing through the front door in time to see the SUV he arrived in speeding out of the parking lot. Vera had left the vehicle idling by the front door where she waited patiently for Draper to strike out searching for her. Once he did, she ducked in to seize her handbag then tore out to make a swift getaway. She left him standing at the vacant taxi stand waving his hands in the air erratically. "That's what you get for calling me a bitch," she spat angrily. "Think about that while you're walking home, punk!"

Vera hit the Interstate interested to know how long Draper had been tailing her and what he'd learned about her investigation. It was obvious that he knew something, although it wasn't nearly as apparent what. He'd risked his career coming after her and his health when marching her into Bullet's bar the way he did. He couldn't have known about Rags or who he was because he would have come out before now, she reasoned. Speaking of Rags, she had to find him immediately and convince him to blow town just as he arrived, very quietly.

Vera called Glow's home and cell numbers but no one answered, so she decided to cruise over to her apartment building and wait. She was relieved when she parked at the curb. Glow's lights were on inside her apartment. Vera jogged up the stairs to bypass the elevator. Huffing and puffing, she knocked at the door, then even louder when it seemed that Glow would rather not tend to it.

"Open this door, girl!" Vera shouted. "I'm standing out here about to pass out."

When the door opened, Glow fastened her silk

housecoat with a pink belt. She cleared her throat before welcoming Vera in. "Uh-hmmm, why didn't you call first?"

"You cannot be serious. I called until my fingers went numb but you didn't pick up once, heffa." Vera peered over her shoulder to see if anyone were lurking about. She entered the den yapping about business until she recognized business and pleasure had been intermingled to suit Glow's taste. "I thought I told you to sit on Rags. How in the hell . . ." she fussed, as Rags exited the bedroom stripped down to his underwear. Vera's eyes flitted back and forth from his cotton boxers to her girlfriend's skimpy negligee. "What the hell," she reiterated disappointedly. "I know I said to sit on him, but damn. I'm out there ditching bad guys and you're popping off a freak fest with my client."

"Hey, Vera," Rags spoke eventually, slightly embarrassed. He would have been considerably more self-conscious had Glow not spent a few hours loosening him up.

"You shut up," she told him, "and Glow, me and you, we'll deal with this later."

Glow folded her arms defiantly. "Whatever. You did say sit on him and I had to make sure he wouldn't try to leave. Well, he ain't trying to go nowhere now."

"Glow, please! Rags, we've got to go. Get your pants on if you can find them," ordered Vera. She noted how the nasty looking surgical scars on his chest and back made a lot of sense. She'd seen other dead men who didn't make it off the operating table with their souls intact, Rags was the first.

While Rags searched for his pants, Vera explained to Glow what she'd gathered over the past four hours and why she felt compelled to get her strange bedfellow off and running. Glow listened attentively, shocked at Vera's new revelations, the latest on Sinton Johnson and how she cleverly shook the evil Frank Draper at The 3rd Round. Even though Vera made her promise to stay put by the phone, Glow had already started making her own plans. She kissed Rags on the cheek and told him that he was twice the man he thought himself to be. He blushed, turning beet red.

"If y'all are finished playing *Guess Who's Coming to Dinner* we should go," Vera grunted in the doorway. "Remember what I said, Glow. Stay put and answer the damned phone. I might need you later."

"Girl, I hear you," she quipped with attitude. "'Bye, Rags," Glow sang like a gluttonous mistress. The tall cowboy tipped his hat and grinned politely.

Vera cocked her head in utter disbelief. Rags acted as if he were stoned. He hadn't said two words since she showed up. "I see that the cat's got his tongue, but how long has he been like this?"

Glow was blushing then. She leaned against the door and sighed. "About as long as he's been here. He doesn't do his best talking with words necessarily, if you get my point."

With her eyes locked on Rags's satisfied grin, Vera recognized it. She sneered at Glow. "Yeah, I get your point all right, trifling cow," she said jokingly. "Just better hope neither of y'all traded something you can't get rid of."

Rags wore that stupid albeit satisfied grin all the way to Vera's SUV. When he saw the shattered window, he stopped cold. "What happened to your truck?"

"Oh, now you got something to say? Shut up and get in, lover boy," Vera teased. "There's a place you need to revisit." Vera kept quiet about the news that was busting to get out. Rags knew she was on to something and almost blew a gasket when she not only refused to share it yet, but added insult to injury by demanding he pipe down so she could think. "There are some things you just don't blurt out," she told him, in a way he'd understand. "Hold still a while. Trust me, it'll keep." Rags chewed on his fingernails until they parked in front of Vera's office. When he started around the rear of her truck, she stopped him. "Uh-uh, over there," she uttered, motioning toward the Leftovers diner across the street.

"But I'm not hungry," he whined, like a cranky child. "Just tell me what you dug up and I'll be all right."

"You'll be more than all right and full off what I'm about to feed you." Obediently, he followed her. Like a ghostly scene from an old movie, rain began to fall much like it did the night of the shooting. Vera eased further beneath the restaurant awning to stay dry. Instinctively Rags moved in closer to hear her out. "This is going to be a lot to swallow so try and relax until I'm finished." After he gulped nervously, she started in. "It was a night like this one. You know why rain always comes down by the bucket in your dream? Because that's the way it happened when a police detective named Warren Sikes was killed, right over there." Vera pointed at an imaginary spot in the road, unsure exactly where the attempted murder ruse played out, although an educated guess was close enough.

"Linda Klaus was the waitress who called in a holdup. Sikes and his partner Frank Draper responded very quickly to the call—too quickly. They chased the robber on foot, up that away." Vera studied Rags's eyes intermittently, waiting on a sign of recognition to show itself in them. "Both cops were dirty. A sizable contract was taken out on Sikes by a very wealthy Mexican drug lord, Bolda Guzman. Sikes's partner set up the whole show to make it look as if he'd gotten killed in the line of duty." Rags's eyes were red and blank. He was listening but none of it registered so Vera continued. "Susie Chow, an emergency medical tech came to help but she figured it was too late. She told me how nobody could have survived the blood loss from the shooting but she was wrong. Sikes's body was mistakenly taken to the back dock of the county hospital, where they take the Dead on Arrivals. Covered in blood stained sheets, Sikes's was laid on a gurney waiting for his turn to meet the coroner, until the FBI agents he was plotting with to flip on his partner and Guzman found him, half dead but hanging on by a very thin thread." Rags gulped again. He was more apprehensive than he could have imagined.

"Good thing that Sikes fella was a fighter," he mused, when it felt like the right thing to say.

"You don't know how good a thing that is," she asserted. "Listen up. A Detective Beasley told me there was an Internal Affairs investigation looking into the death of the slain cop."

"But I thought you said the Feds saved him?"

"The cops don't know that," she confirmed, with a raised brow. "The Feds plucked him right out of hell's gate, got him fixed and prepared to suit him with a new identity. Guzman wanted proof of Sikes's burial before he'd call off the dogs." Vera could see that Rags's pulse was racing. "Don't stress, Guzman's kid brother croaked him shortly after Sikes disappeared. That's right, the Feds lost him. Seems he up and walked away before they got him to turn on his drug buddies. There're only three people who know where he is tonight: you, me and my girl Glow."

Rags frowned as he ran the series of events around in his cluttered mind. Again, Vera watched as the wheels spun. His mouth popped open like a man who'd been sucker-punched in the stomach. "I hear what you're saying but I can't believe it. It's too much."

"I'm sure it is and that's why I had to get you here. Turn around, look into this window and then close your eyes. What was the last thing you saw?"

"Light, a reflection, my reflection," he answered slowly.

"Yeah, and that's one of the last things Warren Sikes saw before two shots put him down." Vera felt a haunting chill skate up her arms and down her spine. "You said the man in your dreams, Sikes, was saying something like "Why?" He knew the only person who could have shot him in the back was his partner. What he couldn't understand was why? You were going to roll on him. Draper knew that. He had to take you out first. The reason you came to me," she said, with a pregnant pause attached, "seeing the sign on my building from flat on his back was the last of Warren Sikes's memories, dead or alive."

"Bravo," Detective Draper chuckled, as he stepped out of the shadows near the building's edge. He cocked his service revolver, wielding it at Rags. "That was one hell of a story. Too bad nobody else is going to hear it. Get across the street before I drop you both." He aimed the barrel of his gun at Rags. "You know I'm good for it. Ain't that right, Warren?" Rags stared at Draper, the pistol in his hand, and the predicament staring him in the face. He still found it hard to comprehend.

"You shot Sikes?" he asked somberly. "You tried to kill me?"

"Yeah, yeah, yeah, Tex," Draper rattled disparagingly. "Let's get along now or I'll be forced to plug you again."

Vera noticed how steam had covered the inside of the diner windows, like the restaurant manager said it had when the robbery took place. That's why no one witnessed the shooting that followed and why no one saw them being held at gunpoint now. Reluctantly, Rags headed for the street. Vera stalled. "Don't be in such a rush, Warren. Some things never change. He's going to kill us, you know. After he gets what information he thinks we have."

Draper snarled. He shoved the gun into the small of Vera's back. "Another county heard from. Who told you to say anything? I still owe you for the trick you pulled at the bar."

"I still owe you for that bitch comment," was her heady comeback. "And I always pay off. That little stunt of mine was nothing. For manhandling me and busting my car window, I'm gonna mess you up." On the outside, Vera appeared harsh and unscathed. Inside, she counted her every breath, praying the next wouldn't be her last.

Eighteen

Once inside Vera's office, Draper held a weapon on Rags while he tied her up with twine. Fear saturated the room. Wet from walking in out of the rain, Vera whispered to her client not to be a chump or it would be the end of them both. When Rags scanned the room for something with which to attack Draper he felt a sharp pain racing through the back of his head. His former partner had clapped him with the butt of his pistol, sending Rags tumbling down to the floor.

"Why'd you have to do that?" Vera squealed. "You might have killed him."

"No, I just lulled him a bit. He'll come around but he's going to have one hell of a headache."

Vera squirmed as Draper propped Rags in the chair next to her. Within minutes, Rags was bound with both arms constricted. Because he didn't shoot them right away, Vera was certain of Draper's plan to walk away with what he'd come for, incriminating evidence against him. She clawed at the ropes around her wrists, trying to loosen them. Draper sorted through boxes of files he'd ripped through previously, thinking he'd missed something. Had he known Vera committed everything to memory that Rags told her, he'd have executed them already and then slinked away clean.

"Where is it?" Draper barked, time and time again. "You've been to the firehouse, talking to that goofy chick who took Warren away. You've been meeting with Donald Beasley too. Yeah, I saw you. What did you tell the Feds tonight, huh? I should have popped you before you had the chance." As Draper searched throughout her desk for a second time, Vera felt violated. Fear that previously had a hold on her relinquished its grip. She was filled with anger now. There wasn't any room for panic.

"You always been the type to go through women's things?" she asked, purposely antagonizing him. "Hey, Draper, is that your bag? I keep extra underwear around too. Wouldn't that be more your speed? Cops and perps are a lot alike, both torn by their sickness within." Draper kicked over a grandfather's clock standing against the wall. It was the one decent piece of office furniture Vera owned. "Maybe I was all wrong about you. Violence, that gets you off, huh, Draper? I know a lot of cops who get a kick out of hurting women. Sharon Sikes, she like it rough?"

When Vera struck a cord by bringing Warren's wife into it, Draper charged her with his hand raised in the air. Vera winced as he hovered over her. She yelled out before planting her size ten boots in his groin, Draper toppled over at her feet. "Ahhhh, you bitch!" he wailed loudly, writhing in the fetal position. "I'll kill you."

Vera wrestled with the twine feverishly, kicking at

Draper to keep him down. "I told you about that bitch stuff," she heckled, scooting her chair closer to him. "I'm not ready to die tonight. I'm going shopping tomorrow." Draper staggered to his knees, raising his pistol at Vera. She rocked the chair back and forth, then threw herself against him. Vera, the chair she was tied to, and Draper all went tumbling on to the carpet. Vera sank her teeth into his chest. He fought to push her off. Draper bellowed in pain but she wouldn't release the hunk of flesh she'd bitten down on.

"Ahhh, let me go!" he demanded furiously, working to pry her mouth from his ravaged nipple. Vera managed to hold on until Draper began pounding on the top of her head with his fist. Eventually she fell off, her eyes watering. The crooked cop howled. His chest heaved in and out while he massaged the patch of skin, bleeding through his shirt. "I knew I should have snuffed you out that day you came to Sharon's," he babbled sorely.

Vera's eyes crossed. She was woozy and disoriented. "You want me to turn my back so you can do it now, punk? Coward!"

"See, that's where you're wrong about me. I want to see your face when I blow it off." Draper cast a devilish grin, raised his gun then steadied it.

"What about the money, Frank?" Rags interrupted, his voice low and hoarse. He'd regained consciousness like the man who clunked him said he would, with one hell of a headache.

"So the dead has risen," Draper mocked. "I'll deal with you next."

"You'll deal with me now," Rags replied firmly. "Ouuuch, what did you hit me with?"

"Don't worry about that. What money are you talking about?"

"Yeah, what money are you talking about?" asked Glow. She had eased in behind Draper and pressed a sharp blade against his throat. "And don't let your ego get you twisted. If I have to go to slicing, you won't get to be the same fool twice," she threatened. "Vera, are you all right?" Glow shouted, when her friend began to groan on the floor. She scraped the blade against Draper's neck to nick him. "Man, I ought to split you wide open."

"Unh-unh," Vera grunted. "Not unless you have to. He's a cop."

Draper chuckled fiendishly. "Finally, somebody's talking sense. My whole department is going to be here in a minute. I called for backup."

"Frank never calls for backup," Rags smarted. "Vera was right, some things never change. Ol' Frank never did like other cops around his action. Then he might have to share all that he finds. Huh, Frank?"

"Warren, Warren, Warren," Draper said, still holding his gun on them. "Always the sap. Let's see how this plays out. She takes me down and I get you."

"That suits me fine," Glow hissed. "This scalpel guarantees you don't make it. Who knows, Rags might. But, in case he doesn't, somebody's gonna tell me about the money he was offering when I came in." Glow liked to get her kicks. However, she was an opportunist after all. "What gives, cowboy?"

"Glad to see you too, Glow," he said, slightly disappointed with her tone. "Me and Frank here, we made over three-hundred grand working for Guzman. We had a safety deposit box. I took the money and hid it the day I learned he was sleeping with my wife."

Glow manufactured a fake frown. "Rags, you're married?"

Vera sighed heartily. "No, but Warren is."

"Ohhh, Rags," Glow sang, playing along. "You've been talking in your sleep, sugar, but you didn't say nothing about a wife. Oomph, and after all we meant to each other. Now I really don't care if he shoots you."

Draper's eyes blinked rapidly, he was deciding on what to do but delayed while he thought it over. "If I hadn't heard it, I wouldn't have believed it. Warren Sikes in the flesh." Beads of sweat rolled down his forehead and into his eyes. "Look at him. The Feds sprung for his new face, new body and new life. Huh, taking two slugs from me was the best thing that could have happened to you. All the booze and blow you sucked in, that old sad sack you tried to pass off as a body wouldn't have lasted another year. Fifty pounds ago, you weren't hardly worth a damn. I did you a solid, Warren; where's the gratitude? You were better off dead."

"Then that makes two of you," chided Special Agent Yogi Easterland, with her shiny automatic handgun locked in on Draper's head. "I just missed busting you when the Guzman family ties got in the way of business, then later got in the way of Bolda's breathing. What do you say, Frank? You've got one choice really, to help me take down Bolda's younger brother Raphael or not. After what I heard you admit to, you're looking at life for attempted murder of Warren Sikes, whereabouts unknown." The federal agent smiled when showing her appreciation for Rags's help and for a second chance to do right by him.

As Glow tightened her grip on the sharp blade, she glanced up at Yogi. "Nice suit, glad you finally made it. I could save everyone lots of trouble by doing this jerk right now. Warren Sikes is dead and won't nobody cry over this one for going the same way."

"Okay, okay. I'll take the Fed's deal," Draper stammered nervously. He flung his gun across the room then threw his hands up. "I know where Raphael's smuggling drops are and when the shipments come in. Please, just stop this crazy broad from sticking that thing in my neck."

Agent Easterland turned her gun on Glow and shrugged her shoulders. "What do you think, Glow? You did call me to help sort this out. I would really owe you big time if you turned Draper over to me. I've got two units waiting outside. He'll keep his part of the bargain. I promise you that."

Vera sat up on her elbow. "Come on, Glow. I'm okay. Stop playing doctor and drop the scalpel."

Glow considered her options before working the means to justify the ends. "Easterland," she growled. "Me, Vera and the cowboy, we walk away clean but what about the money, the three-hundred thousand these two racked up?"

"Money?" Yogi said with a pretend puzzled smirk. "What money?"

"Yeah, that's what I hoped you'd say." Glow lowered the blade from Draper's throat. He clutched at his neck then crawled toward Yogi. "Take him, Special Agent Easterland, he's all yours."

Draper was handcuffed and taken away. Glow used her shiny manipulator to cut through Vera's ropes. "Tell me where it hurts, then I'll tell Bullet for you," she joked. "Sit up here and don't move until I get some ice from the diner to put on it." Next Glow turned toward Rags. "What's this I keep hearing about you having a wife?" She was very happy to see both of them alive and just as thrilled to be coming into some money on the back end of a very bizarre case. Vera peered over her office. Broken furniture littered the floor and hundreds of papers were tossed about. It hurt a bit when she thought about the way things turned out, but for once, everyone got what they had coming to them and her client got what he needed.

Rags went home with Glow and slept for two days. Although his rest was uninterrupted by terrible dreams, he continued to talk in his sleep. Glow listened to every word. When he awoke rested and hungry, he was reunited with the steel box which she personally dug up in Warren Sikes's backyard. Glow went on to share how she almost informed his wife that she should be expecting a petition for divorce but thought better of it.

"What wife?" Rags chuckled. He rubbed the knot on his head when his own laughter caused it to hurt. "Warren is history and Rags is single."

Glow giggled while pulling off her clothes. "Hee-hee, that's what I hoped you'd say."

Bullet scolded Vera for excluding him in her plans to shake Draper at the restaurant. He didn't care how it ended, reasoning that she should have asked him to solve her problem. Just like a man, he felt left out and useless. That is, until Vera felt up to her old tricks, all of which included him. She apologized in every way she knew how. Bullet found a way to forgive her after each one.

One week later, Vera and Rags settled up. He offered to give her a third of the loot but she wouldn't accept more than fifty thousand. Rags hugged her tightly at the bus station. He was determined to leave town the same way he rode in, on a slow Greyhound so that he'd have time to think. Frank Draper was right about one thing in his summation: Warren Sikes was better off dead than alive. Yogi made good on her long-standing promise to provide Rags with a new identity. With his past tucked in his back pocket, he looked forward to loads of easy sleep from then on.

*Enjoy the following excerpts from
Victor McGlothin's latest novels*

Available now wherever books are sold

Down On My Knees

1
Flextime with Tyson

Grace Hilliard sauntered into the lobby of the Hotel Carlyle just as she had done once a month for the past year. Her canary yellow skirt swayed in step with her confident strut. An impish grin danced on her full lips when the doorman stopped dead in his tracks to inventory the most attractive curves he'd seen all day. Upon stepping inside the elevator, Grace turned around slowly, wearing a self-assured smirk befitting a woman who was quite accustomed to drawing attention. She wasn't in the least bit surprised when she noticed that the doorman hadn't moved an inch from the very spot where his curiosity had rendered him defenseless. He had seen Grace on several occasions, gliding past with a patented, carefree ease that accompanied her like a silken shadow. Regardless of how often he'd viewed that perfectly framed picture, the way she moved captivated him every time.

Although Grace was attractive in her own right, including being blessed with radiant skin, the deepest shade of chocolate conceivable, she would have been categorized as overqualified in the assets department compared to America's flawed idea of beauty. Fortunately, she wasn't the kind of woman who wasted her time trying to live up to fashion-industry standards. She was way too busy working her shapely size twelve like a part-time job to give it much thought at all. Grace wore self-confidence as if it were a badge of honor. In fact, she was honored to be a proud black woman, although she'd discovered wearing that particular designer label was at times as much a blessing as it was a curse after having to deal with male business associates, who rarely knew how to manage a working relationship to benefit both parties involved. She had discovered for herself some time ago that manipulating circumstances as a means to an end offered better results when it wasn't personal, but rather for the sake of business. Because of her strong work ethic, Grace didn't allow anyone to confuse one with the other under any circumstances.

Likewise, Grace wasn't the type to become disillusioned immediately following casual, albeit mind-blowing, sexual acrobatics. After experiencing her share of disappointment, she understood the high cost associated with permitting her emotions to climb into the same bed she shared with a man that wasn't hers. "Check your emotions at the door, girl," Grace whispered softly, to remind herself, whenever tempted by the silly notion that casual sex, no matter how physically rewarding, ever resulted in anything other than what it actually was, fun and games.

That's exactly what Grace had in mind with Tyson Sharp, the epitome of fun and games, sensual bliss, and good times, when suddenly, her purse began to vibrate. She slid her hand inside the brown leather tote bag dangling from her manicured fingertips. While fishing around inside it, her heart rate quickened. "Oops, that is not a cell phone," she chuckled quietly, after discovering that it was another battery-operated device vying for her attention instead. She flipped the "off" switch and then wrestled it back to the bottom of the bag. "Got to be more careful. Ain't that right, Big Mike?" she said jokingly. No sooner had she stepped off the elevator onto the ninth floor, than her bag started up again with another chorus of "Good Vibrations." This time, it was the flip phone summoning her.

"Hey you," Grace cooed seductively into the tiny handheld. "I'm running a bit late, so I knew you'd be calling. How did I know? Because you always get impatient when you want some. Yes, I do like that about you. Huh? What else? Oh, don't trip; isn't being my sex slave good enough?" Grace strolled down the long corridor leading to room 921, their favorite pleasure nest, where Tyson was undoubtedly undressed, cocked and ready for her arrival.

"Hey, I'm here. Yeah, right outside," Grace confirmed, anxious and aroused. "What, you want me to knock? All right then, get your naked self out of that bed and open up."

When the door swung slowly from the inside, Grace tilted her head to catch a glimpse of what wasn't concealed behind it. "Ooh, is all that for me?" she asked, knowing that it was.

Tyson's smile widened. "Every inch. Just tell me how you want it," he answered cunningly, with the same dose of spirited verbal foreplay that Grace had initiated. As he hung a DO NOT DISTURB sign outside and locked the door, she leaned against the mahogany armoire to watch him. Tyson's muscles seemed to gather together in all the right places when her eyes traveled his entire body. She studied his dark skin, deep set dark brown eyes, sculptured arms and thighs, washboard abs beneath a developed chest, broad shoulders, and the tightest butt she'd ever seen. And as usual, Grace blushed seductively with her gaze trained on the talent.

Imagining what the opening act would be when the talent show began, Grace became giddy with anticipation, knowing that sooner or later Tyson Sharp always got around to doing what she liked best of all. Today, however, Grace was hardly in the mood for appetizers. She slipped out of the skirt and let it hit the floor, noting how Tyson's eyes narrowed when they landed on her thighs. "What you looking at?" she teased as he took two measured steps toward her.

"Everything I see," he told her convincingly.

"Tyson," Grace whispered urgently, her white silk blouse falling onto the cloth-covered chair near the thick drapery. She fell back on the bed, pulling Tyson down with her. "Mmm, what are you going to do to me?"

"That thing you like," he answered softly, tracing her body with his soft lips and fingertips. "That thing that keeps you running back to me."

Grace caressed his bald head gently until the irresistible urge to guide it between her legs refused to be denied. "Ooh, yeah, that's it," she moaned passionately. "That's it. That's what I want."

Of course, Tyson knew exactly what Grace wanted, as well as how she wanted it. He'd made time in his busy schedule to get away from a thriving financial services business to do just that, before she returned the favor with unrivaled proficiency. While Tyson was a brilliant money manager, drop-dead gorgeous, and generous to a fault, at age thirty-five, he had yet to grow into the kind of man who possessed the maturity required to look past his own accomplishments in order to applaud someone else's. He wore shallowness like the impeccable designer suit tailored to perfection that hung in the hotel-room closet. Other than that, Tyson Sharp was a single woman's dream, and a married woman's fantasy.

Hours after receiving more of what she wanted, Grace was staring at her own reflection in the large rectangular bathroom mirror, once she'd wiped the steam away with a bath towel. She opened the miniature makeup kit she'd brought along, then paused to get a glimpse at what a single and satisfied woman looked like after an afternoon rendezvous with one of Dallas's finest bachelors. Grace ran her fingers along the ridges on her supple breasts, admiring how they were still holding their shape and fullness after thirty-six years. Then she giggled quietly when she noticed her hair sticking up in a hideous telltale just-got-laid fashion. She quickly made herself presentable, collected her clothing, and exited the lavish den of sin, with Tyson sleeping off the aftereffects of Grace's naughty nimbleness. The thought of snuggling up next to him zigzagged through her mind, but she chased it away before it caused her to do something stupid, something emotional, something she would have regretted. Grace had to remember that flextime with Tyson was simply an exercise in futility, nothing more. Besides, she was already up against Friday evening traffic. She was forced to hurry to make it home in time for dinner with the one true love of her life, her thirteen-year-old son, André.

It was half past five when Grace zoomed out of the hotel parking garage. During the thirty-five-minute drive home, she grew increasingly uneasy. Having feelings of culpability and exhilaration, an edgy twinge gnawed in the pit of her stomach. As she pulled into the driveway of her two-story buff-colored brick home in a well-to-do subdivision, it occurred to her that she had forgotten to pack a spare pair of panties. In such a hurry to make her scheduled appointment, it didn't cross her mind until then.

Grace parked her Volvo SUV in the garage and entered through the laundry room, with intentions of slinking past André undetected. She tiptoed around the cherrywood dinner table and eased into the mouth of the hallway leading to the master bedroom. When it appeared the coast was clear, Grace quickly realized that the jig was up.

"Hey, Ma," André said loudly, with his hands fastened to the controls of a PlayStation video game, his elbows resting on his bony knees.

Grace smiled awkwardly as she entered into the den. Deliberately, she moved directly behind the evenly brown-hued teenager when she answered his standard salutation. "Hey, yourself," she replied pleasantly to the gangly boy evolving into a young man before her eyes. "And what did I tell you about that 'Hey, Ma' stuff?"

André continued wrestling with the video-game controls until he realized what she'd said. After placing the joystick on the coffee table, he climbed off the walnut-colored sofa. Grace panicked when he approached her from the opposite side of the broad sectional. "Where are you going?" she stammered, fearing the inevitable.

"To say hello proper, like my mother taught me."

Grace wanted to back away as he reached out for her, but she couldn't think of an acceptable excuse for doing so. "You didn't have to get up," she said, in an exasperated tone. "All I expected was a sensible acknowledgment."

"I know. That's what I got up to do," André told her, with a warm embrace. "How's that?"

"Uhh, very refreshing actually," she answered, then immediately changed the subject before her peculiar behavior was called into question. "So would you like to go out later, or should I whip up something for dinner?" Suddenly, André leaned away from his mother, wrinkled his nose, then sniffed the air.

Oh my Lord, Grace thought to herself, hoping to high heaven that her child didn't recognize the remnants of grown folks' business or have a clue what she'd been up to on the other side of town.

"Mom, you smell kinda funny," he said as he continued sniffing around her. "Kinda like those stinky little soap bars from that hotel on the San Antonio Riverwalk that gave me a rash."

Frozen in her humiliation, Grace played it off as best she could. "Don't be silly, Dré. I haven't been anywhere near San Antonio." She was thoroughly relieved that he hadn't learned enough about life to ask whether she'd been anywhere near a hotel. Immediately following a narrow escape, Grace snatched up the telephone and hit "2" on the speed dial to order a pizza. Then she slid into the shower again to rinse away the incriminating evidence. While languishing in her solitude, a single tear streaked down her cheek. It occurred to her that André was no longer the boy she'd said good-bye to that morning before heading off to work. His senses were sharpening, and there wouldn't be many years left to offer motherly advice or see to it that his homework was completed to her strict specifications. She wasn't prepared for André's ascension into manhood or having to increase her level of cleverness to get around his impending understanding regarding her indiscretions with men. Grace remained in the shower for quite some time to conceal her sadness and troubled soul with undeniable traces of gratuitous sex hiding just beneath it.

Borrow Trouble

Chapter 1
Night Train

Ａ tortuous evening of bowing and shuffling had gotten the best of Baltimore Floyd, just like a one-armed boxer's desire to climb back into the ring got him knocked out every time. Flashing that cheesy grin he hated had left the smooth tan-colored drifter with a mean streak thicker than train smoke. Smiling back at countless blank faces of discouragement while serving a host of ungrateful, highbrow travelers in the last two dining cars on the Transcontinental Steamer had him wishing for better days and easy money. In the winter of 1946, times were hard. That meant tips didn't come easily, and come to think of it, "please" or "thank you" didn't, either. Hearing the train's whistle blow when it crept slowly across the Missouri state line put an awkward expression on Baltimore's face, one that almost slighted his charmingly handsome good looks. Agreeing to sign on at the railroad company as a waiter for an endless collection of snooty voyagers, with nasty table manners and even worse dispositions toward the Negro help, was simply another in a string of poor decisions plaguing Baltimore, who was a professional baseball player hopeful mostly, and a man with troubles certainly.

He'd seen nothing but rotten luck during the past month. The worst of it had happened when the gambling debt he couldn't pay off came haunting around his rented room to collect at about three o'clock in the morning. Two pistol-toting "go-getters" is what Baltimore called the hired thugs who broke down the door at Madame Ambrose's boardinghouse, aiming to make him pay the devil his due or else send him straight to hell if he couldn't. It was a good thing the lady with the room directly across the hall from his didn't like sleeping alone, or he'd have been faced with meeting the devil firsthand that night. With three dollars in his pocket, every cent of it borrowed from the gracious neighbor lady, Baltimore had lit out of Harlem when the sun came up. He'd hitchhiked south, with a change of luck in mind and a bounty on his head.

Unfortunately, the change he'd hoped for was slow in coming, and his patience was wearing as thin as the sole on his broken-in leather work shoes. That awkward expression that welcomed Baltimore into Missouri melted into a labored grin when his best friend, Henry Taylor, a sturdy, brown-skinned sack of muscle, popped into the flatware storage room, balancing two hot plates weighed down with porterhouse steaks, mashed potatoes, and green beans. Henry, just as tall as Baltimore and substantially brawnier, presented the dinner he'd undoubtedly lied to get his hands on or outright stole, while maintaining his professional, "on the time clock" persona. His black slacks held their creases, the starched white serving jacket was still buttoned up to the neck, and his plastic Cheshire cat grin, which the customers always expected, made a dazzling appearance.

"Dinner is served boss and not a moment too soon," Henry announced, once the door was latched behind him.

"You ole rascal, I don't care what you had to do to come up with this meal fit for a king, but I hope your eyes was closed when you did it," Baltimore teased, salivating over a dinner much too expensive for the likes of them. "I can't wait to get my hands on—," he started to say before hearing a light rap against the other side of the storage room door. "Here. Put the plates in the bread box, Henry," whispered Baltimore, fearing another waiter wanted to share in their late-night treasure. Some of them were unscrupulous enough to make waves by reporting thefts to the crew supervisor if they didn't get a cut.

"Shut that cupboard door all the way so's they can't smell the taters," Henry mouthed quietly as the light tapping grew into more insistent knocks.

When Henry opened the storage room door slowly, he was surprised to see a white face staring back at his. The man, who appeared to be nearing fifty, was fairhaired, with pale, blotchy skin. He was thinking something behind those steely blue eyes of his, Baltimore thought as he leaned his head over to see who was disturbing the first decent meal he'd had in a week. "Sorry, mistuh, but the dinner car's been closed for hours now," uttered Henry, guessing that was what the man wanted. "We's just putting the dishes away."

"Either one of you boys interested in making a few dollars, fetching ice and fresh drinking glasses for me and some sporting friends of mine?" the intruder asked, fashioning his remarks more in the manner of a request than a question.

"Naw, suh, I'm . . . I'm really whooped," offered Henry in a pleading tone.

"Hell, naw," was Baltimore's answer. "We's retired for the evening, done been retired, and besides, you don't see no *boys* in here." Venom was dripping from his lips after slaving deep into the evening only to incur some middle-aged white man getting between him and a four-dollar plate of food, with an off-the-cuff insult. "You best get on back to those sporting friends of yours," Baltimore added when the man didn't seem too interested in budging.

Henry swallowed hard, like always, when Baltimore got it in his head to sass a white man to his face. He swallowed hard again when this particular white man brushed back his green gabardine jacket just enough to reveal a forty-four-caliber revolver.

"Yeah. You'll do rather nicely," answered the man in the doorway. He was leering at Baltimore now and threatening to take his bluff a step further if necessary. "Now then, I'd hate for us to have a misunderstanding. The head conductor might not like that, especially if he's awakened to terrible news."

Baltimore squinted at the situation, which was brewing into a hot mess he'd have to clean up later. He was in deep because he'd already decided just that fast to lighten the train's load and teach the passenger a lesson about respect he would take to his grave. Considering that the train wasn't due to arrive at the Kansas City station until eight a.m., only a fool would have put his money on that particular white man's chances of breathing anywhere near 7:59. "Well, suh, if'n you put it that way, I guess I'm your man . . . uh, your boy," Baltimore told him, flashing the manufactured beaming smile he was accustomed to exhibiting when bringing customers their dinner bill. "Just let me grab a bite to eat, and I'll be along directly."

"You'll come now," growled the uninvited guest. "And button your clothes. You look a ruffled sight," he added, gesturing at Baltimore's relaxed uniform. "I'll be right out here waiting."

"And he'll be right out, suh, right out," promised Henry, pulling the door closed. "Baltimo', what's gotten into you? That's a white man, and he's got six friends in that pistol, waiting to do whatever he tells 'em to."

"He ain't gonna shoot nobody," Baltimore reasoned as he fastened his serving jacket, huffing beneath his breath. "A stone killer does the doin' and don't waste time on the showin'. I'll be back tonight. You go on and have at my supper, too. Ain't no use in letting it get cold. Be too tough to chew then, anyway."

Henry put his face very close to Baltimore's in order to get his undivided attention. "Ahh, man, I know that look in your eyes, and I hate it. You got trouble in mind, but you told me you was through with that sort of thing."

Baltimore sighed as he eased a steak knife into the waistband of his black work slacks and pulled the white jacket down over it. "Don't appear that sort of thing is through with me, though, does it? Think of me when you eat my share. It'll make me feel better knowing you did."

Waiting impatiently in the aisle, the insistent passenger raised his eyes from the silver coin he'd been flipping over his knuckles when Baltimore came out of the tiny closet, holding a stack of glasses on a round tray. "Good. I was starting to get concerned about the two of you." The man was fond of the joke he'd told, so he chuckled over it, but neither of the black men found it amusing in the least. Both of them saw a dead man pacing in the other direction, wearing an expensive suit and a brown felt hat, and playing an odd little game where the stakes were dreadfully high. It was a skins game, Baltimore's favorite. Killing the white man on their way to the smoking car crossed his mind, but he suspected there'd be money to be had at the end of the night, maybe a lot of it. Before he chased those demons away, he told them to come back later, when he'd have need for them.

"I'm going to say this only once, so pay attention," the man grumbled. "When we get inside, I don't want you to speak, cough, or break wind. There are some very important people in there, and they won't stand for an uppity nigger interrupting their entertainment," he warned Baltimore. "I'll give you ten bucks for your time, when I'm convinced you've earned it." When Baltimore's gaze drifted toward the floor, the white man viewed it as a sign of weakened consent. He had no idea just how close he came to having his chest carved up like the porterhouse left behind in the flatware cabin. "Good," he continued. "Don't make me sorry for this."

"I'm already sorry," Baltimore wanted to tell him but didn't. Instead, he played along to get along, but soon enough he found himself wishing for a seat at that poker table. As the night drew in, and the smoke from those fancy cigars rose higher, so did the piles of money. Baltimore had learned most of the gamblers were businessmen heading to Kansas City for an annual automobile convention. He'd also discovered that the man who'd coerced him into servitude went by the name of Darby Kent, and for all of his gun-toting rough talk, he was the sorriest poker player this side of the Mississippi and spitting out money like a busted vending machine. Darby often folded when he should have stayed in, and then he often contributed to someone else's wealth when everyone reading his facial expressions knew he had a losing hand. After three hours of fetching and frowning, Baltimore was really disgusted. The way he looked at it, Darby was shoveling over his money, the money Baltimore had planned on relieving him of after the fellows were finished matching wits.

"Darby, looks like a bad run of luck," one of the other men suggested incorrectly. It was a run of overgrown stupidity.

"I'll say," another of them quipped. "Gotta know when to say when." After watching Darby toss back another shot of gin, he shook his head disapprovingly. "On the other hand, if you don't mind fattening my wallet, I won't, either." That comment brought a wealth of laughter from other players sitting around the musty room, smelling of liquor, sweat, and stale tobacco.

"I'll agree that the cards haven't exactly fallen in my favor up 'til now," Darby said as he grimaced. "Perhaps I could use a break." He laid the cards on the table, next to a mountain of money Baltimore guessed had to be close to ten thousand dollars. "Come on, you," Darby ordered his reluctant flunky, while motioning for Baltimore to collect his serving tray and an extra ice bucket.

Leaving all of that loot behind was like pulling teeth, but Baltimore forced himself to walk away.

Had he not been confined to a moving train, there would have been a golden chance to stick up the card game and make a fast getaway. Unfortunately, there wasn't a hideout to dash off to afterwards, so the idea passed just as quickly as it had entered Baltimore's head. Baltimore fumed every step of the way he followed behind Darby, staggering and sullen. He was mad at himself for not going with his first mind to end their arrangement before Darby had all but opened his billfold and shook out a big stack of money for the better-suited players to divide amongst themselves.

When they reached a nearly depleted icebox inside the abandoned dinner car, Baltimore began filling one of the wooden buckets. Darby steadied his shoulder against the door frame to light up a cigar. He huffed and cussed that he should have been more conservative with his wagers.

"I'm beginning to think, maybe I've taken those other fellows too lightly," Darby opined openly, as if Baltimore gave a damn what he thought. Tired and angrier now, Baltimore sought to put that silly notion to rest.

"Say, Darby, lemme ask you something," Baltimore said, seemingly out of nowhere. He was facing the man while holding the bucket firmly at his side with his left hand, keeping his right one free. "Do you always lose your ass after showing it? I mean, you have got to be the dumbest mark I've ever seen." Baltimore watched Darby's eyes narrow disbelievingly after hearing a much cleaner diction roll off the black man's tongue. "See, the way I figure it, you resort to pattin' that pistol of yours when men like me don't step lively fast enough. I'll also bet the ten dollars you owe me that you're all bark and no bite.

Ain't that right, suh?" Baltimore added, showing him how black men were skilled at adapting their speech to fit the occasion. When Darby stopped puffing on the stinky cigar poking out of his mouth, Baltimore smiled at him. "Ahh-ahh, not yet. I'll also bet you a nickel to a bottle of piss, if you go pulling that heater on me, you'll be dead before your body drops."

Darby spat the cigar onto the floor as he reared back and went for the revolver. Baltimore slammed the heavy ice bucket against his gun, snatched him by the throat, and then punched the steak knife into Darby's gut so hard, the handle broke off. Darby's mouth flew open as he anguished in pain. Baltimore watched intently as the white man gasped for breath like a fish out of water and clutched at the opening in his stomach. When Darby fell onto his knees, pain shooting through his body, he began to whimper softly. Baltimore was quick to stuff a bar towel in his mouth to shut him up. "Uh-huh, I knew you were all bark," Baltimore teased as he removed the pistol from Darby's shoulder holster and began riffling through his pockets. "Let's see how much you still have, you sorry bastard. Seventy-two dollars?" he ranted. "I knew I should have stuck you sooner." Suddenly, Baltimore heard someone coming, but there was nowhere to hide, so he raised the dying man's gun.

"Baltimo', that you?" someone uttered from the shadows. "Baltimo', it's me. Henry."

"Whewww, man, I almost blew a hole in you, thinking it was one of them white boys coming to see about the ice," Baltimore cautioned his closest friend. "Here. Hurrup. Help me get his jacket and pants off him."

Henry's eyes grew as wide as saucers. "Why you want to go and do that?" he asked apprehensively.

"'Cause he's just about my size, this here is a damn nice suit, and I don't want to get no blood on it," Baltimore told him flatly. When Darby's upper body started convulsing, Henry was ordered to stop it. "Come on now. Hold his head still."

Struggling to hold the man down, Henry was forced to snap his neck when the groaning grew too loud to bear. After realizing what he'd done, Henry fell over on his behind like a repentant sinner. "Now you done got me involved," he fussed.

"Being my friend is what got you involved, Henry," Baltimore corrected him. "And you came through for me. I won't forget that. Now, let's get him off this train before somebody comes."

Reluctantly, Henry climbed to his feet and helped wrestle off the dead man's suit. He spied the fancy wing-tipped shoes on Darby's feet, but he could see right away, it wasn't any use to take those. Darby's feet were nearly four inches shorter than his. Then, he caught a glimpse of a shiny gold ring on the man's finger as they opened a dining car window to ease his body out onto the countryside. "Hold up, Balt. I'ma take this here ring for my troubles."

Baltimore pulled Darby's legs up to the sliding window and pushed against the cold January winds. "Naw, don't take the ring. It's the same kind the other fellas had on. That could come back to haunt you. Leave it on him. Hell, let the coyotes get it." Henry considered what his partner in crime had told him, pretended to agree, but then decided to swipe it, anyway. He eased the ring off and slipped it into his pocket behind Baltimore's back. As the train whipped around a bend, the wind howled. Henry closed the window while Baltimore neatly folded Darby's suit under his loose jacket.

"Where're you going now?" Henry asked, as he rolled out a mop bucket to clean up the mess they had made doing away with the corpse.

"To sleep so's I can get to dreaming about that steak that's been calling my name," Baltimore answered, slapping thirty dollars in his accomplice's palm. "Send somebody to wake me when we pull into Kaycee. Boy, I sho' am tired." He patted Henry on the back and started off, with a carefree saunter, as if he hadn't moments before goaded a man into a fight and ended his life as a result. Baltimore's ice-cold veneer aided him in sending Darby to another world altogether, but it didn't do a thing in the way of shaking off that bad luck shadow dogging him from town to town.

Sinful

Prologue

"Everybody's got a weakness," was Dior's quiet proclamation. Sighing wearily, she stared at her ragged reflection captured by the dusty hanging wall mirror inside of the tiny room at the Happy Horizons mental care facility where she'd been sentenced for psychiatric evaluation. *The difference with me is,*" Dior continued to herself, *I claim mine and ain't never tried to put it off on nobody else.*

After sweeping hair in desperate need of professional attention underneath the baseball cap her favorite cousin Chandelle had brought along, Dior smirked at her tired expression. Her eyes seemed darker, murkier, than she remembered them, but her flawless cinnamon brown complexion and attractive features hadn't waned one iota. She was still just as fine as she was when they checked her in and took her belt and shoelaces away.

"You're a Wicker, too, Chandelle," Dior spouted adamantly. "Or else you used to be. Deep down, where it makes every bit of difference, you still are, so don't go thinking that swooping me from this giggle factory on my early release day makes you any better than me."

Dior sighed again, turning away from the image of a troubled 25-year-old with a pretty face. She placed the last of her personal belongings into a stolen designer travel bag and then snapped her fingers in a snooty chop-chop fashion. "Get that bag for me, Chandelle, before they try to hold me for the full two-week bid. I wasn't loony when that stupid judge sent me here, but I swear I ain't wrapped too tight now. Go ahead on and get that bag off the bed; it's checkout time."

"Humph, you ain't that crazy," Chandelle chuckled under her breath as Dior paused to sneak another glimpse of her tightly fitted low-rise jeans in the filthy mirror. "Look, Dior, you're my girl as well as my blood, but you'd have to be up in here a lot longer than eleven days for me to feel sorry enough to be your personal valet. I don't even carry my own bags."

Dior's attempt to obtain her closest friend's pity didn't go over well because Chandelle was one of two people who often knew her better than she did herself. The other person was Dior's fraternal twin, Dooney.

"I know you have issues but they have nothing to do with me," Chandelle contended. "You're the one who . . ." she began to say before realizing her own words waxed judgmental. "You right about one thing. It is way past time to get you out of here." Chandelle, the color of ginger peach and fashion model tall, with the looks to match, stood up from the cloth-covered chair placed by the door. Although she tried mightily to avoid the inevitable, it was utterly impossible. She found herself primping the chic, angular hairstyle framing her face in the same dirty mirror. Chandelle's stunning beauty, beset by round brown eyes and anchored by full voluptuous lips, beamed back at her with a brilliant approving smile. "Yes, just as I suspected. Beauty knows no bounds."

"If you ask me, they had the wrong one locked up," Dior heckled from the hallway. "Come on, cuz, let's get out of here. I'm hungry for some real food. Something dumped in grease."

"Ooh, Dee. That's the sanest thing I've heard all day. Let me get your bag."

1
Exodus

The brisk fall Dallas air brushed against Chandelle's cheeks. "It's too cold to be early October," she shrieked. The mink jacket she slid out of a slick plastic covering from the trunk of her car, the one she'd sufficiently convinced herself that she couldn't live without, hugged her shoulders as they approached the front doors of the Alley Cat'n Restaurant parking lot.

Dior caught the hint. She peered over the hood of the car at the dark brown collection of expensive pelt and escalating debt. Chandelle sashayed casually in the ridiculously overpriced fur as if the hefty bill, including a truckload of finance charges, wouldn't be arriving in her mailbox within the week. "Look at what the cat drug in," Dior howled. "That's a nice coat." She stepped around the front of Chandelle's two-year-old Volvo to run her fingers along the velvety sleeves. "Uh-huh, soft as cotton too. Who boosted it for you?"

Highly offended, Chandelle was outdone. "Boosted? Don't get the way I do business mixed up with how you handle yours. I don't get my hands dirty like that anymore, and if I did, I wouldn't appreciate you putting it out there like that."

After Dior smacked her lips, she turned her nose up at Chandelle's refusal to pay the drastically discounted prices for stolen goods like she had done in the past. "I's just saying, I know Marvin didn't let you run up his credit cards with no department store mink. Even I'm smarter than that."

Chandelle flipped the collar over her ears and huffed. *Shows how little you do know. Marvin didn't let me because he doesn't know about it yet,* she thought. "Let me deal with my husband. He doesn't tell me what I can buy with my own money," she contended in an irritated tone.

Still fuming over having been chastised by a streetwise headache after their entrées were delivered, Chandelle quietly picked over a deep-fried fish basket while Dior dove into hers face-first. Instead of listening to her cousin recount the events that landed her inside of the county-funded facility for observation, she was having second thoughts of treating herself to the exotic jacket now saturated with oily catfish odors. It was all right, Dior explained only what she was willing to share, there were always incriminating details she'd purposely leave out. And despite how often Dior managed to get herself caught up in a web, it was never, under any circumstances, her fault.

"See, what had happened was, that trick of a store manager couldn't hold off long enough to see things from my standpoint. It would've been cool if he'd have just listened to me and then let me bounce. Besides, it was a victimless crime anyhow. After being poked and pinched in that loony bin they put me in, I'm the victim." With a half-eaten hush puppy in one hand, Dior used the other to illustrate how she'd been wronged yet again by the system, although she was caught dead to rights shoplifting in the department store restroom. Fourteen sets of lingerie items, in assorted sizes, were stuffed inside her jogging suit when an employee began pounding on the door. Dior's eyes had bugged out as the realization of serving jail time popped into her head. That was a fate worse than death as far as she was concerned. Knowing that the jig was up, she worked feverishly at pulling the bunched undergarments out of her pants while reattaching them to hangers scattered about on the floor. "Just one minute," she pleaded, before a large, brooding white man opened the door with his master key. When Dior heard him warn that he was coming in, she acted fast. She snatched her jogging pants down past her knees and plopped down on the toilet seat. The scream she hurled at him reverberated throughout the women's clothing section of the store. "Get out!" she shrieked. "Police! Police!"

Immediately detained in the manager's office, Dior readily explained how she'd never felt so violated before and that she'd never intended on stealing a single garment, but rather how she'd innocently taken the items to the restroom during the fleeting hours of a "once a year" sale because she couldn't risk losing her great finds to other shoppers with similar taste. Soon enough, the police arrived, heard Dior's outrageous story, and as quickly as they appeared, sped away with her handcuffed in the backseat of their squad car. She pled her case vehemently while traveling downtown for central booking. "I'm serious, officers!" she clamored loudly. "I couldn't wait for a store employee to come and watch the clothes for me because I got a condition, uh-huh, a weak bladder." After being reassured that the officers had no plans for letting her go, the cagey criminal decided to build a case for insanity by leaving a urine sample on the vinyl seats of their squad car.

"You know what, Chandelle? I ought to sue," Dior contemplated, from the other side of a forkful of fries. "I just might win, too. You know I can lie real good. Humph, I can make a stupid bunch of jurors believe me like I fooled that judge who signed my crazy papers instead of sending me to county."

Chandelle sat across the table. She stared at Dior as if she had been released too soon. "Don't tell me you thought you could pee your way out of that too?"

"Why wouldn't I?" she questioned. Wetting her pants had gotten Dior out of numerous tight spots before, and it still worked.

"How many times are you going to use that stupid defense as a 'get out of jail free' card?"

"Until they take it away," Dior answered quickly. "That pill-popping palace they call Happy Horizons is the closest I've ever gotten to doing real time. Well, except for that one night, when I almost get snatched up. That cop caught me behind that night club trying to get back in good with Kevlin. Girl, I had my skirt hiked up when he shined the light on us. Shoot, I squatted so fast it nearly ruined the officer's shoes. Sure did, told the law how Kevlin was back there to keep a lookout so nobody would bother me. Uh-huh, the same bad bladder scheme was on and popping then too."

"You're getting too old to be showing out like that with Kevlin."

"That's what you think," Dior smarted back. "I'll

never be too old to hike my skirt up whenever I feel like it."

"You are too old to be doing it in back alleys with some brotha who won't half call you afterward. And all of the scheming you're so stuck on has gotten you tossed into that asylum. Dior, nobody even knew where you were until you called today begging for me to pick you up."

"That's why I had to go about the schizted route. I couldn't risk you or Dooney showing up there talking about 'she ain't crazy, just too sinful.' That's been the bad rap all of my life, and I don't deserve it. I'm just misunderstood."

"You mean misdiagnosed."

"Whatever. You say po-tay-to. I say to-may-to."

Chandelle glanced up when she replayed Dior's mishandling of the common cliché. "You mean po-tay-to, po-tah-to?"

"Why would I say the same thing twice? That's stupid."

"Yeah, and so is this conversation," Chandelle replied, realizing it about thirty minutes too late. She massaged her temples with all ten fingers, agonizing over the slim chances of returning a mink coat that reeked of deep-fried fish. Since Dior didn't elaborate on how she'd successfully proved to clinically trained psychologists that she wasn't harmful to herself or others but not likely to harbor the propensity for shoplifting either, Chandelle assumed she'd pulled off yet another ruse whereby urinating her way out of it. Unfortunately, this time around, Happy Horizons was only the beginning.

Chandelle fought with further attacking her cousin's dirty deeds while maneuvering through the streets of Dallas. She wondered if beating a dead horse would have amounted to much, if anything, in the way of setting the mixed-up sister straight. When Dior insisted that Chandelle zoom past her apartment, she didn't question it until they were speeding off in the other direction. "What's gotten into you?" she yelled, feverishly glancing in the rearview mirror.

"Just keep driving!" Dior cried out, whipping her head around to see if they were being followed. "Make a left up there at the corner." Chandelle did just that; she kept her foot on the gas pedal and followed directions until entering a drug-infested neighborhood off the interstate. On the outer ring of a densely cluttered assortment of aging apartment complexes, commonly referred to as "Crack City" by the local police, Chandelle pulled her car into a convenience store parking lot, and then slammed on the brakes.

"I've been quiet long enough, Dee. This is as far as I go until you tell me what's got you too scared to set foot into your own spot and has me all jacked up and ready to jet from this one. I'm trying not to end up on the news, gunned down in a drug bust gone bad."

"It's not that serious, Chandelle," Dior argued, although reluctant to face her. With her head down, she fiddled with the suede tassels hanging from her Navajo Indian–style purse. "You wouldn't understand if I told you, so I won't even try."

Now, Chandelle was seething too much to lay eyes on her salty passenger. "So that's it? I just fled the scene like some kind of fugitive from justice and that's the best you can come up with to justify it? I'm not moving another inch unless you tell me what you're running from and why you've chosen this crack alley of all places to hide."

"You're lucky, Chandelle, always have been. You

might no longer be what you used to be, but I am. This thing hanging over me ain't up for discussion. Feel me on this, pop . . . pop . . . bang. It's dead and buried. Trying to go home again was my fourth mistake of the day, so please let it rest in peace."

Chandelle lips pursed into a firm pucker. "Fine, if you want to go at your demons alone, then so be it. I'll drop you off, but don't come beating down my door when Kevlin decides to throw you out with tomorrow's trash." When Dior's eyes widened, Chandelle laughed. "Huh, sure I knew you've been creeping back to him every chance you got out. Your never-agains don't hold any weight with me, baby girl. I'm still slicker than you'll ever be without even breaking a sweat, so save it. All I needed was one time for a man to paint me stupid and then go upside my head because I called him on it. That grew me up quick, fast, and in a hurry. We'll play it your way, but this is where I get off of your constant collision with catastrophe. You need to grow up, too, and get your head on straight before Kevlin knocks a hole in it."

A sigh escaped from Dior's lips, making it apparent to Chandelle that the words she spoke were ignored. Dior's eyes gradually rose to meet Chandelle's icy glare. "What makes you think I want to grow up, huh? What makes you think that just because you made college and marriage work, that I want the same things? Besides, ain't no guarantees, Chandelle, not for a sistah like me. What, am I supposed to grow up and get shackled down to some brotha selling toasters for a living while trying to make a slave outta me? I already know I don't look cute chained to a stove."

"You just keep on pressing your luck, trying to get

over without putting the work in," Chandelle said, before issuing a stern warning. "And you got one more time to criticize my man."

"You're right, my bad going there about Marvin, but don't forget I've *done* the nine-to-five thing and it didn't suit me. My heels were too long, my lunch breaks were too short, folks didn't like my clothes being too tight, and somebody was always complaining about something I was doing wrong. Listen to me close, I can't do the square life and can't use no square love."

Caught between a hard head and her better judgment, Chandelle refused to let Dior's difficulties in the workplace go unchallenged. "That may be so, but every black woman deals with the same issues until they realize it's not always about us. I wasn't gonna say anything, but you know who you sound like talking all pitiful and woe-is-me?"

"I know who you bet' not be thinking of," Dior spat ferociously. "Leave her out of this. I'm not going to end up like Billie." Her mother was doing a ten-year bid in the state penitentiary on a welfare food stamp charge. Dior had yet to forgive her for getting caught. Hustling was a way of life she'd grown accustomed to, but a woman leaving her family behind was unacceptable under any circumstances.

"Dior, you might not plan to but that's where the road you're headed down leads. Me, I love being a *square*. Need I remind you that you're in my whip? My square job and my square husband help to keep me rolling in it. Thank God."

"Whatever, I'm just saying . . . can't do the square thing."

"Here's a note for you, cousin, we all have to grow up sooner or later."

"I hear you, just ain't ready yet. Anyways, all that stuntin' I do, it's cool because it's like I've heard you say, that God of yours knows my heart."

"Listen at you. *He knows your heart.* That's another reason for you to check yourself because He does know about the stuff you're too ashamed to tell me." After Chandelle got her dig in, she backed out of the small parking lot and proceeded toward the apartment she'd sworn never to revisit, Kevlin's den. "I can't believe I'm doing this," she huffed. "Nothing good can come from getting mixed up with him again. He's a snake, poison."

"Bump that, Chandelle. Kevlin said he was sorry, and that's what's up. Let me out so I can get what I've been dreaming about for almost two weeks." Dior hopped out and wrestled her bag down the walkway to an open gazebo-style beige-colored brick building with three doors on either side. She knocked at the nearest door on the right. When a yellow-toned, muscle-bound man wearing a long gangster perm and sagging blue jeans opened it, Dior's eyes floated up in a begging-please-take-me-in manner. Chandelle, looking on from the street, shook her head disapprovingly. Kevlin's expression was undecipherable to Chandelle as he stared at Dior and her bag resting at his doorstep. Then he leaned out to clock whoever was watching their reunion from the red Volvo idling in the road.

Yeah, I'm the one who told Dooney you were putting hands on his twin. Uh-huh, the same one who's responsible for him posting you up at the car wash and had you crying like a li'l punk, Chandelle thought, as she rolled down the window so he could see her face clearly, displaying her unmistakable contempt for him and men like him. *Yeah, the stitches and the lumpy hospital bed, that was all on me.*

After mean-mugging Chandelle like he wanted to return the favor, Kevlin nodded his head respectfully instead, pecked Dior on the lips, and then ushered her inside.

"That's what I thought," Chandelle mouthed triumphantly, before making a fast U-turn to get out of the area as quickly as possible. Although Dior was willing to brave the climate of the low-rent apartment district, she wasn't in the mood to reminisce on the life she led before leaving it all where it belonged, in the past.

Ms. Etta's Fast House

1
Penny Worth o' Blues

*T*hree months deep into 1947, a disturbing calm rolled over St. Louis, Missouri. It was unimaginable to foresee the hope and heartache that one enigmatic season saw fit to unleash, mere inches from winter's edge. One unforgettable story changed the city for ever. This is that story.

Watkins Emporium was the only black-owned dry goods store for seven square blocks and the pride of "The Ville," the city's famous black neighborhood. Talbot Watkins had opened it when the local Woolworth's fired him five years earlier. He allowed black customers to try on hats before purchasing them, which was in direct opposition to store policy. The department store manager had warned him several times before that apparel wasn't fit for sale after having been worn by Negroes. Subsequently, Mr. Watkins used his life savings to start a successful business of his own with his daughter, Chozelle, a hot-natured twenty-year-old who had a propensity for older fast-talking men with even faster hands. Chozelle's scandalous ways became undeniably apparent to her father the third time he'd caught a man running from the backdoor of his storeroom, half-dressed and hell-bent on eluding his wrath. Mr. Watkins clapped an iron padlock on the rear door after realizing he'd have to protect his daughter's virtue, whether she liked it or not. It was a hard pill to swallow, admitting to himself that canned meat wasn't the only thing getting dusted and polished in that backroom. However, his relationship with Chozelle was just about perfect, compared to that of his meanest customer.

"Penny! Git your bony tail away from that there dress!" Halstead King grunted from the checkout counter. "I done told you once, you're too damned simple for something that fine." When Halstead's lanky daughter snatched her hand away from the red satin cocktail gown displayed in the front window as if a rabid dog had snapped at it, he went right on back to running his mouth and running his eyes up and down Chozelle's full hips and ample everything else. Halstead stuffed the hem of his shirttail into his tattered work pants and then shoved his stubby thumbs beneath the tight suspenders holding them up. After licking his lips and twisting the ends of his thick gray handlebar mustache, he slid a five dollar bill across the wooden countertop, eyeing Chozelle suggestively. "Now, like I was saying, How 'bout I come by later on when your daddy's away and help you arrange thangs in the storeroom?" His plump belly spread between the worn leather suspender straps like one of the heavy grain sacks he'd loaded on the back of his pickup truck just minutes before.

Chozelle had a live one on the hook, but old man

Halstead didn't stand a chance of getting at what had his zipper about to burst. Although his appearance reminded her of a rusty old walrus, she strung him along. Chozelle was certain that five dollars was all she'd get from the tight-fisted miser, unless of course she agreed to give him something worth a lot more. After deciding to leave the lustful old man's offer on the counter top, she turned her back toward him and then pretended to adjust a line of canned peaches behind the counter. "Like what you see, Mr. Halstead?" Chozelle flirted. She didn't have to guess whether his mouth watered, because it always did when he imagined pressing his body against up hers. "It'll cost you a heap more than five dollars to catch a peek at the rest of it," she informed him.

"A peek at what, Chozelle?" hissed Mr. Watkins suspiciously, as he stepped out of the side office.

Chozelle stammered while Halstead choked down a pound of culpability. "Oh, nothing, Papa. Mr. Halstead's just thinking about buying something nice for Penny over yonder." Her father tossed a quick glance at the nervous seventeen-year-old obediently standing an arm's length away from the dress she'd been dreaming about for weeks. "I was telling him how we'd be getting in another shipment of ladies garments next Thursday," Chozelle added, hoping that the lie sounded more plausible then. When Halstead's eyes fell to the floor, there was no doubting what he'd had in mind. It was common knowledge that Halstead King, the local moonshiner, treated his only daughter like an unwanted pet and that he never shelled out one thin dime toward her happiness.

"All right then," said Mr. Watkins, in a cool calculated manner. "We'll put that there five on a new dress for Penny. Next weekend she can come back and get that red one in the window she's been fancying." Halstead started to argue as the store owner lifted the money from the counter and folded it into his shirt pocket but it was gone for good, just like Penny's hopes of getting anything close to that red dress if her father had anything to say about it. "She's getting to be a grown woman and it'd make a right nice coming-out gift. Good day, Halstead," Mr. Watkins offered, sealing the agreement.

"Papa, you know I've had my heart set on that satin number since it came in," Chozelle whined, as if the whole world revolved around her.

Directly outside of the store, Halstead slapped Penny down onto the dirty sidewalk in front of the display window. "You done cost me more money than you're worth," he spat. "I have half a mind to take it out of your hide."

"Not unless you want worse coming to you," a velvety smooth voice threatened from the driver's seat of a new Ford convertible with Maryland plates.

Halstead glared at the stranger then at the man's shiny beige Roadster. Penny was staring up at her handsome hero, with the buttery complexion, for another reason all together. She turned her head briefly, holding her sore eye then glanced back at the dress in the window. She managed a smile when the man in the convertible was the only thing she'd ever seen prettier than that red dress. Suddenly, her swollen face didn't sting nearly as much.

"You ain't got no business here, mistah!" Halstead exclaimed harshly. "People known to get hurt messin' where they don't belong."

"Uh-uh, see, you went and made it my business by putting your hands on that girl. If she was half the man you pretend to be, she'd put a hole in your head as sure as you're standing there." The handsome stranger unfastened the buttons on his expensive tweed sports coat to reveal a long black revolver cradled in a shoulder holster. When Halstead took that as a premonition of things to come, he backed down, like most bullies do when confronted by someone who didn't bluff so easily. "Uh-huh, that's what I thought," he said, stepping out of his automobile idled at the curb. "Miss, you all right?" he asked Penny, helping her off the hard cement. He noticed that one of the buckles was broken on her run over shoes. "If not, I could fix that for you. Then, we can go get your shoe looked after." Penny swooned as if she'd seen her first sunrise. Her eyes were opened almost as wide as Chozelle's, who was gawking from the other side of the large framed window. "They call me Baltimore, Baltimore Floyd. It's nice to make your acquaintance, miss. Sorry it had to be under such unfavorable circumstances."

Penny thought she was going to faint right there on the very sidewalk she'd climbed up from. No man had taken the time to notice her, much less talk to her in such a flattering manner. If it were up to Penny, she was willing to get knocked down all over again for the sake of reliving that moment in time.

"Naw, suh, Halstead's right," Penny sighed after giving it some thought. "This here be family business." She dusted herself off, primped her pigtails, a hairstyle more appropriate for much younger girls, then she batted her eyes like she'd done it all of her life. "Thank you kindly, though," Penny mumbled, noting the contempt mounting in her father's expression. Halstead wished he'd brought along his gun and his daughter was wishing the same thing, so that Baltimore could make him eat it. She understood all too well that as soon as they returned to their shanty farmhouse on the outskirts of town, there would be hell to pay.

"Come on, Penny," she heard Halstead gurgle softer than she'd imagined he could. "We ought to be getting on," he added as if asking permission to leave.

"I'll be seeing you again, Penny," Baltimore offered. "And next time, there bet' not be one scratch on your face," he said, looking directly at Halstead. "It's hard enough on women folk as it is. They shouldn't have to go about wearing reminders of a man's shortcomings."

Halstead hurried to the other side of the second-hand pickup truck and cranked it. "Penny," he summoned, when her feet hadn't moved an inch. Perhaps she was waiting on permission to leave too. Baltimore tossed Penny a wink as he helped her up onto the tattered bench seat.

"Go on now. It'll be all right or else I'll fix it," he assured her, nodding his head in a kind fashion and smiling brightly.

As the old pickup truck jerked forward, Penny stole a glance at the tall silky stranger then held the hand Baltimore had clasped inside his up to her nose. The fragrance of his store-bought cologne resonated through her nostrils for miles until the smell of farm animals whipped her back into a stale reality, her own.

It wasn't long before Halstead mustered up enough courage to revert back to the mean tyrant he'd always been. His unforgiving black heart and vivid memories of the woman who ran off with a traveling salesman fueled Halstead's hatred for Penny, the girl his wife left behind. Halstead was determined to destroy

Penny's spirit since he couldn't do the same to her mother.

"Git those mason jar crates off'n the truck while I fire up the still!" he hollered. "And you might as well forgit that man in town and ever meeting him again. His meddling can't help you way out here. He's probably on his way back east already." When Penny moved too casually for Halstead's taste, he jumped up and popped her across the mouth. Blood squirted from her bottom lip. "Don't make me tell you again," he cursed. "Ms. Etta's havin' her spring jig this weekend and I promised two more cases before sundown. Now git!"

Penny's injured lip quivered. "Yeah, suh," she whispered, her head bowed.

As Halstead waddled to the rear of their orange brick and oak, weather-beaten house, cussing and complaining about wayward women, traveling salesmen and slick strangers, he shouted additional chores. "Stack them crates up straight this time so's they don't tip over. Fetch a heap of water in that barrel, bring it around yonder and put my store receipts on top of the bureau in my room. Don't touch nothin' while you in there neither, useless heifer," he grumbled.

"Yeah, suh, I will. I mean, I won't," she whimpered. Penny allowed a long strand of blood to dangle from her angular chin before she took the hem of her faded dress and wiped it away. Feeling inadequate, Penny became confused as to in which order her chores were to have been performed. She reached inside the cab of the truck, collected the store receipts and crossed the pebble covered yard. She sighed deeply over how unfair it felt, having to do chores on such a beautiful spring day, and then she pushed open the front door and wandered into

Halstead's room. She overlooked the assortment of loose coins scattered on the nightstand next to his disheveled queen-sized bed with filthy sheets she'd be expected to scrub clean before the day was through.

On the corner of the bed frame hung a silver-plated Colt revolver. Sunlight poured through the half-drawn window shade, glinting off the pistol. While mesmerized by the opportunity to take matters into her own hands, Penny palmed the forty-five carefully. She contemplated how easily she could have ended it all with one bullet to the head, hers. Something deep inside wouldn't allow Penny to hurt another human, something good and decent, something she didn't inherit from Halstead.

"Penny!" he yelled, from outside. "You got three seconds to git outta that house and back to work!" Startled, Penny dropped the gun onto the uneven floor and froze, praying it wouldn't go off. Halstead pressed his round face against the dusty window to look inside. "Goddammit! Gal, you've got to be the slowest somebody. Git back to work before I have to beat some speed into you."

The puddle of warm urine Penny stood in confirmed that she was still live. It could have just as easily been a pool of warm blood instead. Thoughts of ending her misery after her life had been spared fleeted quickly. She unbuttoned her thin cotton dress, used it to mop the floor then tossed it on the dirty clothes heap in her bedroom. Within minutes, she'd changed into an undershirt and denim overalls. Her pace was noticeably revitalized as she wrestled the crates off the truck as instructed. "Stack them crates," Penny mumbled to herself. "Stack 'em straight so's they don't tip over. Then fetch the water." The week before, she'd stacked the crates too high and a strong gust of wind toppled them over. Halstead was furious. He dragged Penny into the barn, tied her to a tractor wheel and left her there for three days without food or water. She was determined not to spend another three days warding off field mice and garden snakes.

Once the shipment had been situated on the front porch, Penny rolled the ten-gallon water barrel over to the well pump beside the cobblestone walkway. Halstead was busy behind the house, boiling sour mash and corn syrup in a copper pot with measures of grain. He'd made a small fortune distilling alcohol and peddling it to bars, juke joints and roadhouses. "Hurr'up, with that water!" he shouted. "This still's plenty hot. Coils try'n'a bunch."

Penny clutched the well handle with both hands and went to work. She had seen an illegal still explode when it reached the boiling point too quickly, causing the copper coils to clog when they didn't hold up to the rapidly increasing temperatures. Ironically, just as it came to Penny that someone had tampered with the neighbors still on the morning it blew up, a thunderous blast shook her where she stood. Penny cringed. Her eyes grew wide when Halstead staggered from the backyard screaming and cussing, with every inch of his body covered in vibrant yellow flames. Stumbling to his knees, he cried out for Penny to help him.

"Water! Throw the damned . . . water!" he demanded.

She watched in amazement as Halstead writhed on the ground in unbridled torment, his skin melting, separating from bone and cartilage. In a desperate attempt, Halstead reached out to her, expecting to be doused with water just beyond his reach, as it gushed from the well spout like blood had poured from Penny's busted lip.

Penny raced past a water pail on her way toward the front porch. When she couldn't reach the top crate fast enough, she shoved the entire stack of them onto the ground. After getting what she went there for, she covered her nose with a rag as she inched closer to Halstead's charred body. While life evaporated from his smoldering remains, Penny held a mason jar beneath the spout until water spilled over onto her hand. She kicked the ten-gallon barrel on its side then sat down on it. She was surprised at how fast all the hate she'd known in the world was suddenly gone and how nice it was to finally enjoy a cool, uninterrupted, glass of water.

At her leisure, Penny sipped until she'd had her fill. "Ain't no man supposed to treat his own blood like you treated me," she heckled, rocking back and forth slowly on the rise of that barrel. "Maybe that's cause you wasn't no man at all. You just mean old Halstead. Mean old Halstead." Penny looked up the road when something in the wind called out to her. A car was headed her way. By the looks of it, she had less than two minutes to map out her future, so she dashed into the house, collected what she could and threw it all into a croaker sack. Somehow, it didn't seem fitting to keep the back door to her shameful past opened, so she snatched the full pail off the ground, filled it from the last batch of moonshine Halstead had brewed. If her mother had ever planned on returning, Penny reasoned that she'd taken too long as she tossed the pail full of white lightning into the house. As she lit a full box of stick matches, her hands shook erratically until the time had come to walk away from her bitter yesterdays and give up on living out the childhood that wasn't intended for her. "No reason to come back here, Momma," she whispered, for the gentle breeze to hear and carry away. "I got to make it on my own now."

Penny stood by the roadside and stared at the rising inferno, ablaze from pillar to post. Halstead's fried corpse smoldered on the lawn when the approaching vehicle ambled to a stop in the middle of the road. A young man, long, lean, and not much older than Penny took his sweet time stepping out of the late model Plymouth sedan. He sauntered over to the hump of roasted flesh and studied it. "Hey, Penny," the familiar passerby said routinely.

"Afternoon, Jinxy," she replied, her gaze still locked on the thick black clouds of smoke billowing toward the sky.

Sam "Jinx" Dearborn, Jr., was the youngest son of a neighbor, whose moonshine still went up in flames two months earlier. Jinx surveyed the yard, the smashed mason jars and the overturned water barrel.

"That there Halstead?" Jinx alleged knowingly.

Penny nodded that it was, without a hint of reservation. "What's left of 'im," she answered casually.

"I guess you'll be moving on then," Jinx concluded stoically.

"Yeah, I reckon I will at that," she concluded as well, using the same even pitch he had. "Haven't seen much of you since yo' daddy passed. How you been?"

Jinx hoisted Penny's large cloth sack into the back seat of his car. "Waitin' mostly," he said, hunching his shoulders, "to get even."

"Yeah, I figured as much when I saw it was you in the road." Penny was one of two people who were all but certain that Halstead had killed Jinx's father by rigging his still to malfunction so he could eliminate the competition. The night before it happened, Halstead had quarreled with him over money. By the next afternoon, Jinx was making burial arrangements for his daddy.

"Halstead got what he had coming to him," Jinx reasoned as he walked Penny to the passenger door.

"Now, I'll get what's coming to me," Penny declared somberly, with a pocket full of folding money. "I'd be thankful, Jinxy, if you'd run me into town. I need to see a man about a dress."